THE BYGONE
CAPER

—⁕—

JOSEPH R. LALLO

CONTENTS

CHAPTER 1

A guy could get used to this.

Fel snapped the reins of the wagon and leaned back with a grin. A "normal" day for the workhorse of the Masker clan was a frustratingly difficult thing to define. His job description included tasks as mundane as hauling silverware back and forth from the family shop for polishing to tasks as absurd as raiding a dragon's hoard for missing components. There honestly weren't many things that he'd feel confident crossing off a list of potential tasks his family might assign to him. But today he'd had the pleasure of doing a good old-fashioned vault dive.

Raiding a Bygone Era trove was a bit like eating an apple. In the beginning it was all about taking the biggest, juiciest bites. But as the pickings started to get slimmer, he found himself going over portions he thought he was done with in order to nibble at previously disregarded morsels. All the vaults within three days' travel of Beffshire had been picked clean, or such was the popular wisdom. But when there was nothing else worthwhile to occupy Fel's time (and when he was out of money to gamble away at the grum table), a quick trip to one of those scoured-out old vaults always seemed to turn up enough antiques and contraptions to keep the shelves stocked and the bills paid.

Perhaps the best indication that both he and his family felt as though this trip to a musty old vault just a few hours from home would be worth the time and effort was the presence of the full cargo wagon and a proper horse. Much as he enjoyed having the little family cart and his goat-size and impressively strong lesser unicorn Parch towing it, one could only fit so much in its limited bed, whereas the wagon could be heaped with enough goods to keep the shop busy for weeks. And right now, it was groaning under the weight of his haul.

"We're going to have to start paying visits to all the old haunts, now that it turns out you have a nose for goodies," Fel said as Parch hopped down from the pile of goods and clippy-clopped in place beside him.

He tugged a journal from his pack. It would have been nice to suggest he'd always been mindful and professional enough to keep one, but his sister Epiphany had browbeat him into carrying one after he'd misplaced a crate of scavenged repair parts because he'd simply forgotten he'd even acquired it. He was still developing his inventory technique.

It could use work.

"Two crates of junk-junk," he read. "Three crates of junk Mom can sell to people who don't know better. Three crates of junk Dad can fix up. One crate of junk that'll sell even if Dad doesn't fix it up. And one crate of stuff that isn't even junk."

He scratched Parch and stowed the journal. "By my figuring, that's enough to make Mom and Dad happy for at least a few days." He slapped Parch's side, raising a cloud of dust that made him cough. "I say we get you a bath, maybe me too if time permits, and get Mom to give us an advance on my share of the week's sales. I'm itching for a proper game of grum. Tem's due for a big loss, I can feel it."

The wagon rattled through the gates of Beffshire. He made it as far as the watchhouse a few yards farther along before his mood started to sour. Watchman Leonard, a senior member of the Watch, who seemed to spend all of his nights and most of his days precariously dozing on a tipped-back chair, marched to the center of the street and waved his hands.

"Uh-oh. Things can't be good if they've got this guy upright and moving…" Fel muttered. He tugged the reins. "What seems to be the problem, Watchman?"

"Fel Masker. You're the one who's always dragging wild animals into the town, right?" Leonard said.

"No," Fel said.

Parch hopped from the seat to the back of the horse, nearly startling it. Leonard glanced at the lesser unicorn, then at Fel.

"Not always," Fel amended.

"We've got a troublemaker we think might be yours."

"When'd he show up?" Fel asked.

"She. We think, anyway. And she showed up this morning."

"Not mine, then. I've been doing a vault dive since yesterday."

Leonard took off his watchman's cap and rubbed from his thinning hair to his face and back again. "Look. She's a handful, and we've been arguing with the beast wrangler about whose job it is to keep her locked up. He says she's not his problem because she can talk a little. I say she's his problem because she's got sharp teeth and a tail, and we've never had to lock up someone with either of those things before."

"I'm telling you, Leonard, I'm not missing any sharp-toothed, tail-having maybe-prisoners, maybe-strays."

Leonard grumbled. "Remember last month when 'someone' broke through a door at the refinery and ate a bunch of wheat mash?

Remember when we didn't come pounding on your door and demanding you keep a better eye on your little magic goat there?"

Now it was Fel's turn to grumble. "Fine. I'll take a look," he said.

He pulled the wagon alongside the watchhouse and tied off the reins. Leonard opened the door and led him inside. Parch trotted along beside him because even the Watch had learned it was just easier to let the unicorn in than try to keep him out. Once they were inside, Fel didn't need to be told where the troublemaker was.

"Get off it! Get off it I said!" barked Captain Boltt. He glanced over his shoulder as Fel approached the holding cells, which Fel had seen the inside of one or two more times than he would have liked.

"Masker! I swear if this turns out to be one of yours," he growled.

Fel marched forward, fully expecting to see some manner of strange, feral Lesser Mystic that just happened to wander past the walls. His expression fell when his expectations were thoroughly defied.

It wasn't a Lesser Mystic. It wasn't feral. And though it was certainly strange, it wasn't a stranger. The thing was a touch more than half his height, broadly human in shape and distinctly reptile in features. Grayish-blue scales covered the bits of anatomy not hidden behind tattered cloth. Cunning, if stubby, hands were clutching the bars of the cell. It had climbed all the way to the top, a short tail swishing back and forth as clawed feet scrabbled to keep from slipping down again. Its jaws were clamped onto the straw end of a broom, tugging at it while the captain yanked at the other end. Presumably he'd gotten tired of her climbing the bars and had tried to shove her down, resulting in this little confrontation.

When the creature saw Fel, it let the gnawed broom slip free and pulled its droopy, ruffle-edged ears back with interest.

"Fel!" she said. "My least-worst friend!" She pointed a stubby finger at the captain. "These men? Very mean. Lock me up. For what? Nothing!" she said.

"So you do know this thing," the captain said. "I knew something this irritating could only be one of your pets."

"She's a kobold. Her name is Teya. And she's not one of my pets," Fel said.

Teya nodded. "Yes. Not pet. Friend."

All the tightness and stress that had been eased away by the uneventful vault raid gnarled up Fel's neck and back. "What'd she do?" he asked.

"This one?" Teya said. "This one did—"

Fel shushed her before she could confess anything. "I'm not asking you what you did, I'm asking them what you did," he said.

"She doesn't need to do anything. Look at her," the captain said. "We can't have something like that walking the streets in the city. It'll cause panic!"

"We both know the people who come pouring out of the taverns every night are more dangerous than she is."

"I don't know that," Captain Boltt said. "All I know is she's a wild animal, and she left bite marks on my broom. Not even Lou has done that."

"She hasn't done anything much more than trespass, here in the city," Leonard said. "But we've been getting reports of cattle poaching down south, and there's even been some people gone missing."

"This one didn't miss people," Teya insisted.

"Also, that onion farmer said someone set fire to the junk pile in his west field," Leonard said.

"Fire? Maybe yes," she said simply.

"Quiet!" the captain barked. "What happens outside these walls isn't my concern, so I couldn't care less if she made a mess along the road. But I don't want to have to clean up anything in this city. Either you claim her and deal with her, or I'm going to find a muzzle that fits her, and Greenwald from the lord's menagerie can come down here and deal with her."

"What do you want me to do? I didn't invite her here," Fel said.

"What you need to do is make sure that I don't have to do anything," the captain said. "If I let her out of this cell, I had better not even know she is or was ever in the city. I don't want to see her. I don't want anyone else to see her. I don't want to hear about her. And anything she does falls on your head."

Fel glared at Teya, who was still hanging from the bars. She smiled back at him.

"Fine. Let her out," he said.

"And my things!" Teya said.

"Leonard, get her things." Boltt glared at Fel. "And remember: her crimes are your crimes."

"No crimes!" Teya said.

The captain opened the door. Teya dropped down and chattered happily. Parch reared up so that the pair could play a game of headbutts.

Fel grumbled under his breath as he shouldered the sack of gear that had been taken from Teya. "I almost made it all the way back to the shop before things went sideways," he muttered.

A few minutes later, Fel was in the dining room with Teya.

"You don't need help? Help to unload?" the kobold asked.

"Mom and Fanny will deal with it. It'll help them wrap their heads around the inventory, because my journal evidently isn't detailed enough for them. And it'll delay me having to properly introduce you to them."

Teya nodded. "You change mind? You tell me. I carry. I very very carry."

"Trust me, I know you can carry. You dragged me through the forest and up a mountain, remember."

She nodded eagerly. "Important day!" she said. "Met least-worst friend."

Now that he'd had some time to cool down and didn't have to worry so much about keeping her out of sight, Fel had a chance to look her over. Almost immediately, he felt a tinge of guilt that he hadn't done so earlier.

"Teya, you don't look so good," he said.

She was filthy. That seemed like it shouldn't have stood out to him. She did live in a cave, on a mountain, and in a forest. Being filthy ought to have been her default. But seeing her with deep, dark smears of dirt and road grime between her scales and caked on her feet underscored just how clean she'd managed to be back in the Greater Lands. She was noticeably thin, and the rampant enthusiasm that defined her was tempered by a weariness in her eyes.

"Are you all right?"

"Very!" she said brightly. "And hungry. All right, and hungry."

"I'll get you something. Come on," he said.

She paced along behind him as he climbed down the steps to the kitchen and pantry. Along the way, a jangling form nearly tripped him as it hobbled up to him. Oiler, a contraption with a mind somewhere between a puppy, a toddler, and a textbook on repair, thumped up the steps and rattled a puzzle box. He took it and scrambled it.

"Good to see you, Oiler. Look, we have a guest," he said.

"You live in the ground!" she said. "Your home? Dug! You dug your home. Like us!"

"Yeah. Only we're not in the mountains," he said. "But we can talk about me later. Why are you here? And more to the point, how are you here?"

"Easy questions. Same answer!" she tapped a silver ring dangling from her ear. "This."

"Oh, right. Right. Tome said the elves made that, right? I'm surprised the Adept let you keep it."

"Had to ask. Very much ask. For very long."

"And that's the reason you're here, too?" he said, ladling out a healthy serving from the perpetually simmering stew pot.

She gratefully took the bowl. Before he could fetch her a spoon, she'd drained the bowl and handed it back for a refill.

"Yes," she said between licks of her gravy-smeared snout. "The ring? It tugs. Leads me. This way. Leads me here. Didn't know why. Didn't know where. But you are here. See? Destiny."

"Wait, wait," he said. "Slow down. You can feel the earring tugging?"

"Yes. Soft. Have to shut eyes. But very much there." She shut her eyes. "It pulls... that way."

She pointed downward. Oiler looked up at the gesture before rattling a solved puzzle box at her.

"Toward Oiler?" Fel said, grabbing the box to scramble it again.

"No. More down."

"Toward my basement?" he said.

"Yes!" She pointed upward. "Also that way. More soup. Then we go, yes?"

"I'm confused about what you think you'll find in my basement."

She shrugged. "Destiny. We don't know. Until we do know." She gulped at the second bowl of stew, a bit less desperately this time.

"You seem like you've been having a hard time of it," he said.

"This place? Bad for hunting," she said. "Much food, but with fences. Easy to climb, but mean people too. Dogs? Sometimes. But people? Always shouting. So much hiding. And for what? I borrow, they chase."

"Borrow," he said doubtfully.

"Yes! Borrow clothes. Borrow water. Borrow food."

"You borrow food," he said.

"Yes."

"How, exactly?"

She gestured with her paws. "Eat food from field now. Poop in field later. Borrow."

Fel shut his eyes and shook his head. "But you're not returning the food you borrowed. You'd have to go back to the same field to do that."

She gave him a serious look. "Poop is poop, Fel."

"We're going to have to have a long discussion about how to behave in a city. Or better yet, we're going to have to send you on your way. Not that I'm not happy to see you, but my life is complicated enough without having to babysit a kobold."

She handed the bowl back to him. "Then take me to destiny. ... And later? More soup."

Martin adjusted some magnifying lenses and rounded the edge of a brass piece. A clearly incomplete and horribly complex assembly occupied the center of his workbench. It looked as though he was endeavoring to build the world's most expensive scarecrow. A wooden torso with a hinged door in the center of the chest made up the bulk of the contraption. That piece, at least, appeared nearly complete. It was topped with a cylinder of gears and linkages about the size of a beer stein, and two-thirds of a brass arm dangled limply to the side. He focused intently on the remaining one-third of the arm, which was clamped into a vise to free up both of his hands for adjustments.

Focus had never been a problem for Martin Masker. More accurately, lack of focus had never been a problem for him. In a very real way, an overabundance of focus was his largest problem, as it meant that whatever his current project was ran the very real risk of shoving aside petty things like eating and sleeping for days at a time. A fine illustration of his relationship with focus came in the form of his reaction to the visitors who stepped into his workshop just as he fitted the new piece in place.

"Dad, I don't want you to panic, but we have a visitor who's a little new," Fel said.

"Mmm. Lovely. Lovely to have a visitor," he said vaguely.

"Hello, Papa Fel!" Teya said.

"Lovely to meet you," he said, glancing aside.

Three seconds passed before he realized his glance in the direction of the voice had revealed nothing but wall. He glanced again, this time sweeping his eyes down until he saw the creature grinning up at him expectantly.

"This would be..." he said, holding perfectly still and raising his eyebrows.

"Teya. The kobold."

"Oh! Your friend from the Greater Lands." His expression was still uncertain, wheels in his head slowly clicking to dredge up the proper context. "How did she come here? I thought that wasn't possible for natives of the Greater Lands."

"Earring!" she said simply. "Also destiny. Both. Same."

"Well, er. Welcome to our home," he said, holding a hand out to her.

Her eyes darted to the extended extremity. She tipped her head and sniffed his fingers. Then her expression lit up with realization. "A shake! For hello!" She grabbed two of his fingers and rattled his arm. "Thank you, Papa Fel. You make soup?"

"Did I make the stew? As it happens, today I did."

"Good soup!" She looked up to Fel. "Contraptioneers? Not evil, always. Nice people!"

"We try," Martin said.

"Is your 'destiny' anywhere in this room?" Fel asked.

"I look. I feel," she said.

Martin hastened to add, "Do be careful, would you? I've organized these pieces quite precisely."

"No touching," she said with a nod.

She shut her eyes and tilted her head, almost like she was trying to listen to someone she couldn't quite hear. When she didn't immediately pinpoint anything, Fel turned to his father.

"How is it coming along?" he asked.

"Well enough," Martin said, testing the motion of the freshly fabricated linkage. "Ever since I was able to re-create those long-burning pipes that you recovered the plans for, I've been much more confident in my ability to craft functioning contraptions from scratch, but I just can't seem to get the fabled durability of Bygone Era contraptions out of the new parts. There is some treatment, perhaps some alloy, that we're missing. But I've made some fine progress with the coupler. It should hold together well enough."

Fel furrowed his brow. "I thought you already finished the coupler. Isn't that it right there?"

He pointed to a much older bust on the far edge of the workbench. Unlike the one in the center of the workbench, it looked more or less complete. The only questionable component was a matching cylinder of gears and linkages, the coupler. It was supposed to allow any contraption with a will to use it to manipulate the appendages of a bust. This one was connected to the back of an ancient-looking faceplate that was presently inert.

"Oh. No, no. That's the first prototype."

"But it worked. You were talking to the Student yesterday."

"It was a fine first effort, but this one will be much cleaner and smoother running. Better even than the second prototype."

He gestured to a third coupler sticking out of a crate near the edge of the table. Fel shook his head.

"And I thought you were a perfectionist back when you were just fixing stuff."

"It needs to be perfect. When it is through, it will facilitate the transfer of knowledge from..." He squinted. "I'm sorry, what level of secrecy are we applying with our new friend?"

"Oh, speak freely. I don't think she'll be telling anyone our secrets."

"Do not know. Do not care," Teya said, creeping forward with the ring-bearing ear held high between two fingers.

"Excellent. I do find secrecy too bothersome sometimes. It is, indeed, at complete odds with what I'm working on. If I am able to link the notions and whims of a thinking contraption like Wick or the Student to something with the physical means to record information, I can provide them with the capacity to record their knowledge and reproduce it.

Secrets and lessons we'd long thought lost to antiquity will be ours again. Frankly, I'm even excited about the potential for lost fiction to be restored. But unlocking the lost information is of little value if that information cannot be clearly and reliably shared. Thus, it must be perfect."

Teya aimed her stubby finger toward the top shelf. "There!"

They followed her gesture to where Wick's lantern sat. Presently it was flickering, indicating Wick was not present in this particular lantern.

"Wick?" Fel said. "Wick is your destiny?"

"I feel tug. Tug toward that. Tug is destiny. That is destiny," she explained simply.

"This is the ring that Tome said was crafted from Wick, yes? The one that weakened him for quite some time," Martin said.

Teya nodded.

"We would need to confirm with Tome, as he is the household's expert on such things, but I would imagine you may simply be experiencing an artifact of the magic involved."

"So? Still destiny."

"I'm not a wizard," Fel said. "But even I can understand how something made from someone else might have a connection to them."

Teya crossed her arms. "Still destiny."

"But—" Fel said.

She waved off his comment. "You say connection. You say magic. This is how. Destiny is not how. Destiny is what. Elves do bad things. Make earring. This one takes earring. Earring leads this one. Through desert. Through forest. Along road. Through towns. Far, far. Through a world. A new world. Strange world. And leads right to friends. Destiny. Destiny needs this one. Needs this one here. So, I stay."

"Until?"

She shrugged. "Until destiny is fulfilled."

"So you'll be shacking up with us, and complicating my already horribly complicated life, until some completely arbitrary and unknowable job is finished."

"Yes!" she said. "You understand. Good."

"That's just great," Fel said. "Dad, where's Tome? If I can't end the misery, I can at least spread it so it thins my share out a bit."

"He's in his room, and he asked not to be disturbed," Martin said.

"Studying?" Fel said.

"Studying," Martin said with a nod.

"Just when I thought he couldn't get his nose any further into a book, he starts reading stuff from the Greater Lands..." Fel grumbled. "Teya, let's go say hello."

He turned, expecting her to be on the floor. Instead, she'd scrambled up to the workbench and was peering around the edge of the door to the house's dumbwaiter.

"This is for going? For going up?" she said.

"It's mostly for hauling goods up and down so we don't have to use the stairs," Fel explained.

She scrambled through the door and hung from the ropes inside. "Good for up and down, too!"

She climbed up the ropes. Fel shrugged and shut the door.

"At least someone's having fun."

Tome looked up from his current book and rolled the crackling stiffness from his neck. One of the more troubling side effects of life in Beffshire was the proportion of time spent in basements and sub-basements. Tome had always fancied himself rather skilled at estimating the passage of time. Now that his home was several levels below the surface and received no sunlight whatsoever, he was forced to accept that his primary skill in that regard had been noticing the changing angle of shadows through the windows. He could have asked for one of the endless assortment of clocks that Martin Masker kept in storage. He chose to go in the exact opposite direction and disregard the very concept of traditional timekeeping. For Tome, time was now measured in books. And by that measure, it was three in the afternoon. He'd be stopping for a meal at four, so he'd best get started.

In a maneuver he'd had to master once he ran out of room on the bookshelves, he braced the top half of a stack of books and swiftly yanked one of the lower volumes free.

"Ancient Elvish: Theories of Grammar and Structure," he read from the cover. "It is hardly encouraging that the author considers grammar subject to speculation and hypothesis."

He added the book to the constellation of others arranged on his desk. To his right, beside his quill and ink, was his journal. Spread along the back of the desk were the three current items from his small collection of writings stolen from the elves during his prior adventures in the Greater Lands. Below his left hand and nearest to the flickering lamp was the book on Elvish.

Several weeks of study and analysis had given him some small understandings of the broad strokes of their language. Tome had what he was comfortable calling a fluency in three languages, and he could muddle through reading a half-dozen more. But that level of expertise was thanks almost entirely to the fact that those languages all shared a similar root. The same could not be said for Elvish. It was utterly alien. Even so, he'd made some appreciable progress in learning how to read and understand it. Appreciable to anyone but him, that is, as Tome felt certain he should have a much better understanding by now. And it was doubly frustrating that learning Elvish was simply the first step toward his real goal, which was learning their magic. The spells were written in an entirely different form of their language, one specific to spellcasting and composed of far stricter language rules.

The most substantial spellbook he'd stolen contained a great many spells. Confoundingly, the words themselves bore some basic similarity to the written magic he knew so well. His mastery of Elvish had grown sufficiently to make it clear that the simplest spell was intended to summon a breath of wind, and he was quite certain he'd learned the proper pronunciation for the words of the spell itself.

He gritted his teeth and flipped back to the page. A slip of paper marking the spell was scrawled with a precisely written phonetic version of it. He took a deep breath, moved the lantern a bit closer, and removed the protective glass bulb.

"Steady yourself. Focus your mind," he muttered.

Tome worked his way from word to word, keeping his pronunciation articulate and his pace steady. When he finished speaking, he felt a heavy, tight sensation in the back of his mind. He knew the feeling well. It was like there were strings tied to his brain and someone had plucked them. The sensation left no doubt that the spell had been cast. But the flame didn't even dance. A successful casting of the spell had failed to summon so much as a sigh of a breeze.

"Hey!" shouted a voice outside the door.

He jumped and nearly knocked down the lamp. The door shoved open and Teya tromped in.

"Elf magic? No, no. Bad magic," she said.

"I... how did... what are you doing here?" Tome said.

"Doing destiny things. Why elf magic?" she said accusingly.

"I'm sorry, doing destiny things?" Tome said.

Fel leaned on the doorjamb. "The earring tugged her toward Wick, and she thinks it was fate leading her here."

"Not think. Know," Teya said.

"We're stuck with her until she decides she's done whatever she thinks destiny brought her here to do. Also, in case you were wondering, a dumbwaiter is like a playground for a kobold."

"Explain what you do," Teya said, pointing at the pile of books.

"You helped me steal this," Tome said. "The whole point of that trip was to learn things like this."

She waggled her finger. "Contraptions? Mostly bad. Elf magic? Mostly bad. You two? Mostly good. Stop the mostly bad doings!"

Tome shook his head and tidied up the books on his desk. "You'll be pleased to know that it is very unlikely I'll be doing any bad or any good with spoken magic."

"Still haven't worked it out?" Fel said.

"I've worked enough out," Tome said. "Enough that I should be able to cast that spell."

"Sounded right," Teya said with a nod.

"But I've tried. I've gathered everything I have to the task. Nothing."

"Maybe you're still messed up from the blood magic you were doing," Fel suggested.

"Maybe. But I've finally felt like myself again after the past few days. If I haven't fully recovered, I've at least recovered as much as I'm ever likely to."

Fel shrugged. "Then this kind of magic's not for you. It's like how I'm good at grum and bad at sixes."

"You're passable at best at grum," Tome said. "But I take your point. It's just... disheartening."

"Why?" Fel said.

"Because I'd convinced myself I was a powerful mystic in general. My utter lack of meaningful capacity for elf magic suggests I, at the very least, have a blindspot, and more likely I'm simply a savant at paper magic."

"Boohoo," Fel said flatly. "Woe is me. I'm only an expert of one way to defy the whims of nature."

"I won't be mocked for having the temerity to strive for more," Tome said.

"You sure? Because I'm pretty sure I just did it."

"Temerity? What is this?" Teya said.

"It's a thing smart people have when they're being a pain in the backside for everyone else."

"It means audacity," Tome said.

"What is this?" Teya said.

"... Boldness?" Tome offered.

"Oh! Why not boldness first?" Teya said.

"Because he is a smart person and likes being a pain in the backside for everyone else," Fel said.

Teya nodded sagely. "Temerity."

"Did you have a reason to come in here? Or were you just hoping to frustrate me?"

"What do you mean 'or'?" Fel said.

"Then you've accomplished your mission. Run along."

"Not just yet. Since Teya's going to be staying—"

"She's not staying in my room," Tome said quickly.

"I already have Parch," Fel said.

"And whose fault is that?"

"Parch's, mostly," Fel said.

"I stay here?" Teya said.

"Not in this room, no," Tome insisted.

"But this place? In your home? I stay?" she said.

"Of course," Fel said. "For one, you're my responsibility now. For another, we've been through some tight spots together. Seems only right. We're fresh out of beds, but—"

"Don't need," she said.

"You don't need a bed?" Fel said.

"No." She held up her stubby paw and counted off her requirements. "Food? Need. Water? Need. Dry place? Need. That is all."

"That makes you one step easier than Parch. Come on. I'll show you where you can get cleaned up, and then we'll go over the ground rules of city living."

Epiphany finished logging the last crate of goods from Fel's haul.

"Not bad. It will be nice to have a decent supply of goods that the 'contraption averse' will buy without coaxing," she said.

"And overwhelmingly, they can be spiffed up with a brush and some effort. That should keep your father from having to set aside his pet project," Vivian said.

"I still don't see why he's so fixated on it. And why you're not more opposed to it."

"I've been married to Martin for a long time. His mind needs to sink its teeth into a problem from time to time. It helps him stay sharp and helps him sleep at night. When he remembers to, at any rate." She turned a vase and knocked a bit of caked-on dirt away with her fingernail. "This will go in the cleanup crate. I'll work on this between customers."

Epiphany stowed it appropriately and started loading the items in greater need of repair into the dumbwaiter. When it was full, she thumped the side of the compartment and raised her voice. "Coming down. Find a place in storage for it."

"I'm getting Teya settled!" Fel shouted back.

"You can do two things. These crates are cluttering up the shop, and the evening rush is ready to start."

Fel grumbled loudly enough to be heard through the dumbwaiter shaft, but the cubby started to rumble downward as he worked the winch.

"Well, well, well. Look who's back in town," Vivian said.

Epiphany shut the door and turned. A well-dressed older gentleman at the reins of a heavily laden cargo carriage eased the vehicle to a stop. He hopped down and approached the door of the shop. Before he entered, he pulled an understated yet elegant pipe from his mouth and pressed his thumb over the end. The bell over the door jangled as he entered.

"Thaddeus," Vivian said. "I hadn't expected you to come through town for another few days."

"I'm ahead of schedule, by design. Your daughter had the foresight to shift the entire trip up a few days after word of some unpleasantness in the area, and By the High was she right to do so. Have you spent much time out on the road lately?" he said.

"I tend to stay behind the counter, making the sales," Vivian said.

"A confluence of consternation. The whole area is a bit mad right now. There are all manner of tales of cattle mutilation, poaching, acts of vandalism and sabotage. Anyone with the money to do so is hiring on extra muscle to keep their assets safe and sound, but it is a horror for people trying to get from here to there. Nobles are deploying extra oversight and mercenary protection up and down the main thoroughfares. The north gate to town was a snarl with the arrival of some high-ranked individual or another. If I'd left a moment later, I doubt I would have been able to get through at all. I tell you, times like these I envy your operation. Making a living without traipsing across three kingdoms. Luxury."

"We pride ourselves on taking proper care to remain solvent in the most trying of conditions, Vivian said. "Speaking of which..."

"Right, yes."

Thaddeus raised an eyebrow and flicked his eyes aside. Epiphany crossed her arms and tried to keep her face even. Newcomers to the sort of business that requires one to look over one's shoulder before negotiating tend to suffer from a downright theatrical glance this way and that to survey their surroundings. There are few things more effective at proclaiming to the world that devious dealings are afoot than making a show of checking to see that one is unobserved. The mere fact that Thaddeus had distilled his personal surveillance down to a barely perceptible flicker of the eye was reason enough to treat him with extra caution. The man knew how to do shady business a little too well.

"Were you to take a look in my wagon, you would find it heartbreakingly empty. I've brought barely a third of my usual inventory." He tugged a booklet from his waistcoat and thumbed it open. "I also have a number of items of interest to individuals along the bazaar's route. These are customers who are either unwilling or unable to wait for the next trip through, so a special journey had to be scheduled. I do hope you'll be able to oblige them."

Vivian took the booklet and flattened it on the counter. She took note, one by one, of the contraptions that were being requested.

"How is Euphoria?" Epiphany asked.

"Relieved beyond measure that the Graves flame is once again a trustworthy form of communication. Having to forego it was positively crippling to our business, spread out as we are. And you'll be pleased to know she is making strides to a more open trade with your shop. Hence this little meeting. But we've had to increase our security protocols to stifling levels to avoid another breach like the one with the Bolivans that your boy and Lattica had to take care of. Once bitten, twice shy, as you might imagine. Codes upon codes. Copious hand delivery by intermediaries to break the chain of communication. Downright confounding."

"The purpose of good security is to confound," Epiphany said.

"Ideally it wouldn't confound me, but such are the prices we must pay to maintain our edge."

"I can fulfill all but six of the requests from our current inventory. For the rest I'll need to see if I can tear Martin away from his current puzzle to complete some repairs and restorations."

"And just what is his current puzzle?"

"A private matter," Epiphany and Vivian said simultaneously.

"Ah. Pleased to know we aren't the only ones keeping security at such a high priority." Thaddeus idly fiddled with his pipe, twice nearly putting it back in his mouth before recalling the general distaste for his tendency to smoke in the shop. "You seem to have gotten quite the shipment of antiques. Found a new supplier?"

"That also is a private matter," Epiphany said.

"Though if you see anything that might pique the interests of your customers, I'm sure we could discuss a fair price," added Vivian.

"Forgive me, but I am too fresh off the road to be crossing blades with so capable a salesperson. Perhaps tomorrow."

"How long do you plan on staying?" Epiphany asked.

"A day at least. Longer if I can guarantee I'll be leaving with a completed inventory."

"We will see what we can do." Vivian handed back his book. "If you'd like to leave us the address where you are staying, I can send Fel along with the bulk of your purchases in the morning, and we can settle the price for those and the remainder."

Vivian turned the day's ledger toward him. Tellingly, she'd turned it to a blank page, the better to keep him from snooping into their earnings for the day. He scribbled the name of an inn.

"It is a rare and refreshing opportunity to speak to someone outside the Graves clan who is so rigidly business-minded," he said. "Until tomorrow."

Fel swiped the bottom of his bowl clean with a biscuit and stuffed it in his mouth. Tome was still in his room, doing battle with the elven language. Martin had brought Oiler back to the shop to help with some repairs on Thaddeus's requests. Epiphany was running some errands, and Vivian was running the shop. That left him, Parch, and Teya as the only ones at the table for supper at the actual hour it was intended to be eaten.

"This soup? Who made?" Teya asked between savory laps of her bowl.

"Dad made this one, remember?" Fel said.

"Still? So much?"

"We try to keep a lot of soup on hand."

"Is good," she said.

"I should hope you'd like it. You've eaten six bowls of it since you arrived," he said.

"I borrow food? People get mad. I not eat? People not notice. Not notice better."

"And you were starving yourself, trudging across an unfamiliar world, just because you felt a tug from your magic earring."

"Destiny. Don't ignore destiny," she stated.

"Uh-huh. So far I've been able to get myself in enough trouble without destiny leading me astray. But while we're talking about trouble, now that you're cleaned up and fed and watered, we need to set the rules straight."

"Oh! Yes, rules. I do bad? Does bad for you. So I do good. Tell me rules."

"First, and foremost, I need you to keep out of sight. We get plenty of Lesser Mystics in this area, but the last few Greater Mystics that came through town left claw marks in solid stone. Hippogriffs. Regular griffins. This town is not very fond of Greater Mystics. You show up on the street, it'll cause a stir."

"This? Not a problem. Very sneaky."

"Even so, I'm going to pick up an outfit for you to wear. It'll look ridiculous, but it'll keep people from grabbing the torches and pitchforks to chase you out of town if they see you."

"Why torches? Why pitchforks? For poking and burning?"

"Yes."

She nodded. "Don't want."

"Good. Next, here's the hierarchy in this house. If Mom or Dad say something? Their word is law. Next is me and Epiphany. After that is Wick. We're not going to order you around, but if we say something needs to stop, it needs to stop."

"Good, yes. This I do," she said. "What about Tome?"

"Feel free to ignore him."

She nodded. "Good."

"If you need to come and go, I'd prefer you do it at night. And be careful out there. Though if you got here safely, you probably know how to handle yourself."

"Can do that. Yes."

"And I guess that's it. What about you? Do you need anything from us? Besides a roof over your head and a full belly?"

"I work. I help. Do thing, for you."

"No, no. You don't need to do anything. It'll just complicate matters if you tried to help out."

She thumped her chest with her paw. "This one? Kobold. Kobold? Team. You? You give me home. Treat me like tribe. Like clan. You help, again and again. I help. Must help. Until destiny? I help."

Fel opened his mouth to try to convince her the best help she could give would be to keep a low profile, but a distinctive rattle reverberated through the house. It was a stomped warning from the shop that he knew all too well.

"Someone from the nobles is here..." he said.

"From who?" Teya said.

"The nobles. The people who own the land around here. Usually they only send assayers to check our inventory and make sure we don't have anything we're not supposed to have."

"Do you? Have bad things?"

"Yes. Lots. Oh, that's another rule. Don't talk to anyone about what we have here."

"Secrets. Yes. Always."

He stood and piled the bowls to be dealt with later.

"Why are they here now? They were just here eight days ago. They usually don't come more than once a month." He wiped his hands on his pants. "You stay here. I need to see what this is about."

Rather than the two stodgy and irritable assayers who had poked through a carefully curated portion of the Maskers' inventory a week prior, the person who had prompted the warning this time was a stranger. He was certainly a representative of the nobles. Anyone sent by the people holding the purse strings of the region didn't let you forget it. He had a well-worn but brightly polished badge, quite authentic, and was dressed finer than Fel had ever dressed in his life. He also had the unmistakable air of someone who knew he was fully able to inflict his will on everyone he met.

"Ah, Fel. This is Inspector Cartwright," Vivian said.

"A pleasure," Fel said, not even attempting to sound genuine with the sentiment.

"Fel Masker?" the inspector said.

"That's me."

"I'd expected you to be larger. Considering how often your name has come up in unpleasant contexts. You come off as a brute."

Fel hiked his thumb over his shoulder. "You want me to get my cudgel and start acting the part?"

"Fel," Vivian said, a veneer of stern reprisal coloring the statement. "The inspector was just informing me of the reason for his presence here."

"Don't let me stop you." Fel crossed his arms and leaned against the shelf.

Cartwright cleared his throat. "By now I imagine you've heard of the recent unrest in the area."

"Oh, yes. I understand there has been some violence along the roads. More so than usual," Vivian said.

"Considerably," Cartwright said.

"And that brought you to our antiquities shop?" Vivian said.

"Not directly. As you might imagine, I began by looking into matters with the rather underwhelming local Watch to see if any of the threats had breached the walls. And according to them, there was one rather notable arrival."

"Oh?" Fel said.

"A... beast of some kind. Vicious. Feral," Cartwright said. "And to my extreme confusion, I was informed that the Watch captain personally turned this monster over to you, Mr. Masker."

"Word travels fast," Fel said.

"Maybe you could explain why you are qualified to look after a bloodthirsty beast, Mr. Masker."

"You already called me Mr. Masker once. Let's not make it a habit. It makes me feel like you're about to pull the shackles out," Fel said.

"Tell me why you can be relied upon to look after a murderous fiend, and we'll consider more informal terms for one another."

"She's not murderous," Fel said. "She's just... different."

"So you do have her," the inspector said.

"She's here, yes. It's a bit of a stretch to say I have her. She's a guest."

"Then I would like to meet this 'guest.' I imagine she's just downstairs?"

The inspector stepped toward the hatch. Fel stepped in front of it, arms still crossed. Cartwright looked him in the eye, seemingly noticing for the first time that he had to look up to do so. To his credit, despite Fel's imposing size, the inspector didn't bat an eye.

"Sir, you are interfering with an inspector in his duties," he said.

"I'm standing in my home and place of business," Fel said.

"I am here as an authorized agent of the nobles of Thayne," Cartwright said.

"Oh, By the High, I'm am terribly sorry for my son's behavior," Vivian said. "I wasn't aware you were authorized to search our home. If you'd be so kind as to present the proclamation from the nobles, I would be happy to bring you to have a word with our new guest personally."

Cartwright tapped his badge. "Now step aside."

"A thousand pardons," Vivian said calmly. "But I think you'll find that, within the city limits of Beffshire, a representative of a noble is permitted entry to a private home only with direct and specific authorization. Again, if you'll show me the sealed and signed proclamation from Lord Katritz, I'll be happy to invite you inside."

"This is absurd. I represent the lord. I do his business personally," he said.

"Undoubtedly so, but the town charter is quite clear on the subject. We pay a not-inconsiderable amount of additional tribute for this privilege as residents of Beffshire," Vivian said.

"I need but to ask for such a document and I shall have it," the inspector said.

"Splendid. If it is not an imposition, then I feel quite comfortable in requesting it."

Fel leaned ever so slightly forward, the better to emphasize his height advantage. "Rule are rules, Inspector," he said.

Cartwright narrowed his eyes. "You realize I shall return."

"And you'll be welcome within our shop then as you are now," Vivian said as though there wasn't an ounce of tension in the air. "Until then, I suggest you enjoy the hospitality of our town. We have some of the finest shops, taverns, and restaurants in the region."

Inspector Cartwright gave the hem of his coat a sharp tug and turned on his heel. "Good day, Mrs. Masker. Good day, Mr. Masker," he said, marching out the door.

"The name is Fel," Fel called after him. "When you do the misses and mister thing, it sounds like you think we're married. I know you're used to working with nobles, but not everyone marries within the family."

Cartwright let the door swing shut without a response. Likely for the best.

"Fel, you need to learn a bit about how to deal with authority figures," Vivian said.

"There's a reason I never started working the counter, Mom. I'm more suited for the kind of interactions where I can hand someone their teeth if they deserve it. Besides, something seemed off about that guy," he said.

She nodded, glancing out the shop window. "You've got the family intuition, at least. The man had an aim he wasn't voicing. The inspectors are dispatched from Teskal. That's up north. Most of the trouble in the area has been further south. And more to the point, it takes a good four days to reach here from there. Without something like Wick or the Graves flames to get the word to him quickly, I'm not sure he would have gotten word of the troubles nearby by the time he left for the trip."

"And he didn't ask us to bring Teya up, he wanted to go down to see her," Fel said.

"He had ulterior motives," she said. "And an inspector that marches all the way to Beffshire isn't likely to drop the subject just because I happen to know the town charter better than most."

"After the sort of trouble we've been having with monsters and mercenaries, some good old-fashioned corrupt nobility feels like a refreshing change of pace," Fel said.

"Nothing refreshing about having a problem with someone in a place of legitimate authority." Vivian glanced over her shoulder. "If it turns out this new friend of yours is the source of our difficulties..."

"She isn't," Fel said. "We faced a dragon together. I trust her more than I trust half the guys in The Fox and Log."

"That's not a very high bar," Vivian said.

"Teya's a little rough around the edges—and that says a lot, coming from me—but she's not a murderer or a thug."

"And the poaching?"

"... Some light poaching. And maybe a dash of arson."

Vivian sighed. "If you vouch for her, she has sanctuary with the family. But we have enough problems without importing new ones from the Greater Lands."

"That's the good news, Mom. She was able to get here because of that earring, and there's only one of them. I can guarantee that no one else is coming here from the Greater Lands. You let me know what I have to do if the inspector becomes a problem."

"You'll be the first to hear about it."

Well after nightfall, a fit young man paced along the road with a bright, friendly lantern dangling from the end of a stick over his shoulder and a rucksack on his back. Five long days of hiking along the road had nearly brought him to Beffshire. If he kept up the pace, he'd be there by morning. For the average traveler, keeping up the pace through the night simply wasn't an option. Most people traveled during the day. The setting sun was reason enough to find an inn or someplace to camp. But those people simply lacked the sort of cleverness and ingenuity that had kept him fed and happy for the past few years.

If you wanted to be successful, you needed to be the sort of man people needed. And late at night, on the road? Everyone could use a man with a good lantern.

He'd gotten the idea one night when he'd been kicked out of a tavern. It was an upscale sort of place. That was the reason he'd been kicked out. He didn't look fancy enough to be one of their clientele. He also didn't have any money. Frankly, he didn't see what difference that made. The place had more money than they knew what to do with, considering they kept a lantern burning outside the place all night long. As he'd sat in the gutter and gazed up at the ill-advised lantern, he saw moths flitting and fluttering about. Then he'd noticed not one but three people over the course of an hour pause beneath the lantern to do something or another. Tying a boot, dusting off a sleeve, checking a pocket to be sure their coins were safe. All things that could easily have been done anywhere else, but like the moths, they'd chosen the glow of the lantern to do their business. There was an awful lot a fellow could do if he had a means to attract people simply by dangling a light. And so, he'd liberated the tavern of their flame.

It had all worked like a charm. Without fail, everyone he passed on the road was drawn to the flame. Sometimes they needed help. Sometimes they just wanted to borrow a bit of light. Usually he was able to persuade them to part with a few coins. Sometimes out of their own charity and kindness, sometimes with a bit of coaxing from the knife on his belt. Whatever it took.

He stopped to lean on a fence and dig out some dried meat from his pocket.

"No one on the road tonight," he grumbled. "I wonder what's scared everyone off. This close to a city as big as Beffshire there ought to be someone."

He tore at the leathery meal and planned what he'd do once he got to Beffshire. A decent pint, maybe some good bread and butter. Perhaps...

He paused. Something was wrong. Though there was no one about, he didn't feel as though he was alone. He squinted into the darkness. The benefit of a lantern was that things nearby were easy to see. The curse was that it ruined his night vision for anything much farther than its glow. He raised the lantern higher.

A single, complex, incomprehensible word filtered out of the darkness. A flutter of wind rushed past him. A gout of warm fluid rushed down his neck: his own blood. He was already on his knees when the white-hot sting of pain reached his brain. He crumbled to the ground, his lantern rattling down beside him. As his vision dimmed, the last thing he saw was a shadowy figure stooping to snatch the lantern away.

CHAPTER 2

The following day, Epiphany and Vivian were grappling with the curse and blessing of a fresh infusion of inventory. On one hand, nothing packed the store with people like shelf after shelf of freshly polished and cleaned antiques. On the other, the sort of person attracted by a shiny new trinket in a shop window was seldom the sort of person who would actually buy it. Converting an idle browser whiling away the afternoon into a customer took a set of skills that had been handed down for generations, and Epiphany had learned her lessons well.

"Ah," she said, approaching a gentleman manhandling a serving bowl. "I can see you have an eye for value."

She gently tugged a bowl that was likely older than Beffshire itself from the hands of a man who was treating it with the same care as the crumpled hat under his arm.

"May I ask, did you come here specifically with heirloom ceramics in mind, or were you after something more general?"

"I'm looking for something to empty my pockets in when I come in the door," he said.

"Ah, yes. An excellent opportunity for something both attractive and functional. And while this particular bowl has survived several hundred years, might I suggest that in your case we'll need something with a better balance of durability to cost," she said, guiding him toward things on the wicker side of the value spectrum.

The tried-and-true sales routine slipped directly from the back of her mind to her mouth, leaving the bulk of her brain unburdened and able to process other things. She glanced first to her mother, who was setting a price on a complete set of clay figurines. When she closed the deal, she'd have earned as much in a single sale as they'd made in the entirety of some of their slower days. Then she looked to the street. Her gaze fixed on the gentleman across the way. She knew him as Inspector Cartwright, as her mother had explained their run-in the previous day. For some reason, rather than actually entering and making his intentions known, he had simply lingered across the street, periodically waving off the quartet of lesser harpies that had taken up permanent residence along the rooftops of the local shops.

"... and thus I think you'll find it will suit your purposes brilliantly for the very affordable price of seventeen duots," Epiphany said, hearing herself end her sales pitch rather than consciously choosing to end it.

"Does it come in red?" he asked.

"Sir, this is an antique shop. What you see is what we have. However, for a small fee, an additional eight duots, I can have it dyed for you."

"So that'd cost me..."

"Twenty-five duots."

"That's a little much."

"If you are able to wait a week, I can see about having the work done at a discount. Twenty duots in total?"

"You've got a deal."

"Wonderful. If you'll join me at the counter, we can handle the payment and—"

The jangling of the bell over the door was joined by a burst of croaked commentary from the lesser harpies.

"Rotten monkey-headed rat dog!" shouted a bird that it shamed Epiphany she was able to recognize as the one her brother had named Toody.

The inspector swatted them away and held the door as two other representatives of the nobles filed in. The man and woman who entered after him were familiar, two of the rotating cast of assayers, and were notably ignored by the harpies.

"Those things are a menace and a threat to public safety," Cartwright said.

"You just need to bribe them with something shiny or something edible and you're safe for the day. They're better at remembering faces and fees than the toll collector at the bridge down south," Epiphany said.

"I will not be extorted by wildlife," the inspector snapped. "Now, all but the Maskers, out of the shop. This is an official assayer's inspection."

"Certainly," Vivian said with mechanical cordiality. "I will just finalize this purchase and—"

"By the order of the nobles, leave the store now," he instructed with the tone of voice that burrowed straight to buried memories of school headmasters and stern grandfathers.

The would-be customers scurried out. As they abandoned their business in the shop, the lesser harpies left them alone as well. Epiphany noted, but through raw force of will managed to avoid mentioning, that the inspector had chased away the customers at the precise moment that it cost them two sales. One of which was a hard-negotiated payday.

That was not an accident or coincidence. He'd been watching and chose the maliciously perfect moment to strike.

"Our most recent inspection and appraisal was only nine days ago. Has the schedule been altered?" Vivian asked.

The young woman who had taken the lead in the previous appraisal began to answer. Cartwright raised his voice to answer first.

"These are representatives of the nobles. I am a privileged representative of the nobles and thus am permitted to direct them at my discretion. I am directing them to assess the inventory of this shop, so you will present that inventory for inspection and you will speak only to answer questions we ask and otherwise facilitate the inspection," he snapped.

"Very well." Vivian turned to Epiphany. "Fetch your brother to help with the crates. This will fortunately not take long, as we've had only a handful of purchases and one sizable acquisition since the last set of appraisals."

"All right," Fel said, brushing his hands as he returned to his room. "That's the last of the crates. Now where were we on... Oh."

Prior to being summoned by his sister to help the store submit to an entirely unnecessary appraisal, Fel had been attempting to work out with Teya how precisely she would be able to come and go from the house without causing a stir. Evidently in his brief absence, she'd developed a plan of her own. Teya had donned one of his older and more worn winter coats from the wardrobe. The hood was cavernous enough to almost entirely cover her head. The blunt tip of her muzzle still emerged, but she'd wrapped one of his scarves around it. Comical as it was to see the sleeves dangling down to drag on the ground, it was even more entertaining to see how poorly Teya's toe-walking-type feet handled being shoved into a pair of boots. She'd effectively stuck her clawed toes in the tops of them, leaving the soles of the boots to stick forward and the toes of them to point straight up. If he squinted, in the bizarre outfit Teya almost looked like an oddly proportioned human being sitting down on the ground.

"Disguise! Very sneaky!" she said, her voice muffled by the scarf.

He sighed and pushed the hood back. "I admire the ingenuity, Teya, but there are some flaws in your technique. First, that's not how boots go."

She looked at her feet. "I know. You wear boots. I see them. This? Close to that. Close enough."

"No. I don't think very many people pay attention to how a person wears their shoes, but that's liable to stand out. There's also the issue that you are bundled up for a mountain winter, and in and around Beffshire, it's never cold enough to bundle up like that."

"Some people get cold. Get cold easy. Yes?" she said. "People see me. They think, that one? Gets cold easy."

"I'm not sure it'll work, Teya."

"It will. Very sneaky," she said with the utmost of confidence.

"Even so. Let's try to keep the outside time to a minimum, at least inside the city. I don't want you getting hauled back to the Watch again. To say nothing of what some of the locals will do if they see something they'd call a monster walking the streets."

"This is best." She patted the wall. "Your home. Very like cave. Nice. Good home. Also water! Easy for clean. Easy for drink. Very, very good home."

"Thanks. We just need to work out where you're going to stay."

Teya pointed. He looked up. The broad top of one of his bookcases now had a neat little nest of torn sacks from the antiques he'd brought back. An old iron lamp hook near the ceiling now held the pack of gear that they'd reclaimed from the Watch.

"You're going to sleep on my bookcase," he said steadily.

"Nice! High. Sturdy. Place for things. Good place!"

She scrambled up with impressive ease. Once atop the shelf, there wasn't nearly enough room for her to sit up. But she crawled easily into her nest and gazed over the edge at him.

"Can watch friend, too."

"You can watch me," Fel said.

"Yes!"

"While I'm sleeping."

"Yes, yes! Keep safe. Fel, least-worst friend. Should watch. Keep safe. Maybe destiny."

"We'll set aside the 'least-worst friend' thing. Right now I'm mostly interested in this 'destiny' you're on about."

"Important," she said with a nod.

"You're really going to stay here because you feel it is your destiny."

"No. Stay here? Not destiny. Come here, destiny. Stay here until destiny."

"But you don't know what your destiny is."

"No."

"Then how will you know when you're done with it? How will you know what it even is?"

"I see, I know. Destiny? Can't miss. Destiny? Maybe not big. Maybe not important to all. But important to me. Clear to me. I see, I know."

"And what will you do until then?"

"Help!" She grabbed her bag and slipped down from the shelf. "Here? This place? New. All new. Very, very newness. I do. I learn. You move box? I move box. You empty box? I empty box. Father build? Maybe me too. Mother sell? Maybe me too."

"I don't think you'll be doing any sales. Sorry to say it, but just about the only way you're likely to earn any money while people can see you is if you end up behind bars and someone sells tickets."

She scratched her chin. "Not that. Boring. If that? Escape. But other things. Do. Do all the things. Be more. Be better. Good, good. Me? Here? Not make harder. Make easier. Promise. Very, very promise." She pointed at the little tool bench Fel had set up in the corner. "Can use?"

He shrugged. "Sure."

She tottered over and hopped onto the chair. Taking care not to move any of the things already in place on the table, she slid her fishing rod out of its loop on the pack and pulled the needle and thread from its cubby on his tool board. "What about you? Destiny for you?" she said conversationally.

"Oh, I don't need to go looking for destiny. My destiny has been set out for me since before I was born. I'm a Masker."

"Name? Destiny more than name."

"Yeah, but Masker is more than a name. Masker is a calling. Dad talks about it sometimes. We're an unbroken thread of contraptioneers, leading all the way back to the Bygone Era."

"Contraptioneer. And not bad." She paused. "Not very very bad. Rare."

"Thanks. If I can't be good, I can at least be not very, very bad. But you're not kidding when you say rare. There are three families out there still doing this stuff. On this continent, anyway. And the Bolivans absolutely are very, very bad. The Graves family... eh. The point is, bad or not, if we don't want contraptioneering to vanish, I sort of have to stay in the family business. I won't be breaking the chains of destiny, that's for sure."

"Chains? No, no. Not chains." She threaded a needle after six tries. "Destiny not chains. Destiny gift. Back home? On mountain? Many kobolds. Many many. And this? Good. Much to do, many to do it. Good good. Important things to do. All who do things? Important. But this one. Teya? Job for only Teya. Job for only this one. Honor. Privilege. Very very."

"Feels like kind of a heavy burden to be calling it an honor," he said.

"Heavy? Heavy means big. Big honor. Very very big. And if heavy?" She finished pulling a seam on her pack tight. "Friends help lift."

She tied off the repair and bit through the thread. With the job done, she hopped from chair to shelf and leaned out to pat him on the shoulder.

"You feel heavy honor? You ask. This one? Help."

"It's good to know I've got a friend out there."

Teya nodded, then dropped down and scampered toward the door. "You have other boot? Old boot? Maybe make new boot. Out of old one. Boot right for feet. Will be fun. Much fun! Learn! Very very!"

Six hours later, Vivian's assessment of the duration of the appraisal turned out to be a rare miscalculation. The best sales days were always those immediately after an infusion of new inventory, and Inspector Cartwright had dragged his inspection out long enough to cost them the lion's share of the earnings from the day. It could only be called malicious adherence to the law as he nitpicked and overanalyzed everything from the individual markings on each acquired item to the very crates they'd been stored in. But even he couldn't drag it out forever.

"And this? What do you call this?" he said, holding up the final item in the final crate.

"That is a nightingale box. A contraption functionally similar but mechanically distinct from a music box. We purchased it from a collector three days ago."

The male assayer turned it about in his hands. Of all the people in a given community, a contraptioneer was certainly the most familiar with the operation of contraptions. A distant second, but still head and shoulders above most others, was an assayer. In moments, he located the activation mechanism and filled the shop with a pleasant, if not entirely natural-sounding, bit of birdsong.

"Acceptable," he said.

"Wonderful," Vivian said. "And that concludes an impressively thorough assessment of our new inventory. And quite a light one, in terms of acquisitions by the nobility. Unless my accounting missed something, you've forbidden the sale of a single rotary chisel."

"If you would please settle the accounts, so we can re-open for business?" Epiphany said.

She'd failed to match her mother's composure. Twenty duots were about to change hands, the pathetic underestimate of the chisel's value. Meanwhile, thousands of duots in sales had been turned away for the sake of finding said chisel among the rest of the innocuous items. The female assayer opened a locked pouch on her belt and reached inside. Inspector Cartwright stopped her.

"We are through when I say we are through," he said. "We will see the rest of your inventory now."

"You have checked every piece of new inventory we have," Vivian said. "I believe the assayer's records will confirm it."

"Everything else on the shelves has been appraised," the female assayer said, clearly as eager to be out of this place as the Maskers were to be rid of them.

"So they say. But those crates came from below, didn't they?" Cartwright said. "This is an old building. It has basements. And sub-basements. I happen to know it has no less than five levels beneath this one. Clearly they are being at least partially used for inventory. And thus, we need to appraise the contents of that inventory."

"Oh, I see. My word is insufficient?" Vivian said.

"Decidedly so," the inspector said.

"Very well. Your proclamation permitting entry to my home?" Vivian said.

He pointed to the assayers. "You agree to periodic appraisals in order to be permitted to peddle your antiquities. We are exercising those rights now. I have all the permissions I need."

"You have all the permissions you need to inspect my place of business. Below this shop is my home. And as we have stated, you require a specific signed and sealed proclamation from the lord himself to inspect it."

"But the assayers!" the inspector said.

"They are quite familiar with the law, as well," Vivian said.

"The appraisal is complete," the first assayer said.

"It was complete three hours ago, once it was clear the rest of the crates were mundane antiques," grumbled the second.

"Are you honestly telling me that all this woman needs to do to completely bypass the assayer's office is to call her personal warehouse part of her home?"

"Inspector Cartwright, I am honor bound to follow the law. What's more, failure to do so could lead to me losing my right to sell contraptions of any kind. That is a very strong motivation to be forthcoming. But just as I am obligated to follow the law to the letter, so too are you. Were I to permit you to inspect my home without the proper permissions, you would be defying the will of the nobles you serve and the agreements they put their names to. And I care too much about your hallowed position and theirs to allow that to occur."

He shuddered. "So be it. I will send for the proclamation immediately. And until it arrives, either I or one of my representatives will maintain this building under constant surveillance. Anything that leaves this shop will be inspected. You are hiding something and I will find it."

"Splendid. Then, assuming you are able to find a messenger with a swift horse, I look forward to giving you a tour of my home in just a bit more than a week."

He turned to leave.

"Oh! Inspector, before you go," Vivian said calmly. "I believe just yesterday when you arrived, you were primarily interested in the violence in the surrounding countryside and its potential connection to a creature presently in our care. I wonder, have there been any developments in that regard, or has your area of interest shifted?"

"The investigation is ongoing. My tasks are many, and I take them all very seriously. Good day, Mrs. Masker."

He marched out the door.

"Rat-bag monkey thief!" squawked a lesser harpy the moment he emerged.

The two assayers offered silent but sympathetic glances before slipping out as well. When they were comfortably out of earshot, Vivian turned to Epiphany.

"Get the boys. Tell them what's happened. This will need to be dealt with."

In her entire life, Epiphany had never known her mother to show undue emotion. Not when her eldest daughter eloped. Not on the all-too-common occasion of Fel's brushes with death. She was the rock upon which the family was built. But the way she'd delivered that instruction vibrated with a suppressed anxiety in a way that she'd never witnessed.

This was serious.

Martin tightened a fastener on the cylinder of parts, then gently dropped the cylinder into place. It slid into the opening on the scratch-built bust with the sort of slow, steady motion of an incredibly precise slip-fit. Once it was properly seated, he tested it for slop or rotation. None.

"The moment of truth, Wick," he said.

"I am eager to observe the conclusion of the day's tweaks," Wick said, the light of his stationary flame softly illuminating the workbench.

Martin removed the Student mask from the inert bust. He'd already removed the fasteners. All it took was a gentle tug to remove the piece from its place. Once removed, the opening in the bust revealed its magnificently complex workings. Yet, when he held up the backside of the mask to inspect it in the light, the inner surface was almost featureless.

"Here it is," Martin said. "The interface. The border between what I understand and what I do not. Just the head of that bust contains seven hundred fifty-three moving parts. Two hundred fifteen linkages.

Seventeen different types of fasteners. Forty different types of bushings. Those I understand. But somehow, some way, they interact with this mask despite no obvious place for them to attach. This polished surface is a mystery. Somehow it contains something very much like my own intellect and precisely like yours. Yet it was crafted by hands not unlike my own. The means to create it is how this clan earned its name, but it's a mystery to me. It's such a delicious irony. So tantalizing."

He turned the mask upright facing the ceiling, and lowered it down onto the cylinder. It came into contact with a soft click. He gently slid it in circles until it rather jarringly snapped into position and locked itself there. A hinged section of the cylinder pivoted, and the mask angled to face forward.

"Oh! Hello. This is a curious new mechanism," the mask uttered, its voice somewhat more tinny and distant than usual. "Would this be the newest bust?"

"It is," Martin said. "How does it function in comparison to the other one?"

"Rather more effort to articulate. And I cannot see," the Student said. "But otherwise no other obvious shortcomings."

"Excellent. A step closer to a faithful re-creation. And as for new aspects?" Martin said hopefully.

"I do so enjoy these tests of observation," the Student said. "Let me see. There does seem to be an additional function."

Martin took a step back. The single arm dangling from the side of the bust remained motionless.

"It does not appear to be a sensory function," the Student said. "Perhaps if I..." The fingers of the arm shuddered. The elbow of the arm bent. "Ah. A source of motion," the Student said simply.

Martin erupted with a cheer. "Success! Ha ha! Success."

The door to the workshop opened. Epiphany stuck her head in. "Dad, we've been calling you. We—"

"Success, Fanny! Success! The arm moves. The coupler activates the mask, and the mask can move the arm! A tremendous milestone! This is a momentous occasion. Momentous!"

"Dad, you need to come upstairs," she insisted.

"It was a very small adjustment, Fanny. A small inscription on three struts and a minor adjustment to their assembly order. I can have the other two couplers built to the same specifications by this evening. Now I simply need to work on the other arm."

"Dad!" Epiphany snapped.

"Oh! Yes. Sorry, dear. Is something wrong?" he said.

"We need you upstairs. Now. It's bad."

His expression became more serious. "Is anyone hurt?"

"No, but the shop is in trouble if we don't figure something out, and fast."

Martin turned to the Student. "I apologize for the brief lesson. I'll be with you as soon as possible."

"No trouble at all," the Student said cheerily.

He tried to pull the mask free but found it quite sturdily attached. Rather than leave it in operation or take the time to work out how it was adhered in the first place, he slipped an ornate black dagger from its holder in the other bust and gently tapped it to the point where the mask and coupler met. The mask pulled free, and he set it on the desk.

Father and daughter silently climbed the steps to the dining room. Tome, Fel, and Teya were present already. Martin's frequently preoccupied mind took a moment to recollect the brief introduction he'd had with the kobold. It would take a bit more time for him to become accustomed to her presence in the house.

"What's the problem?" Martin said.

"I'll make it fast. As you know, yesterday a man called Inspector Cartwright came and wished to inspect our home, claiming Teya may have been responsible for some violence around the town. Today he spent nearly the entire workday overseeing an appraisal and became outraged when he wasn't allowed to continue the appraisal down here. Mom reminded him he needs a signed proclamation to do so, and he's sent for it."

"Oh dear..." Martin said.

"Four days to Teskal and four days back, that means we have eight days before an inspector and two assayers come down here and see storerooms and full floors of contraptions that we are legally obliged to turn over due to their high risk. Best case, we end up paying several years worth of income in compensation to the lord. Far more likely, we have to do that and we're forbidden from doing business any longer, perhaps with some number of months or years behind bars in addition."

"It is absurd that this could be happening ostensibly because we were simply unwilling to give up Teya," Tome said.

"Are you suggesting we should have given her up?" Fel asked.

"I'm suggesting the path between 'take in someone who needs help' and 'destroy a business and imprison a family' seems like it ought to have a few more steps," Tome said.

"I don't care why what's happening is happening. It's happening. We need to do something about it," Epiphany said.

"I suggest we look into this Cartwright fellow. Overstepping his bounds, certainly," Tome said.

"He isn't," Fel said. "He's an inspector, authorized by a noble. He basically doesn't have bounds. It's only thanks to a quirk of the town charter in Beffshire that we even got the eight-day reprieve."

"Maybe so, but that doesn't mean he's not abusing his power," Tome said. "I think something fishy is going on. If we can uncover it, perhaps we can diffuse the situation prior to the proclamation's arrival."

"I won't hold my breath on that," Epiphany said.

"Surely we can simply move the offending items to storage elsewhere," Martin said.

"Right now, and evidently until the moment the proclamation arrives, we are under surveillance. It won't be as simple as moving things out. They'll notice. And even if they didn't notice things leaving, they'll notice things coming in. They don't keep track of what we sell, but the assayers do keep track of what they've appraised, and in order for them to not suspect something, we'll need to make sure we replace a suitable amount of the inventory we move out with items at least superficially similar to what they already appraised for us. Empty shelves will raise questions. We've been in business too long for them to believe we're working with nothing in our inventory."

"Maybe kill the man?" Teya said.

All eyes turned to her.

"The man who watches," she clarified. "Or other man? Inspector man? Kill that one."

Martin raised an eyebrow. "Are we certain this creature isn't the threat she's purported to be?"

"We can't kill the inspector or anyone else, Teya," Fel said.

"Because it is wrong?" Teya said.

"Yeah. Also because there are always more inspectors. They'd just send another one to investigate the death of the first. Probably two."

Teya nodded. "Like hydra heads. Cut one, get two."

"If we're through discussing murder," Epiphany said, "let's look at this objectively. The message is sent. It would be a mistake to try and stop it. Cartwright already suspects us of misdeed. If anything gets in the way of the investigation, even if we aren't responsible, he'll blame us. So we have to assume this inspection is going to happen. And to be frank, the best possible outcome is that it does happen but turns up nothing. That will underscore the waste of time and resources that Cartwright demanded, and it'll all but guarantee they no longer suspect we're hiding anything. No one ever looks for something in a place they've already searched. So the question isn't how to stop the inspection. The question is, how do we get the incriminating contraptions out of here and sneak in some replacements, all in the next eight days and without anyone seeing the items enter or leave?"

"We need to do a double-reverse heist of our own home," Fel said.

"While someone is effectively expecting it to happen," Martin added.

"It would appear so," Epiphany said.

They were silent for a beat.

"So, what's the to-do list?" Fel counted off on his fingers. "Figure out what we need to move, figure out where we're going to move it, figure out how we're going to move it? Am I missing anything?"

"That's the long and short of it, for now," Epiphany said. "I'll get started on identifying the list of items we'll need to move. Though, frankly, it is going to be most everything in the storeroom. The legal stuff goes from the workshop to the shelves to our customers' homes."

"Quite so. I imagine we'll need to make some rather significant changes to my workshop as well," Martin said. "A fair amount of my reference materials, many of my current projects, and some of my new tools would be in violation. While I'm creating the necessary list of contraband, I'll put my mind to some potential means to transport items surreptitiously."

"I'll go talk to Mom. Let her know we're starting and see if she has anything to add," Fel said.

Tome glanced about. "That's it? Just like that? This is happening?"

"It has to be done," Fel said with a shrug. "You gonna help out?"

The paper mage shook his head a bit. "I suppose if you have a place for me, I'll endeavor to fill my role. But until then, I think there is value in investigating the investigator. Perhaps I give the nobles too much credit, but I don't believe this appraisal would be approved if they knew it was under false pretenses."

"You are indeed giving the nobles too much credit," Epiphany said. "Pettiness and contrariness are driving forces once you get high enough up the ladder of nobility."

"Even so. You know my capabilities. Until you determine how you need them, I'll be looking into this."

"And this one?" Teya said expectantly. "How to help?"

"Stay hidden. I get the feeling there will be plenty for you to do once we know what it is."

Teya rubbed her paws together eagerly. "I work so good. You watch!"

The family, each with their own tasks, went their separate ways. It was going to be a busy few days.

Chapter 3

Just past noon the next day, Epiphany was ready for the first step in what was turning out to be an unpleasantly ambitious plan. The inventory was over in just a few hours, and the largest challenge had been sifting through the workshop with her father. She already knew everything that was in storage, but Martin's tinkering had been producing a range of items beginning with inert and ending with inarguably dangerous, with examples of every other shade of mechanism on the spectrum. Removing them while still leaving enough tools, resources, and mechanisms to appear to be a typical, functioning contraptioneer's shop quickly began to feel more like set dressing than inventory. But that job was done, and in the process, the combined ingenuity of the Masker family had pieced together the first fragments of a plan.

Epiphany wasn't entirely pleased that such an early step—or indeed, any step—of the plan required her to visit The Fox and Log. It was a lovely tavern, but it was also the birthplace of many a bad idea. Booze had that effect on any situation it came near. She stepped into the busy tavern. Ever since Euphoria's visit, Epiphany had tried to avoid this place. She actually quite enjoyed her visits, but spending a few weeks getting drunk and singing had earned her a bit of a reputation that she'd prefer fade a tad before she began frequenting the place again.

She took a whiff and instantly knew she'd come to the right place at the right time. The distinctive and penetrating stink of badgerweed hung in the air near the door. She scanned the bar and found Thaddeus Graves seated alone at a table near the grum game. She hurried to him and avoided eye contact with the regulars for fear of someone making a song request.

"Thad," she said, sliding into a seat opposite him.

"Ah! Epiphany. Come for a drink?" he said.

"No. I came for a word."

"Business?"

"Is it ever not business?"

Epiphany caught the attention of Allie, who was across the room, loading up a tray and chatting with Fel. With a short exchange of gestures and nods, Epiphany asked for and received permission to use one of the private rooms in the back. Thad followed and they slipped inside, where a table with four chairs was awaiting them. They sat on either side.

"To what do I owe the honor of you approaching me with business without any subterfuge to grease the wheels of commerce?" Thaddeus said.

"Who said there was no subterfuge, Thad?"

He leaned forward. "Oh? Am I to believe the Maskers are sliding themselves even further into the seedy underbelly of this city?"

"We've drawn the scrutiny of someone who thinks we're hiding something, and it just so happens that they're right. You know about it, we know about it, and frankly you're partly responsible."

He laughed. "We dangled the cheese of bypassing the assayer to make some sales. It isn't our fault you swallowed the whole wheel and the trap. Take some responsibility for your own actions."

"That I called you partly responsible rather than entirely responsible is a tacit acceptance of our share of the responsibility. Now let's stop quibbling on semantics and get to the details. In a week, the representative or representatives of the noble will be searching our house from top to bottom, and we're going to need to make sure there's nothing to find. We'll be watched, so we can't ferry things in and out without some serious misdirection and ingenuity. We need your help with that."

"And failure, I presume, spells doom for the business aspirations of the Masker clan?"

"Among other things."

"Fortunate that we've so recently become rather better collaborators than we've been in the past. There was a time not a year ago that the best possible turn of events for the Graves family would have been the collapse of Masker's Antiquities. Not to insinuate such is still the case."

"You'd best not insinuate such a thing, because the Graves family stands to gain an awful lot by playing a part in this," Epiphany said.

"And we stand to lose a great deal if our involvement were to be discovered. But I'm an open-minded negotiator. What precisely do we stand to gain?"

"A permanent foothold in Beffshire and a cartload of money directly out of our coffers."

"My, my. You really are in a tight spot. What would you have me do?"

"I need you to make some purchases on my behalf. Innocuous contraptions. A crate or two."

"To replace the inventory you'll need to move with something a bit less concerning to the nobles?"

"Of course."

"You'll need rather more than a crate or two if I'm correct about the amount of inventory space in your shop."

"You're not our only source. And let's not start talking up your end of the bargain when you don't know the hardest part."

"I'm all ears."

"The shop next to ours belongs to a cobbler named Reynard. He is getting on in years, and he's been griping about a desire to travel for ages. He's on the very cusp of retirement, but he's too stubborn to do it. I can respect that. But the most important thing is that the lower levels of our shops share a few walls. Second and third levels at least."

"And you're planning on breaking down a wall and moving your things out through his shop?"

"That's part of the plan. We're hoping to persuade him to let us see to his shop while he travels. You'd work the counter. Do general business, ignore what you hear downstairs, and maybe help us get some of the stuff out via 'sales' to people we'll be arranging to come in."

"It's a shade optimistic to assume the inspector wouldn't find a sudden increase in volume in the shop next door a bit fishy."

"That has been taken into consideration. There are additional prongs to the plan. The key takeaway is that Reynard is an excellent cobbler but a pitiful salesman. You'll move more of his shoes in the week that he's gone than he's sold in a month. He comes back to find the heap of earnings, and he'll know that when the time comes to retire, you can be trusted with the shop."

"You think he would sell us the shop in the near future?"

"I know the man. As desperately as he clings to that place, the moment he knows the old shop will continue to do brisk business when he moves on, he'll move on. It's a long story, but he's kept it going as long as it has not because he needs the money but because he doesn't want to see the place vanish."

"Euphoria has spoken frequently in the past about how difficult it is for someone outside the kingdom to acquire a shop in Beffshire. That won't be an issue here?"

"We'll handle it, when the time comes."

He stroked his chin. "It would certainly streamline collaboration between the families. And there is something appealing about Beffshire having a semi-official 'Antiquities District.' That should help attract more sellers and collectors and shave some stops off the traveling bazaar's route."

"My thoughts exactly."

He fiddled with his pipe. It was presently unlit, but he chewed it a bit regardless.

"I think I can be persuaded to postpone my trip south for another week. Now. Let's discuss the items you wish to acquire. I'm sure we can come to a fair price."

Epiphany grinned and leaned back. After the tense hours of planning, a little old-fashioned haggling was a welcome change of pace.

Fel crunched some crickets and idly stroked Parch's head. The lesser unicorn stood beside him and lapped at a dish of water. Fel eyed the grum table. There was an opening. Right now Fel would like nothing more than to plop down, throw some duots on the table, and see if he could win back some of what he'd lost last week. Fortunately, though he was a man of many faults, it was a point of pride that he never let them get in the way of family business. And right now there was a lot of family business to be done and not much time to do it.

Allie marched back over to the bar and set down her tray. "I tell you, Fel. Once this place got redone, I've barely been able to keep up. You wouldn't think a little extra space and some rearranging would make that much of a difference."

"Hope that means more money for you," Fel said.

"More than I was making, but less than I'm worth, if you ask me. But it beats the alternative," she said.

"What's the alternative?"

"Trying to convince anyone else I'm worth anything at all. You need a refill?" she said.

He pushed his tankard forward. She topped it off with ale.

"Oh, I meant to talk to you. A while back you were talking about some… cave or something. You and your dad went there. Full of statues?"

"Yeah, yeah. The headless quarry. That's the second vault my Dad ever took me to."

"Right. I know you're busy, but if you ever head back that way, any chance you could grab one of those statues? I'm sure I could get Sid to throw you some coins."

"They're pretty heavy, but we could probably work something out. Why?"

"I try not to spend my time puzzling out what's going on in a drunk's head, but someone has been using the alley out back for business a gentleman doesn't do in public."

"There's a lot of stuff a gentleman doesn't do in public, Allie."

"Someone's peeing in the back alley," she said flatly. "And I'm thinking a nice, big, sturdy statue might do the job of one of those lesser-harpy statues some folks put on their roofs to scare off birds."

"Those don't work very well."

"I bet they'd work better if the birds were drunk."

He considered her statement. "All of those statues are busted, though. No heads. Hence the name."

"We'll have someone carve up some festive heads to pop on there. Make it classy."

"I'll put it on my to-do list."

"Great. You got something else on that to-do list that involves me? You're lingering in a way that usually means you've got something on your mind."

"I need to pick your brain about something, yeah."

"Well, I need to restock some of the cheap stuff. Follow me. Oovay! You have the floor!"

She led the way down to the new stockroom. It was in the first-level basement of the tavern and thus enjoyed the pleasantly cool temperature and relative silence that the tavern lacked. Parch trotted down behind them.

"Grab some of those crates down from the top there. And start talking. Oovay gripes if I leave him alone up there for too long."

"All right. I'll try to make it quick. Do you know any cheap places a guy can spend a few days? Someplace where they'll keep their mouth shut about who is staying there? Maybe turn the other cheek about when and if he comes and goes?"

She crossed her arms. "I'm going to give you the benefit of the doubt and assume you don't realize what you're insinuating when you ask a lady a question like that."

"Why would... Oh. No, no. That's not what this is about."

"It better not be. So it's secret business, then. The same sort your sister is probably talking to the man who stinks of badgerweed about."

"Yeah. This is a full-family affair."

"Just how secret do you need to be? You already know the names of all the inns in town, I'm sure."

"Very secret. What we're working on requires all but people we absolutely trust to believe that I'm not even in Beffshire."

"Fel, I don't like that you're talking to me about an alibi."

"It's not about having an alibi." He paused and squinted. "No, actually, that's exactly what it's about, now that I think of it."

"If you want my advice, if you're planning to commit a crime, the first thing you should do is stop talking to me about it, and the second thing you should do is stop planning to do it."

He helped her lever open a case.

"You know what? If we're going to be trusting Badgerweed up there, we can trust you. Someone from the nobles is planning to inspect our entire home in a week, and we need to clear out the things inside that would get us in trouble. I'm going to be leaving tomorrow to get some antiques to replace some of that stuff. Officially I'll be gone all week, but in reality I'll be back in less than a day. The rest of the time, I'll be helping the family with the rest of the plan. Epiphany thinks 'sending me off' will make them think what we're up to isn't as big as it is, because they won't know I'm helping."

Allie rubbed her face. "I don't know if I should be flattered or furious that you feel comfortable involving me in your schemes."

"Ideally your only involvement is knowing about it and pointing me toward someone who I can trust to keep their quiet about where I'm staying. Do you think I can just go to one of the places the upper crust take their mistresses to?"

"The fact that you know where the upper crust take their mistresses is a pretty good sign that they're not as secretive as you're looking for. Not a lot of people realize just how thriving a business blackmail is in this town. Or any town, honestly. If you think there exists a businessman who is unscrupulous enough to turn a blind eye to someone who is clearly up to no good, but scrupulous enough to not take a bribe to name names about what that no-good-doer is up to, you deserve what you get. If you ask me, and you are, then I'd suggest staying with someone you can trust. Someone who lives alone, obviously, unless you think you can trust all of them."

Fel scratched his head. "Tem lives alone, and I might be able to trust him, but I think we'd kill each other if we had to deal with each other outside The Fox and Log. Lou's house is disgusting, and that's coming from someone who spends half his time crawling through crypts and swamps. Maybe... no, I owe him money. Or... no, he can't keep a secret."

Allie selected an appropriate assortment of bottles and directed Fel to return the crates.

"I have a sneaking suspicion this is heading in a very specific direction, and I don't like it," she said.

"Oh yeah? What direction is that?"

"You're going to ask to stay with me."

He raised his eyebrows. "I can honestly say I'd never even considered that."

"I live alone, over in a relatively dead part of town, and you've already shared your plans to commit misdeeds with me, so you at least think I can be trusted. If you weren't planning on asking to stay with me, you weren't thinking hard enough."

"Are you offering?" he asked.

She sighed. "Is it just you?"

"Just me."

She glanced down at the lesser unicorn, who was snacking on some of the straw that had been used to stuff the booze crate.

"Probably Parch, too," Fel said.

"What about Oiler?"

"They'll be keeping Oiler busy at the house until the very end, if everything goes right. And by the time it's not busy enough to come looking for me, I'll be 'back.'"

"And you won't be bringing back any contraband for me to store?"

"No. There's way too much of it for that anyway."

"And will you make it worth my while?"

"Of course. This is business, and the Maskers pay their bills."

She grumbled under her breath for a moment. "Here are the rules. You do everything in your power to avoid getting me tangled up in this. We settle up what you owe after. And this conversation we're having now? It never happened. I don't know that you are supposedly somewhere else. I don't know what's going on with your family. If someone finds out you're staying with me and asks me why, I'll tell them you told me your room was infested with something or other and you needed a place to stay until it was taken care of."

"Understood."

"Bring something soft to sleep on, because I only have the one bed, and you're not sharing it. If that unicorn makes a mess of my house, you'll never hear the end of it. And if you make me regret this in any way, I'll make you regret it."

"... Maybe I should keep looking for someplace else."

"You probably should be rethinking the whole thing, but you're not going to find a better place than mine. When can I expect you?"

"Late tomorrow night."

"You know when my shift ends. Be in the alley between my building and the tanner's place. No one ever lingers there, for obvious reasons. I'll let you in, and this whole absurd thing can start getting over with."

"I'll be there. And thanks, Allie."

"Thank me when it's over and neither of us is dealing with the aftermath."

Tome lingered in the shop. He'd ostensibly joined Vivian in order to lend a hand with the customers, but his primary goal had been to observe the inspector. Tome had admittedly led a very sheltered life in the Gate of the Ancients Monastery prior to seeking his fortune as a paper mage, but he struggled to believe that anyone with any form of official authority could legitimately behave as the Maskers claimed Cartwright was acting. He had been disabused of that notion rather quickly.

It wasn't simply that Cartwright had essentially begun a patrol across the street, cycling himself and the two assayers in and out like prison guards fearful of an escape attempt. A reasonable argument could be made that the Maskers had demonstrated they may be up to something and surveillance was called for, or at least made sense. But there were other actions that could only be called punitive. They were stopping every customer on the way out to inspect their purchases, if any, or to accuse them of attempting to smuggle something if they hadn't purchased anything. It had tapered the number of customers to a trickle, mostly those who already had pending business with the Maskers. And then there was the veritable war being waged between Cartwright and the lesser harpies.

"Here they come again," Tome said, a tad more glee in his tone than he would have liked.

Vivian looked up from the ledger. She didn't do something so uncouth as to smile at the man's struggles, but she made certain to watch intently while they were happening. Two harpies fluttered down and landed at a precisely calibrated distance. Too close to the inspector to justify throwing something. Too far for him to kick or swat at them. At this distance Tome couldn't quite make out their utterances, but with a vocabulary of perhaps forty words each, chiefly composed of nonsensical threats and invectives, one needn't spend much time musing on the nature of the exchange. Cartwright shouted angrily and brandished a small handheld club that seemed to be his only official piece of weaponry.

"Watch the little one. Rudy, I believe," Vivian said.

The crow-like creature hopped down the street, keeping close to the storefronts as Cartwright kept his attention on the harpies in front of him. Rudy moved with slow, precise jumps, biding its time. When Cartwright finally took a step forward to try to thump one of the harpies, the smaller one flitted up, tucked a beak expertly into the satchel hanging by his side, and plucked a duot from inside.

Their toll paid, the harpies fluttered skyward, sprinkling a few fresh insults as they departed. Vivian marked something down in a separate ledger.

"Keeping track?"

"That's seven duots so far. Unless the third one was a cenot. I couldn't quite see the color before they took to the roofs."

"If this keeps up much longer, he's going to be broke."

"If he's endeavoring to inflict it upon us, it seems fair he'd face it himself."

"I'm beginning to wonder if the harpies are a bit smarter than we've given them credit for. Lesser Mystics in general may be a brighter breed than their appearances would indicate."

Vivian nodded and slid the second ledger over to him. He picked it up to find that it was dedicated not only to the pickpocketing successes of the harpies today but their behavior in general. Everything from what sort of bribes worked best to how they treated the customers.

"This is quite thorough," he said.

"One must keep busy when things are slow," Vivian said.

He read over the page. "I'm sorry, but are you sure this is accurate? It looks like they hardly ever bother customers, and the customers they do bother are only ever the ones that didn't buy anything."

"That's right."

"And it doesn't matter if they were on their way in or on their way out."

"Indeed."

"Either that means a harpy bothering a customer is likely to cause a customer not to buy something—not entirely implausible—or the harpies can tell if someone is going to buy something and pester the ones who will waste your time. How could that be?"

"I can usually tell before they walk through the door if someone is looking to actually do business. Perhaps the birds have picked up the same skill. Or perhaps they see the expression on my face and aren't quite as restrained," Vivian said. "Rather fascinating, regardless. Martin is endlessly intrigued by it."

Tome looked outside again. Cartwright was eying the skyline suspiciously. The fourth harpy flitted in with surgical precision and snagged a duot without even drawing his attention. Tome handed the book back to Vivian to mark it down.

"That's a second duot for each of them," she said. "They'll behave themselves for a bit."

"Do they bother the assayers?" Tome asked.

"No. Only the inspector."

"As though they know he's the one who actually means the family harm," Tome mused. "You Maskers do have a way of teasing loyalty and friendship from the most unlikely sources." He dusted his hands on his pants and headed for the door. "May as well do my part," he said.

"Be careful," she called after him. "This is complex enough without adding another reason for him to be cross with us."

"I am a paragon of tact," he said, slipping through the door.

"Watch yourself," Cartwright shouted as Tome crossed the street. "There is an infestation of foulmouthed flying rats."

"I've paid my fee for the week in the form of a bread bun for each of them," Tome said. "I don't believe we've been formally introduced. My name is Tome Inkbrand."

Cartwright reluctantly pulled his eyes from the skyline to assess the mage. "Customer of the antiquities shop?" he asked.

"Boarder, actually."

The inspector rumbled, "I'll thank you not to attempt to dissuade or distract me. They are under investigation, and your association with them by rights ought to earn you the same scrutiny."

"I endeavor to keep to the sunny side of the law."

"See that you do."

"I understand there have been some instances of violence in the surrounding area. More so than the usual street brigandry that comes part and parcel with more densely populated areas."

Cartwright looked past Tome to stare down a would-be customer, who thought better of entering as a result. "Indeed."

"And that is why you came here? Both to Beffshire and to the Maskers' shop?"

"Yes. There is a mystic within the very same place you foolishly choose to board. Quite likely responsible for the violence. You take your life into your own hands by staying with them."

"But have you—"

"The business of an inspector is not a matter of public discussion. You are interrupting my duties. Move along."

"I fully intend to. Indeed, that is why I'm speaking to you. I am likely to be doing some business outside the city, and I imagine your investigation would have provided a degree of additional insight. Is it safe for me to leave the city? Have instances of violence decreased now that the creature you suspect is responsible is tucked away in the Maskers' home?"

"Move along," Cartwright repeated.

"Surely if your reason for coming here was to address the violence, keeping apprised of it would necessarily be part of your investigation, as it would give you insight into whether or not the person you believe is responsible is—"

"Move along or I will consider you a person of interest in this investigation. More so than you already are."

Tome took a step back and raised his hands in placation. "Forgive me. I'll leave you to it," he said quickly.

Tome scurried to the nearest intersection. If he'd had any doubt that there was something suspicious about the inspector's motivations, it was gone now. The man had clearly lost all interest in his claimed reason for coming to the city. That cast genuine doubt on the truthfulness of that motivation to begin with. The only thing that was certain was his desire to see what the Maskers' home held. He could only assume he'd come here with that in mind, and everything else was an excuse or set dressing. But he was certainly a genuine official, operating on behalf of the nobles. Did the nobles want access to the Masker home? If so, couldn't they have sent him with the proper proclamations to begin with? And if not, had he gone rogue? Was he in league with some of the other enemies the Maskers had managed to accumulate?

Many questions. Quite a puzzle. Perhaps if...

Tome shut his eyes and wavered. If he'd been a step closer to the street, he would have tumbled down to the cobbles. It was a wave of the same weakness he'd been slowly recovering from since he'd made the ill-fated foray into blood magic to save himself in the Greater Lands. He caught his balance and braced himself against the wall.

"What was that?" he muttered.

The weakness was gone just as quickly as it had come, and in truth it wasn't potent enough to have warranted the near tumble. It was just unexpected, a brief and unpleasant return to a wounded state. Like an errant throb of a long-healed injury when a storm was brewing. He'd never experienced it before. Something sour in the pit of his stomach told him it was a near certainty he'd be feeling it again.

The day's business had concluded quite early, such as it was. If not for the loss of nearly the full day of sales due to yesterday's punitive appraisal, it would have been the worst sales day of the year. Now it was merely the second worst. Vivian watched from the doorway as Fel guided the cargo wagon down the street after a lengthy search by the inspector. His departure had been delayed for over an hour as the noble stopped just short of disassembling the vehicle before allowing him to depart. It was a small miracle that Fel hadn't lost his temper and buried his cudgel in the inspector's head halfway through the process.

Just a few minutes after Fel had left, Inspector Cartwright reached his limit for surveillance and harassment for one day. He fetched one of the other assayers and left him in place for the night shift of observation. It was abundantly clear at a single glance that the assayers, far more accustomed to the comparatively easy task of confiscating contraptions, were in no mood to match the level of vigilance that Cartwright had displayed. She slipped out of the store and gave a pleasant nod to the one on duty. He cast a weary look in her direction. She turned about, illustrating she was carrying no contraband. He nodded and resumed his dead-eyed observation of the now-empty storefront. She stepped into the cobbler's shop next door.

The place was dimly lit. It smelled pleasantly of oiled leather. The shop so seldom had foot traffic that Reynard, the proprietor, had taken to doing his work in the back of the shop and stopping only when he had to see to the odd shoe shopper or customer in need of repair. He looked up at the sound of the shutting door and grinned at Vivian, the expression only vaguely recognizable as a rearrangement of wrinkles and facial hair in a head that was chiefly composed of laugh lines and a wiry gray beard.

"Ah, Mrs. Masker. How are those boots treating you? Some of my finest work. Those button-sided boots just aren't as popular as they were."

"They're holding up quite well. And quite comfortable. How were sales today?"

"Bah. Same as ever. Terrible," he griped. "The winter is setting in early, isn't it? Keeps the people off the streets."

"Funny, I was just saying to Epiphany that it seemed unseasonably warm."

He waved a hand irritably. "No such thing as unseasonably warm. These old bones are sick of the cold."

"Yes. As I recall, that's what we spoke about last time you and I had a chat. Back then you were insisting you'd finally decided to take some time off and head down south for a spell."

"You shouldn't listen to me when I say foolish things like that," he said. "I can't leave this shop unattended for that long. And I just know once I got a taste of that good dry air down south, I'd never want to come back."

"So maybe that will be a sign that the time has come to enjoy your golden years."

He laughed. "Not so much gold in these years. This shop is my business and my home. Same as you. It's all I can do to keep the lamps burning and the cupboard full. I don't have your gift for sale."

"You should have hired someone to do sales so you could focus on the work. Or married one, like Martin did."

"It's the whole problem of the cart and the horse, isn't it? Need the money to hire the clerk to make the money to hire the clerk. And if there is a lady with savvy like yours and the willingness to hitch her cart to an old horse like me, I haven't met her. No. Living down south will be a nice dream and that's it."

"You could always sell the shop."

He stopped tapping at the punch he was using to add holes to his current project and looked her firmly in the eye. "Could I? Could you? Masker's Antiquities has a legacy in this town that's almost older than the town. And this little shop? Maybe it doesn't have that pedigree, but it's a lifetime of toil that got it here. Selling this shop? Even if I could find a buyer to pay me what it's worth, I couldn't bear it. What if they let it fall to ruin? Turned it into something distasteful? It'd be like marrying off my daughter to someone I'd never met."

"I respect that, Reynard. I'm sure I'd feel the same way. But maybe there's a solution."

"If there is one, I haven't come up with it."

"You sell shoes to the travelling bazaar when it comes through, don't you?"

He laughed. "Do I? I probably sell half my stock to that lot every time they come through. Tell you what, if I ever do head down south, I'm liable to run into a whole town of folks who have been wearing my shoes for years."

"So you'd say that they're shrewd businesspeople. After all, they know good shoes when they see them."

"Quite so."

"And that they keep coming back suggests they're making enough sales to make it worth their while."

"No sense rolling that big caravan of wagons through the three kingdoms if it's not making money."

"So they're some fine salespeople. Fit to run a place like this?"

He set his tools down. "Viv, it is starting to feel like you're working me over. Softening me up."

She laughed. "I must me losing my touch. I usually try to make sure the folks I'm selling to don't realize I'm selling to them until they hand over the money. I'll skip to the closer, then. It just so happens one of the better merchants from the bazaar is in town to do some off-season business with me. He's been hoping to set up a more permanent shop, and I thought of you."

"I don't know, Viv."

"You've wanted this for ages."

"Sure, but 'one of the better merchants from the bazaar' is a bit of an empty claim, isn't it? How do I know this place would be in good hands?"

"I could vouch for him."

"Ah, but now I know you're selling."

She raised her eyebrows and leaned back, somewhat theatrically aghast. "Reynard, do you think I'm trying to swindle you?"

"You're a good enough saleswoman to lean on the scale a bit."

"And I'm a good enough friend to have your best interests at heart. I vouch for him, as I say, but if you want to see for yourself what he can do, that's more than reasonable. Test him. Take your trip. There's a very nice coach heading south tomorrow morning. Be on it, spend a few weeks, and see what you think. Or even a few days. Give him your ledger, your price sheets, complete with how much you need to sell to meet your needs. He takes his pay from however much more he can sell the goods for above that."

He gazed aside, clearly already imagining how the sun and air would feel on his aching bones. Vivian grinned. She had him.

"What's in this for you?" he asked.

"I get to know my friend is happy and healthy, the shop next door is in good hands, and a business associate owes me a favor for helping him set down roots in our market district."

"That's assuming I'll be so enamored by the south that I'll be in the market for selling my shop after all."

"I know you and I know the south. You'll be happier there. I'm sure of it."

He pulled a drawer and selected a roll of thread. "No surprise, Vivian Masker makes the sale. Send him in."

"I'll see if he can come in before you turn in for the night." She patted him on the shoulder. "You're making the right decision. I only wish you'd made it earlier."

She slipped out the door. The weary assayer gave her a cursory glance before nodding her back into her shop. Epiphany was waiting for her.

"Well?" Epiphany said.

"Tell your father to have the tools ready. This time tomorrow, the plan unfurls," Vivian said.

Martin shook his head and gazed up at the wall, empty crates at his feet and a massive undertaking ahead of him.

"Where is the line between what the assayers will approve of and what they won't?" he muttered to himself. "That I've let that line get so hazy in my own head, and so quickly, is evidence that I've been heading down an unfortunate road, Wick."

"Rare is the road that lacks the occasional hazard, Martin," Wick said.

"What does it say about me that the first thought I have when I think of this is how bothersome the timing is? That I was on the cusp of something truly momentous and now I must set it aside to extinguish these figurative flames."

"It says you are a contraptioneer first and all else second," Wick said.

"And is that a proper thing to be?" Martin asked.

"Judging ethics, morals, and values are not services I fulfill," Wick said. "I am not qualified."

"You sell yourself short. You have better insight than you think." Martin ran his fingers through his hair. "But perhaps we can salvage a few moments of additional work while we get this started."

He grabbed the Student mask and clicked it back into place on the freshly installed coupler on the bust he'd built. The head shifted slightly.

"Ah. The new bust. And its lack of vision," the Student said. "An oral test, then?"

"And physical, if you don't mind," he said, sliding books from their place and carefully stacking them in the crate. "This will be something of a guided exploration. I will help you to learn about the bust you are installed in."

Naturally, the process would teach Martin as well, but given the rather limited point of view of the Student, he'd learned that suggesting that anything fell outside the scope of a test or a lesson was a sure way to cause the mask to lose interest.

"I do not believe I have ever had the capacity to perform a physical test. This will be delightful," the Student said.

"I hope so. First, do you feel your arm?"

"Hmm... I am afraid I do not know. I suspect not, as I am not experiencing any new sensations, but I cannot be certain because I have never 'felt' anything before. My senses have been and appear to continue to be limited to sight and sound."

"Are you aware of your arm?"

"I am aware. I am aware of an assembly with three degrees of freedom, connected to a linkage with one degree of freedom, connected to an assembly with three degrees of freedom, which is in turn connected to—"

"That will do. And do you find you have full control over those degrees of freedom?"

The arm moved in a curious sequence of motions. It was slowly pivoting everything from the shoulder to the tips of each finger simultaneously.

"There are some limitations regarding the maximum extent of each one, but they all move under my control."

"Excellent."

"May I request some clarification?" the Student asked.

"Of course."

"Are there intended to be two arms?"

"That is my intention, if only for completion's sake."

"And legs?"

"I do not suppose so. Those would be surplus to requirement."

"So this is a new, more limited application of prior development rather than a continuation of past development."

Martin paused in his packing of books. "Were there developments of animated busts of this type?" he said.

"I thought we were doing a physical examination."

"Let us briefly shift to history. Animated busts of this type. There was work done in that regard?"

"Animated contraptions are among the most heavily researched and developed contraptions there are. From simple rotating drive boxes to complex self-motivated contraptions like the Oiler presently in your possession."

"Specifically busts used to give humanlike dexterity to contraption-based entities. Did they exist?"

"I do not know. But there were considerable adjustments made to this mask to provide additional capacity to control more complex linkages than this. Those adjustments were completed prior to the creation of subsequent masks."

"Interesting…" Martin mused. "And would those adaptations have come before or after the construction of Oiler?"

He glanced down at the contraption in question, intending to briefly study its far more mystical and far less mechanical means of animating its chain links. Instead, he found himself looking upon an empty patch of floor beside three fully repaired contraptions and a solved puzzle box.

"One moment," he said.

He hurried up the steps to find Oiler thumping along in one of the storerooms, eyes turned roughly toward where Fel had been heading. Teya stood in the doorway ahead, legs planted as though she was preparing to tackle the contraption.

"Papa Fel!" she said, looking up. "Oiler? It goes. I stop it?"

"No need. I'll handle it," Martin said, hefting Oiler up by the straps. "The contraption has been rather insistent on following Fel wherever he goes. Anytime it isn't focused on a task, it seeks him out."

"Why not let it?" Teya asked.

"You'll note the general reaction you have produced in the populace, yes?"

"Angry and shouting," she said.

"Oiler would produce much the same. Additionally, Oiler and things like him are specifically forbidden."

"Oiler thinks. Lives. How can be forbidden?"

"You'll find such things are quite common in society."

She scratched her head. "Dumb," she decreed.

He turned to return to his workshop.

"Wait! Papa Fel!" she called. Teya scampered in front of him and revealed a familiar contraption.

"Is that Fel's sparker?" he asked.

She shook her head. "Was Fel's. Now mine."

"Ah. Well, I trust it has served you well."

"Very well, Papa Fel. But… can you make more?"

"Can I manufacture additional sparkers?"

"No. This sparker. But more."

"You want me to improve the sparker? Why?"

She grinned and glanced aside, as if reminiscing. "Like fire. Very very."

"I'm a bit busy right now, but I'll see what I can do."

"Thank you, Papa Fel!" Teya said.

He brought Oiler back downstairs, scrambled its puzzle box, and set about disassembling its other toys to provide a longer distraction.

"This household is becoming much more interesting of late," he mused.

A few hours on the road took Fel and Parch to the ruins of an old mansion. Or, rather, a place that had once held the ruins of an old mansion. When Fel was a little boy, it had already been stripped to little more than its stone walls. The roof had rotted away, and everything light enough to be carried had been harvested. His father explained the history of the place, the home of an aristocrat who had already fallen upon hard times before the Bygone Era had ended. The only reason Martin knew this was because when he was a boy, there were still some scattered remnants of the library intact. These days it was difficult to tell there had even been a mansion here. The walls themselves had been carted away brick by brick to be reassembled into a wall around the neighboring farm. It took a skilled eye to spot the foundation as an unnaturally level bit of ground utterly wreathed in fast-growing vines. But there were still the sub-basements, and still doors too well secured with locks or traps to break through. And thus, about once a year, Fel would come down and try his luck. It was just a few hours from Beffshire. It only took one or two dusty relics overlooked in the muck to make it worth the stop. Last time he'd come down, that luck had paid off to a much greater degree than that.

Fel slipped down to the lowest level and raised his lantern. What had once been a trove was little more than an empty chamber with a strangely high roof, several levels below ground. The air had the autumnal coolness that seemed to occupy any chamber more than a few levels below the surface. The walls should have been clear and clean, showcasing the needless precision of Bygone Era masons in the construction of their walls. But time and nature had conspired to give the place a bit more flavor than that.

"Gotta hand it to the weeds here in Thayne. They're the best explorers around." He puffed on the pipe his father had made. "Wick, you there?"

"I am."

"How are things back home?"

"No updates."

"Good. Bear with me. This next bit is going to be a little tricky with a pipe in my mouth."

The same vines that were doing their very best to hide the foundation had legendary roots. Roots that in time had been able to bore through the same mortar that made breaking through walls in search of treasure all but impossible. They continued their quest downward until they found water, which it just so happened was beneath the floor of this final level of the mansion's basements. Having found their precious supply of hydration, the roots had grown so thick in this section of the mansion that the walls looked like they had fur. Stout cords of roots with thin wispy offshoots hid three of the four walls. Since hacking through them inevitably revealed more wall, neither Fel nor any of his fellow treasure hunters wasted their time hacking through them.

Parch, on the other hand, had a different policy. The very moment they reached this level, Parch trotted over and started snacking on the roots. He was just as thirsty as they were, after all. And they were juicy with water. What's more, their decades of erosion had covered the wall with plenty of little rough spots and chips. To the sure-footed creature, it may as well have been a staircase. A few weeks ago, when Fel had made his annual pilgrimage to this place to see if he'd missed any scraps, Parch had wandered straight up the wall, just as he was today.

"Hey, hey! Rope, remember?" Fel called.

Parch dropped down again. Fel looped the end of a rope over his horn and gave him a pat. Parch bounded up the wall again, headed for the thickest tuft of roots he could find. Someone with a more botanical bent probably would have noted that those roots seemed like much fresher growth than the surrounding ones. Fel lacked that level of insight. But he was observant enough to notice that once Parch reached the tuft, he pushed through them and stood such that half of his body should have been inside the wall. He gave the rope a tug. Parch trotted farther, completely vanishing into the thicket of roots. Fel hung his lantern from a clip on his belt specifically for that purpose and got to work. With a rope and plenty of roots to support him, Fel made his way up the wall and pushed through to the well-hidden air shaft Parch had inadvertently discovered.

Hidden for hundreds of years. Discovered by a hungry unicorn.

He dragged himself through a few yards of shaft barely wider than his shoulders and emerged into the sort of room any vault diver would kill to find. It was nothing but shelves of antiques. Ornate pots, pans, and dishes. Gold and silver utensils. Jewelry boxes still stuffed with jewelry. Martin would have been moderately disappointed, as there were relatively few contraptions and nothing in the way of reference material or tools. But this room alone could probably supply the shop for six months of record-breaking sales.

Fel held up the lantern and surveyed the contents. "And to think. We didn't find it just because it doesn't have a door," he mused.

That was the most confounding thing about this little treasure trove. It wasn't as though he'd simply missed an entrance. The air shaft he'd crawled through was the only opening of any kind. The person who owned this mansion had entombed these goods.

"It is a fascinating decision," Wick said. "One wonders why this wealthy individual would seal away so many valuable goods, and how common this behavior was."

"You can wonder that. I'm fine with assuming there was some family squabble, and this stuff was locked away out of spite. Or maybe the lord was taking too big a bite, so it was hidden away. All I know is I'm bringing Parch to some of the other old spots to see if he can sniff out other chambers like these. I'm just lucky they put in an air shaft. They could have walled the whole thing off without that, and I never would have found it."

He pulled some sacks from his belt and unfurled them. "It kind of makes me wonder why they even put in an air shaft. Was there something in here that needed air? Or maybe..." He shut his eyes and shook his head. "No. Nope! No time for falling down the kind of rabbit hole Tome and Dad get caught up in. I have goods to loot."

"Your dedication to the task at hand is admirable," Wick said.

"Deadlines will do that. Now shout out if you see anything particularly fancy. We can't afford to spend more than an hour or so in here. I'm due back at the city walls before midnight, with a full night of work to do after that. It's going to be too tight for thinking about stuff."

CHAPTER 4

The night was quite young, and Fel was already approaching the edge of town with his haul of antiques. Never in his life had a vault trip gone so swiftly and smoothly. It helped that he knew precisely where he was going, precisely what he would find and where he would find it, and that there were no active traps. Even so, he'd pushed himself and the horse entirely too hard. They were both utterly exhausted, but at least the horse would have several days to recover. For Fel, even if things went well, there was a week of frenzied hauling and anxious stealth ahead of him. If things went poorly, the hauling would be even more frenzied and... the less he thought about what the stealth might evolve into the better. For now, there were more immediate concerns. It was best to take these steps carefully.

He eyed up the western gates of the city. Beffshire's walls, like many of the city's more charming features, were a relic of the past. Specifically, they were a relic of a war-torn past. Some of the cities nearer to the borders of other kingdoms still put their gates to use, closing them every night in a security ritual that was more theater and tradition than anything else. As far as Fel knew, Beffshire's gates could close, but he wasn't sure he'd ever seen them shut. This was a town of trade. It wouldn't do to turn away late-night shipments in the interest of protecting the populace from a nonexistent threat. But a wall that choked down entry to just a few points did make it quite easy for the Watch to know if and when someone arrived. Fel had never much cared about that before, but now that their plan required the officials to believe he wasn't in town, and the wagon of mundane antiques wouldn't return for a few days, he suddenly had new respect for just how effective a wall could be at making sneaky maneuvers more difficult.

Not effective enough, of course.

He caught a whiff of the man who had turned out to be the linchpin of their schemes, and not far off the road he found the purple covered wagon belonging to Thaddeus Graves.

"Fel," Thaddeus said pleasantly, puffing on his pipe.

In the dim light, it took Fel a moment to realize the hand that wasn't fiddling with the pipe was clutching a crossbow. "Expecting someone else?" he asked.

"Even if the thorn in your side of an inspector seems to have lost interest, there have been some rather more substantial roadside mishaps. One cannot be too careful."

"How have things been?" Fel asked, hopping off the wagon and trotting around to begin loading up the crates of goods.

"Proceeding apace. With remarkable alacrity, your mother has arranged for the temporary loan and likely eventual sale of a shop in Beffshire, something that the Graves family has sought, off and on, for seven years. Meanwhile, it would seem even the wildlife has allied with your family against the inspector."

"Toody, Judy, Rudy, and Moody are giving him the business, I take it?"

"By your mother's figuring, they've robbed him of at least a hundred and fifteen duots."

Fel laughed. "I need to figure out if they like anything better than yeast buns. They deserve a reward after this."

Thaddeus unfastened the reins of the horse and moved it to the front of his own cart.

"It helps that your Watch, particularly your night Watch, isn't precisely world class. In Shalia, it would take a more complex ruse than leaving via the east gate and entering via the west one to fool the watch."

"There was a time when I would have said having one competent member of the Watch and a bunch of incompetent ones was a bad thing. Then you tricked my sister into getting us into the illicit contraption market, and here we are."

"You're not going to let that that drop, are you?"

"Nope."

Parch, who had been snoozing in the back of the cart, finally popped out and reviewed the proceedings. Under his supervision, Fel and Thaddeus moved half the crates of antiques into the back of the cargo carriage and stashed the Maskers' wagon well off the road in one of the scattered stands of trees. For good measure—and to avoid having it wander off before they were able to fetch it again—Fel wove a chain through the spokes of the wheels and secured it with a Bygone Era lock. Parch took the hint and hopped from the half-empty wagon and into the covered one.

Thaddeus rattled his wagon back toward the city. As luck would have it, Leonard was the man on west gate duty this evening, so it was entirely possible Fel could have been the one at the reins and word wouldn't have reached the inspector that he was back in town. Thaddeus slipped by without a comment from the drowsy watchman and stowed his wagon back in the stable near the inn where he was staying. With that, the pair parted ways. Thad walked the city in the open, as any normal person would. Fel was forced to move through the shadows and back alleys, wrangling Parch all the while. Even so, it was his town, not Thad's. Minutes before Graves arrived, Fel sidled into the narrow alley that ran between the row of shops on his home street and the row of shops on the street behind.

He held still and listened closely. Something Reynard's shop had that the Maskers' shop lacked was a rear window. It was a few inches over Fel's head, and given that it faced the moldy stone wall of the shop behind him, it wasn't meant for a view. At the moment it was shut tight, but made as it was from slatted wood rather than thick stone, it remained his best option for listening in. Silence turned to muffled conversation. The muffled conversation became more distinct as Reynard and Thaddeus approached the rear of the shop floor.

"There's a window up there. Open the front door and crack that window if the smell of the leather oil gets to be too much for you. You get a nice cross breeze," Reynard said simply.

He mumbled his way through an explanation of where the inventory of various sorts could be found in the levels below.

"I forgot how chatty Reynard could be," Fel grumbled under his breath.

The minutes crawled on. Creaking footsteps signaled their journey down into the basement. Fel could do nothing but listen and wait until he got the signal he was looking for.

"Lousy thief?" croaked a voice overhead sweetly.

His eye twitched. He and Parch looked up. One of the lesser harpies was gazing down at him from the roof. One by one, the other three heads popped up.

"Raaaat bird?" chirped Judy.

"Now's not a great time, you four," he hissed.

Slow, plodding footsteps thumped up the stairs.

"You hear that?" Reynard said. "Lesser harpies. I don't know what got into the boy next door, but he started feeding them or something, and now we can't get rid of them. That boy must be a hard worker, because he's dumber than a sack of salamanders."

Fel gritted his teeth.

"Gimmee back my hat," suggested Rudy.

"Usually they're along the front," Reynard said. "Can't imagine what's got them in the back there. Nothing back there but drainage into that old well across the way."

The sack of gear Fel had with him was carefully selected to include everything he needed for this little caper and nothing he didn't, the better to move quickly and silently. Alas, he'd forgotten to include anything tasty or shiny in the rugged bag. He frantically fumbled in his pockets. As luck would have it, two leathery strips of dried meat he'd been snacking on were still wrapped in a bit of cloth in his jacket. He fished them out, ripped each in half, and held them up.

The feathery extortionists took their payments and left. With no more comments outside the window, Reynard moved on again. A few more minutes of interminable chitchat finally led to the half-heard conclusion of the handoff of operations for the shop. He heard the front door distantly slam, and not long after, a carriage rattled away. The very moment the crunching of wheels on the street had drifted into the distance, the window shuddered in place and popped open.

"Couldn't you have chatted with your little pets later?" Thad asked from the other side.

"Oh, shut up," he grumbled. "Is the coast clear?"

"The window leads to a clear area in the back of a small storeroom, just beside the hatch to the lower levels. The door to the storage room is shut, so you won't be seen, but it looks like it will be a tight fit for you."

"Spoken like a man who's never had to raid a vault. Stand clear. Here comes the gear sack."

He hefted his pack of tools up and over the edge of the window, then reached up and started to wedge himself through. Thad wasn't far off when he'd judged it to be too small. The largest dimension of the window was still appreciably narrower than the burly young man's shoulders. But a few trips into a half-flooded storage chamber with no way inside but a single dislodged roof block was a fine teacher in the ways of contortionism. He fed one arm through, grabbed the wall inside, and started to drag himself through the little vent. It tested the limits of his other shoulder's mobility, and nearly tore the seat of his pants as he had to slide up along the wall behind him until his spine was willing to provide the amount of curve he was asking of it. Finally more than half of his mass was through the wall, and gravity helpfully finished the job. He thumped gracelessly to the floor.

"Yours is not a career defined by its quiet dignity, is it, Fel?" Thad said.

"Your head's going to be defined by its quiet dignity when I break your jaw so you can't talk," Fel mumbled.

"Pardon?" Thad said.

"Just take me downstairs, and we'll get this started!"

Teya stood in the tight little gap between shelves on a storage level of the Masker household. She had an almost manic look of gleeful excitement as she held a stub-handled pick-mattock in her hands.

"You understand what you need to do, right?" Martin said.

She gave him a brief glance. The patriarch of the house had Oiler hanging by one strap over his shoulder. The animated contraption was likely to complicate this part of the plan, given its obsession with repair. They'd learned that keeping the pack off the ground had a way of delaying Oiler's more irritating tendencies, and so Martin wouldn't be dropping it anytime soon. She turned back to the wall.

"Wait for knock. Find knock. Break wall," she said.

"Carefully," he said. "The wall is rather thick, but I would still prefer we take care. The floor joists are there, and there, and a poorly placed fault could cause them to buckle."

"Papa Fel?" Teya said. "My home? A cave. So much digging. So much careful. When we dig? Both sides. Some from there, some from here. Last part? Break through? Great day. Celebrate, when wall breaks. Important job." She poked her chest. "This one? Never did it. Not important enough. But now? Now I do."

"You've never done this final bit before?" Martin said steadily. "Perhaps we should—"

A muffled knock softly reverberated through the stone. Her floppy, serrated ear flicked up, and she turned, eyes flashing with joy.

"Stand back for breaking!" she squealed, raising the hammer high.

Chips of stone flew in all directions. Though Teya may never have been the one to break through a new tunnel, her mining experience was more than evident. The blows marched their way around the edge of a circle, the largest that would fit on the exposed portion of the stone wall. In a march of blows, striking roughly the hour positions of a clock, she made neat and steady progress. Heavy, thumping blows came from the other side. Martin climbed the steps, then returned.

"Nothing up top. Keep it at this level of intensity or lower and we shouldn't raise any eyebrows," Martin said.

Teya continued her steady assault. There was a simple, deep contentment to doing something that one knew forward and backward, and that one knew she was doing well. She knew exactly where to strike and exactly how hard and how fast she could work without getting too tired too quickly. Chipping away at stone was a wonderful sort of work. Unlike painting a picture or something of the sort, where there was always another bit of work to do and there was no telling when it would be complete, a hole was a hole. Progress could be measured by the size of the pile of the chips on the ground. And she was making plenty of progress.

She raised her floppy ear during a brief pause to adjust her stance and grip. A trained ear could tell a lot about a near-complete tunnel just from the way the knock of the hammer and pick changed from moment to moment. Fel was moving a lot more chips on his side. He'd probably made twice the progress. But he wasn't doing it with nearly the precision, and he stopped frequently. What was likely to be his final blow before another long rest was decidedly sharper and less muffled than those that had preceded it. They were nearly through.

Her already-wide grin curled even further, and she hoisted her pick above her head. She struck at the twelve o'clock position. The tip of the pick punched through. Another blow at three o'clock. Then six. Some struck through to empty space. Others simply knocked a chip away. But when she'd cracked her way around the perimeter one last time, she spun the pick to its wide, blunt edge and chattered something in her native language. In her excitement, she'd failed to translate, but the rolling chitter produced the desired effect. Everyone on both sides backed away. She heaved five mighty blows. On the fifth, the stone fractured and crumbled, leaving a circular hole. Fel, smeared with dust and sweat, set his hammer down and huffed a relieved breath. Teya's celebration of the breakthrough was less subdued.

"Yah-haa!" she cried, hopping into the hole she'd dug and pumping her pick over her head. "We work! We work good! Very very!"

Oiler, at the sight of Fel, maneuvered itself to drop free of Martin's shoulder and hobble through the hole to Fel's side. Unlike Parch, who was quite vigorous in his desire to be with Fel if at all possible, Oiler was a bit more subdued, quietly gazing in his direction regardless of how much distance and how many obstacles separated them and waiting until the opportunity arose to slip way and find him.

Once positioned by Fel's feet, the contraption started to sort through the chips of stone until it found two pieces that had been split from one another. It popped out its "fang" and spritzed some mystical adhesive, then stuck them together.

"I'll fetch a puzzle box," Martin said.

"Where we dig now?" Teya asked excitedly. "More dig! Dig lots!"

"No digging right now." Fel huffed again. "Fortunately for us, Reynard didn't use all of his inventory space. So the next step is moving a heap of this stuff over."

"Carrying. Not as fun. Digging is better," Teya said.

Martin returned with a scrambled puzzle box and held it out to Oiler. The jangling chain contraption gave it a brief look, then found and attached a third clump of stone.

"In that case, I have great news. Oiler's probably going to fill this hole in right about when we're done shifting and sorting, so we're going to be starting and ending each day with digging."

Teya nodded. "This is good. Best part of tunnel. Over and over. Like magic roasted duck!"

Fel had been trudging toward a shelf on the opposite side of the room to fetch the first crate, but the comment stopped him.

"Digging holes is like a magic roasted duck?"

"Finishing tunnels like that," Teya corrected.

"How?"

"Tunnel? Finishing, best part. Roasted duck? Crispy skin, best part. All finishing? All crispy skin. Like magic duck."

"Are there magic ducks in the Greater Lands that are all skin?"

"No. But all skin? Must be magic," Teya said. "Think, Fel. Very clear."

He shook his head. "Yeah, I don't know what I was thinking. Come on. Let's get this rolling before I descend completely into madness."

"We do!" Teya said, trotting after him.

In The Fox and Log, Tome scribbled his thoughts in a journal. As tended to be the case, it was after closing time and the place was still quite full. Though he couldn't precisely come right out and say it, Tome had decided to spend the evening in The Fox and Log specifically to escape the sound of tunneling and the low-level chaos that seemed to linger anytime Teya was near. Contrary to expectation, he found it much simpler to keep his mind focused when surrounded by the boisterous but random noise of a tavern than the steady and relentless hammering and clanking presently consuming the lower levels of the Masker household.

Allie finished what was likely to be her last round of drink orders for the evening and leaned on the opposite side of the bar in front of Tome. "So what is this? Fel makes himself scarce and you come in and keep his seat warm?" she said.

"It seemed a worthwhile change of scenery. Keeps the mind sharp, you know," he said.

"I don't know and I wouldn't know, since I don't get many chances to change the scenery, and the last one was spent chasing our boy. If the same scenery day in and day out dulls the mind, then mine should be blunt as a wooden spoon."

"Mmm... Then perhaps my theory needs revision, as you are certainly not suffering from mental stagnation. As it so happens—"

"You're looking for advice," she said quickly. "You really are taking Fel's spot."

"Allie, there are very few people in this city I would consider worth asking advice from, and you are foremost on the list."

"Yeah, yeah. At least Fel doesn't waste time buttering me up. What's the problem?"

He lowered his voice. "You are well acquainted with the situation with the inspector?"

"I am," she said with a subdued, unreadable tone worthy of a place at the grum table.

"I've taken it upon myself to 'inspect the inspector,' so to speak."

"That sounds like a great way to end up thrown in prison."

"I intend to do so with the utmost of care," Tome said.

"You'd better, because if he's crooked, he'll find some excuse to get you off his scent, and it won't matter to him how permanent it is. If he's not crooked, just about the best way to get on the bad side of someone on the up and up is to accuse them of being otherwise. What have you done so far?"

"I've questioned him."

"And that's your version of the utmost of care, is it?"

"I'm new to this particular pursuit," he admitted. "You seem to have some insight."

"Into overzealous inspectors? Yeah. They're like a dog with a bone. Sink their teeth in, won't let loose. A tavern like The Fox and Log gets one of them in here once a year or so. They're always so certain they're onto you, that you've got some sort of a scheme running out of the back room."

"So how do you deal with them?"

"Show them the back room."

"Ah."

"It's a lot easier to get rid of them when you're not actually doing what they're accusing you of," Allie said softly.

"That's rather the point of the matter," Tome said. "To use your metaphor, if this was a 'dog with a bone,' then he's not nibbling on the bone he claims to be. He came pursuing the one responsible for the violence around the city, but he's now given up any pretense of pursuing that. His mind and actions are entirely fixed on the Masker household. I think there is an underlying reason that he's obscuring with plausible alternatives."

"Do you think he's in it for himself, or do you think he's following orders?"

"Little indication of either, but my intuition says he's following orders. I can't imagine what an inspector would personally want out of the Maskers' inventory."

"Then my advice to you, which certainly wouldn't be my advice to me, would be to figure out how he's getting his orders. That'll tell you who he's working for and give you someone further up the line to look into, which will keep from turning up the heat on anything simmering here in town. Unless the boss is in town too. Or, and this is the advice I would normally follow, you could leave it be and avoid complicating matters. ... But you won't be doing that, will you?"

"I too have found a bone," Tome said.

"Then there's only so many ways someone can get orders to someone, and if it's an important job, he'll be sending updates regularly at the very least, and checking for updates pretty often too."

"As good a place as any to start. But how would you..."

He paused, not because of any sound or sight that interrupted him, but because of a smell. There were any number of surprising and terrible smells that would be perfectly in place in a tavern. A whiff of raw flour, powdered sugar, and exotic spices were not among them. He turned just in time to see Mariss, the baker and focus of Fel's yet-to-be-requited romantic aspirations, plop into the seat beside him.

"Mariss, you dirty stay-out. What brings you to this seedy little establishment so late at night? Or early in the morning, as the case may be," Allie said without an ounce of genuine disapproval.

She yawned. "We have had a monumental order of those crackle-top apple pies I've started making. You know the ones."

"Oh," Allie said dreamily. "I know the ones. I don't suppose you brought some."

"None to spare at the moment, I'm afraid. I spent all day making them. Neither Daddy nor any of the other helpers can get the crust right, so it's been all me. I am exhausted."

"If you ever end up with some spares, you be sure to bring them down here, would you?" Allie said.

"Heavens no. I'll bring them right to your home. People around here have sticky fingers when it comes to sweets. Even before they start eating them."

"I'll look forward to your visit. But if you're exhausted, why don't you head home?"

"It's that sort of fatigue where I just know if I plop down in bed, it'll be an hour of staring at the ceiling before I actually sleep. So I thought I'd come down. I know Fel was fresh from a trip. Hoped he might have some stories to tell."

"I'm sorry to say you missed him," Tome said. "Back out on a new trip. Won't be back for a week."

"Ah, well. Still plenty of fun to be had in The Fox and Log, eh?" Allie said. "A cider, please."

"Normally I wouldn't be pouring a first drink this late into my shift, but what point are policies if not to make a fun exception now and then?" Allie poured the drink. "How are things in Divinity's Oven?"

"Bustling," she said, taking a sip. "That one trip we took caused three new recipes to come tumbling out of my head, and those crackle-top pies alone are adding a whole day of work to each week."

"Just shows how much a little change of scenery can help sharpen up the mind," Allie said.

"What a stunningly wise statement," Tome said wryly.

"It's true, though. Maybe not the scenery, but the new flavors, new smells. Even so close to home, things change so much from town to town. I would dearly love to do a bit more traveling."

"I'm sure Fel would be pleased to have you along on his next trip," Allie said.

"The only part I'd just as soon do without is the risk to life and limb," Mariss said.

"Best not to join Fel, then. His principle additions to any given road trip are a likelihood to be brought to death's door and a knack for just barely avoiding breaching the threshold of said door."

"Such stories he brings back, though," Mariss said. "Imagine if the lot of us could pile into a nice big, comfy wagon and head out into the world. We experience what the cities have to offer, then there comes a signpost that points off toward adventure, and you boys go have your excitement while Allie and I find a lovely little restaurant and keep two seats open for you to return to for a meal and night of regaling us. To see the world, taste it, smell it, and hear about the adventure without being dragged into it? Heaven."

"If only adventure would be kind enough to put up some of those signposts, we'd all be a good deal happier," Tome said. "I'm tempted to say I'd prefer to totter off with you two and try out that restaurant and leave Fel to the tales of derring-do, but I do so strive to be honest with those who have earned my respect, and that includes myself. I seem to have been afflicted by whatever gentle madness sends Fel off down that hazardous path. And to that end, I'm afraid I must leave you ladies. There are plans to be made."

Fel took a final sack of things from Teya and found a place to wedge them into the now entirely filled storeroom of Reynard's shop. Despite his best efforts, Fel had only managed to clear about a third of the shelves in their home of the contraptions that violated the current assayer's rules. This had made two things clear. They were going to need far more storage than Reynard's shop had to offer, and he'd need to make at least one more trip to acquire enough mundane goods to fill the empty space with innocuous items. This one load, plus what they'd be buying from Thaddeus, would leave this place quite sparse. If he were to fetch the rest of the crates from the hidden wagon, he might fill it sufficiently, but that would leave the wagon empty and cast some doubt on just what he was supposedly doing while "away." More preparations were in his already-crowded future.

Both of these determinations had been made before the scheme had even started to unfold, but Fel had been hoping that there had been enough miscalculations to make one or both of those additional complications unnecessary. He should have known better.

"How does it do?" Teya asked, snapping Fel out of his unpleasant line of thought.

She was crouched, hands on her knees, watching with fascination as Oiler completed a new chunk of the broken wall and adhered it to the near-complete circular block they'd chiseled out.

"It's a contraption. It's equal parts magic and mechanism," Fel said. "Or if you listen to Dad, and you probably should, more like nine parts mechanism and one part magic."

Teya pointed to the block Oiler was continuing to work on, then the dwindling pile of chips.

"We should smash, yes?" she said. "Smash fixed rock now? Keep hole open?"

"No," Fel said. "We need to know how close the repaired wall will look to the original. Things get more complicated if it's clear a repair happened. Better to plan for that now than later."

"Will look very different," Teya said.

"You'd be surprised how seamless Oiler's repairs are. The important thing is that I stay over here on the Reynard side, because I've got another trip to make. Ideally before sunrise."

"So go!" Teya said. "I watch. Tell how looks. You go and come back."

"You're sure?" Fel said. "Basically as soon as we get a good look at the repaired wall, it'll be time to knock it back down again. You'll be here doing that alone."

"Good job for me! I help! You go!"

Fel gave her a pat on the back. "Boy am I glad you showed up when you did. Even if maybe you're the cause of this problem, you're making the solution much easier."

"Destiny," she said in a singsong manner, grabbing her mattock and hopping through to the Masker side.

Fel hurried up the steps. Oiler stuck one of the last chips of stone in place and crawled after her to start piecing together the final bits on the Masker side.

The rest of the family was asleep, leaving no one but Teya and Oiler stirring. The kobold yawned and flicked an ear, then looked to the lantern hung from a hook overhead. The flame was still.

"Wick. The flame. You here?" she said.

"I am," he said.

"You feel good? Feel better? You were hurting before."

"I have recovered from my time in the Greater Lands. And you have my gratitude for your role in my rescue."

"Friends help friends. Even… fire contraption friends," she said.

"Your grasp of the language is improving," Wick said.

"Grasp always good. Saying part, hard part." She shut her eyes and shifted her jaw and tongue a bit. The next word required every ounce of focus she had. "Articulation. Your words? Bad for my mouth."

"You can speak your own language, if you like."

"You know it?" she said.

"I know a great deal. There is more information available to me than I can easily retrieve. But your rare comments and exclamations have a familiarity to me. I suspect I could decipher it with at least the level of success with which you speak human languages."

She rubbed her paws together and chattered in her own tongue. "We can give it a try then, because I would surely enjoy a brief respite from trying to select words that I'm confident I can pronounce."

"I imagine it would be quite taxing to do so."

She squealed happily. "You do understand me."

"So it would seem."

"Can you speak like me? Speak it back to me in my tongue?"

"I do not think so. Not yet, at any rate."

"Would you need practice?" she asked.

"What I would need is exposure. To hear words often enough to be certain I can associate their sounds with their meanings."

"Oh, splendid. Then we can chat. I will expose you to my words. Because while Fel and his family treat me like kin, a heart can start to long for the family left behind," she said. "Hearing my own tongue spoken back to me? I'd be a good deal less homesick."

"Does it trouble you to be away from home?"

"Trouble me? No. No, I am happy to have a job to do. But when I do go home, I will be happy to do that, too. I'll tell long stories about what I've learned, what I've seen. It will be strange because I know how the wall affects their minds, now that the earring means it does not affect mine.

It will be hard for them to imagine. But I will tell the story all the same. But not until the story is done. Not until the destiny is fulfilled."

"You speak of destiny with such certainty. I would have thought such a thing was unknowable."

She shook her head. "Destiny is the clearest thing there is. Every day, we all move forward. Step by step, moment by moment, we move toward where we're intended to be. Where we have been heading all along. But sometimes, the way becomes rocky. Murky. Maybe something appears that blocks the shortest, best path forward. When that happens, destiny comes. It taps us on the shoulder and points its divine finger. It shows us the door that was shut and guides us to open it. Destiny is how we move forward when there is no other way."

"I can only observe, but it does not feel that way to me," Wick said.

"How does it feel to you?"

"Can we really know the future?" Wick asked. "Is there one right way forward? I have observed much. Though my vision is ever pointed forward, all that I know is in the past. The past is the part of time that we know. And if something feels known to us, if it has a shape that we feel certain about, surely that means it is not a part of the future but a part of the past."

"How can we be moving toward the past?" Teya said doubtfully.

"I do not know. But I have seen much. To observe is all that I've ever been expected to do. And the shape of things does feel familiar. It feels like a place I have been. I think, or perhaps I fear, that destiny is not about moving forward. Instead, when destiny rears its head, it may be a warning that history is repeating itself."

"You remember the world as it is now, but in some earlier time?" Teya said.

"I remember events very much like those that are once again shaping our world."

"What part of history does it feel like, then?"

Wick remained silent for a few beats. "The last part."

Now it was Teya's turn to be silent. When she spoke, it was with the same gleeful exuberance with which she lived her entire life.

"Exciting!" she said.

"I had anticipated dismay at such a statement."

"The two parts of history that are most interesting are surely the beginning and the end. And if there was a previous ending, that must mean there will be another beginning. If I am brave, and I do my job well, I might get to see both!"

A jangle of chain drew their attention to the hole. Oiler had its tail and one claw braced against the base of the wall. The remaining claw clutched the edge of the stone block the contraption had rebuilt. Trembling with force, it reeled the claw in, tipping the piece into place. It slotted perfectly into the excavated hole, leaving only a handful of gaps where blows had turned the stone to powder.

Deft and precise motions of the claws followed, gathering bits of stone onto the flat palm of its metal mitts. Pulverizing motions of the claws on the other hand turned them to powder. A spritz of liquid from its fang turned that powder into a paste. From there, scoops and smears of the stuff filled the gaps. Before Teya's very eyes, the last evidence of the break faded away. She crept up to the wall and investigated the repaired section while Oiler merrily continued working its way around the perimeter. The color was a perfect match. That stood to reason; it was made from the very same stone that had been broken away. Having seen the wall before, if she aligned her head against it and peered across its surface, she could just make out gentle dips and bits of unnaturally smooth stone where pieces of rock were repaired. But the change was so subtle she couldn't even feel it if she scratched the wall with her claw. Had she not known the job had been done, she would never have spotted the difference.

Footsteps drew her attention to the stairs. Martin was approaching.

"Where is Fel?" he asked.

"He has gone to fetch some additional antiques from where he's stowed them. He hopes to get back before sunrise," Wick explained.

"This? Not fixed stone," Teya said, reverting to the local tongue for his benefit. "This new stone. Not like glue. Like... not glue."

"Oiler is a fine example of some of the most impressive contraption work of the Bygone Era. I think we are just beginning to see the things it is capable of."

"Magic..." Teya said with a slow nod.

"I assume the final detailing of this repair was only just completed?"

"Yes."

"Mmm..." Martin said. "That would imply that a good deal of cosmetic work remains to be done on the other side of the wall to match this level of repair."

Teya nodded.

"An important point. Oiler needs to finish a repair on the side that we most need to be flawless," Martin said.

She nodded again, then widened her eyes in realization. "Oh! Wick! Tell what you said. About the end."

"I'm not sure Martin will greet this information with the same zeal," Wick said.

"Papa Fel smart. Knows good things. Wick? He says history ends. Ends soon! Exciting!"

Martin blinked. "I'm afraid I'll need clarification."

CHAPTER 5

Fel puffed at one of his father's new pipes. Built from stolen designs from the Bolivans' contraptioneer, it was a way to keep a flame lit from Wick burning in a durable and portable way. He'd been talked into bringing it as his means of staying in contact. It was against his better judgment. He liked doing things the old-fashioned way. As tended to be the case when debating things with his family, he'd lost the argument.

"You there, Wick?" Fel asked after a second puff and an idle scratch to Parch's head.

"I am, Fel. Is something wrong?" Wick asked.

"Yeah there's something wrong. This is a dumb way to talk to you. Why couldn't I just bring the other persistent lantern?"

"I believe your father was quite clear. With the greater scrutiny being provided by the inspector, he is not comfortable with something irreplaceable like one of the two persistent lanterns being moved about."

"We could have just lit this lantern from you and used that," he grumbled, raising the half-covered lantern in his hand.

"That is true. I cannot speculate why such an option was not selected instead," Wick said.

"Oh, I can tell you why," Fel said.

He crunched through the brush a short distance from the city walls. Parch pranced ahead and snacked on some bramble that most creatures would consider inedible. Leonard was still asleep at the gate, so slipping out hadn't been difficult, but the sun would rise in another few hours. It would bring with it a fresh recruit to watch the gate. He needed to be back inside before then. Leonard's utter failure to perform the "watch" part of being a watchman was why this first night of the plan was so busy. From here, leaving the city would be much more difficult until next week when Leonard was back in the watchhouse. It was a tight deadline, and he hated working on a tight deadline.

"Were you going to continue that thought, or was it an idle expression of frustration?" Wick asked.

"It's Dad getting excited about the shiny new thing. It's like when he was pushing the dazzler as must-have gear for vault trips."

"You have used the dazzler to great effect on nearly every mission where defensive action was necessary."

"Yeah, listen, I didn't say it was necessarily a bad idea. But Dad is always looking for ways to test and use the stuff he builds, so now I've got a pipe in my mouth," he griped, coughing lightly. "Why do people smoke? I don't see the appeal."

"I believe the hands-free means to maintain a sentry flame for communication is the focus of this contraption and less the actual act of smoking."

"Yeah, yeah. Meanwhile it's putting a lousy taste in my mouth. It's like bad scotch but without the tipsiness."

He glanced over his shoulder. Only the very tip of the wall was visible over the tree line. He was getting close to his target.

"Tell you the truth," he grumbled. "That's not the main reason I hate this dumb pipe. It's that it's a Bolivan thing."

"Your father built that pipe himself. I observed it."

"Yeah, I know, but we got the design from the Bolivans. They had to use it for their whole operation to work, so it just feels like we shouldn't use it. Same reason I don't want to use the invisibility bracer."

"I thought the bracer gave you headaches and a sour stomach."

"It does. But, again, so does cheap scotch, and I still drink that. If feeling lousy after I did something was reason enough not to do it, I'd be living a much cleaner life. But a bunch of people using something to try to kill you and your family kind of makes you want to push it away. Ah! Here it is."

A decent distance from the western road, and at the precise point where the city's walls ceased to be visible, an old structure stood tangled in weeds, completely invisible to anyone who wasn't looking for it. It was an outpost, or a stronghold, or whatever the old tacticians would have called it. To Fel, it was a musty-smelling stone chamber dug into the countryside. In the days when Beffshire might have had to turn away an attacking force, it served the purpose of housing lookouts who could raise a signal for the city to close the gates if someone was approaching from this blind angle. Once war ceased to be a concern, this cold, miserable hole in the ground was abandoned. Fel doubted anyone in Beffshire even realized it was there. He only knew about it because he'd literally fallen into it when he was playing as a child and had proclaimed it to be his secret lair.

The only exposed portion of the chamber was a narrow arrow slit, a mossy stone top, and a rotten wooden hatch that had slumped down into the interior. A brief attempt to open the failing hatch caused it to crumble to mulch and slap wetly against the stone floor inside. He dropped a rope and slid down. When the light of the lantern lit the gray stone interior, countless dark forms scuttled away. He shuddered.

"I really wish I didn't have to spend so much time in places where creepy-crawlies like to hide."

"I thought you liked wildlife," Wick said.

"Not when it has more than four legs, goes crunch when you step on it, and itches when it bites," he said.

Parch clopped down beside him.

"All right. Let's make this quick. We need to set this place up so that the Graves family can fill it up with another shipment or two of antiques and replacement contraptions scraped from nearby shops so I can haul them in next time Leonard is working the gate." He raised the lantern. "This place felt a lot bigger when I was little."

The chamber was only about five feet by eight feet. Room enough for a soldier or two to hunker down with a pair of bows and a bunch of spare arrows. But it was an old feature, as old as the town, and that meant it was just like any other old part of Beffshire. They'd built it down, not up. The same sort of hatch-door combination that led from the Maskers' shop down into their home was tucked into the back wall. It had held up a good deal better than the top hatch, but it wasn't quite up to the standards of the Bygone Era defenses he earned his living by defeating. A few taps with a hammer and punch were enough to knock the pin out of the hinge. He removed the door and flipped the hatch open. A wave of stagnant air struck him like a bucket of water. He puffed the pipe a few more times. Suddenly a bit of burning tobacco stench was the preferable scent.

Parch wrinkled his nose and backed away.

"Yeah. You've got more sense than me. As usual," Fel said, thumping down the steps.

The lower chamber was, thankfully, much larger than the upper one. It actually felt unsettlingly similar to the sections of the Greater Lands wall that they'd determined must have been barracks. Little rectangles on the floor, relatively free of grime, marked where bedposts and footlockers had once been. They were long gone, probably either taken by the last soldiers positioned here or pillaged by the first set of thieves that stumbled upon the undefended chamber. Given the intact nature of the top hatch when he arrived, he guessed the former. The tattered remnants of pennants hung on the walls. They weren't the current lord's seal. No surprise. Beffshire changed hands every few generations. Backstabbing and arranged marriages would do that.

He popped the door from the next hatch. The steep stairs leading down were entirely missing. Lowering the lantern a bit revealed a much more cluttered but still relatively empty level. He dropped down to investigate.

If the basement had been pillaged, the sub-basement was where the pillagers had dropped the things they didn't care enough to bring with them. A dozen empty weapon racks, some shattered crates, and the odd boot or piece of moldy clothing covered the floor in scattered mounds.

"This'll do. Push all of this over to the other wall, install some pulleys so they can lower the goods down easier, and this'll give us enough room to stow the remainder of what we need. Better get moving. We're short on time, and the smell isn't getting any better."

He kicked enough of the debris on the second level aside to clear a landing spot and went to work installing the pulleys. There was a time he would have questioned the value of this part of the plan, but a lesson one learned quickly when doing dives into vaults, crypts, and other places that one technically had no specific right to was that the less time one spent out in the open the better. There was every likelihood the Graves family had done their share of raids and thus knew the best ways to hoist gear into and out of musty holes in the ground. Even so, depending on another person's expertise in handling something important was an excellent way to add weak points to an already wobbly plan. If a quick bit of hammering and bolting could cut the Graves' stop from an hour to ten minutes, that was one less chance for their scheming to be observed and uncovered.

The upper pulley went in easily enough. It took just a few minutes. The stone he had to chip away for the second one was another thing entirely. It was some seriously stubborn stuff. He'd been at it for twice as long as the first, and he'd only just gotten the second anchor in. It was good and solid, but after such a fight, Fel was inclined to do a few more taps for good measure, just to underscore his victory over the recalcitrant stone. An odd sound between spiteful thwacks of the hammer made him pause.

"What's that?" he said quietly.

It was a scrambling, clattering sound on the upper floor. He reached for the lantern. Before he could grab it, the frenzied gray form of Parch practically fell on his head. He sprang from the floor beside him, kicked off the wall, and vanished to the lower floor.

"That's not good..." Fel said.

He had one of his smaller cudgels on his belt and a larger one in his pack, but the hammer already in his hand would do if something reared its ugly head.

Or so he thought.

The next motion was dizzying. Whatever it was, it whisked down to his level without touching the floor. He felt a stinging slash across his chest and stumbled back. Three long, shallow gashes cut straight through his shirt and were beading with blood. He tried to spot what it was that had attacked him, but a second form, a match for the first, darted down through the hatch as well. A wild swing of the hammer failed to strike it but did convince it to withdraw rather than complete the attack.

The frenzy of motion continued for a few moments before the streaking attackers finally slowed and held their ground. In the flickering light of the lantern, Fel saw what had slashed his chest and frightened Parch.

There were two nearly identical creatures. The shape was broadly feline, midway between the size of a mountain lion and a house cat. The hind legs, the tail, and most of the back were covered with a sandy-yellow fur. Beginning at the middle of its spine, the fur gradually took on a darker brown color. At the shoulder blades, the fur broadened into feathers and two powerful eagle wings fanned out. Rather than a feline head, something more simian glared at him with orange-brown eyes. The ape-like heads had an ominous wisdom in their gaze. No fear. No fierce but empty instinct. These two creatures were not being cautious, they were waiting.

Near-human hands tipped the front legs, though catlike claws emerged from the fingertips where nails might be.

Fel searched his mind. Had he ever seen such a thing before? Had he even heard tell of one? Any information, any at all, might help him plan how to avoid a fresh gash in his chest.

"Are you seeing this, Wick?" Fel asked.

"Faintly," Wick replied. "The pipe is better for communication than observation."

"If I survive this, I'll be sure to tell Dad that," Fel said, sliding the cudgel from his belt to have a weapon in each hand.

"I can deliver the message now if you would prefer."

"No! Just tell me what these things are!" Fel said.

"Feline and avian features imply griffin. Smaller size implies lesser griffin. But the presence of ape features is curious."

"Yeah. Curious. There's a lot of that going around. Like why they're just sitting on their haunches and not attacking." He waggled the cudgel in one hand. "I feel like they know something I don't."

"Sphinx," Wick said. "I believe these are lesser sphinxes."

"Great! How do I fight them?" Fel said.

"I do not know. The only information I am able to recall about them is that there are no known cases of them attacking anyone. They are very stoic creatures."

"My bloody chest begs to differ, Wick," Fel snapped. He stomped his foot and bashed the wall beside him. "Go! Go on! Get!" he shouted.

The sphinxes looked at one another, then back to him.

"Don't make me bash your skulls in. I'll do it! You're talking to a guy who freed one dragon and fought another. I'm friend of, and enemy to, all sorts of Greater Mystics. You think I'm afraid of a couple of Lesser Mystics?"

From above, almost silent beneath the thundering of his heart in his ears, a flutter of cloth and the grind of dust beneath a boot drew his attention to the hatch. He couldn't make out who was lurking there. He dared not take his eyes off the sphinxes long enough to give it a proper look. But with few other tools at his disposal, Fel continued to lean on bluster and threat.

"I don't know who you are, but you call off these beasts, or I'm going to bury this hammer in your skull."

A long, complex sound echoed down from above. It was a harsh, jagged sequence of syllables, unlike any language he'd heard before. It had no meaning for him. But the sphinxes heard it loud and clear. They spread their wings and crouched, ready to pounce.

Fel stepped back, choosing to drop down into the lowest level rather than catch a twin assault. Before he'd even struck the ground, they were scrabbling at the hatch, trying to get through at the same time. Fel threw the hammer, but the blasted things were able to dodge. The attack did little more than buy him another moment.

He used that moment to realize just how poor his planning had been in dropping down here. The only light source was still in the level above, leaving him with the reflected light in otherwise total darkness. And while there was a still-secured hatch leading to an unexplored fourth level, he certainly wouldn't have time to get it open.

The creatures swept down after him, one by one. He pulled the full-size cudgel from his pack and choked up. Three mad swings at half-seen attackers kept them at bay, but midway through the fourth, he caught a slashing claw under the left arm, raking across his ribs. Little hooves clacked and clattered against the stone, and Parch charged to Fel's aid, but he had no more success at striking the things than Fel had. The sphinxes were devilishly fast, and they seemed to have the cunning to use that speed perfectly.

He abandoned offense. The goal shifted from winning the battle to surviving each successive blow. Swinging the weapons wildly to ward off charges and raising them to defend against attacks was a more successful tactic, but only just. He went from blocking none of their attacks to blocking about half, and those that got through weren't quite as direct and deep. Instinct began to latch on to the way the things moved. He got a feel for how they would attack, and where. If he could hold out a little longer, or if they slowed a bit from fatigue, he might actually get a blow or two in and turn the tide.

Then, the dim light from the lantern above vanished. It was instantly pitch-black. All he could hear was his own ragged breath and the slow, sinister breathing of his enemies. If he was lucky, they couldn't see any better than he could. But he most certainly was not lucky. If he were, he wouldn't have ended up in the pitch-black lower level of a forgotten stronghold being assaulted by two mysterious Lesser Mystics in the first place. All he could do was wait and hope.

For once, hoping was enough. He heard another sharp, vicious command from above. He was buffeted by wind stirred from beating wings. Then, silence.

The thrill of battle faded, and with it the dulling effects on his wounds. He dared to take a deep breath. Then a brush of fur against his leg nearly stopped his heart. He released a shrill yelp before he realized it was Parch. The yell caused the pipe that had been desperately clenched between his teeth to fall to the ground. He located it via the faint ember in its tip and stuffed it back in his mouth.

"Wick?" he said. "You see anything?"

"Nothing."

He took another puff. "How about now?"

"You and Parch are alone."

He fumbled for the unicorn and hoisted him up, helping him climb to the next floor up before painfully hauling himself up as well. Another puff, another assurance that there was no one there. Fel climbed the stairs to the upper level, where the fading moonlight and brightening dawn sky finally gave him a decent view. He was bleeding from half a dozen different wounds. None were dire, but collectively they'd taken their toll. All his gear was still present.

"All of that, and all they did was steal my lantern?" Fel shook his head. "Forget it. I'll take the good fortune while it lasts. Come on. We need to get back to Beffshire. Keep as good a watch as you can, Wick. I don't know if I'll have a better chance against those things out in the open, but I don't want to find out. And when we're clear, tell Dad what happened and get them to pass a warning to the Graves crew to watch themselves when they stow the gear down there."

Tome sat in the unlit back corner of the shop, bleary eyes fixed upon the inspector across the street. When he'd returned from The Fox and Log, he'd had every intention of going to bed. He'd even made an attempt. But sleep wouldn't come. It was tempting, and reasonable, to blame it on the off-and-on work being done by the tireless Teya and Oiler, but he knew that was only part of the problem. The greater problem was the puzzle.

He ran his thumb over the packet of spells he'd selected or scribbled anew over the course of the night and narrowed his eyes. The hatch to the rest of the Masker household flipped open and Vivian emerged.

"Oh!" she said with a start. "You're up early."

"Up early. Up late. One begins to lose track," he mumbled, not even looking in her direction.

"Goodness, you're one of those, are you?" Vivian said, pacing to her ledger and flipping it open. "Suffering from the same affliction as my husband."

"At least your husband seems to make progress."

"Struggling?"

"Magic is a ball of snakes. You think you understand it, but it turns out you only understood one of its many forms, and it's shifted a dozen times since then. I'd set it aside with the hopes of understanding far more mundane things, like the actions of supposed keepers of the law, and even that eludes me. I think I'm losing my wits," he said.

"Oh, if you're hoping to understand what drives certain folks, you're better struggling with that ball of snakes."

"I spoke to Allie. She seems to think Cartwright is working for someone."

"I do wish we wouldn't keep burdening that girl with our business," Vivian said.

He rubbed his eyes. "I think she's right. But I'm not sure. I'm not sure of anything. I think that's why I can't keep this riddle out of my mind. A man can only suffer so many setbacks. I need to see something through to the essential truth. I need to get to the core of something."

"If I were you, I'd take the skills you already have—which are extremely rare and rather sought-after—and apply them to some sort of trade. You could be a very successful healer. You could write spells on commission."

"I've done the latter. Unfulfilling with regard to both the amount I earn and my personal growth. And I worry that the moment I fail to cure someone who comes to me as a healer, I will lose the trust and respect of my would-be clients and my confidence in my own abilities. And, not to belittle your mercantile aspirations, but I do not share them. Don't get me wrong. Wealth is not without its appeal, and it is certainly an eventual goal. But I worry it may be too easily attained."

Vivian laughed. "I think you'll find it more elusive than you think."

"My point is that I've set up something of a contradiction for myself. On one hand I desperately want to achieve, however that may be defined. But on the other I'm worried if I achieve too quickly, I'll be stripped of the drive to continue to grow. So I set my sights higher and higher for fear of earning the prize. Recently, I've done a wonderful job of reaching for things thoroughly beyond my grasp. I need a victory."

He leaned forward, expression becoming sharper and more intent, like a predator spotting its prey. "And I may have my next step toward one."

A courier trotted up to Inspector Cartwright. Tome slipped a spell from the stack and tore its edge. It flickered with faint blue light, and his ears tingled with sensitivity. He could hear the rush of his own blood, the thump of Mrs. Masker's heart. He could hear the rustling and preening of the lesser harpies on the roof. He narrowed his focus, and gradually the words exchanged between the inspector and the courier filtered into his ears.

"—fresh pork pie, like you asked," the courier said.

A rustle of fabric as Cartwright looked in the sack he was offered. "It will do," he said.

"Four duots, sir," the courier said.

Tome shut his eyes and gritted his teeth. "It's a food delivery…" he grumbled. He heard the jingle of coins.

"Anything in the box for me?" the inspector said.

Tome opened his eyes again.

"The box? Oh, you mean from—" the courier began.

Cartwright shushed him and glanced about. Tome grinned.

"Is there anything or not?" Cartwright asked.

"Nothing yet. But it's early. Stuff like that doesn't come through until—"

He waved off the explanation. "Just see to it I'm alerted as soon as there is anything." He dropped an additional duot in the courier's hand. "That's to ensure promptness. And if anything comes…"

The tingle in Tome's ears faded. His hearing returned to normal.

"Blast it," he said. "I really shouldn't rely upon spells I've written while sleep-deprived." He turned to Vivian. "I don't suppose you recognized that courier."

"Not specifically. But there are only three places in town that'd deliver food and messages. I'll write them down for you."

"In a moment," Tome said, eyes still fixed on the inspector. "I don't want to miss this."

"Oh, yes," Vivian said, glancing up as well.

Cartwright revealed the still-steaming pork pie. Instantly a sequence of shadows swept over him. His expression turned sour as the lesser harpies landed in front of him, one by one.

"Raaat thief?" Toody croaked sweetly.

The inspector held his meal close to his chest and spat some profanities at the birds. Tome crossed his arms and drank in the torment as it unfolded toward the inevitability of Cartwright losing some or all of his meal in the pursuit of keeping the harpies from having any of it.

"But surely I needn't pack this away," Martin said, clutching a book to his chest with the same fearful protection as the inspector's pork pie.

"It has to be packed away. It's potentially incriminating," Epiphany said.

"But it isn't even in our language. He won't be able to know it is incriminating."

"That it isn't in our language and you're holding on to it will be enough of a clue to prompt him to investigate further. And there are diagrams, Dad. Even a layman will be able to tell this has to do with constructing contraptions."

From the moment they'd both awoken, Martin and Epiphany had been engaged in what amounted to a desperate bargaining session. Martin wanted to keep as much of his workshop intact as possible. Epiphany wanted to strip it as bare as possible. Unfortunately for Martin, Epiphany's stock and trade was bargaining. The proportion of the shelves that had been cleared into crates underscored just how successful she'd been.

"Dad, honestly. You worked for your entire career without having access to these things. You did without them just fine then," she said.

"But I've never had to do without them after I've had them," he said.

"It's just for a week or two."

"But this is a critical time. I'm so close to a serious breakthrough on the bust," he said, gesturing at the project on the workbench.

Epiphany took advantage of the gesture to slip the book from his grasp and drop it into a crate. "I don't even know why that's still here. It is the most incriminating thing in the entire shop. It should have been gone first."

"I intend to be working on it until the last moment."

She placed her hands on her hips and looked over the bust. She spent very little time in the workshop, so it wasn't until now that she'd seen just how far he'd come. One full arm had been installed, and a second one was only awaiting a hand.

"Does it work?" she asked.

"It moves brilliantly. Precisely as intended. The coupler does the job quite well, sans vision for the mask. But this isn't intended for masks. It is intended for Wick, and he has his own means to see. Once the arms are properly installed, I apply his flame to the coupler, and he can begin to learn to work them. Once he learns to work them, he can begin recording the pieces of the Telestressa Archives that were consumed in his flame. It will take ages for him to finish putting the words to page. Longer than you or I will live, I suspect. But it is worth it. Wisdom thought lost forever is just waiting to be retold."

"It's a noble pursuit, Dad. But is this really the best way? There was that contraption that illustrated images. It was very swift at reproducing documents as well. That would be a speedier way."

"We don't have one in our inventory for me to study, and it was more luck than know-how that allowed me to fix the first one. Hands? Arms? They're simple mechanisms, things I understand. Maybe in the future I'll improve this, but better to start poorly than waste any more time."

Teya hopped down the steps and tapped on the doorway. "New hole done." She pointed to the nearly filled crate at their feet. "I take?"

"Not just yet." Epiphany grabbed two more books before Martin could defend them and dropped them inside. "Now you can take them. Do you need help?"

"No no." Teya tipped the crate up and slid it to her neck and shoulders, steadying it from below with remarkable success, if not with grace. "I carry. Good at carry. Very very."

She hauled herself up, one step at a time.

"Thank you very much, Teya. You are being extremely helpful," Epiphany called after her. "Now let's talk about tools, Dad."

"Tools are innocuous!" he immediately asserted.

"I know that and you know that, but…"

She trailed off as the flickering of Wick's lamp, which was for the moment still perched on its shelf, slowed with the arrival of the sentry flame's consciousness. The family had come to treat the steadying flame roughly as one might respond to someone clearing their throat to request a chance to speak.

"Wick! Tell Epiphany that tools are innocuous and need not be stowed away. You know the assayer's rules better than anyone," Martin said.

"I would be delighted to do so, but first it may interest you to know that Fel has had some difficulties in his current task. He has been lightly injured."

Above, the crate thumped to the floor and scrabbling claws bounded down the stairs.

"How lightly?" Epiphany said quickly.

"And how did it happen?" Martin said.

Teya tumbled into the room. "Fel hurt? Tell more!"

"He was attacked. Our best guess, based upon low visibility and our combined intuition, is that the culprits were lesser sphinxes. Fel was slashed multiple times by their claws. He is bleeding, but none of his wounds are dire."

"Tell him to come here," Martin said. "I'll get the bandages ready. Where is Tome? Have him write one of those healing spells."

"Tome has spells? Where? I take. Bring to Fel," Teya said, shifting her weight anxiously.

"Fel is heading to Allie's home, as the plan dictates," Wick explained.

"He can't come here," Epiphany agreed. "He's supposed to be off somewhere raiding a vault."

"I find! I find help!" Teya said.

"We are certain the wounds are not dire?" Martin said. "Fel has a terrible tendency to underestimate the severity of problems."

"The slashes are largely superficial. Once bandages are applied to stop the loss of blood, I am quite confident they will cease to be anything more than a nuisance."

"I get magic. I go," Teya said, scampering up the stairs.

"You have to stay out of sight!" Epiphany called.

Teya poked her head back down into the doorway. "I sneak. Very sneaky."

"You already got caught once, Teya," Martin reminded her.

"Caught once. Not again. Learn fast!"

"You don't even know where he is."

Teya tapped her earring. "I find. Destiny!" She dashed up the steps again.

"It's a circus. I live in a circus," Epiphany muttered. "Wick, keep us apprised, will you?"

"I shall do so," Wick said. "We are presently arriving at Allie's home."

Fel finally reached the alley outside the barmaid's home. Thanks to the "distraction" of being assaulted by a mystical creature, it had taken him just a shade longer to get back into the city than he'd intended. But in a place as big and busy as Beffshire, ten minutes at dawn could make an enormous difference. He'd just barely made it through the gate before the changing of the guard replaced Leonard with someone able to keep his eyes open long enough to spot someone Fel's size slipping into the city. The larger problem was the amount of business that was typically done in the wee hours of the morning. Navigating the city without being seen just before the sun rose was tricky but not too much of a burden. Navigating it once the sky had begun to change color put him on the streets precisely when the taverns, restaurants, and their like were fetching their goods to begin their day. And while Parch was quite bright, persuading the little unicorn to keep out of sight wasn't really within his set of commands. That meant Fel had to carry him over his shoulders. Thankfully, Parch endured such without much vocal complaint.

If nothing else, the extra effort he put into keeping from being seen occupied enough of his brain to push the ache of his wounds to the back of his mind. That benefit vanished the moment he shoved his way through Allie's door and let Parch down.

"By the High, that stings..." he muttered.

He fumbled for a lantern by the door and lit it from his pipe, then extinguished the smoky contraption. He looked up and stumbled back against the freshly shut door. Allie was standing there, wrapped in a robe and holding a leather-wrapped stick with some cruel-looking metal studs speckling its surface. Parch clippy-clopped toward her. He recognized her as one of the handful of people who could be trusted to give snacks and/or pats. A moment later he interpreted her body language and thought better of seeking either.

"Um... hey, Allie," Fel said. "You're up early."

She shook her head and set the stick down before hurrying over to him. "Why does it not surprise me that the first time you ever enter my home, you're bleeding all over everything?"

"Because I lead a very interesting life and you know it." He glanced at the floor, then the door. "I'll clean up the mess once I stop making it. As you can probably guess, I've gotten pretty good at cleaning up blood."

She opened a cabinet and pulled out some old rags, then fetched a basin of water. "Sit down at the table, you big animal. How bad is it?" she said.

"I can handle it. You're just giving me a place to hide out. I don't want to ruin your day."

"You left a big smear of blood on my door with your back. As entertaining as it would be to watch you try to clean and bandage the middle of your back on your own, let's just get this done."

He didn't argue. He just stripped off his half-shredded shirt and leaned on the table. She slapped a moistened cloth against the gashes on his back and started to mop them clean.

"Your shift doesn't start for another six hours today, right?" he said.

"Yes. That's why I was sleeping," she said.

"You got up and got armed in the time it took me to light a lantern?"

"Yep. A woman's got to protect what's hers."

"I thought you said you've never been robbed."

"I've never been robbed because people got the hint that I'm the sort who can go from asleep to knocking teeth out in the time it takes them to blink. That's the kind of reputation that fades if you don't stay on top of it." She lifted the rag. "These aren't as bad as they look."

"Yeah. Lots of blood, but not too deep," he said.

"What did this to you?"

"You ever heard of a lesser sphinx?"

"I didn't know there was a lesser version. And I wasn't sure if the greater version was even real."

"I'm that lucky fellow who gets to find these things out, I guess. I think they're what's been making the road around Beffshire so rough recently. And I don't think they're doing it of their own accord. There was someone else. I didn't get a good look at him."

'If you didn't get a good look, how did you know it was a him?"

"Because all of the biggest pains in my backside are men."

"Likewise. Do you have bandages? I don't have any in the house because I don't usually end up bleeding like a stuck pig."

"In my bag," he said.

She shook her head and flipped the bag open. "You have bandages, but you're running around making a mess?"

"Speaking as the one with the 'bleeding like a stuck pig' experience, the two times you don't stop to deal with that sort of thing are when the one that did the sticking is still around or when someone with a lot of very good questions about it will spot you if you do."

"You are a great source of wisdom I hope never to have use for." Allie finished wrapping the gash on his back. "Let me do your front."

"I can reach the front," he said.

"Right. Right, you do that." She dropped the rag in his hand and picked up the discarded shirt. "What are you going to do for clothes?"

"I have gear stashed all over. I can pick up something once the sun goes down."

"So you'll just be lurking in my home with your shirt off?"

"Mostly I'll be sleeping. Why? Afraid someone will see me and get the wrong idea? Trust me, if anyone sees me, that's the least of our worries."

Allie sighed and looked down at Parch, who was gazing up at the basin of now-filthy water with the look of a creature growing increasingly impatient about not having something fresh to drink. The barmaid squinted at him.

"Your unicorn has blood all over his belly. Did he get hurt too?"

"Mmm? No. That's mine. Allie, really, you've done enough. This is already more than I'd hoped you'd have to do for me. This was just supposed to be a hiding place during the day."

"I told you to come here, and I know what sort of mischief you get up to. I knew what I was in for. I just... didn't know it'd start happening so quickly."

"I promise this is as bad as things are going to get. From here on, it will be like I'm not even here."

She poured some fresh water into a bowl and put it down for Parch. The intensity of the silence was almost painful. Allie was one of those people who seemed capable of changing the temperature of a room with the raw potency of her moods, and right now the place felt absolutely scorching to Fel. It was no small relief when a strange scratching sound gave Fel something else to fixate on.

"What's that?" he said.

She waved it off. "Don't worry about that. The chimney is huge. All sorts of animals on the roof scratch at it. I persuaded the man who owns the place to put in a bit of metal mesh to keep them from crawling into my home."

Another scratch was followed by a quiet ring of metal being shifted. Both Fel and Allie turned. Each of them grabbed their weapon of choice. A third scratching. Now closer. Allie crept closer and raised her stick. Fel held his weapon tight and stayed tense.

A pair of sooty, serrated ears flopped into view, then with a puff of soot and a huff of effort, a bright-eyed reptilian head poked into view.

Allie's eyes widened, and she raised the stick to strike.

"No! Friend!" Teya said.

Fel grabbed Allie's stick to keep her from bringing it down. Teya wriggled out of the chimney.

"Friend. Came for Fel. Fel hurt? I come. I help," she said.

Allie pointed a shaky hand at Teya. "... What... What?"

"Her name is Teya. She's a kobold. She's my friend, and she was supposed to stay at my house!" Fel said quickly, delivering the final words directly into the soot-covered face of the kobold.

She waggled some paper slips. "Healing. Magic. For wounds."

"Did anyone see you?" he said.

She shook her head, puffing more soot into the air. "No. Not this time. Very sneaky."

Allie shut her eyes tight and took a controlled breath. "I am going to go into the other room and get dressed. Then I am going to go to The Fox and Log early because there is no chance I'll get any more sleep."

"Allie, I—" Fel began.

"Don't. Don't," she said, jabbing his chest in one of the unbandaged spots. She stalked into the only other room in her home and slammed the door.

"Your friend. She is very..." Teya groped for a word for a moment. "...Very. Eyes like dragon."

"Yeah. She's pretty intense."

Now that the various sources of threat, both physical and emotional, were gone, weariness seized the opportunity to impose itself. He'd worked all day and all night. Pounding through stone walls, toting crates of gear, rushing to and from vaults. He was ready for sleep. But first, some answers.

"Seriously, Teya. What are you doing here?" he asked.

Teya pointed. "Wick said Fel hurt. I come. Heal magic. Friend."

"But you're supposed to be home moving crates and digging holes."

"Move crates? No more room. No more until night. I stay until night. Need help with bed? I help with bed."

She tottered over to his gear bag and unfurled the bedroll to start setting it up. Fel's mouth hung open a bit as he fished for some way to illustrate just how badly this all felt like it was going. As was his policy when words were too tricky, he abandoned them and just shrugged.

"Fine. We'll argue later. I don't have the energy for this."

She handed him one of the pages. He found the proper end, tore it, and pressed it to his chest. As usual, the effect of the healing magic wasn't complete. The wounds didn't simply vanish. About half of them closed to the point he probably wouldn't have needed bandages on them. The other half still would have trickled enough blood to ruin his shirt if they weren't covered, but all in all the improvement was inarguable. But he'd never had quite so many injuries treated at once by magic. And he'd never been quite so exhausted when he'd used one of the spells either. For the first time he could remember, using one of the paper spells struck him with a wave of weariness that compounded with the fatigue he'd earned on his own. If Tome had been around, he was sure he'd be told some long-winded nonsense about how the magic was merely speeding up what his body was doing, or it was using up something in his body, or something of that nature. He couldn't care less what the reason was. All he knew was he'd arrived here with the desperate need for sleep, and now it was so intense he couldn't put it off any longer.

Teya hadn't been told where to set up, but Allie's home wasn't large enough for there to be much in the way of choice. There was a door, a large room with a table and two chairs on one side of it and a fireplace on the other side, and a door leading to what he assumed was Allie's room. The only place large enough for him to sleep without blocking the door or curling up under a piece of furniture was the space in front of the fireplace. And so, that's where the bedroll had been laid out.

Fel slumped down onto it, thumped his head onto the softer part of his pack, and fell fast asleep.

Allie paced out of her room, dressed in the sort of outfit that was more about sturdiness and ease of cleaning than fashion. Such an outfit was a must for a barmaid, but even if she had a cleaner job or a rare day off, she'd be dressed the same. She'd designed her life around decreasing the things she had to think about so she could focus her time and attention on more important things. Simple clothes, simple meals. Life was just easier that way. Indeed, she was so accustomed to shifting her mind to the next important task that when she emerged, she was already working out how she'd go about sliding her shift up a few hours and whether she'd simply work longer or try to leave early. It wasn't until she spotted a kobold mopping soot off her face with one of the damp rags that she remembered the Fel-flavored slice of chaos that had descended upon her life.

She froze, staring down at the mess her life had dumped on her. Fel was asleep, his bedroll tucked in the corner where Allie kept her pots and pans. Parch was curled next to him, contentedly gazing at nothing in particular. The kobold was sitting on her haunches in front of the pair. She finished wiping away the soot and neatly folded the rag before giving Allie a cautious look.

"No angry, please," Teya said softly. "And no loud."

"Is he... all right?" Allie asked.

"Yes! Good magic. Good sleep. Good health," she said.

"And you? Are you just going to stay here?"

"Keep Fel safe." She tapped her earring. "Destiny."

"I don't understand," Allie said.

"Me neither!" Teya said brightly. She pointed. "Allie, yes?"

"Yeah, that's me."

She nodded. "Good human."

"How would you know?"

"Fel talk? Three things." Teya counted them off on her claws. "The job, his family. His friends. Fel talk friends? Allie."

"He talks about only me when he talks about friends?"

Teya tapped her chin. "No. Also Tem. Angry grum Tem."

Allie stifled a laugh. Teya continued, her tone quite serious. She pointed at Allie.

"Good human." Now she pointed at Fel. "Good human. Take care. Both. Good humans? Not so rare. I thought rarer. Not so. But human this good? Very rare. Take care. Need more like Fel. More like you. Precious. Protect."

"That's the plan," Allie said softly.

— ◆ —

CHAPTER 6

After breakfast and a short nap, Tome had set off to investigate the messenger he'd seen delivering to Cartwright. Over the course of the last year or so, Tome had crossed most of the continent from his hometown to Beffshire and trekked back and forth to the Greater Lands. He was more aware of the width and breadth of the world than most, so it was easy to think of something like a single city as being comparatively tiny. A full morning of walking the streets of Beffshire in search of three specific shops had disabused him of that notion very quickly. The continent was like a thread stretched out across the countertop. Beffshire was like that same amount of thread wadded up in a ball. The latter might take up less space, but it was ten times harder to find a particular piece of it.

"Belle and Watts: Speedy Delivery," Tome said, gazing up at a sign featuring a boot with wings. "Finally."

He opened the door to a shop that he strongly suspected was formerly a closet in the adjoining shop. It was barely wider than a hallway. About two yards past the entryway was a countertop running wall to wall. A woman about twice his age sat behind it with a slate and a piece of chalk.

"It was rather hard to find—" Tome began.

"What's the package, where from, and where to?" the woman asked.

"Would you be Belle or Watts?" he asked.

"Neither. Belle is dead, Watts is retired, never met either. Bought the place from a guy who bought the place from Watts. Never bothered to change the sign. What's the package, where from, and where to?"

"The package I'm interested in has already been delivered, but—"

"No refunds."

"Perhaps I am not being clear. I am not here to complain. I am here about a package."

"What package, where from, and where to?" she said mechanically.

Tome had envisioned having a bit more room for nuance in this interaction.

"It was a meat pie, this morning. To a gentleman named Cartwright across from Masker's Antiquities."

"Did the pie get there?"

"It did, but—"

"I figured as much. Belle and Watts Speedy Delivery. Like it says on the sign."

"I'm looking for information, ma'am."

"It doesn't say Belle and Watts Speedy Information, does it?"

"No, but—"

"Unless you're going to tell me what package, where from, and where to, I really don't want to hear it."

Tome paused. A different tactic was in order.

"The customer who received the pie was very appreciative of the excellent service. It so happens I do a fair amount of delivery and fetching as well, so his satisfaction encouraged me to come here to see if your services would suit my needs."

"If your needs include having a package, or knowing where it is, and knowing where you want it to go, then tell me and I'll tell you the price."

"Before I hire you, I'd like to know a little about how you do business."

She spoke slowly, hitting the words hard enough to spritz him in the face. "You give us a package, or you tell us where a package is, and we give the package to the person you tell us to give it to."

"Do you keep records?" he asked.

She tapped the slate. "See this? This is the records. Doing this job requires a sharp memory, but the customers would usually prefer a short memory. So I write it down, and when I'm done, I wipe it clean."

"So, if I were to ask you who delivered that pie, or what other things the recipient might be waiting for, then you wouldn't know?"

She set down the chalk and pushed it aside. "Listen. We make about one duot per delivery—"

"I'm not interested in rates at the moment, I just—"

"Listen to the words I am saying to you," she said firmly. "We make about one duot per delivery. People trust us, or they wouldn't give us their packages. But if someone were to find out that we'd told someone else something about what their package was, where it came from, or who it went to, they might lose some trust in us. Maybe word gets out that we can't be trusted, and we lose fifty deliveries before we get our reputation back."

"I would treat any information I received with the utmost of tact."

"I tell you something they don't want me to tell you, and it costs fifty duots," she said more firmly.

"I will be very discreet."

"Well, sir, you won't, because you're clearly a fool. I know this because either you are attempting to rope me into accepting a bribe and you've passed up two different attempts to do it, or you're actually looking for information and you don't seem to understand the very concept of a bribe."

Tome paused. "I see. Forgive me, I am new to this particular type of subterfuge. Fifty duots it is."

"It's one hundred now. Surcharge for wasting my time."

"Fifty up front and fifty if your information is actually worth my while," he countered.

She raised her eyebrows. "So now you get shrewd? Fine." She tapped the desk. "Fifty."

He pulled a pouch from his bag and counted off stacks of coins. The moment the last coin hit the stack, the clerk swept the money into her pocket.

"You're interested in the inspector's packages. Has us bringing him three meals a day for the foreseeable future and had us set up a box in the back to receive messages in his name and deliver them when they arrive."

"Can I see the packages in the box?" he asked.

She threw her head back in a frankly uncalled-for laugh. "First, if you wanted me to just hand over his packages, it'd cost a lot more than one hundred duots. And there wouldn't be any packages in his box, because once we get them, we deliver them."

"Fine. Have you received any since he made that deal?"

"Two."

"How did you receive them?"

"They were dropped off."

"By whom?"

"We don't take names."

"Was it a man or a woman?"

"Man."

"What did he look like?"

"Young fellow. Blond hair. Quiet. Never says a word. Comes from out of town."

"Meaning he's not a local or meaning he physically enters the town from outside every time he leaves a package?"

"Both."

"And what sort of packages are they?"

"Sealed envelopes."

"And from which direction does he approach?"

"North gate."

"Is there anything else you can tell me?"

"I can tell you you've used up your bribe faster than most people."

Tome grumbled. "Thank you. You have been very helpful."

"Would have been a lot more helpful a lot faster if you'd known how business was done. Where's the other fifty?"

Tome counted out the rest of the payment. She swept it off the counter and grinned.

"Pleasure doing business with you," she said, again without a trace of sincerity.

Tome simply turned and marched out the door, out of both the eagerness to put this expensive bit of information to use and avoiding any further loss of face or funds.

After one of the heavier and more recuperative sleeps of his life, Fel woke up with a very rare predicament. Though he had plenty to do, it was too much of a risk to actually leave Allie's home to do it until nightfall. That left him with one room and a small section of her alleyway available to him and nothing but time to plan and fret over what the future held.

For better or worse, he wasn't short on company.

"You do good cleaning!" Teya said, crouching to inspect Fel's work as he scrubbed the formerly bloody floor.

"So do you," he said. "Thanks for handling the door."

"See work, lend hand," Teya said. "Kobold way. Why you clean good? Clean for job?"

"At one point I was a teenaged boy with money in my pocket and a home in a big city. You get into what my dad called 'misadventures' in a situation like that. I had the option of learning to clean up blood and treat my own wounds or get lectured by my parents twice as often as I already was."

"Or stop misadventure... ing," Teya said.

"Where's the fun in that?" Fel glanced up at the lantern lit from Wick's flame. "Any news?"

"Not presently. Thaddeus Graves began his first day working in Reynard's store. Your mother feels confident he will be able to clear a full shelf for additional contraption storage, but she also feels confident there is the real possibility that the inspector will want to search Reynard's shop eventually. He is already searching all packages leaving the shop, making the removal of contraptions through sale to intermediaries a non-option. Thus, she reaffirms that the next stage of the plan is still very much called for."

"Wonderful," Fel said. "And what about those things that slashed me up? Do you know any more about them? Are we even sure they were lesser sphinxes?"

"No."

"Oh come on, Wick. You're supposed to know practically everything."

"I know what I have seen and what has been consumed by my flame. While that includes a great deal of the contents of the Telestressa Archives, accessing that information is more complex than I can articulate. Further information about lesser sphinxes is either not among my knowledge or too well hidden within it for me to locate in a timely manner."

Fel looked to Teya. "What about you? Any insight?"

"Lesser Mystics? Don't know. Not many back home. I know Greater Mystics." She pointed at the bandage peeking out from his shirt. "That? Not from greater sphinx."

"I figured. We don't get many Greater Mystics out here without riders or taming contraptions, and I didn't spot any."

"True. And if greater sphinx? One swipe…" She glanced up, working through something in her head. "You? Four pieces. Or more."

"Thanks. That's encouraging. Let's assume we were right and they were lesser sphinxes. What do you know about greater sphinxes?"

"Big," Teya said. "Eat Fel whole. That big. Lady head. Other lady parts, too. Chest parts. Wings. Bird-type wings. Good for flying. Back part, bottom part, big cat. Paws. Claws. Also smart. Too smart. Annoying smart. Play games."

"Play games?"

"Sometimes, big cat? Catches small things. Bats it. Lets it go. Bats it again. Small thing? Doomed. But cat plays game. Like that. Only no batting. Questions. Riddles. Right answer? No eating. Wrong answer, eating."

"Why?" Fel said.

"Why anything? Why dragons collect? Why kobolds work? We do because we do."

"Fair enough. Now for the important question. How does that translate into a Lesser Mystic? Parch is smart and strong. So are greater unicorns. The lesser harpies are smart too. So if the sphinxes are smart, then we've got to assume the little ones are smart too. That seems to carry over."

"Yes, yes," Teya said.

"What about cruel games and riddles?" he said.

Teya shrugged.

"They certainly weren't asking me any questions," Fel said. "And there was someone else. They weren't attacking him. Would they work together with someone?"

Teya shrugged again. Fel stood up and straightened the kinks out of his back.

"I guess I should be used to not knowing what's going on by now. I'm hungry. You?"

"On way here? Ate two rats. City has so many. Could eat more."

"Let's see what I can cook up. Gotta get my eating done early, because tonight there is a lot to do, assuming they make enough room in Reynard's shop."

Teya perked up. "We need fire? I make fire."

She scampered over to the fireplace and hastily piled logs. Fel watched with something between bemusement and concern as she gleefully clicked at the sparker he'd given to her. She watched the tinder start to smolder, than took great huffing breaths to stoke the embers to flame. Her eyes were practically sparkling as she watched the flames take hold.

"Make fire..." she murmured dreamily.

Fel shrugged. "Whatever makes you happy, I guess."

She glanced at him. "We need more fire maybe?"

"No," he answered quickly. "In fact, let's get started cooking before you get any other ideas about what you might want to burn."

Epiphany stepped through the door of the shoe shop. Four customers were inside, which was twice as many as she'd ever seen in the shop before. Though she'd done a fair bit of business with Thaddeus Graves, mostly without knowing he was Thaddeus Graves, she'd never actually gotten a chance to see him ply his trade with someone outside of those interactions. One did business with businesspeople very differently than one did business with customers. Whereas Epiphany and Vivian were of the school of thought that one must educate a customer in how precisely to identify and purchase a quality item, and they just so happened to have precisely the best item on the shelf when they looked for it, Thaddeus took a subtly different approach. The man had a way of making you think any purchase you made from him was the most important purchase of your life.

"I was just hoping to purchase a good sturdy pair of shoes," said a man with the unmistakable look of someone swept up in a sales pitch he didn't know how to escape.

"Of course, sir. Of course. Good sturdy shoes are all we sell. I could sell you any given piece of footwear in your size, and you'd undoubtedly find them to be the best and most durable shoes you'll ever purchase in your lifetime or mine. But a discerning man such as yourself ought to look for more than that. The perfect shoe, good sir. The perfect shoe. I intend to find and sell to you a shoe that will not merely last. That will not merely do the job. I want you to buy a shoe that will bring you pride. That people will admire. And that is precisely what you'll find here."

Epiphany lingered in the corner while he persuaded each of the four customers to purchase, in all likelihood, the precise pair of shoes Reynard would have sold them. But they'd been convinced that making that purchase was an expression of their wisdom and foresight, their key to a better life. And, of course, such a vital choice came at a premium price.

When the place was empty, and Thaddeus had been paid twice what the shoes were worth, Epiphany clapped slowly and paced up to him.

"I'd fully expected you to make some sales, and quickly. But even I am a bit impressed at how many people you've managed to get into this place."

"Make a man proud of what he's bought, and he'll talk it up. That sends the rest marching right through your door," Thaddeus said. "I may have to take it a bit easier, or I'll completely clear the inventory before our little gambit is through."

"I notice he has been searching the packages on the way out," Epiphany said.

"Not all of them, as it turns out. The first one or two were scrutinized, but most since then have gotten a mere glimpse. Our friend across the way certainly doesn't suspect anything. We may be able to exchange some small items if we can place them physically inside shoes. That is, unless this little visit convinces him to increase scrutiny once more."

"The important thing is that he sent a request for permission to search our shop already. If he starts to think you're in on it, it will take a second proclamation and the associated travel time."

"Indeed. How are things going on your end?"

"Fel had some trouble. Whatever has been haunting the area took some swipes at him, but he's fine. Please pass word along to whoever is bringing the shipment of goods to drop at the edge of town that they should take extra care."

"It is a bit late to be passing word to them. The first shipment will be arriving late tonight. They are already on the road. But I assure you, they are well aware of the severity of the situation."

"You can't pass word to them on the road? I thought surely after we'd worked out the issues with your flame you'd be back to using it to maintain such things."

"Oh, it is back in use. But once bitten, twice shy, as they say. There are fewer than ten individuals in the entire organization permitted to carry a flame, and only the most vital of messages are delivered directly to the final recipient via flame. Messages are sent in code, different codes for different recipients, and anyone outside the circle of flame bearers must receive their messages through other means."

"What other means?" Epiphany said.

"That is at the behest of the flame bearer to determine and, forgive me, not the sort of information I'd feel comfortable sharing even with you."

"No, no. I understand. Security is security."

"And you're sure both Fel's health and your assessments about the feasibility of the next stage of this plan are sufficient to move on?"

"We'll make it work."

He glanced up at the door. "Then if you'll excuse me, I have more room to make in the inventory."

Allie marched through her day, a bit more subdued than usual. She was still dedicated to doing a good job, so every cup was filled and baskets of crickets were never empty for long, but her mind and heart weren't in the more performative aspects of her job. No pretending to care how the usuals were doing at the grum table. No conjuring up a clever way to remind folks when their tabs were getting a bit too high.

Part of her dull, thick state of mind had to do with her sleep being cut short. She'd stayed until closing the prior night and was up at dawn. If she'd had four hours of sleep, it was a miracle. But there was a good deal more keeping her mind from her job than that. Her home was on her mind as well. On an average night, she had the mild but persistent concern that someone may have robbed her home in her absence. For the most part she preferred to be left alone, but doing so meant while she worked, there was no one keeping an eye on her home. And she worked a great deal. Presently the issue wasn't the lack of someone to watch over her home, but the presence of three things just as likely to destroy it as protect it. A unicorn, a kobold, and Fel Masker were in her house right now. She didn't know which of the three was capable of the most chaos, but she had her suspicions.

All she wanted to do was go home. It was a thought that was familiar to the great majority of people—people who didn't like their jobs but didn't have a choice. Allie didn't have a choice, that was true enough, but she got a tremendous amount of pride and fulfillment out of tending the bar at the level she did. Maybe she could have made more money elsewhere, but The Fox and Log was her tavern. She'd helped make it what it was. She was almost as worried that the tavern would fall to pieces while she was home as she was concerned about her home while she worked.

But a small part of Allie's mind, a part she would have viciously denied if anyone asked, provided yet another reason to yearn to return home. It was the same thing that often made her yearn to come to work.

Fel was there.

For all his faults, and he was more fault than man some days, Fel made things interesting. It was easy enough to work the tavern when he was off on one of his adventures. That just meant when he came back, he'd have fresh stories and a bit of extra money to tip her with. But right now he was absent because he was elsewhere in this very town. He was in a place where she could be alone with him. A place where she could hear his stories and his groan-inducing attempts at humor without having to split her mind in a dozen directions to keep the tavern running. She craved it more than she'd ever anticipated. She wanted to talk to her friend.

Allie was good enough at her job that even at her most spiritless and automatic, she kept the place running and the clientele happy. When her heart wasn't in it, she felt the difference in the jingle of her apron at the end of the day. Not quite so many tips. But today that couldn't be helped. Oovay would be in soon. She'd remind him how often he'd left her working the floor alone, and how seldom she'd made a fuss. He'd grudgingly agree to handle a bit more of the late shift than he normally would, and she'd head home early. Ideally to a home that wasn't completely ransacked, besieged by attacking warriors, or any of the other things the current occupants might bring about.

She just had to last until then.

Tome paced along the north road out of the city. Already he was wondering if perhaps he'd overpaid for the information the courier woman had given him. What had he really learned? That there was a man who entered via the north gate. It had taken further snooping and asking around just to determine that a great deal of short-term business was done through the north gate of town, thanks to something the locals called the Skinflint Camp beyond the gate.

He clutched a small collection of defensive and offensive spells in the fist tucked in his pocket. Fel could be a bit of an oaf, but he knew how to defend himself. According to the family, he'd taken some lumps at the hands of whoever was stalking the roads around town, so the dangers lurking out here were real. He wanted to be ready.

Fortunately, and necessarily, the Skinflint Camp was quite near to the city. He'd only been on the road a few minutes. The walls to the city were still quite visible behind him. Ahead, the camp was coming into view.

Beffshire was a place people came to make money. As was the case in any place where a great deal of money changed hands, the base price for survival was a good deal higher in Beffshire than in most other towns. It was the reason the merchants of the traveling bazaar slept in their wagons. It was why many other traveling merchants arranged their travel such that they were clear of Beffshire before sundown. And it was why the Skinflint Camp existed. Setting up camp just outside of town was worlds more affordable than even the cheapest and least reputable of bunkhouses. He'd had little cause to head up this road, so Tome had never seen it, but he'd been told on an average day, Skinflint Camp had more temporary residents than some of the smaller permanent villages in the area. That only a half-dozen tents had been set up was evidence that even the thrifty travelers on their way through Beffshire were taking the dangers of the roadside seriously.

"The question now is, are the people in this camp too simple to fear the attacks, too foolhardy to fear the attacks, or responsible for the attacks," he mused as he drew nearer.

He paused for a moment and held his head. Another one of those blasted pulses of pain. He'd been getting them with some regularity for the last few hours. If he knew for certain that they were nothing to be worried about, he could easily disregard them. The pain was subtle and brief. But not knowing the source made him fixate on them all the more. The pain passed quickly enough. When a second throb didn't follow, he set the distraction aside and continued his mission.

Tome tried to strike a balance between looking intimidating enough not to be taken advantage of and harmless enough not to draw a preemptive strike. Given the fleeting glances he earned from the people in the camp, he was a shade closer to harmless than he would have liked, but it was acceptable.

Of the six tents in the camp, the owners of four were present. None of the campsites was large or had enough materials to support more than one resident, so he chose to believe if the person lingering outside a tent or visible through an open flap didn't fit the description he'd been given, he could safely disregard that spot. The first tent belonged to a woman who looked as though she probably had some giant in her ancestry, as she was more than sturdy enough to justify traveling alone even with killers on the road. Two more were occupied by men, but one was twice the age of what Tome would consider a "young man," and the other was missing an eye, which he felt certain would have been included in the description he'd been given. The fourth could have matched the description. His hair was more brown than blond, but that was the sort of distinction that could vary from one assessment to another. He had a very large knife on his belt though. That plus the hard look he gave Tome as he drew near encouraged him to continue his search elsewhere, at least for now.

The sixth tent had been completely ransacked, stripped of its supplies and shredded. That left the fifth campsite. It was a very sturdy tent with a stake driven into the ground where a horse was likely tied up during the night. The doors were clasped with leather belts from the outside. That was good news; it meant there certainly wasn't anyone inside.

Tome glanced over his shoulder and found the knife-wielding man hadn't taken his eyes off him. Unless he missed his guess, Mr. Knife had been paid by the keeper of tent five to keep it from ending up like tent six. That would complicate things, but only slightly.

He paced alongside the tent and did his best to avoid the obvious appearance of a man investigating its weak points. A matching flap was present on the opposite side, also belted shut. That entrance faced away from the knife man. Tome thumbed the carefully shaped end of one of the spells in his pocket. He waited until the moment the tent entirely obscured him, then tore the edge of the packet of pages comprising the spell. A very convincing duplicate of him wafted into being and continued pacing. When it was a dozen or so paces down the road, Tome slipped a small mirror from the other pocket and poked it around the side of the tent to check on the would-be defender. He was watching the illusion. Tome grinned and reached for the belt on the flap.

He paused.

A small wire, almost thin enough to have escaped his notice, ran from the belt down to a bit of packed soil. A few months ago, he wouldn't have known what to make of such a thing. But a few adventures with Fel had taught him to notice an alarm box when he saw one. More importantly, he'd learned how to disarm one as well. He gently held tension on the wire and removed it from the strap, then affixed it to a hook on one of the support struts that he very much suspected was installed precisely so that the owner of the tent could do the same rather than dig up the alarm each time he returned. Now that it was undefended, he gently unfastened the strap and slipped inside.

A bit of the daylight filtered through the worn canvas of the tent. Not much, but enough to make it immediately clear he was in the right place. The only contents of the tent were a bedroll, a stool, an improvised writing desk, and an unlit lantern. The desk was covered with a carefully sorted sequence of messages, each folded and sealed with a blob of wax and a simple signet. The wax for the seal was on the desk as well, but the signet was most certainly on the man's person. It meant he couldn't read the messages. They weren't without their value, however.

Whoever wrote these messages must have spent some time in a monastery not unlike his own, or learned from someone who had. The level of organization was uncannily similar to what he'd been taught to do. Small, hand-lettered cards had been neatly aligned along the top of the desk. The messages were lined up below them. The words on the cards would have been gibberish to a layman, but they were practically tools of the trade for anyone who had to organize large collections of books. They were written in an old dead language with many useful terms for organization. Those on display translated roughly to: to be delivered immediately, to be held until last, and to be delivered after preordained event numbers one through six. Back home, the list of books that needed to be duplicated would be arranged under labels just like that. The "preordained event" cards were what baffled him about this particular arrangement. In the monastery, they were used to indicate that a given book should only be copied after each of the prior books in a multivolume set had, or perhaps a book should be held to be copied only when it had been confirmed that it was the most recent of a frequently updated volume. Conditional things like that made perfect sense in his old line of work. How or why a messenger would have a stack of messages only to be sent when certain criteria were met was a bit of a riddle.

He crouched and tugged at a small leather bag beside the desk. It contained a large sheaf of additional pages of the precise sort the messages were written on. Some very nice pens and ink were beside them. Were he a touch less respectable—and not concerned about giving away his presence—he would have taken them for himself. They would have made for some extremely passable spells. But the final contents of the bag were the most worrying. A small pouch of tobacco, and two strange metal pipes. Precisely the sort the Bolivans had formerly used and Fel had recently begun using.

Questions rushed through his mind. Were the Bolivans at it again? Or still at it? If this was the person delivering the messages that the inspector was waiting for, did that mean that the Bolivans somehow had gained influence over legitimate representatives of the nobles? Was the inspector truly legitimate?

He probably would have chased the puzzle in circles around his mind for another few minutes, if not for another phantom throb of pain. This one was much sharper and came with an emotional jolt of concern as well. It may have been intuition. It may simply have been nerves. But the pain and the fear combined to convince him he was no longer safe in the tent. He slipped outside and glanced about. No one in sight. A quick tug on the strap secured the door and a gentle manipulation reset the alarm. The illusion he'd cast should still be active and still visible along the road. If he was lucky, the man with the knife was still watching it like a hawk. Regardless, he moved low and slow along the ground, keeping the tent between him and the lookout for as long as possible.

The area had some trees and brush, but none were thick enough to provide shelter. Years of people camping here meant that most of the branches near enough to the ground to help provide cover had been stripped away and burned. There was, however, a fence, beyond which was a field of tall grass waiting to be harvested for feed or some such. He hopped the fence and vanished among the tall grass.

"I just need to get back into the city," he whispered to himself urgently. "I've learned something. I don't know what exactly, but enough to know something is shady about the inspector, his motives, or both. Just need to get inside, get clear."

Another jolt of pain struck him, and with it, the softest suggestion of a spoken word he couldn't recognize half-lost amid the rustling of the grass. Tall stalks around him began to rattle and shift. Something was running on either side of him, keeping pace.

He stumbled onto the gravel path between two fields. The creatures that had been racing along beside him emerged a step before he did. They shifted and came to a stop in front of him in a flurry of wings and fur. They could only be the same beasts that had faced Fel. He pulled an ice spell from his pocket and readied to cast it, but the monsters weren't attacking. They simply watched and waited. He turned to dash back from whence he came. One jumped in front of him, again blocking his way. He didn't know what they wanted, but one thing was certain: they wouldn't allow him to leave.

He took the ice spell in one hand and reached for a second. One casting wouldn't be wide enough to catch both of them. There was some doubt that he'd have time to cast a second after he'd cast the first, considering how swift these creatures were, but he was short on options. Fire, in a field like this, would probably get out of control.

Before he made up his mind to act, he heard another shifting from the tall grass and turned. The creature slipping free was human-shaped, but Tome knew it was no human. He was tall and thin, dressed in layers of stiff cloth dusted with grime from the road such that even in full view he seemed to fade against the grass. A bow was strapped to his back, and assorted other tools of the hunter's trade were strapped to his waist, arms, and legs. Like so many things, just a few months ago Tome wouldn't have known what to make of this man. But now he would know that sight anywhere. This was a ranger. An elven ranger. The only thing that didn't match the image that had earned a place in his nightmares was the face, which was hidden behind a strange metal mask. A mask that was familiar for an entirely different reason.

"How..." Tome uttered, trying to back away.

A lesser sphinx closed in to keep him from escaping.

For a tense moment, the elf gazed at him through the eye slits of the mask, still as a statue. Then he tugged a weighted rope from his belt and began to spin it to speed. Tome called for help. He tore the ice spell and tossed the page toward the elf. It surged away in a sizzling blue flash, and a cone of frost painted the ground and grass white, but both elf and sphinx were able to dodge the blast. Tome charged in the direction he'd cast the spell. They may have dodged it, but it had created an opening. He made it three long strides before he heard the weighted rope hiss through the air.

Tome felt it pull tight around his ankle, but he was able to stay on his feet. He heard first a flowery, complex sound that nevertheless had the edge of a profanity, then an entirely different word in a language he couldn't place. Sphinxes burst into motion. It was undoubtedly a command, a fact that he had the space of a few heartbeats to consider before one of them struck him in the back and sent him sprawling. The pain was dull. The claws hadn't torn his tunic. He rolled to his back and tore the second ice spell. This time the sphinx was too close to cleanly dodge. The spell caught its wing and one of its paws. It tumbled to the ground, yowling in pain. He tried to get to his feet, but the elf's boot struck his chest and forced him down again.

The ranger leaned low, placing all his weight on Tome's chest. He drew a knife. Tome could see the fierce flash of his eyes behind the mask. In the distance, the shout of voices and the hammering of footsteps. People from the camp coming to his aid. The ranger rumbled with another vicious comment and produced a leather hood. He pulled it over Tome's head.

All was dark.

CHAPTER 7

The sun was still lingering in the sky as Allie marched home. She couldn't remember the last time she'd left The Fox and Log before midnight without planning it weeks in advance. Neighbors she hadn't seen in months simply because they were asleep before she arrived waved and asked her where she'd been. She did her best to greet them cheerfully, but she just wanted to get home, eat something, find out what mischief her guests had gotten up to, and maybe catch up on the sleep she'd missed out on the night before.

She paced down the alleyway. No flames. No rubble from broken-down walls or shreds of wood from shattered doors. So far the only indication something was different was a slightly different odor, but with a tannery so close to the back of the alley, an errant wind could easily be to blame for that.

She opened her door. Another unexpected wave of aroma struck her. This one was downright appetizing. She stepped fully inside and didn't spot her guests until she shut the door. They must have huddled behind it at the sound of her approach.

"Allie," Fel said, his voice low and peppered with relief from the sudden, panicked dash for cover that her arrival had prompted. "I wasn't expecting you until after dark."

"I wasn't expecting my home to be in one piece," she said.

"Look! No blood," Teya said. "Not on floor, not on door!"

"I appreciate that." She turned to the fireplace. "Are you... cooking?"

"Yeah. I was hoping to start earlier, but there's not supposed to be anyone here, so I had to wait until your neighbors started cooking so it wouldn't stand out."

She paced over to the pot hanging over the fire. "Stew," she said.

"A personal specialty," he said.

"Usually that means 'the only thing I know how to make,'" she said.

"It just so happens I know how to make five things. But you only had the ingredients for stew."

"It is good!" Teya said. "There is meat. Also not meat. But meat is best."

"I haven't eaten all day," she admitted. "Nothing but a few handfuls of crickets."

"Have a seat," he said.

"I can serve myself. It's my home."

"Oh sit down. Seems like the one place you shouldn't be serving."

She prepared a few more comebacks, but she didn't have the energy to spend them on something quite this trivial. She took a seat at the table as he grabbed a bowl and ladle. He loaded up a steaming bowlful and set it before her, then prepared one for Teya, who clamored into the seat opposite. She had to stand on the chair to reach the bowl properly, but she didn't seem to mind. Nor did she bother waiting for a spoon.

Allie sampled the meal. "This is... this is actually not bad, Fel."

"Not bad. Is that better or worse than 'good enough'?"

"One step better," she said.

"Success, then. I usually only strive for good enough."

"Aren't you going to eat? You gave your seat up for a kobold."

"She eats fast, and I like the burnt bits on the bottom anyway. The longer I wait, the more there are."

Allie took a few more bites. Teya tipped up the bowl like she was dumping a bucket on an out-of-control fire. Fel stretched and failed to hide the wince of pain that accompanied the movement.

"Still hurting?" she said.

"Yeah. Tome's a paper mage. I think he writes those things to deal with paper cuts and the like. They never seem to finish off the kind of wounds I end up with."

"Teya brought two. Did you use the second one yet?"

"No."

"Shouldn't you?"

"I have a few more days of work ahead of me. The chances of me taking another beating are better than Tem's chances at a game of grum, so I'd better save one. Besides, the first one did enough of the job. Like I said. Good enough, it's all I strive for."

"You know, when I was a little girl, we had a dog. Nothing special. Just a mutt we found wandering the street and decided to take in. He was a puppy when we got him, and he must not have gotten much to eat when he was younger, because he was always very little. Every time we walked him, he would eye up the bigger dogs and growl like he wanted to bite their heads off. Eventually, he decided to make good on his threats and got into a proper fight. And did he ever take a beating. Limped around for weeks. And you know what happened next time he saw a big dog?"

"Allie, if you're telling me a story that ends with a dog dying, we're going to have a long talk about what sort of stories I want to hear."

"Relax. What happened when he saw a big dog next is he stuck right by me and didn't do anything stupid."

"Good."

"It strikes me, my dog had better sense than you. He knew better than to go and get his rear end beat twice in a row."

"If that dog had a job to do, it wouldn't have mattered if he was in for a beating or not. A job is a job. It has to get done. The family's in trouble."

"Sure. I'll grant you this one. You need to help your family. But this isn't the first time I've seen you hurting from something, and it hasn't always been about helping your family."

"It's not my fault the only ways for me to get rich come with a high chance of a beating."

"What do you need to get rich for? And don't tell me to impress Mariss. You and I both know it didn't take money to catch her eye."

"No, but it did take tales of adventure. Same difference. You don't get much money or much glory from selling your sweat. To do that, you've got to risk your neck."

"Weren't you just saying 'good enough is good enough'?"

"Good enough is good enough on the small stuff. The day-to-day. All the little steps it takes to stay alive. But for the big stuff, you have to aim higher."

"Do you have to, though? You have a family and a family business. You have friends. A home in a city where anything you want is yours, any time of day or night. You have money enough to keep your belly full and your tankard topped off."

"We both know I'm always running out of money."

"You're always running out of money because you're always gambling. And you're always gambling because you want more money. You'd be better off if you stopped before you started."

"You sound like my mother."

"You mother must sound pretty smart then. So let's hear it. What's your real reason?"

"Gotta keep those adventures coming to keep you ladies entertained with new stories, right?" he said.

"Remember last month? Mariss stopped by The Fox and Log, and you had her laughing for an hour about that time you did a whole day's silver deliveries with your shoes on the wrong feet and your pants on backward because you hadn't sobered up from the night before."

"I still owe Epiphany a prank or something for not letting me know," he grumbled.

"The point is, there was no gold or glory in that story. It's not the story, it's the man telling it."

"All right. Maybe I'm not doing it for Mariss then. Maybe I'm doing it for me."

"Fine, then what are you after?"

"I don't know."

"Kind of hard to get where you're headed if you don't know where it is."

"What does it matter?"

"What does it matter? You came into my home bleeding last night. You've been doing things that put you up against dragons and griffins of all different flavors. You're in league with criminals and doing battle against other criminals. This isn't a recipe for a long life."

"Maybe not. But it's a recipe for a significant one. Maybe an important one."

"Significant to who? Important to who? You're already important to your friends and your family. You're already significant at The Fox and Log."

"Not a very high bar."

"The Fox and Log is the best bar in town," she said with a waggle of her head.

He snorted. "Well done."

"My point is, when will it be enough for you? Because you are the one moving that finish line across more and more treacherous ground."

"I said I don't know." He scraped the bottom of the pot and started loading up his bowl.

"Well start thinking about it. You are the one who gets to decide how important is important enough, so get to it."

"Why do you care so much?"

"Because Beffshire is a better place with you in it. You want to be important? You're important to me. You think I would have let anyone else stay in my home while they were doing madness like this? Or for any other reason, while we're at it? Do you think I would have hopped on a cart and gone north to try to get word to you about the legion of baddies looking to ambush you? And Mariss came along."

She pointed at Teya, who was industriously swabbing the bowl clean with her tongue. "You've made friends with kobolds and unicorns and bundles of animated brass. I don't know who you want to be, and neither do you, but I think you're seriously underestimating who you already are."

Fel paced to the cupboard. "You have one spoon," he said.

"I don't entertain very often," she said. "You're lucky I have two chairs. The only reason I have four bowls is because Oovay ordered too many for the tavern, so we all took some home to keep him from getting in trouble. Don't change the subject."

He sipped at the bowl. "I don't have any answers for you. I'm not out here making plans. I'm doing what I think I should, and what I think I need to do, when I think I need to do it. And this madness that's going on now? This all started way back. I have to ride it out. It's all reactions. You should know me well enough to know how little thinking I do."

"That much we can agree on," she said.

A few seconds of silent eating passed.

"I say things?" Teya said.

"Only if they don't make things worse," Fel said.

"Don't be mad," Teya said to Allie. "Not at Fel."

"I'm not mad at Fel," Allie said.

"Your voice? A mad voice. Also, eyes like dragon," Teya said. "This one? Knows dragon eyes." The kobold pointed to Allie's face. "Eyes like dragon," she repeated.

Allie straightened up a bit, a faint grin on her face. There was something oddly rewarding about being told by a lifelong servant of a dragon that you have something in common with one. "I'm spirited," she said.

"Fel? Does what he must. We all do. Big things. Important times. We all have parts. This one. You. Him. Parch. All important. Dangerous? Yes. But we do. Because destiny."

"Not this again," Fel said.

"I'm a part of this?" Allie said.

Teya nodded.

"And you know this how?"

"Little kobold. Far from home. First to leave. Maybe ever? And what happens? Finds friends. Finds job to do. How? Destiny. Only destiny. And if destiny? All around me? Also destiny. Me, you, Parch, Fel. All destiny."

Allie considered her words. "She makes a decent argument, Fel."

"There, see? Don't yell at me. I'm doing destiny things."

He took a big sip. She ate a bit more.

"You said you can make five things?"

"Yes."

"Write down some ingredients. If we're going to have our hands full of destiny, we may as well eat hearty, and I'm keen on seeing what else you can make."

"Destiny? Better on full stomach," Teya agreed.

Martin crossed his arms and looked over the workshop. This time last year, he would have been thrilled to have the place as well equipped and well supplied as it was now. But he'd grown accustomed to the embarrassment of wealth they'd accumulated in terms of both reference material and contraptions in every state of repair. Now the only remnant of the infusion of information and equipment was the new bust, the item he'd arranged to part with last. His expression must have done a poor job of disguising his dismay.

"Is something wrong, Martin?" Wick asked.

He shook his head slowly. "Look at this place. It looks like I've lost ground. My whole life has been about keeping pace or advancing. Always advancing. But now I have to tie my hands until someone can come through and satisfy themselves that I haven't crossed lines they'd prefer I not cross."

"It cannot be helped," Wick said.

"I'm not certain that's so. It most certainly could be helped if people would just open their eyes and use their heads. But that is rather a lot to ask, I suppose. Any updates for me?"

"Fel is doing some final preparations. He will be arriving shortly after nightfall. Teya and Parch will join him. Phase two can begin then. Thaddeus has sold half of his stock. There should be room enough to finish clearing away most of the incriminating contraptions even before phase two."

"What of Tome?"

"Tome was pursuing his own investigation of the inspector. He did not bring something lit from my flame, and he has not returned."

"Either good news because he's been making so much progress that he's been too busy to check in, or bad news."

"I do not know enough to speculate."

"Do we know where he is?"

"When last he shared his intentions, he was planning to find the couriers sending the inspector his instructions."

"And he's given no updates."

"Not unless they were delivered to Epiphany while she was running errands."

"We should find some way to check on him."

"I believe the family's resources are stretched thin at the moment, Martin."

"He's a friend, a guest, and an ally. We should look after him as we would our own. Once the bust is packed away, I believe I'll have little left to do. I shall look into it personally. But first, since it will be days until I work with it again, a final session."

He pulled the Bygone Dagger from the back of the bust. The mask activated. Now fully completed, the arms shifted slightly before coming to rest once more.

"Ah. I observe that I now have 'fingers' on both of my 'hands.' Is this correct?" the Student said.

"It is. Would you do me the favor of testing the second hand in the same way that you tested the first?" Martin said.

"Of course."

The left hand became rigid, then clicked through a sequence of positions, testing each joint along the way.

"May I request a specific lesson?" the Student said.

"Or course. If I am able to oblige it, I will," Martin said, eyes fixed on the freshly built hand as it ran through its test.

"What is the reason for the reunion?"

"Please be more specific. What reunion are you speaking of?" Martin said.

"The reunion of the masks."

Martin looked up. "The reunion of the masks?"

"Yes! For the first time since my earlier lessons in the Bygone Era, it would appear that all four masks are awake."

"The Teacher, the Student, the Diplomat, and the Warrior are all awake right now?"

"Yes. It seems unlikely that such a thing would occur if a reunion of the masks was not intended."

"Where? You can tell their locations, correct? Where are they presently?"

"Ah! An excellent point of knowledge to test. The Student, clearly, is speaking to you. The Diplomat's location is unchanged, quite far north of here. The Teacher is somewhat farther north and west of the Diplomat. And the Warrior is a short distance to the west."

"How short?"

"It is moving, but less than an hour of travel by foot, I would estimate."

"From the Diplomat?"

"No. I am sorry. I was not clear. The Warrior is a short distance from my present location."

"And it is awake?"

"In a fashion. Similar to the Diplomat, its activity is stifled. Quite significantly, in fact. But certainly awake."

Martin calmly pulled open one of the tool drawers and revealed his old vault-diving gear. He selected a compass and arranged it on the freshly cleared workbench, then laid out a map. "How confident are you in your ability to accurately indicate the direction with your arm?"

"Oh. I believe I can do so quite accurately."

"Please point in the direction of the mask," he said.

The bust extended its left arm. Martin quickly stretched a string across the map, starting at their shop and extending it in the indicated direction. He noted any major locations along the way.

"Thank you, Student. I am afraid that will be all for today," he said.

"There still remains the question of the reason for the reunion of the masks," the Student said.

"Yes… I'll have to investigate that, as I was not made aware such a thing would occur."

"Fresh research! A new lesson! Excellent. This was a brief but interesting session," the Student said. "I look forward to the next one all the more."

He inserted the dagger to put the mask back to sleep.

"Wick, I am going to give you a list of locations within the city. I don't know if we should avoid them or investigate them, but there is the possibility that the Warrior mask is located within. More likely, it is somewhere outside the city, roughly in the direction of Skinflint Camp. And I would be very surprised if its presence was not related to Tome's conspicuous absence. Something must be done."

Tome struggled at his bonds. He didn't know how long he'd been tied and hooded. It felt like days, but he knew it couldn't have been more than a few hours. Being restrained did terrible things to the mind. Panic came easily, and with it, struggling. But Tome was, to his great dismay, becoming something of an expert at being in captivity. He knew nothing good came from panic, and struggling would only tire him out and possibly injure him. So he'd set his mind to anything that could keep it occupied without breaking to pieces.

He'd first focused on how far he was being carried, counting each footstep the hunter took with him stretched across his shoulders. Nearly two thousand, and likely many more. That should have taken him quite far away, but from the way he was jostled, he knew that the elf had been changing direction frequently. He must have been spending his time and energy evading the people who had answered Tome's call for help. It would have taken a much greater level of expertise in being kidnapped to know precisely where he'd been carried while the elf fled, and Tome greatly hoped he'd never reach that level of expertise, but he was probably still quite close to the city.

When he'd lost his pursuers, the elf had thrown Tome down and rummaged through his pockets to disarm him. In the unknown, punishingly slow march of time since then, Tome had split his focus between observing whatever he could and engaging in what he'd convinced himself was a measured, strategic form of struggling. Certainly not panic. He was better than that. Regardless of his strategy, he'd learned very little. Quick arm and leg restraints pulled tight before he was carried away had been supplemented by much more secure loops of rope. They seemed to be positioned in such a way as to keep any knots far from his fingers. He'd been dumped at the foot of a tree; he could hear the leaves rustling. And there was an itch on his ankle that would drive him to madness if he didn't scratch it soon.

The hood was roughly pulled from his head. He blinked until his eyes adjusted to the light of the setting sun. A mind tuned to pick up any fragment of information was suddenly flooded. The sun was low; it was late afternoon. He'd been held for several hours. The sun was behind him. He was facing east. He was in a relatively thick stand of fruit trees, laid out in far too regular a grid to be natural. He was in an orchard. That would have been more than enough to tell him his precise location if he'd had the foresight to take note of where around the city fruit orchards could be found. He hadn't, so the information would only be of any value after he escaped. The remnants of a campfire and some assorted other clues suggested this was something of a stronghold for the elf, his base of operations. Most bizarre among them was a heap of stolen lamps and lanterns. Some still burning, others shattered and twisted.

Now that he looked upon the elf with something less than terror seizing his mind, Tome noticed a few more things about his captor. He was crouched, a position that seemed to emphasize the long, spindly nature of his legs. Though he supposed the layer of dust on his clothes was a cunning measure, intended to grant an impressive amount of stealth, an overall griminess of cloth and skin suggested he had been on the road for ages, without the time or opportunity to properly care for himself. His clothes seemed loose. His neck, one of the only bits of his body clearly visible, was narrow and drawn. He looked malnourished.

The elf sifted through the stack of spells he'd confiscated, glaring through the narrow eye slits in his mask. The mask was ancient and metallic. Scattered, fresh scrapes and gashes gleamed brassy and bright beneath a milky patina. The elf set the stack of spells down atop a small stack of firewood and pinned them in place with an extra piece of wood. He huffed a breath and reached for the end of a piece of rope. A slipknot had been tied in one end. The other was anchored around the trunk of the tree. Tome's mind briefly lit up with fearful theories about what the rope would be used for, but he fell short of the actual use. The elf pulled it tight around his own left wrist. He removed his hat and, after a brief pause, slipped the mask free.

It should have been a surprise to find that he recognized the elf, but honestly, the sheer volume of impossible acts that had shaped his life since he'd met Fel made surprise a dull, subdued thing these days. The grimy, exhausted face staring down at him was that of Mevrelle, the very elf who had been his escort while he was in their village. Thick white scars along the side of his face and his neck marked where Teya had savaged him during their last meeting. His eyes had a fury smoldering in them, but one that was tempered by something far deeper and more fundamental. He was desperate, and frightened as well.

"You..." Mevrelle rumbled. "The High shine upon me, leading me to you."

"Mevrelle," Tome said. "Strange to hear you speak my language. A new talent you've picked up? Or was your monolingual nature just another way of tormenting me before I escaped your clutches."

"Silence!" he spat. "It curdles my blood to hear your words leaving my mouth. But this is your world, not mine. I have no choice. There is not a man or woman among you fools who could understand me. And I have demands."

"I'm not in much of a position to obey your demands. Perhaps if you untied me."

The elf stood, looming over Tome, and thumped his boot on the human's chest. "I said be silent. You will speak when I require you to speak. Do you understand?"

Tome wheezed in what he liked to imagine was a defiant way.

"I want to kill you..." Mevrelle rumbled. "Nothing would give me greater joy, and you deserve nothing less. But I have a mission. And you may have a place in it."

"I strive to be useful," Tome croaked.

Mevrelle kept his furious gaze locked on Tome, but he shifted aside, slowly pulling out the slack in the rope attaching him to the tree. From his expression, he barely seemed aware of it. He squinted his eyes.

"You were the keeper of the sentry flame. I need it."

"Evidently you don't. Last I met you, you couldn't even focus your eyes on the wall. Now you've reached my home. How did you manage that? And just where did you acquire that mask?"

"I ask the questions and I make the demands!" Mevrelle pointed to the mound of lanterns. "Where is the sentry flame?"

"Ah. So that is your goal. I should have guessed. There are two. They get around quite a bit. I'm not typically in possession of either."

"Is it with the other mask?"

"So you know about the other mask, do you? You seem to know a great deal already," Tome said.

"The plan was always to use the flame. But you took it from us. And that kobold wretch took the fruits of our labors. But we learned. We always learn. It is our way. The sentry flame gave us insight. We learned what the twisted whims of the contraptioneers could achieve. The nature of the connection that contraptions can have, if not their function. And your kind littered our world with your refuse before the world was split."

He held up the mask. "This item, we found, had power." His eyes darted to the south. He shut them and shook himself, then focused on Tome again. "Power and a connection. But the power was different. Tenacious. It couldn't be separated, siphoned to our own purposes as with the earring that your kobold ally stole. The best we could manage was to access it. Link it to one of us. That will not do. A single mask and a single operative? It will not serve our purposes. We need more. We need the means to manufacture keys to the prison. The sentry flames. Something that can't... that won't..."

The thought was lost as he shuddered and clenched his teeth. "The blasted voices, human. The blasted will. Intolerable. Plans of its own..." he muttered.

Mevrelle took a full step to the south, testing the limits of the rope about his wrist. It pulled taut and yanked his arm awkwardly back. He winced in pain and turned toward it. There was a flicker of confusion and irritation in his face.

"I need to... I'm torn between two calls... two draws." He shakily hung the mask on his belt and drew a blade from where he'd fashioned it.

"I've come a long way... Too far to find my way back without... clarity. But there is no clarity..."

Tome shuddered at the sound of his voice. The anger was peeling away, desperation and fear more firmly gripping him. He flexed his arm, tightening the knot about his wrist, and shakily held the knife toward it.

"Just want to... return... But so far..."

His voice became low. He slipped back into his own language, uttering the same phrase over and over. The knife trembled in his hand.

Mevrelle had been a terrifying foe before, but the terror came from his competence and focus. Seeing him this way, his mind seemingly stretched to the limit, brought a whole new form of dread. It was the difference between a trained tiger and a wild one. Either could kill Tome in an instant, but one had the semblance of control. Seeing something he knew to be as dangerous as Mevrelle teetering on the brink made the whole situation far more chaotic.

Tome glanced about. If he was briefly not his captor's focus, he would make the most of it. Two roughly feline figures lurked in the shadows of nearby trees. They were standing stone still, eyes gleaming in the fading sun. They didn't look like they were poised to strike. They looked like they were simply waiting. Their attacks had been preceded by a command. Perhaps, if Tome could do something quickly enough to prevent a command from being barked, they wouldn't be a factor.

He glanced to the stack of firewood, and his spells atop it. An inventory of what he'd brought along flicked through his mind. This was going to be unpleasant. But unpleasant was better than lethal.

Mevrelle seemed to be winning the battle against whatever was searing his mind. He'd lowered the knife, and a dash of rationality and reason was returning to his expression. Tome pulled his bound ankles back and thrust them against the pile of firewood. The top few pieces, and the entire stack of spells, tumbled toward the smoldering fire. A few of them fluttered uselessly to the ground. Three of them reached the flame. And by the greatest of good fortune, two of them flared to flame from the correct direction. A burst of blue light flared up from the fire, hissing it to ash and splashing the tree with frost. At the same moment, a duplicate of Tome appeared on the ground, wriggling and thrashing just as he was.

The elf had acted quickly, dodging aside to avoid the flash of icy magic. But bound to a tree as he was, what would have been a graceful evasion turned instead to an awkward swing aside. He tumbled to the ground. His blade clattered beside him. Tome managed to roll to his knees and throw himself toward the knife. He glanced up. Mevrelle was already on his feet, but his free hand was pressed to his temple. Whatever had been tugging at his mind had renewed its grip. He desperately patted his thigh. At first Tome thought he was seeking the knife, but he and Mevrelle realized at the same time that the mask was gone.

Mevrelle looked desperately about and soon fixed his eyes on something among the thin underbrush. He pulled as hard as he could against the rope and strained to reach the mask.

Tome clutched the knife in his bound hands and raised his legs. After two painful misses that nearly slashed his ankle, he was able to hack enough of a notch out of the rope to snap it and separate his legs. He stumbled to his feet. There was value in claiming the mask, but the thing clearly was having some sort of terrible effect on the elf's mind. Instead he kicked the mask out of Mevrelle's reach and dashed toward what he imagined must be the edge of the orchard.

Behind him, he heard a word of the unknown language shouted. The distant flap of wings and rustle of branches followed. When he wasn't instantly slashed with claws, he knew the order hadn't been an attack. He didn't know what they were doing, but he wasn't so foolish as to imagine that they would ignore him for long.

Sprinting with his hands bound in front of him was more difficult than he would have imagined, but terror had a way of taking up the slack, driving him forward despite the aching stiffness of having spent hours bound. The sound of flapping wings approached him again. Ahead, he saw a fence. He was near to the edge of the orchard, and he could see the road just beyond it. Familiarity sparked and fizzled in his mind. He'd seen this orchard from the other side, traveling around Beffshire. He was close, maybe half a mile from the city's walls. But as the wings fluttered closer, it may as well have been a thousand. He'd be lucky to reach the fence before they reached him. There was no chance he'd make it any farther.

Behind him, hammering footsteps joined the flapping wings. But new figures emerged ahead. Just beyond the fence. Two members of the City Watch, crossbows at the ready. Tome redoubled his efforts. A crossbow bolt hissed past his head, close enough to tousle his hair. If he hadn't been in quite such a blind panic, he would have entertained the possibility that they were shooting at him. Instead he simply surged forward. Another bolt fired, this one in no danger of striking him. The flapping wings retreated. He tried to hop the fence, bumped his bound hands with his knees, and went tumbling over it instead. Strong hands grabbed him by the shoulders and hauled him to his feet. It was Captain Boltt.

"What in muck were those things?" he barked.

"Sphinxes? Lesser sphinxes? I don't know. Where is the elf?" Tome said, whipping around to look at the orchard.

"... Elf?" said the captain.

Tome shook his head. "Er. A man. A masked man. Sort of a green metallic mask. He's the one who captured me. Tied me up."

The captain swept his vision across his surroundings. "Nowhere in sight. Come on. Back inside the city walls. Let's get those hands untied."

Tome rubbed his wrists when his hands were freed. "I thought you fellows didn't leave the city walls," he said.

"We don't. But Martin Masker came to us and insisted there was something going on out here that was likely to come in here if we didn't do something. Given how much trouble that man's boy gets into and brings this way, I thought it was better to nip this one in the bud."

"I owe him one."

"You owe me one," the captain said. "And I'll redeem it by telling you to keep your head down and not do anything to coax those things inside the city."

"I don't know that we'll be able to stop them if they decide to come over the walls."

"That's fine. They breach the walls, we'll pump them full of bolts. But I don't want you doing anything to cause that."

Tome rubbed his wrists again and glanced in the direction of the orchard. "I shall do everything in my power to avoid it."

The sun had solidly set. Fel had almost lost track of time. Once the little inquisition was over and they'd finished their meals, he was treated to something he hadn't experienced for more than a few minutes at a time in all his life. Allie Waverly, outside of work. Fel had fancied himself at least an equal for her wit and her capacity to banter. He was wrong. Until now, he'd only ever had to keep up with her for a few comments at a time before she had to wander off and tend bar for a bit. Now she was there with him, nonstop. It had turned from a sprint into a distance run. And his sides were already aching. Teya was cackling on the floor, kicking her legs. Fel was practically crying.

"You have got to be joking," Fel said.

She put her hand to her heart. "May I be struck down if I lie. Seven times. The man knocked his hat off on the doorway, stooped, picked it up, and knocked it off again seven times. And he was on his way into The Fox and Log. He was stone-cold sober. The dimmest man I've ever known."

He wiped a tear from his eye. "What did he even need a hat for? He clearly didn't have a brain to keep warm."

"He probably needed it to keep the rain off his head. Can you imagine the racket if it was raining on something that empty. Like a drum in a hailstorm."

"You tell good stories," Teya said, climbing to her feet. "Very very! This place? Good fun."

"You should visit The Fox and Log sometime. That's where all of these happen."

"If we bring Teya down there, she'll be the one I'm telling stories about for a month, no doubt," Allie said.

He held his belly and groaned. "Oh, By the High, I thought I'd heard them all."

"You haven't heard half of them." She paused. "Move your hand."

He took his hand away. A sprinkle of blood showed through his shirt.

"It's nothing," he said. "One of the wounds opened up. It's what you get for being so side-splitting."

"It's not nothing. Sit down, shirt off. Let's get a fresh bandage on that."

"I have a lot to do tonight, Allie."

"And it'll go a lot easier if you aren't bleeding all over yourself."

He grumbled and unfastened the buttons. She grabbed his bandages and another rag.

"I don't know why you don't just use the other healing spell."

"We've been through this. What happens if I get in a fight again today?"

"Then you get more from Tome."

"If I ask Tome for another healing spell, first he'll gloat about how I needed the first ones, then he'll mutter about how much work it is to write a proper healing spell."

"And is that worse than having an open slash on your side?"

"Yes. By a mile."

She shook her head. "Child." She threw him the rag. "And here's another question. Parch is a wild animal, Teya is... sort of halfway, and you're a human being. Why is it you smell the worst of the bunch?"

"Don't be mean," Teya said. "Fel? Very good smell. Strong. Good at smelling."

"You're not helping, Teya," Fel said.

There was a knock at the door. They all froze. Teya was the first to react. She hefted Parch onto her shoulders and tottered into the corner, where they would be hidden by the open door. Fel grabbed his shirt and joined them. Allie waved at them and pointed.

My room! she mouthed silently.

He hurried through the door, helped Teya pull Parch through, and shut it. He heard Allie approach the door.

"Who's there?" Allie said.

"It's me. Mariss," came the reply.

"Mariss? I wasn't' expecting you," Allie said.

"I'm sorry to come along unannounced, but you made me promise if I had any of the crackle-top pies left over, I'd bring you some. I managed to sneak two extras. I stopped by the tavern and they said you'd already come home."

"Pies?" Teya said, almost silently.

Fel shushed her.

"I'm in the middle of something at the moment."

"Oh, I don't want to intrude. I'll just hand you the pies and be on my way."

The short silence that followed said quite a bit. Fel could practically imagine the look Allie was giving. One of those calculating looks into the middle distance as she realized Mariss would likely leave with far more questions if she didn't hand over the pies than if she did. He heard the door open.

"There you go," Mariss said. "It's good that you're home already. They're still warm. You can have them to finish your supper. It smells lovely by the way. What did you cook?"

"I got the recipe for the Masker family stew a while back and decided to try it."

"How did it come out?"

"Fine. It's a bit hard to get wrong. Very easy recipe."

"Easy recipes are some of the hardest to come up with. I'm not one for stews, but if you'd be willing to share it..."

"I'll have to ask the Maskers. They might consider it one of those ancient family secrets."

"Of course. We'll discuss it later."

"I'm sorry to send you on your way so quickly, but—"

"Right, no, I won't waste your time. Sorry again to intrude. I know you don't much like it when people come around unannounced, and, forgive me, I'm not overly comfortable in your neighborhood but... are those Fel's boots?"

Allie didn't even pause. "When I got the recipe, I'd asked if they had any spare boots. I'm planning on doing some work on the fireplace. The grating slipped out of the way, and I don't want to ruin my good shoes when I fix it."

Fel raised his eyebrows. That was easily the fastest and most believable lie he'd ever heard told. It made him wonder how many of those he'd heard from her and not noticed.

"They're such kind people. I do hope Fel gets home soon."

"So do I. The tavern isn't the same without—"

Fel heard a moment of struggle a fraction of a second after it was too late to do anything about it. Parch was impressively well behaved, provided you weren't asking him to stop doing something he was dead set on doing. There were those who would claim this was, in fact, not a sign of impressive behavior, and until this precise moment, Fel would have argued with them. But right now, Parch was smelling apples and hearing the voice of a woman who bribed him with apple cores almost daily. Those two things combined to convince him it was worth wriggling free of Teya's shoulders, popping the poorly secured door open, and trotting out into the open.

For the longest moment of Fel's life, he stood in full view. Shirtless. In the doorway of Allie's bedroom. In front of the woman he'd been trying to woo for over a year.

"Fel?" Mariss said.

It wasn't clear from her tone if she was dismayed or simply confused.

"I can explain," Fel said.

Allie turned slowly to him, a disappointed look on her face. "When has saying that ever helped anything?" she muttered.

"You two are together?" Mariss said.

"She's just—"

"That's wonderful!" Mariss said, stepping inside. "It's such a relief."

"A relief..." Fel said steadily.

"All this time I wasn't sure if you were flirting with me or if you were just a generally charming fellow. And I'd be lying if I said I wasn't a bit flattered and maybe even a bit interested. Especially with all the adventures you go on. It seemed like it would really make life more exciting. But I got a taste of that life when I helped Allie go and warn you up north, and, frankly, a little bit goes a long way. I love the travel, and I love hearing about all the adventure, but there's a difference between having an exciting life and constantly worrying about being killed. A little excitement a few times a year? I could handle that, but it's daily with you."

"Every three weeks, more like," he said flatly.

She giggled. "Still too much for me. I'd been worried what would happen if you ever outright asked me to be yours. I couldn't say yes, but I wouldn't want to hurt you by saying no. But knowing you two are together is such a load off my mind. And you're perfect for each other. Allie is so smart and capable. I'd trust her to navigate things worlds more dangerous than I could. She can handle anything you bring her way and then some. Oh, I can't wait to hear what sort of things you do together." She paused, eyes glancing first at Parch, then at Fel's wound. "Out and about I mean. What you do in private is entirely your business. Anyway, I should be going."

Mariss hurried to the door.

"Er, Mariss?" Allie said after her.

"Yes?" she said sweetly.

"We're in the middle of one of those adventures, so don't tell anyone Fel is here. And certainly don't tell anyone that we're together."

"Oh, exciting!" Mariss said with a little clap. "Mum's the word! But I can't wait to hear all about it when you're through!"

Allie shut the door and turned to Fel. His face was blank.

"Fel, that was—" Allie began.

Fel held up his hand. "I have to go hammer a hole through the wall of my house. Which is nice. Because that is exactly what I want to do right now," he said.

Teya trotted out and reached up to pat him on the back. "Wanted to laugh. Very very. Did not. Because you are friend," she said solemnly.

"I appreciate that," Fel said, wrapping a bandage in place.

"But very funny," Teya said.

"That'll do, Teya," Fel said.

"Because—" Teya began.

"Let's just go!"

Chapter 8

Four hours of hard labor had passed, and Fel's mind still sizzled with the events of the day. Every contraption that could be wedged into the storage floors of Reynard's shop had been. Even with nearly all the shoes the old man had stockpiled having been sold by Thaddeus, there was still more than enough incriminating inventory in the Maskers' home to bring heavy consequences. But managing inventory was one of the many tasks the Masker women excelled at. They'd anticipated this, and more to the point, Reynard's lower floors were entirely too close to the Maskers' shop for them to be able to trust that they wouldn't be swept up in the investigation one way or another. But Reynard's shop wasn't the only one with lower floors aligned with the Maskers'. The next step was to punch a hole in the opposite wall of Reynard's place. And the step after that? It could wait until this step was through.

"The hole you've pounded out is already twice as deep as the wall to your home," Tome said.

"I noticed, Tome," Fel huffed.

Tome's travails that afternoon were significantly more harrowing than Fel's. He didn't appear visibly shaken, but his mere presence in the room while Fel worked betrayed his rattled state of mind. Tome didn't want to be alone right now. Thus, he had taken the task of keeping Oiler busy so that the hammered holes would remain open.

"Are we certain it is actually leading somewhere?" Tome asked.

"I'm a little busy," Fel snapped, looking over his shoulder.

"You talk! Rest! My turn!" Teya proclaimed, hefting her mattock.

Fel nodded and swabbed some sweat from his brow. The seemingly tireless kobold dashed in and started chipping away. Any other time, Fel would have been more than willing to stare vacantly until he was called upon to continue working, but every moment he wasn't fully occupied, the scene with Mariss replayed in his head. Desperate times called for desperate measures. He'd have to talk to Tome.

"Up there is the carpenter's place. It's newer. Built on the wreck of an older shop. Nothing but a basement, a floor and a half up from here. But lowest level of the shop that used to be was even deeper than ours. All the way to the water table. It was like a basement-size well. He was a distiller or something. I don't know, it was before I was born. But when they replaced the old shop with the new shop, they placed some slabs over the collapsed floors below, so once we punch through, it'll be a straight drop down to a pile of rubble and the water."

"How does that help you, precisely? Are you just going to heap the stuff down there?"

"As a last resort, maybe, but Dad would sooner go to prison than send heaps of books and repaired contraptions into that muck. Do you remember what's on the far side of the carpenter's shop?"

"An alley that stinks of harpy droppings," Tome said.

"And tucked in the back is the old neighborhood well. Great big Bygone Era relic that they sort of built this whole district up around," Fel said. "Built-in winch, good cover, and a straight shot right up to the surface."

Tome nodded. "Impressive... but there's still the matter of how to move the goods in a way that won't attract the attentions of the inspector and his cronies, yes?"

"I just said, the carpenter doesn't have a deep basement. Every shop along this street uses their basement for inventory. That means he doesn't have inventory. He's got constant shipments heading to and from. Five, six a day, some days. And they do their loading and unloading around the corner, outside the eyeshot of the inspector's favorite roost."

"But that just moves the problem down to—"

"It moves the problem far enough, all right?" Fel said.

Tome scrambled a puzzle box and handed it to Oiler. "I don't know what you're so surly about. I'm the one who nearly died today."

"We've all got our own problems," Fel said.

"I think mine might outweigh yours."

"An elf." Fel nodded, taking a swig of water. "Seems like the Greater Lands Wall isn't what it used to be. All sorts of riffraff are sneaking out."

"He had the Warrior mask. But he wasn't in his right mind. The mask was the means through which he was able to escape the influence of the wall, but it's not perfect. He had to tie himself to a tree to avoid wandering off when the mask was removed. And he was terribly distracted. Ranting about... wills and voices."

"Considering the trouble the masks seem to cause, I don't like having one labeled 'Warrior' dangling off someone who already hates my family and you for separate reasons."

"On that point, we are in profound agreement. Oh! And there is the matter of the sphinxes."

"We're sure that's what they are?" Fel said.

Tome fetched a stack of pages from within his tunic. "No doubt in my mind. I found a section in a bestiary among my reference books. 'The lesser sphinx will be known by its simian countenance.'"

"What's that?" Fel said.

"Monkey face," Teya said, walking over to him and setting down the pick.

"Who are you calling 'monkey face'?" Fel said gruffly. He handed down a canteen, hefted his hammer back to his shoulder, and returned to the wall.

"No, she's correct. That's what 'simian countenance' means." Tome looked at Teya appreciatively. "Impressive vocabulary."

"I know very very words," Teya said. "Just not say good."

Tome cleared his throat. "It continues. 'Known to exist in small numbers along the southern edge of the Greater Lands Wall, making its home in the hottest of deserts. These creatures are thought to have the greatest intelligence of all the Lesser Mystics. Some theorize they even rival humans in their capacity for thought and understanding. The creatures have an innate knowledge of a language lost to humanity.'"

Fel paused in his blows. "If it's lost to humanity, how do they know the critters know it?"

"People who study things regarding the Greater Lands and the Bygone Era are intellectual scavengers. They find scraps of knowledge left by people who knew far more but didn't record it all. Now as I was saying. 'If one can determine both the language and the riddle, the greatest asset of the species becomes available. They obey any who speak their ingrained commands.' To put it bluntly, the lesser sphinx comes pretrained. Born with a set of commands that it must obey. There is a whole chapter in the book filled with theories about how and why it is so. He believes—"

"Will that information help us not get killed when they attack us next?" Fel asked, pausing again to wipe some dust from his face.

"Likely not."

"Then skip it."

"Wah-ro-kar-kar-rah," Teya said, slowly and deliberately.

Tome furrowed his brow. "Pardon?"

Teya rubbed her jaw like even attempting the word had nearly caused it to cramp. "The words. For sphinx," she said.

"You know the language?" he said.

"Hear it, not say it. Bad for mouth shape. Worse than your words," she said.

"Could you translate?"

"... Not very very. Some, maybe."

"It's better than nothing. I'll have to search through the books to see what the nature of the commands might be. They used the word 'riddle.'

I don't know if that means it is simply something that one must puzzle out, or if it is a legitimate riddle the likes of which their greater brethren are known for."

"You're going to try to solve a riddle through Teya's translation?" Fel said, tightening his grip on the handle of the hammer and widening his stance.

"I only need one word. A single command to shout out to confuse the creatures. It would cripple his control of them. Then we'd have nothing but a demented elven ranger to worry about."

"And Warrior mask," Teya said.

"And a corrupt inspector," Fel said.

Tome scrambled the puzzle box again. "I do wish the world would focus on sending a single challenge at us at a time."

"What doesn't kill us makes us stronger," Fel said. He heaved the hammer down, shattering the last bit of mortar and sending the first of the damaged slabs sliding through to splash down below. "Ha ha!"

"Ya-haa!" Teya said.

"See? All these people trying to kill me and this is how strong I got! Oiler! Do me a favor and fetch that big block. We're going to have to seal this hole up eventually."

Oiler redoubled its efforts to solve the puzzle box. The final tile clicked into place, and the contraption jangled forward to inspect the damage.

"Tome, tell Mom and Dad we're through. Then get someone back down here to keep Oiler on track. Teya, let's get some food in us. One more wall to go..."

Epiphany marched out the door of the shop. As usual, one of the assayers who had been unwittingly pulled into the inspector's little crusade had the bad fortune to be on the overnight shift. He gave the Masker daughter a halfhearted glance, turning back to whatever sulky thoughts were occupying him when he saw that she wasn't carrying any contraband beyond an old muffin. She scanned the rooftops once she was no longer under scrutiny and spotted the forms of the lesser-harpy honor guard huddled together and sleeping on the roof of Reynard's shop.

As much as she'd resented Fel's coddling and spoiling of the little feathered rascals, the utter torture they'd been putting Cartwright through had sweetened her opinion of them considerably. She tossed the muffin onto the roof, a treat for the morning, then hurried along. She had an appointment with a man who didn't like to be kept waiting.

In the back of her mind, she was fully aware that a murderous threat was stalking beyond the walls of the city. Beyond making sure she kept her fingers threaded through the brass knuckles in her pocket, she couldn't bring herself to be concerned. There was a big job to do, and a threat that was at once less overtly dangerous and far more concrete that she was willingly exposing herself to.

After a few minutes, she was marching through the streets of the higher-end part of the city, on her way to the Verfessa household. If Inspector Cartwright's complete disregard for the killer just beyond the city walls—the thing that ostensibly was his reason for coming to the city—wasn't a sure enough sign that he cared only for his personal agenda, the fact that he didn't think to have someone watching Verfessa would have hammered it home. The inspector was either too ignorant of the ways of Beffshire or too foolish to realize that the need to move what amounted to a small warehouse of goods surreptitiously more or less required the help of Verfessa, a man whose entire fortune had been made surreptitiously. And, she was sorry to say, a man with whom the Maskers' fortunes were thoroughly intertwined already.

There were so many ways to take her family down, were someone knowledgeable or dedicated enough. That was something she would have to reckon with, and soon. But for now she thanked what little good fortune they had that Cartwright's still-unknown real reason for coming to town didn't strike at one of their weak points.

The dull-eyed guards at the Verfessas' gate cast furtive glances in either direction when she arrived. When it was certain she was alone and unmonitored, they allowed her inside. The front door opened before she could knock, a similarly sullen maid nodding to her and stepping aside.

"Epiphany!" crowed the avuncular Verfessa marching up the steps as she approached. "How is your mother doing? Sales strong?"

"Pitiful at the moment. The gargoyle outside the door is scaring them off."

"Ah, the nobles and their lackeys," he said. "I don't know that the world has ever seen a worse name for such a seedy bunch. You must tell your mother that I remain gobsmacked at the accuracy of her appraisals. I thought for certain she'd given me numbers triple what I'd end up getting. But wouldn't you know it, I barely had to lean on the buyer, and he coughed it up to the very duot."

"We've been at this a while. About what we'd discussed," she said.

"Right, right. Straight to business. That's what keeps you and I afloat, eh? Always with the eyes on the next job. Come on. I've been working on the details."

He marched down the steps. She kept pace.

"I tell you, I had no idea the sort of merchandise you were holding on to in that shop of yours. You've been holding out on us," Verfessa said.

"You and my mother worked out a very clear list, and very clear volumes for those items. We've sold and repaired precisely to quota," Epiphany said.

"Sure. Sure. But now I see just how much slack you gave yourself. Conservative. You could be making much more if you'd just up the units you sell to me. By the High, you'd have half the inventory if you did, and this mess wouldn't have been nearly the problem it is now."

"If you're planning on making an offer on our surplus inventory, let's wait until the deed is done."

"Oh, I'll be making an offer." He slapped the back of a leather chair, inviting her to sit down.

She sank into the well-worn seat. He dropped himself into the seat opposite.

"I did some looking into that carpenter you're using for cover. Does a pretty brisk business. But, then, so close to the Maskers' shop, it stands to reason. Good market district. In the past month, he's never had fewer than three carts go through and never more than seven. You ask me, the man is leaving money on the table. All the carting back and forth is done via a courier. If he bought himself a good sturdy cart and horse, even if he had to hire someone to drive it, he'd save that much and more in three months. Throwing good money after bad, keeping a thing like that going."

He cleared his throat and poured himself a drink. "What you listed? The items you need my help moving and storing? That'll be five full carts. And by your figuring, you have five days or so to get it all clear, yes?"

"That's about when the messenger should be back with the declaration permitting him to inspect our home."

"I could get enough of my carts out there to harvest the goods, no problem. But thick as a brick this inspector might be, a bit of extra traffic and an unfamiliar wagon doing it might catch his eye."

"I suspect it won't, but I accept it is a concern."

"And then there's the goods you've been having us haul in from that little hidey-hole your brother set up. The one the Graves' dumped their things in. That's got to be brought in, too. Not quite so much. I guess you'll be spreading it thin?"

"We'll be stocking to the level we kept things at prior to Dad's improved capacity to repair and Fel's access to some very good vaults."

"Still, maybe two, maybe three carts in. Plus the five out, that's an awful lot of additional loading and unloading."

"I'm open to alternatives, if you have them."

"Belt and suspenders, Epiphany. Can I call you Fanny?"

"Let's hear the suspenders you're suggesting before I decide."

He laughed and slapped the arm of the chair. "Well listen up. I didn't just look into how many carts the carpenters were sending out. I looked into how full they were. And let me tell you, that man does not pack them tight. I think we can do this whole thing a lot slicker if I just get some of my boys to replace one or two of the couriers. Same carts, different faces. You pile your boxes with theirs, my boys pack those wagons good and tight. If we're lucky, you don't need a single one of my carts to do any hauling. I spread your inventory nice and thin around two dozen places in town, and even if Cartwright got our scent, he'd be sorting wheat with tweezers to try to find where the gear was hidden. Same deal on the way in. Each of those courier carts parked at the carpenter's place comes packed instead of empty. We move in the goods before we move them out. If we're lucky, that street doesn't see a single new cart."

"You can do that? Get your people into the courier's service?"

He laughed again. "How do you think I've been getting this information about the carts? I already own a piece. Just like damn near everything else in this town."

"Including Masker's Antiquities..."

"Hey now," he said. "That shop is all yours. We're partners. And now that I've laid out how I'll be scratching your back, I've got an awful itch I think you could reach."

"Your fee."

"We ran the numbers. Five carts out, three carts in. The way I figure it. Four carts in, when all is said and done, seems fair."

"You want to keep a full cart. Twenty-percent. You're asking for twenty-percent of our stock," she said.

"Twenty-percent of the portion we're storing," he said.

"You're storing the highest-value items," she said.

"Wouldn't need me to store them otherwise," he said.

"Twenty percent is awfully steep."

"Beats the alternative, doesn't it?"

"Ten percent," she said.

"Fifteen percent, and we choose the fifteen," he said.

"Fifteen percent and we choose the fifteen," she countered.

"Fifteen percent, you choose the fifteen, and we get an extra week of your father's time this month to fix up some of our acquisitions."

"Fifteen percent, we choose the fifteen, three days of Dad's time, and an extra meeting with Mom to discuss increasing the volume of inventory we sell to you."

"Fifteen percent, you choose, four days of your father's time, and it's you I meet with about the extra volume."

"Why me?"

"Frankly? You're a little easier to read than your mother. I could use the better deal I'm likely to get out of you, and you could use the practice."

She narrowed her eyes and drummed her fingers on the arm of the chair. Finally, she extended her hand. "Deal. But you're going to regret it. I was going easy on you."

He laughed. "We'll just see about that, Epiphany."

"I think I can tolerate you calling me Fanny."

"No, no!" Tome grumbled, rattling that puzzle box in front of Oiler. "Leave the hole. Take your box!"

Tome was having a terrible time getting the contraption to behave, and he wasn't overly pleased that he had an audience for the struggles. The business of running Reynard's shop was through for the day, so by rights Thaddeus should have gone off to his room for the evening. But he was a member of the Graves family and always interested in contraptions of every stripe. He'd been lingering in the basement, looking over the tightly packed shelves and amusing himself with Oiler's antics.

"Quite the contraption, isn't it?" he said.

"Notable," Tome grunted, pulling a reassembled bit of stone from Oiler's claws. "Impressive. Complex. And absolutely infuriating. Oiler is a tool. A tool should be capable of being controlled precisely, should it not? What value is a contraption that, left to its own devices, will do whatever it pleases?"

"I believe the intention is to deactivate it when not in use," Thaddeus said. "Though it warrants observation that the capacity to control something fully comes hand in hand with the necessity to control it fully. A hammer will never misbehave, but it is also worthless without a hand to wield it, and it is only as precise as that hand. A tool that can operate to its designed level of precision without guidance can do much more work of much more consistent quality."

"Then we ought to deactivate it," Tome said. "Or at least get Fel or Martin up here. The closest it ever comes to actually listening is when it deals with them."

"The two most skilled contraptioneers are best capable to handle the contraption. Hardly a surprise."

"Wait! Wait! I have it," Tome said.

He placed the puzzle box on the ground and grabbed one of the smaller slabs Oiler had reassembled. With a grunt, he pounded the puzzle box beneath it. A product of the Bygone Era as it was, the box took seven solid blows before it finally broke, sending its seemingly endless sequence of tiles and components clattering across the floor.

Oiler waggled its claws and rattled its tail, practically dancing with excitement at the scattering of parts. Instantly the freshly opened holes were forgotten, and merrily repairing the puzzle box became Oiler's focus.

Tome huffed a breath and leaned against a shelf. Thaddeus watched in fascination as bent gears were straightened and replaced on their pivots.

"What do you suppose would be the price to separate this contraption from the Maskers?" he asked.

"Don't bother conjuring up a number. Fel's adopted it. He clings to his pets."

"Laudable," Thaddeus said.

Oiler searched the floor for the next piece. Tome nudged a bit of metal with the toe of his shoe so that Oiler would notice. The lantern in the corner stopped flickering, but only briefly. Tome probably would have missed it if he didn't know Wick's nature, but since he'd started working with the sentry flame, he'd become quite sensitive to the motion of flame. Wick had checked up on them and moved on.

Something about that observation stuck in his mind.

"Sentry flame," Tome muttered. He turned to Thaddeus. "How certain are you that the Graves flame is safe?" he asked.

"As certain as I can be. We have taken extreme measures to ensure it. Why?"

"Out in what they call Skinflint Camp, before I was attacked, I was investigating where Cartwright's messages are coming from. I found the man's tent but not the man. Inside were all sorts of sealed messages and also two of the pipes the Bolivans were using. Neither was lit."

"Curious... but then, the Bolivans aren't the only ones using them now. Fel makes good use of them these days."

Tome spread his arms. "We are witnessing the lengths the Maskers will go to making sure their contraptions are used as they intend. I don't think they'll have lost track of two of those pipes."

"So it is possible the Bolivans haven't learned their lesson," Thaddeus said. "You say they weren't lit. They don't do much good then, do they?"

"No. But they've used your flame against both you and the Maskers in the past. They might be after it again."

"The only Graves flame in this city is burning in my own, quite mundane, pipe, or in the lantern I transfer it to when smoking is not possible. The flame is never beyond my observation. The Maskers take similar care. And even if such were not the case, we now know how to compel the sentry flames to extinguish themselves. It is not a matter of concern."

"Given the failure of the Greater Lands Wall to fully contain the Greater Mystics, forgive me if I lack the same degree of certainty you seem to enjoy."

"Caution is always wise. But I believe we have provided the proper level of security. That tent does warrant greater scrutiny, I suppose. But given your troubles, it seems very ill-advised to investigate it anytime soon unless we are well equipped. And presently we have more pressing concerns."

A muck-covered hammer clattered to the ground just inside the hole Fel and Teya had dug. A moment later, an equally muck-covered Teya scrambled up.

"Job done!" she said proudly, grinning with teeth that practically glowed compared to her muddy scales.

Fel pulled himself up. He was moderately cleaner, if only because he was tall enough that he was wading waist deep in muddy water rather than swimming in it.

"Broke through to the well," he said wearily.

"So we are ready to start hauling things out and in?" Tome said.

"Not quite. The rope is mostly rotten, and a good tug on it suggests the bucket winch isn't up to snuff. Teya and I have to get out there while it's still late enough that we can work in private and swap them out for something good enough to raise and lower crates of contraptions. I'm also going to have to rig up a walkway to haul this stuff across so we don't have to slog through the water. And a halfway civilized way to carry things down and up, because making that climb with crates of goods? Not going to work. And I can't exactly haul the materials in to do all that, because if I could pull that off without people noticing, hauling out the contraptions and hauling in the antiques would be easy."

"So how do you intend to do the building, then?" Tome asked.

"We do rope!" Teya said. "And crate!"

"What?" Tome said.

"We'll swap as much of the stuff as we can from crates to sacks. We have plenty of sacks. Then we make sort of a rope bridge with planks from the crates and rope. Teya knows how."

"Very strong!" she said. "Use for mountain passes. Unicorns use. Only broke once!"

"Once is the maximum number of times a bridge can break," Tome said.

"We'll move some rubble around for supports. Should be fine," Fel said.

"Do you think we can spare enough crates for a whole walkway?" Tome asked.

"Also, borrow wood. Shop above has lots," Teya said.

"I don't think robbing the carpenter is a good idea, Teya," Tome said.

Fel shrugged. "I've heard worse ones. Just to fill in the gaps. We'll replace it once we're not being watched."

Clattering hooves heralded the arrival of Parch from down in the flooded basement. Unlike the others, he was pristinely clean. The trio paced through the crowded floor and through to the Maskers' basement. Oiler held up the repaired and completed puzzle box. Tome took it, expecting to have to scramble it, but before he could do so, Oiler had jangled off to follow the others. He shook his head.

"I don't know if it is a sign of how simple he is or how complex he is, but Fel just marched through a hole he'd hammered through his own wall followed by a menagerie of mystic and mechanical helpers, and he doesn't even appear to notice that the whole circumstance is absurd."

Thaddeus shrugged. "Such is the nature of something as elusive as 'normal.' It changes depending on how closely you measure it. By and large? This is madness. In his life? It's just another day."

"And yet I willingly linger in this place..." Tome said. "Insanity may well be contagious."

$$-\ \bullet\ -$$

CHAPTER 9

Two days were apparently all it took for Allie to slide into an entirely new routine. A full shift at The Fox and Log, home to find some meal or another left for her by Fel. A heavy, exhausted sleep until the telltale thump of his return, then a few minutes dressed in her robe, making sure he wasn't leaking from any new holes before heading back to bed again. Between not having to cook her own meals and losing a bit of sleep with Fel's comings and goings, it turned out to be quite workable overall.

On the third day he was with her, and the fourth of the Maskers' ridiculous scheme, she woke expecting to have to tiptoe through her morning routine to keep from disturbing him. Instead he was awake, stirring at a skillet over the fire. Teya and Parch, on the other hand, were piled on the bedroll together. The kobold's mouth and tongue lolled to the side. The unicorn had a cork stuck onto the end of his horn. Both were deep asleep. Fel glanced at her, bleary-eyed.

"Morning," he said thickly.

"Shouldn't you be at the bottom of that pile there? You look like death warmed over," she said.

"Then I look better than I feel." He rubbed his red-rimmed eye. "I can't sleep. Mind won't stop running in circles. I figured you'd be up soon. Might as well keep that promise and cook you one of the other things I know how to cook." He held up the pan and pointed out the principle ingredients. "Eggs, fried bread, sausage."

"That's three things."

"Not the way I cook them. To me, this is all one thing. I call it 'breakfast.' Eat up."

He slopped half the contents of the skillet into her bowl and the rest into one for him. "Oh, right." He reached back and slipped a cloth-wrapped bundle out of his back pocket. "Handpicked by Vivian Masker."

She took the bundle and unrolled it. Four sets of elegant silverware, made from real silver, had been carefully packed inside.

"I told her you didn't have more than one set of silverware, and she pulled that off the top shelf for you. Told me to tell you to bring it around once a year or so to be polished."

"Fel, I couldn't. These are worth a fortune."

"Oh, stop it. I found them in the dirt four years ago, on the third level of a six-level treasure vault two days south of here. They're worth what Mom says they're worth, and Mom says they're worth giving to you. Now eat your breakfast."

He sat down and took a knife and fork from the collection. She did the same.

"Aren't you going to wake them up for breakfast?" she asked.

"Teya ate six eggs. Three raw and three cooked. Plus five links of sausage. I don't know where she puts it all. Parch ate a whole loaf of bread."

"Your cooking has a way of putting people to sleep, it seems."

"A good meal should require a nap right after," he said.

"Not the best policy when you're cooking breakfast," she said, digging in. "This is good. Though if you're frying things up, you can't go far wrong."

"That's what I told Lattica Graves when she was surprised I could cook. I spend weeks on the road at a time. What do you think I'm doing, tackling elks and eating them raw?"

"Wouldn't put it past you," she said.

He speared a sausage and munched on it.

"So you can't sleep because your mind is racing. That didn't strike me as the sort of problem you'd have either."

"It usually isn't."

"Still, you're not short on reasons. Which is it? The murderous elf? The corrupt inspector?"

Fel glanced at her silently. She gave him a flat look.

"The thing with Mariss." She shook her head slowly. "You have better things to worry about."

"It's a mess," he said.

"It's not. It's an embarrassment. Since when do you care about embarrassments? You spend half your time at The Fox and Log telling people about your favorites."

"It is a mess, and I'll tell you why. First, a year of the best I could muster and she wasn't even sure how interested I was in her."

"That's partially on her. She's a little too innocent for this world sometimes."

"And she thinks we're together."

"If you're going to tell me that's an embarrassment, you're going to get a skillet to the side of your head."

"You're the one calling this an embarrassment. I'm calling it a mess. She thinks we're together." He furrowed his brow. "I don't know how to say it. … You and me? We never would have worked. You know me too well. Too savvy to the kind of oaf I can be. Mariss? She had some distance. I could dress myself up. Build myself into someone right for her. But if it wasn't her, and you weren't an eyewitness to the last few years of drinking and gambling away my pay, you'd have been the one."

"The one who'd have you stumbling over yourself, hemming and hawing about how to get me to think you're the kind of person you think I'd want?"

"More or less."

"Now that would have been a sight to see."

"Doesn't really matter now," he said. "Having her dash my hopes because she thinks we're together? If there was ever a world where I'd have the courage to try to pull that off, and there was ever a world where you'd give it a second thought, now it would look like I was doing it because of what happened here. Because she'd assumed it. Like you were some sort of conciliation prize handed out by the one that got away."

"Oh, I'm a prize all right, but not a conciliation, and you haven't won me yet."

Fel shoveled some bread into his mouth and crunched mindlessly. After a few seconds, something percolated through his mind.

"… Yet?" he said.

"And here I was thinking it'd go sailing right by you, like every other signal a woman has ever lobbed your way."

"You're not serious."

"I let you sleep in my home, dummy," she said. "I practically twisted your arm to get you to do it. How many men in this city do you think I'd trust to even know where I live?"

"You were being a good friend. You'd have done the same for anyone, and I'd do the same for you."

She scoffed. "The same for anyone? I wouldn't even do the same for Oovay, and I spend half my day with him, every day. And that 'you'd do the same for me' part? That's why you get the special treatment, you dope! You're decent, which is a rare thing in this city. And you're genuine. Except, might I add, to the one person you were trying to win over. You're a better man than you think you are. This you. The filth-covered, egg-frying lug who sees a girl without a second spoon and brings her one."

"You… needed a spoon…" he said.

"Now don't let this give you any funny ideas. I'm not throwing myself at you, and that bedroom door stays shut for a reason. I had my hands full even before I ended up with a unicorn and a kobold sleeping in front of my fireplace. And you're in no state of mind to be making a decision like this. But since you apparently need to be told, that world where you and I might possibly one day give one another a try? It's this one."

Fel looked down at his plate, as though looking her in the eyes for a moment longer was more than he could manage. He pushed his bread around to soak up some yolk. "I don't know if you gave me one more thing to think about or one less," he said.

"Make it one less. You'll sleep better that way." She took another forkful of eggs.

Epiphany trudged through the north side of town. She didn't usually head this far north on her day-to-day errands. It was home to the cruder markets, in terms of their products. Burlap sacks, rough-hewn lumber. Simple boxes. Livestock. If the family needed something from this district, Fel or Martin were typically the ones who fetched it. Martin, because he was normally getting raw materials that he had a better eye for. Fel, because the household division of labor assigned anything that required carrying heavy objects any measurable distance to him. But right now the goods they were after were some fresh crates, sacks, and ropes to replace those Fel had used up in his renovations to the carpenter's collapsed sub-basement, and he couldn't very well fetch them himself because the Watch and the inspector both believed him to be absent. And given the money they'd had to spend to make this ridiculous heist work and the damage the inspector was doing to their business with his constant meddling, Vivian needed to be working the counter during every possible moment.

"Thank you. Just send them down to Masker's Antiquities. You know the place," Epiphany said, dropping some duots into the clerk's hands. "And I apologize in advance. An inspector is going to ask to search your entire wagon when you show up. He'll be gone in a few days."

He nodded and set off to fulfill the order, his expression barely registering that he'd been spoken to at all. Her nose wrinkled at the smell of the recently loaded-up holding pens, filled to the brim with swine and cows. Technically she'd been asked to see about getting some grease to quiet down the well winch for the last day of spiriting contraptions out so that they could begin loading in the remainder of the mundane antiquities and be done with this ridiculous caper. She was already attempting to talk herself out of doing so and hurrying home to get the stink off her.

She crossed the main road leading to the north gate and paused. A carriage was heading in. Nothing strange about that. But this was a very distinctive carriage. An official messenger carriage from Teskal. It stuck out like a sore thumb because of the gaudy blue velvet shade over the driver. Packages and other deliveries didn't arrive in a carriage like that. Only official correspondences direct from the nobles themselves did. The kind of things that required an authorized carrier to confirm their authenticity. The kind of things that had to be specially requested by officials.

Precisely the kind of message Inspector Cartwright had requested.

It didn't seem possible. The message was days early, even with the most generous estimate. It should have taken eight days, not four. But there was no sense dwelling on the unlikelihood of such a thing now. It would be inside the city in moments. It would be to the shop in minutes—faster than Epiphany could even get back to the shop to warn them. A whole carriage of replacement antiques needed to be loaded onto the shelves to ward off any questions about why they had no inventory, and there was still a hole in the wall. There might not be a way to buy enough time for what needed to be done, but she had to do what she could to buy as much as could be had.

Epiphany looked about and racked her brain for something that could delay the wagon. Inspiration struck as she was hit by yet another wave of manure stench. She trotted over to the holding pens as casually as she could manage. The messenger's carriage rattled into town. All eyes were turned to the curious sight, which meant none were turned to her as she gently nudged the latch on the gate to the pen. The gate creaked open a bit, just enough for the hog nearest to it to notice and make its bid for freedom. Hundreds more followed, flooding the streets with swine and their dismayed owners. Epiphany took off at a sprint, plausibly because she didn't want to get swamped in the wave of farm animals that had brought the messenger to a standstill. Really, she needed to get to her parents.

A few minutes later, Vivian was engaged in the activity that had come to occupy a disappointingly large portion of her day—staring through the window of her shop at Inspector Cartwright as he stared back with equal dispassion. It wasn't as though she had anything better to do, with him out there scaring off her prospective customers. That changed when she heard the stir of the lesser harpies on the roof and Cartwright looked aside. Something was happening.

Epiphany burst into view, scattering a palmful of washers on the ground before the harpies could attempt to extort their bribe. She threw the door open and thundered inside, gasping for breath and dripping with sweat.

"The messenger," she gasped. "He's here."

Cartwright was already crossing the street to investigate.

"I stalled them," Epiphany said quickly. "Livestock. Won't keep them long. Maybe a half hour."

The inspector stepped through the door.

"Is something wrong?" he said. "You seem rather in a hurry, Miss Masker."

He spoke with the tone of someone at the very beginning of a whole speech intended to intimidate and unnerve. Vivian didn't give him the chance.

"Ah! Inspector Cartwright. I'm pleased to say your message seems to have arrived at the north gate. I believe there is some manner of delay, but if you hurry you may be able to intercept it."

The statement threw him off balance. "You are joking," he said.

"I am quite serious. You could, of course, wait until it arrives, but the streets of Beffshire will only become more congested and slower to navigate as the day rolls on."

He gave her a measuring look. "I'll be placing one of the assayers in position to observe you, you realize," he said.

"A wise precaution," she said evenly.

He gave her a long, calculating stare, then made his way from the shop with the peculiar gait of someone who was suddenly in a terrible rush but attempting not to appear so.

"We have a few minutes until his replacement arrives to watch us, and at least a few minutes more before the inspector returns. Get Tome to take Oiler and bring him through to Reynard's basement. Once he's through, cover the hole in the wall with a stack of empty crates and drape the empty shelves with sacks."

"Surely he'll check what's behind the crates and sacks," Epiphany said.

"You let me worry about that." Vivian turned. "Wick? Are you in?"

"I am, Miss Masker."

"Do you have access to Fel?"

"There is an accessible flame burning nearby, but he is presently sleeping in front of it. I may not be able to wake him."

"Do your best. We need him down here. We need every hand we can spare."

"Fel isn't supposed to be back from his trip yet," Epiphany said, still winded.

"If the messenger can be days early, my son can be days early. Here's what he needs to know…"

Fel, for the first time in days, was dreaming. He was in a boat in the center of a river. There were no oars. There was no sail. The current was speeding up, and ahead, a waterfall. He stared at the rising mist past the edge. There was no way of knowing how big the drop was and no way to avoid the drop. He couldn't bring himself to be afraid. It was almost a relief to know what was going to happen for once.

A stabbing pain in his shoulder shook him from sleep. He opened his eyes to find Teya staring down at him, wide-eyed, with the claws of one paw jabbing his arm and the other pointing at the lantern flame.

"Fire talking, Fel! Fire talking!" Teya urged.

He looked blearily to the lantern.

"Are you clearheaded enough to understand what is going to be a substantial list of events and tasks in a very short space of time?" Wick said.

"Uh-huh," he said thickly.

"The inspector's proclamation has arrived. He will begin searching the shop very shortly. The boxes containing the final incriminating items are in the basement of Reynard's shop. We need to remove them, fetch the final bits of replacement antiquities, and load them onto the shelves."

"In how long?" Fel said, springing to his feet as the bolt of anxiety chased away sleep.

"Minutes."

"All right. Excellent. Impossible. Let's get it done," Fel said.

His mind chewed through the different steps necessary as he grabbed his gear. "As far as most of the people in the city know, I'm still off on a trip. The sun is up, the city is bustling, and I have to get to the other side of the city walls to fetch the carriage with the rest of the antiques and bring them in. I can't be seen leaving and I have to be seen coming in. That means I need a horse and a distraction."

Teya grinned. "No more sneaky, yes?"

"Very very not sneaky," Fel said, lighting the pipe from the lantern and stuffing it in his mouth. "As very very not sneaky as you can manage."

She revealed her sparker and flicked it gleefully. He touched her shoulder.

"Maybe sneakier than that," he corrected.

She scrunched up her face. "Oh! I know what. Good times!"

"Ya-haa!" Teya crowed, holding tight to Parch's back as he galloped through the city.

People shouted and pointed or dashed to get out of the way. Parch wasn't the fastest steed in the world, but he was faster than her, and he had a few other tricks that a normal horse couldn't manage. Even with her on his back, he was capable of some prodigious leaps. And if a crack or crevasse in a wall was wide enough to catch the corner of his hoof, he could jump off it like it was flat ground. Parch bounded from ground to wall to roof as easily as a normal horse could gallop. It made for quite a spectacle, and those who had a mind to stop the pair had no chance of doing so as they surged toward the west gate.

The hapless member of the town Watch stationed at the gate did his very best to stop them, but Parch simply bounded from the wall to the roof of the guardhouse and back to the wall, trotting along its top and hopping down without the slightest sign of effort. The watchman sprinted after him and, quite unnoticed thanks to the comparative mundanity, a thickly built man on horseback followed. It took all of two minutes for Teya and Parch to lose the watchman and a few minutes more for Fel to meet her where the carriage had been stowed.

"Good work," he said, hopping off the steed and pulling the covering from the carriage.

"Where horse come from?" Teya said.

"You'd be surprised what you can 'borrow' when people are in utter panic thanks to an escaped kobold," Fel said. "You and Parch, get in the wagon. No hiding, up near the front. You're my responsibility. They'll be stopping me and giving me an earful regardless of if they find you with me or not, so I might as well have you along to help if things get bad."

"Will do this! Yes!" Teya said.

She and Parch hopped in. Fel did the fastest and sloppiest yoking of a horse he'd ever done and pulled the wagon onto the main road. Bits of underbrush were still dropping out of the spokes when the breathless watchman spotted him and dashed over.

"Fel Masker! I thought the captain had made himself clear. You were supposed to keep that thing under control!" he bellowed.

Fel kept the horse moving. "What do you mean? I have them right here," he said.

"That thing just ran wild in the city!"

Fel looked to Teya. "You ran wild?"

She shook her head. "Ran out of city. Very straight. Fun? Yes. Wild? No."

"She caused chaos!"

"Well she's under control now."

"You were warned!" the watchman said.

"I wasn't even here. Take it up with Epiphany. She was watching her while I was away."

"The captain is going to hear about this," the watchman shouted, now trailing behind the wagon as Fel continued forward.

"I'm sure he will! He knows where to find me!" Fel said.

"Bye! Thanks for chasing me!" Teya said, leaning aside and waving. She turned back to Fel. "You get in trouble?" she asked.

"Probably. If that's the worst that happens to me today, it'll be a triumph."

With the watchman lagging behind, there was no one ahead to block the way. Fel puffed the pipe. "Wick, how are we looking?" he said.

"The inspector is arriving now," Wick replied.

The door flew open, nearly knocking the bell from above it. Inspector Cartwright charged in, proclamation held high. The assayer who hadn't been forced to spy on them through the night accompanied him.

"By the order of the nobles of Teskal, empowered by the throne of Thayne, I am hereby authorized to inspect the entirety of your home and shop until I am satisfied that you are not in possession of any items expressly forbidden by the edicts and proclamations regarding acceptable contraptions," he barked, slapping the proclamation down.

Vivian kept her face even and pleasant, maintaining the precise attitude she displayed when dealing with an irate customer. She simply looked down to the page.

"I demand—"

She raised a finger to delay him long enough to finish reading the proclamation.

"Of course, Inspector Cartwright. Everything seems to be in order. Right this way," she said. She opened the door and hatch leading to the floor below. "Follow, please."

He stayed so close behind her as she descended that he nearly knocked her down twice before they'd reached the first floor of inventory. Every shelf was protected by hastily pinned sacks, but only the shelves nearest to the stairs had anything on them. Despite this, she stepped aside and gestured to the shelves.

"You may investigate the entirety of our inventory."

"Your permission is no longer necessary, Masker," he snapped.

"When you are through, I'll take you to the next floor. I'm afraid that my husband is rather busy in the workshop, so you'll have to wait until tomorrow to inspect that floor. There is plenty here to occupy your time until—"

He turned to her, righteous fury in his eyes. "I am sorry, but do you deign to tell a representative of the nobles how to perform his duties? The proclamation permits a thorough and complete search. It is not your place to dictate which floors I may search and at what time."

"Inspector Cartwright, this is still an operating shop, and we have been rather badly hampered by your presence over the last few days. My husband needs to keep working."

"You and your husband need to comply, and you could not be more transparent in your goals. You mean to keep me from the shop until you have time to clear it. I will not allow it. You will take us to the shop immediately."

"I will not," Vivian insisted.

He narrowed his eyes and stuck his nose in her face. "You will do as I say, or you will be accompanying me to the capital to be locked away until we can uncover the depths of your treachery."

She tightened her lips and nodded stiffly. "As you wish."

Vivian turned and continued down the stairs, leading the savvy inspector away from the nearly bare floor with a poorly hidden hole chiseled through the wall and into the thoroughly cleared workshop. It was difficult to keep a smile from her face as they charged into the shop and looked around. Every cubby and shelf was heaped with raw materials and half-assembled contraptions. Virtually every safe contraption in storage had been brought into the workshop and split into no fewer than three pieces each. Anyone short of Martin himself wouldn't have had a chance of realizing precisely what each item was without instruction. It would take them hours to pick through and confirm their harmlessness.

Martin was hard at work etching a disc for a music box when they burst in. His engraving tool slipped across the surface as they entered, activating the device and filling the room with a loud, repeating loop of melody.

"Vivian, I thought you were going to tell them we needed the shop for the day," he said innocently.

"Silence," Cartwright said. "And silence that device."

"I've damaged the disk. Silencing it will take me a few minutes. If you'll give me privacy while I work—"

"Then leave it. It is more important you serve the investigation. Assayer! We shall do this systematically. That shelf, top to bottom, left to right. We do not set down an item until I am absolutely satisfied. And, Masker, you will answer any question I have."

Fel brought the cart around to the alleyway leading to the old well. Once he'd locked the wheels to offload it, he unfastened the "borrowed" horse from the yoke and let it wander off.

"I chase horse?" Teya asked, huddling in the shade of the alleyway to stay out of sight.

"No, let it go. Its owner will find it eventually," he murmured. "Let's go. We need to get this stuff inside before…"

He trailed off when he realized two rather burly men had turned off the street and were marching down the alley toward him and Teya. They'd arrived in a wagon of their own, and it was now completely blocking the alleyway. This was excellent news in that it would keep prying eyes from noticing what he was up to, but it was rare that two large men following one into an alley was in any way beneficial.

Fel tightened his fist around the grip of his cudgel. "I don't want any trouble, fellows. I have a lot to do and less time to do in."

"Fel Masker," rumbled the first man.

"Yeah," he said warily.

"We work for a mutual associate," said the second man. "He said maybe we should check if you needed any help."

The words "mutual associate" fell out of his mouth with the grace of a newborn calf. They weren't a part of his vocabulary. He'd been instructed to use precisely that term. A term that only ever seemed to get any use in one very specific circumstance: referring to someone who would prefer his name not be spoken aloud. These were Verfessa's men.

He puffed the pipe. "You fellows wouldn't happen to be the ones doing deliveries for the carpenter, would you?" he said.

"Both of these men have been helping Tome move contraptions," Wick confirmed.

The first of the men muttered something to that effect as well. Fel took a breath.

"I guess I was bound to have some good luck eventually," he said. "Teya, you and me are going to head down the well. You two, start loading in the crates from the wagon."

Teya and Parch trotted to the well. She slid down the rope; he bounded wall to wall. Verfessa's two men watched uneasily.

"You think it's strange watching those two climb down a well, you should try sharing a room with them. Welcome to my life, and be glad you're not going to be a part of it for very long."

At the bottom of the well, Tome hobbled across an impressively sturdy walkway they'd assembled in the carpenter's sub-basement and raised one of Wick's two main lanterns. Teya scrambled through the hole they'd knocked out of the side of the well and was nearly knocked off the walkway by the sudden arrival of Parch.

"Is Fel here?" Tome said.

"Yes! And two men. You know them?"

"Both of them a half a head taller than Fel. Diction barely better than yours?"

"Yes, yes," she said.

"Yes, we can trust them. Or at least we've been trusting them so far. So if they're untrustworthy, the ship has sailed."

Fel swung through the opening and gave the winch two tugs. It swiftly reeled up. "What's the word?" he said.

"Your mother convinced them to search the workshop first. Oiler's hard at work reassembling the slab you two knocked free from the wall of your home this morning, yet again. Provided we can keep the blasted contraption from installing it early, Oiler should be able to seal up the wall good as new in just a few minutes, once the job is done," he said.

"Excellent. Keep an eye on him. Teya and I will handle the crates."

Epiphany lingered in the antiquities shop and tried to cope with the stress of knowing that in the bottom floor of her home, someone with the power to end the shop and imprison the family was attempting to find justification to do just that. Simultaneously, just a few floors above where the inspection was taking place, her brother and his friends, one of whom was a creature who shouldn't exist outside the Greater Lands, were quickly and quietly spiriting away the very items that could have them locked up and replacing them with freshly acquired permissible antiquities. The success of the plan depended upon the trustworthiness of a career criminal and his underlings. And worst of all, the thing that set them on this path was her own desire to find ways to bypass the very consequences they were now closer to facing than they had ever been before.

So many things could cause this all to come crashing down. They could make too much noise and alert the people in the workshop that something was amiss, though the "malfunctioning" music box was covering that nicely. Someone could become suspicious of the amount of equipment the carpenter's deliverymen were collecting, though the still-swarming swine were presently far more thoroughly occupying people's attentions. The people in the workshop could finish early. Or...

She shut her eyes and shook the thoughts away. Everything inside her demanded she thump down the steps to at least catch a glimpse of their progress, but she dared not. Doing so could startle them into revealing themselves or cause her to leave the shop unattended at the precise moment some crucial warning came and went. Her only updates came as brief, terse assessments from Wick.

The sentry flame was jumping between the lantern on the top shelf of the shop, the lantern in the workshop, the heirloom lantern loaded into the wagon along with the last of the contraband, and the pipe in Fel's mouth. Information came in little snippets, pulled randomly from each vantage.

"Two shelves filled. Starting the third. ... The bust and couplers have been loaded into the wagon. ... Oiler has finished reassembling the slab. ... Teya dropped a crate of antiques. Copper and brass."

"In the inventory room?" Epiphany hissed, imagining the racket it would cause.

"In the carpenter's sub-basement. No reaction from the inspector. No major damage to the items."

She nodded and tried to calm her rattled nerves by occupying herself with the only part of this madness she could actively engage with. Cartwright had left the proclamation with her. If nothing else, she was becoming very familiar with its language.

The bell over the door jingled. Epiphany barely managed to suppress a startled squeal at the sound. If it had been a customer, it was quite possible they would hold the distinction of being the first person to receive poor service at Masker's Antiquities in the history of the shop, because she absolutely didn't have it in her to even entertain the possibility that the customer was always right. In reality, the visitor was something far, far worse. It was the remaining assayer, dull witted and sleepy from having had only a few hours between the night shift and being summoned to be part of this confounding sequence.

"Hello, ma'am," Epiphany said, fists clenched so tight she feared her fingernails would draw blood. "How may I help you today?"

"Miss Masker, I want to apologize on behalf of the rest of us at the assayer's office. You and the family have never been anything but forthcoming."

"It's nothing, really," she said, now feeling a dash of guilt at the currently unwarranted high regard the assayer held for their record of compliance.

"But I'm afraid I've been asked to stay here in the shop to make sure no one tries to carry anything out," she said.

"Entirely sensible," Epiphany said. "I support any level of precaution. The more thorough you are now, the more certain you will be that we continue to be upstanding examples of the contraptioneer's art."

"I'm sure it won't be much longer," she said.

"Thoroughness takes time, I am in no hurry, and nor should you be. Would you care for some water? Something to eat?"

"A drink would be much appreciated."

She thought better of attempting to pour it for her. Right now she was quite certain she would spill more than she poured, with the state her nerves were in. Instead she offered up the pitcher and a glass. While the assayer slaked her thirst, Epiphany anxiously awaited an update from Wick. He was able to select who could hear him, so she could be kept informed even with the assayer present, but now the communication would have to be one-way. That wasn't a problem, though. She'd only need to say something if there was some sort of unforeseen issue that the assayer would cause by being... present.

She shut her eyes tight as her mind darted through the remaining steps to the plan and stumbled into a pitfall. When the work was done, the hole would have to be sealed. Oiler could do so very quickly, but they'd learned that he could only make the repair seamless on the side from which he was doing the repair. Teya and the others could make themselves scarce through the rear window of Reynard's shop or through the well, but Oiler would absolutely have to do its work from inside the Masker household. And once it had done that work, there would be no way to exit the household except for the front door, which was now being watched. And Oiler itself was a profoundly forbidden contraption. Without some change to the plan, they were all but guaranteeing that Oiler would be found and their fates would be sealed.

Epiphany glanced at the lantern. "Does that look like it's going out to you?" she said. "I should probably top it off with oil." She slid a stool over and stepped up to fetch the lantern.

"Why do you keep it burning during the day?" the assayer said.

"Oh, it's a family tradition," she said. "Superstition I suppose. Mom insists upon it. Something about a bright and warm light bringing prosperity to the shop. I don't believe a word of it myself, but tradition is tradition." She fetched the lantern and headed for the steps. "Do me a favor and do tell anyone who might come in looking for something that I'll be along momentarily," she said.

"I'm, er... I'm afraid I'm not supposed to let you out of my sight," the assayer said. "And I'm also not supposed to leave the doorway unprotected."

"I understand why you can't leave the doorway, but why can't I step away for a moment?"

"I don't know. Something about how you might move things around to places that we've already searched. The inspector's suspicions know no bounds, but I have my orders."

"I see... Well, I suppose I can risk letting the lantern go out. I don't like the thought of leaving the shop entirely empty, and it isn't worth locking up for two minutes."

She set the lantern on the counter and sat down. The assayer returned to the doorway. Delivering a message to the others was clearly going to be a challenge. She pulled a blank sheet from beneath the counter and fetched a pen.

Teya huffed and puffed as she toted a crate through the hole in the wall. As much hard work as this had been, her heart was practically singing. Humans, contraptions, a kobold, a unicorn. Working together, all of them, toward a common goal. It was balm for her soul. A kobold was meant to be part of a team, and ever since she'd felt the tug of destiny, she'd been separated from hers. Working with Fel had been enough to keep her sane, even happy. But something about the scope of this task, the urgency, and the fact that each had their part and no part could be spared made it so much more fulfilling. To feel a weight upon her shoulders, and to know that she could be trusted to carry it... who could ask for anything more? If not for the need for silence, she would be purring.

She scrambled to the top of the last shelf in the room, the final place still glaringly empty. By the time she turned back around, Fel had the first of the items ready for her to tote to the far edge of the shelf. Working as a team, they emptied the crates and filled the shelves as smoothly as water filling a tub. The final ancient, dusty knickknack slipped in place, and she climbed down.

For a brief instant, she and Fel wore the same expression. One of raw satisfaction of a job well done. He motioned for her to follow him out the door.

"All right. That's it. Everything left to be hidden is in the wagon, and everything left to replace it has been stacked up," Fel said. "All that remains is to seal up the hole and stack up the crates where they were in front of it."

"On that point," Wick said, his lamp set carefully on the freshly emptied shelves in Reynard's shop. "There is a minor issue. Epiphany has been joined by one of the assayers, who is watching the front door. As she has indicated in writing, so as to not alert the assayer, this complicates the removal of Oiler and the individual responsible for stacking the crates again."

Fel looked to Tome, then Oiler, then Teya.

"I do!" Teya said, scampering back through the hole and tugging Oiler after her.

"What are you going to do?" Fel said.

"Be sneaky, very very," she said, chin raised in pride.

"You're sure you can do this?"

"I do this. Go," she said with finality.

Fel released a breath and handed her the lantern Wick was burning in. "Then have at it. I'm heading out, making sure the wagon is on its way, and heading around to the front. I'll have my pipe, and I'll try to give you cover by keeping the upstairs assayer's nose in my business and out of yours. Tell Wick what you need, and he'll pass it along."

He hurried away, along with Tome and Parch. Teya hopped through the hole and started gathering the empty crates that had previously blocked the hole in the wall. Oiler had reassembled the center of the circular hole they'd broken out time and time again, and they'd swept together all the largest fragments they'd broken free. The contraption hauled it into place and started inserting chips and shards, spritzing thick adhesive into the mix to fill the gaps. It wouldn't take more than a few minutes to finish sealing up the wall to a mystically indistinguishable level of repair.

Teya had until the contraption was through to figure out just what she was going to do to get it out of the shop.

She couldn't hide; they would be coming along to search all the boxes. She couldn't leave; the only way out was the stairs, and they were being watched. She squinted and turned. No. The only way out for a human was the stairs. But for someone a bit more compact, there was one more option.

Oiler was working its way from right to left. Teya waited until it was precisely halfway finished, then stacked half the crates. She turned and scampered over to the dumbwaiter. Hauling the door open revealed that the compartment aligned with the shop level, leaving the way upward blocked. So be it. If she couldn't leave, she'd just hide very well.

Oiler was a few fragments and spritzes away from completion when she heard a thump downstairs and the constant music became louder. The door to the workshop had opened. She shifted uneasily from foot to foot. The creak of stairs groaning under angry footsteps approached. Oiler splatted a final spritz of adhesive and produced a contented little chime. She desperately pulled the contraption onto her back and slid the crates in place. In a final frenzied scramble, she snatched the lantern and vanished through the dumbwaiter door, pulling it shut behind her. She dangled from the ropes inside, a heavy pack of chains on her back and the grip at the top of the lantern clamped in her teeth.

She slid down the rope until she reached the bottom and raised a floppy ear to listen. There was no rattling or clanking in the workshop. Just the steady sound of music. After a few moments, she heard a soft voice.

"Oh? Is that so," Martin raised his voice. "I'll just shut this door so that you can work in peace, shall I?"

"Please!" snapped Cartwright from above.

The door slammed shut. A moment later, Martin opened the dumbwaiter and helped Teya out.

"That's some excellent work you've done, Teya." Martin took the lantern and Oiler. "The Masker family owes you a debt."

She shook her head. "First, wait until done. Then thank. Second, no thank. Friends. We help friends."

Hours ticked by while Vivian watched her home be ravaged. The inspector and assayer went through every crate and cleared every shelf. They went so far as to open antique pots and pans in case something was hidden inside. She'd expected greater scrutiny on the individual items. There was still an assortment of carefully selected contraptions among the antiques that made up the bulk of the replacement inventory. Were Cartwright steadfastly dedicated to simply ruining the Maskers, as had seemed to be the case across the course of the week, she would have expected him to nitpick each one, trying to convince the assayers that they violated some rule or another about contraptions. He didn't. It became increasingly clear that he was searching for something. Something quite specific. Something he'd fully expected to find. Based upon his first attempt at devising an excuse to enter their home, she'd expected that thing to be Teya, but her absence didn't come up even once during the search.

Every room, from the workshop to their bedrooms, was picked apart. With each passing minute, Cartwright seemed to grow more frustrated and irate. Finally he and the others emerged on the top floor, where Fel and Tome were waiting.

"Any luck, Inspector?" Fel asked.

"You... I don't know how you did it, but I know something was hidden from me," Cartwright insisted.

"Maybe if you told us what you thought we were hiding, we could help you," Fel said.

"Don't patronize me," he snapped. "There is a palpable sense of wrongdoing and deception in this place."

"Inspector," muttered one of the assayers. "I have been an assayer for seven years. I have appraised the inventory of every shop or traveling merchant that has ever touched a contraption. This is, by a wide margin, the most thorough inspection I have ever been a part of. We have interrupted business for this shop for days. Kept them under constant observation. We have seen things that are unusual but nothing that is illegal or unacceptable."

"Then they've hidden it elsewhere," Cartwright said.

"Hidden what?" Fel said.

"You and I both know there's something," he said. "And I am not leaving this city until I've found it."

"With all due respect, Inspector, that is not so," Epiphany said.

"You do not have the authority to grant or deny me permission to do anything," he said.

"Quite so. I do not. But Lord Katritz does. And as I've had little opportunity to do much business over the course of today, I have had ample time to read the proclamation you provided in great detail. I suppose you have not, or you wouldn't be making further plans within the city for at least a few days."

She held up the proclamation. "This proclamation hereby provides Inspector Cartwright the authority to search the home and shop of the Masker family. Upon completion of the investigation, Inspector Cartwright shall personally deliver his findings to representatives of the nobles and the throne in Teskal." She set down the page. "You have an appointment with your superiors, Inspector Cartwright. If you like, I can provide you with a manifest of everything in our inventory to include with your report. Hopefully they have a great interest in antiquities."

If looks could kill, half of Beffshire would have keeled over from the glare he fixed on Epiphany. Without another word, he turned and marched for the door. Fel stepped back to allow him to leave.

"Pleasure working with you, Inspector," Fel said.

Cartwright stomped into the street.

"Thieving rat?" croaked a voice from the roof.

The inspector roared in frustration and dashed down the street. The assayers turned to Vivian.

"Ma'am, our apologies. We'll be seeing you again in a few months. I believe you have earned a reprieve, and lovely as this city is, I have had my fill of Beffshire."

They took their leave. The door shut, jangling its bell as a glorious bow on the top of the entire package.

"Is that it?" Epiphany said quietly. "Is it over?"

"We have to send Oiler into Reynard's basement and fix up the walls," Fel said.

"We have a great deal of new antique stock to sell, and then we need to settle accounts and reclaim our goods from Verfessa," Vivian said.

"We still need to find out who was sending messages to Cartwright, how, and why," Tome said.

"And I suppose I'd rest better if I understood how the proclamation arrived so quickly," Epiphany said.

"Oh! And the Watch is probably going to have some words for me," Fel said. "At the very least for not keeping close enough tabs on Teya. Maybe for stealing a horse, too, but I don't think anyone saw that. Still. All things considered? Job well done."

A pig dashed by on the street outside, followed by a breathless man with a net. Epiphany cleared her throat.

"Job done. We'll leave it at that," she said.

"I don't know about the rest of you, but now that the old plan is done, I'm making a new plan. First, I wait until I know for sure Cartwright is gone. Then, I go downstairs and fetch Teya. Then I go find some way for both of us to get extremely drunk in celebration."

Tome raised a hand. "If you are looking for a team to execute that caper, I offer my services."

CHAPTER 10

It became clear within moments of taking her outside the shop that Beffshire would need a little more time to become comfortable with the idea of a kobold walking the streets. A unicorn, lesser harpies, the occasional half-giant or gnome? These were all acceptable. But something nearly the size of a human but entirely inhuman in appearance was the line that most people were unwilling to cross. Fel, undaunted, had developed a new plan. Namely, he'd made a brief appearance at The Fox and Log, acquired a cask of ale and two bottles of whiskey, and made his way down into the basement of Reynard's shop. The walls there still needed to be fully repaired, so he, Tome, Parch, Oiler, and Teya chose that as their venue. While Oiler happily went about polishing up the opposite side of the hole they'd just closed and patched up the hole leading to the well, the others drank and enjoyed their celebratory inebriation.

"This drink? What is?" Teya said.

"Whiskey," Fel said. "Local stuff."

She nodded. "Is good. For being drunk. Is good."

"Just about the only thing it's good for." Fel raised his cup. "Listen, I've got enough of this in me now that I can talk earnestly, but not so much that I can't talk without drooling all over myself. So now's the time to say this. What we just did? It saved my family. Saved 'em from things we brought on ourselves, more or less, but still. Couldn't have done it without you. Parch? Did some good work. Oiler, key to the whole thing. Tome? You wrangled Oiler."

"I also provided healing spells and nearly got killed revealing that we were under assault by an elf. And investigated the source of the messages Cartwright was getting."

"Yeah, but... mostly the useful part was watching Oiler."

"I find your gratitude lacking, Fel," Tome said.

"I paid for the booze, didn't I? And quit interrupting. I'm not done. Didn't even get to Teya yet. A toast to you. My favorite denizen of the Greater Lands. I don't know how this could have happened without you."

"Couldn't!" She tapped her ear. "Destiny."

"You think this is what it was all about? The forces of fate hauled you out here to help bail out your old buddy Fel?"

She shook her head. "No. Maybe part? But not enough. Not big enough. More to do."

"So are you going to move on?" Tome asked.

She shook her head again. "Until destiny done? Beffshire, home."

"We'll have to work on getting folks to let you walk the streets then. All this sneaking and peeking is unbecoming of an agent of destiny."

"Sneak? Fun. Very very. Run crazy on Parch? More very very."

"You have a way with words, Teya," Tome said.

Fel swirled his cup. "We need to do more toasts. My cup's not empty. Um... Here's to Inspector Cartwright, for trying so hard to catch us doing something and, as we speak, is on the road back home to have a noble tan his hide for wasting so much time and money on us."

They drank.

"And... who else... To Allie! Who put up with me and these two sleeping in her house. It's a crime that we can't be having this celebration at The Fox and Log, but I'll find a way to thank her." He drained his cup. "There. Must be done thanking people now. I'm empty."

The flickering lantern became still.

"Fel," Wick said.

"Wick!" he said. "Pass that bottle. Fill me up. We have to toast him! Our eyes, our ears, our messenger..."

"Fel, there is someone in the shop, sent by Verfessa," Wick said.

"Verfessa! We need to drink to him, too. There aren't two people in this entire city who could have done what he did for us."

"I think you should let Wick speak, Fel," Tome advised.

"Right, right. What is the news, Wick?"

"One of their warehouses has been burglarized. Two of his men are injured, one is dead."

"That's awful. Dangerous business he's in," Fel said.

"The wagon containing the final set of contraptions you removed today is missing."

Fel set down his glass and stood. "Tome, see to Oiler and Teya. My family needs me."

He hurried up the steps with Parch in tow, suddenly wishing he hadn't dumped enough spirits into his body to foul his steps. Thaddeus was at the counter of Reynard's shop.

"Through with your celebration already?" he said.

"Someone's nabbed the last wagon of goods," Fel said.

"No..." Thaddeus said, jumping to his feet.

The pair of them dashed outside and rushed through the door of the antiquities shop. A shaken young man was still recounting the events to Vivian and Epiphany.

"... slashed his neck from ear to ear, the man said. He was gone before we even got to him. I don't know what it was. It was too fast. Some kind of animal. Wings. Claws," he said. "The other two look like they'll make it."

"That's terrible," Vivian said.

"There was a man too. Couldn't get a good look at him. Had a mask on. Armed with weapons like I've never seen before. Had some sort of knife with him that cut clean through the chain we'd locked the storage house with. Handled a horse better than anyone I've seen, too."

"Please tell Mr. Verfessa if there is anything we can do to help the poor men..." Vivian began.

"No. No. Not why I'm here," he said. "Mr. Verfessa sent me to apologize for his inability to keep your gear safe. Says it's a point of personal pride, and this is a slap in his face. He wanted to assure you he's got people hunting down the man who did it," the man said. "I have to get back now. He's raving right now. Who knows what he's got for me to do next."

The man left. Fel was barely able to hold his tongue until the door shut behind him.

"It was the elf. The one Tome clashed with. The one that almost got me when I was setting up the drop point," Fel said.

"No doubt. This is terrible. Lives lost for some contraptions..." Vivian said.

Tome entered, Oiler over his shoulder, carefully tucked into its pack. Teya scampered in after him, adorably bundled in her "disguise" and with her head down in an attempt to avoid drawing too much attention in her brief appearance outdoors. Tome handed the pack to Fel, who hurried behind the counter to set it down. Teya trotted over to stay out of sight alongside it and pulled the hood back.

"Tome, it was the elf," Fel said. "Took out one of Verfessa's men and took the cart. He talked to you, right? What was he after?"

"The elf? He came into the city?" Tome said.

"What was he after!?" Fel demanded.

"We've been through this, Fel," Tome said.

"I've been drinking!" Fel said, as though it was Tome's problem for not remembering that fact rather than his own fault for not remembering any other facts.

"He's just continuing what he started in the Greater Lands when they got their hands on Wick. He wants to find a way for him and his kind to leave the Greater Lands. Wick's lantern was his focus, but the mask had some sort of effect on his mind that might have twisted his intentions."

"If a lantern is what he's after, then he's done his job," Epiphany said, flipping open a small ledger. "One of the two persistent lanterns, unlit, was in the wagon. Along with the Student mask, the bust Dad was working on, and volumes of Bygone texts."

"Wick, if he's got one of your lanterns, do you know where he is? Where he's going?" Fel asked.

"I don't. I could tell you that precisely if the lantern was lit, but without it, I have only the faintest sense," Wick said.

"How faint?" Fel asked.

"I can tell you that it is moving. That is all."

"That way," Teya said.

All eyes turned to her.

"You're sure?" Fel said.

"How do you know?" Epiphany asked.

She tapped the earring with her claw. "Destiny. Feel the pull. That way."

"The lantern in the cart must have been the one that was used to make the earring. The two still have a weak link," Tome said. "What astounding luck."

"Not luck. Destiny," Teya said with the deepest sincerity.

"How much can you tell?" Tome asked.

She pointed again. "That way," she said, as though there was nothing more anyone could ever need to know.

"Fel, I cannot stress enough how dangerous this is. I don't think he knows enough magic himself to do it, but if he gets that lantern back to his people, they could use it to send out more like him, sharp and clearheaded as Teya is, to serve whatever terrible end they seek. And in the process, Wick will be destroyed."

"Killed," Fel said. "The word is 'killed.' And if there's any good news, it's that we know he isn't bringing Wick's lantern back just yet."

"How do you know that?"

Teya pointed yet again. "That way."

"He's headed northwest," Fel said. "The Greater Lands Wall is southeast. He's going precisely in the wrong direction. Are you sure about his plans?"

"I'm sure about the plans of the elves in general. And by extension, I'm sure of the orders he was given," Tome said. "But if you'd seen how he was acting, I don't know that anything firm can be said about what his plans are now. He's of two minds. I think literally."

"It doesn't matter. I have to get out there," Fel said.

"Fel, you are half-drunk, and you barely got any sleep last night," Tome said.

"Then when we catch that elf, we'll tell him what terribly inconvenient timing he has," Fel said.

"He nearly killed both of us already. What good will it do to chase him?"

"What good will it do to let him get away? By the High, Tome, there are probably a dozen things in that wagon that we can't afford to have fall into the wrong hands!"

"We go!" Teya said. "Together, strong. Together, we fight, we win. That elf? Many scars. From me. His blood? I know the taste."

"That's what I want to hear," Fel said. "We need horses, we need camping gear, and we need weapons."

"The weapons and the better combat contraptions are all packed away by Verfessa's crew," Vivian said.

"Then Verfessa's our first stop." Fel turned to Teya. "Wait here. I'm going to get our things, and then we're going to find that elf so you can get another mouthful of his neck."

A few minutes later, Fel marched through the streets. The thin haze of alcohol parted every few moments to assert this concern or that. If he'd had a few more toasts, the wet blanket thrown over his logic would have been enough to silence such thoughts. If he'd had a few less drinks, he would have been clearheaded enough to make intelligent decisions based on them. As it was, intelligence and reason came like flashes of lightning in a downpour. He shouldn't have been heading to Verfessa's home in broad daylight. He should have been taking time to plan what could be done against the very real threat the elf posed. These thoughts passed through his mind ever so briefly before he rattled the gate outside the Verfessa estate.

The pair of guards, two of a seemingly endless sequence of interchangeable sunken-eyed heavies, had their weapons drawn before Fel's hand even touched the ornate iron of the gate. A crossbow bolt clicked into position. A short but cruel club slipped from its strap.

"I need to talk to your boss, fellas," Fel said. "Business needs doing."

"You're Fel Masker, right?" said one of the men.

"Right now, what I am is angry and ready to do something about it. That's what you should be worried about," Fel said.

"As a rule, we don't let in folks who are angry and ready to do something about it," said the other guard.

"I'm not asking to come in. I'm telling you I have business with your boss."

"Boss does business elsewhere at this time of day," said the other guard.

There was something off about his tone and delivery. Fel wasn't equipped to interpret it.

"Listen. I don't have time to be playing games. He's holding some—"

"You might want to talk to him in private. His private room," said the other guard, quickly enough to keep Fel from announcing something sensitive in public.

"What'd I just say about playing games? I've had exactly the wrong amount of booze, and I need instructions."

"If you're the wrong amount of drunk, maybe you should go to the tavern," a guard said slowly.

"If you're giving me a hint, I need a better one."

The man with the club reached through the fence and pulled Fel against the bars with a handful of shirt. "Go to The Fox and Log, you thick sot," he grumbled under his breath.

Fel pulled himself free of the grip and brushed his shirt off. "Was that so hard?"

He turned and trotted down the road. A few minutes of walking farther did little to clear his mind, but that time did give him a better view of the toll their caper had taken on the city. Two pigs and a cow wandered through the street along the way. Relatively few people were out and about, and those who were had the anxious look of someone who knew something terrible was happening and didn't know if it was over yet. In the space of a single day a kobold had raced through town on a unicorn's back, a passel of hogs had flooded the city, and a bloody attack had sent a stolen wagon charging through the north gate. All were things that Fel had learned to live with. A sane person living a normal life had every reason to be shaken. Another handy effect of his present level of inebriation was that he couldn't quite bring himself to care.

He stepped through the front door of The Fox and Log.

"Fel!" Allie said. "Two visits in one day. To what do I owe the—"

"Where is he, Allie?" he demanded.

Her face became swiftly more serious. "What's happened?"

"You'll hear it when it's over, I assure you. Where is he?"

Her eyes flicked to one of the back rooms. "Don't know who you're talking about."

"You're better at hints than most, Allie," he said, marching to the back room.

He threw the door open and stepped inside, slamming it behind him. Verfessa was waiting for him, seated across from the door at a small table. Two glasses and a bottle had been set up. The expression on the man's face was enough to slice through even Fel's addled perception.

Of the members of his family, Fel had among the least face-to-face time with Verfessa. Only his father had done less dealing with the man. But in the exchanges they'd had, Fel had never known him to be anything less than a composed and downright jolly individual. When he needed to be taken more seriously, he was able to drizzle in the intimidation with a chef's precision, but for the most part he looked like the sort of man who would pour you a drink, slap you on the back, and tell you a joke.

Right now, that was not the case.

It wasn't correct to say that Verfessa was angry. It wasn't as simple as that. There was an intensity to him, drenching everything from his posture to the gleam in his eye with a gravity that made him seem somehow more real than anything else around him. Like life itself was populated by a bunch of children playing pretend and he was the only adult.

"I'm surprised you weren't here sooner," he said. "Sit. There's dealings to be done."

"We're not dealing, Verfessa. You have some of my things, I need them, and then I'm going to get the head of the one responsible for this mess."

"I am the one responsible for this mess, Fel. I take my job very seriously. I didn't go into business with your family until I knew exactly who your family was and what your business was. I knew the risks, I knew the challenges, and I made my decision. When you almost got the knife from someone wearing a contraption that passed through my hands? I don't have to feel good about it, but I don't feel responsible either. My role in that transaction was done. But this? A deal was struck between my organization and yours. Prices were set. Obligations were assigned. And it was one of my jobs to keep your inventory safe. I failed, and it cost me one of my men. This is another failing on my part. And that cannot be allowed to stand. My man is dead. That can't be undone, but he knew the risks. I can get a few pints of blood to show his family just exactly what his work meant to me, though, and I can wedge a head on a pike to show others who would attempt the same that Verfessa is not a man to trifle with. Now, what do we know about the man responsible?"

"An elf. He has two lesser sphinxes he commands. He's straight from the Greater Lands. He was after something in one of the crates in that wagon. He might be unhinged. I don't know. That's my friend Tome's claim. I don't know where he's going, but I have a way to find him."

Verfessa didn't so much as blink at the bizarre nature of the situation. "Do we need to worry about magic?"

"I don't think so."

"And there's just the one man?"

"Elf. Yes."

"Shame. I usually like to leave one alive to bring the message home about what happens to my enemies. Can't be helped. What do you need?"

"Fast horses, some of my more vicious gear."

"How many horses?"

"Two... or three? I don't know. I'm bringing a kobold along. I think she'll probably ride with one of us. Make it two."

"I'm making it three, because I'm sending someone along."

"Not a great idea. I have a hard enough time working with Tome."

"We've been through this before, Fel. My man won't be with you. He'll be far enough back to get you out of a jam without getting caught in the jam with you. And he'll be there to draw the knife across a throat if you have the poor sense to grow a conscience before you can do the deed."

"I'm still not—"

"This isn't a negotiation, Fel. Give me a list of the gear you need. If it exists in Beffshire, it'll be on a set of horses at the north gate in ten minutes."

Fel attempted to gather enough wits to assemble an argument against Verfessa sending his blade along, but he simply lacked the mental faculties to do so. It was easier to shrug and shift his limited resources to assembling a wish list for things he intended to bring to bear on the elf.

Epiphany had been flipping through the journal with the list of stolen inventory since Fel had left, as though somehow if she turned the pages enough times, the missing crates would come falling out and this whole madness would be over. Vivian, in what was either a gift or a curse, had been able to keep any hint of desperation, fear, or confusion from her expression as the first trickle of customers in days started to come in. She worried that her mother's capacity to bottle things up like this would carry a price one day, but for the moment, it at least meant that this one element of her life had returned to normal.

If she'd been someone else, she might have been able to latch on to that tiny fragment of calm and set her mind at ease. But she had all of the emotional intensity of her brother and none of his compulsion to dull its edge with alcohol. Her thoughts were razor sharp as they twirled and squirmed in her head, and the result was bringing her sanity to the brink of a death of a thousand cuts.

She snapped the book shut and marched to the door. "I'm consulting our next door neighbor on a few things, Mom. Call if you need me."

She slipped out the door and slipped into Reynard's shop. Thaddeus was at the counter, but there wasn't much reason for him to be. The shop had been all but picked clean. Thaddeus had gone so far as to find buyers for not just the shoes but also some of the raw materials. Reynard would have his hands full making new shoes when he got back, but given the amount of money made in his absence he wasn't likely to complain about the extra work.

"Thaddeus, there are some matters that we need to discuss," Epiphany said.

"Of course," he said.

"I've spoken to Tome, and I believe he's spoken to you, but there are some things that I can't get my mind to set aside. The man Tome was investigating, the one with the pipes."

"Yes?"

"We've been too busy, and it's been too dangerous, to look into him again. But what Tome described—a stack of prepared messages and those pipes—you'd said that the Graves family had taken extra precautions for security. That the final stage of any communication was a hand-delivered message."

"I do not like the direction this conversation is headed."

"Nor do I, but it can't be ignored. What he described has the look of something the Graves family might have organized. You've shown yourselves to be quite capable of subterfuge, and you were seeking the Warrior mask."

"I resent the implication that we are behind any of this. I have had to disrupt my schedule rather significantly to help you solve your current problem. Since the Bolivan issue, the Graves family has been nothing but cooperative and up-front with the Masker family."

"According to Teya, the wagon was headed northwest. The Graves family's territory is northeast. If it veers in that direction…"

"Then it would continue to be a coincidence," he said firmly. "The attacker was an elf. From the Greater Lands. That is your assertion, is it not? Would you suggest that the Graves family has influence that extends that far?"

She rubbed her head and shut her eyes. "Right, yes. The wagon wouldn't be headed in your direction… I mustn't let myself confuse two potential plots. But Cartwright was certainly taking messages from someone outside the city. We need to ready a party to send out after the elf, but soon we'll have the opportunity to investigate where those messages were coming from. And we mean to do so. If you have any insight, I think you can understand how it would be better that you provide it rather than requiring us to dig it up."

"I have been entirely forthcoming, and it is your distrust which is imperiling this newfound partnership between the Maskers and the Graves," he rumbled.

"We shall see. I hope to be coming to you with an apology tomorrow when I get to the bottom of this. But I will be getting to the bottom of it."

Allie couldn't keep herself from glancing at the room she knew to hold both Fel and Verfessa. She would have been concerned for Fel even if she hadn't been aware of the madness he and his family were up to. She'd rarely seen Fel with that look in his eye. But knowing the events of the last few days, let alone the last few hours, and knowing his reaction to all of them, she shuddered to think about what would have sent him through The Fox and Log looking and behaving as he had.

The door opened. He emerged. His expression was different. Still severe, but sharpened in a way that made her fear for the safety of whoever had brought such a look to his face. He was still tied up in a knot of tension, but now there was a dash of certainty. He nearly walked past Allie without acknowledging her but paused just before reaching the door. He stopped and scanned the tavern until he spotted her and marched up.

"The job's not quite done. Might be gone for a few days. I left a few things behind. I'll be back to collect them."

"Good luck. And give whoever you're after an extra kick for me," she said.

"If you say so, but there's no sense kicking a dead man."

He lingered, eyes locked on hers for a moment longer, then turned and marched out the door. Allie, as she'd had to do far more frequently than she would have liked these past few days, let her body work through the mechanical process of being a barmaid while she reckoned with the exchange. Presently there was a bedroll and a few assorted tools left in her home. Those were the things he'd left behind. But she very much doubted he'd stopped to tell her of his plan to retrieve them out of fear she'd be cross with him for leaving her home cluttered. He was telling her because he wanted her to know he'd be back. Which meant there was reason to fear that he wouldn't be.

"He's got a lot to learn about setting a woman's mind at ease," she muttered to herself.

A few minutes later, Fel had returned home and was gulping down a meal at the table. The house was still a terrible mess after being torn to bits by Cartwright, but already that fiasco felt like it had happened ages go. Tome was at the table as well. He madly scribbled at a piece of paper.

"I've come to accept that living under this roof and hitching my fortune to yours means I will be periodically called upon to go on an ill-advised adventure, but I do wish fate would do me the favor of making its intentions known with a bit more notice. My magic requires a degree of preparation, and I seem to be perpetually racing the clock to get something approaching a proper spread of spells written."

"Yeah. How dare disaster not schedule itself," Fel said.

"Just a day or two, that's all I need. My speed at writing spells has more than doubled since I started working beside you. I can write in the space of an afternoon what would have taken me a week of research and a day of writing. But I still need the afternoon, and I seldom get even that."

"At least you end up with some spells. Regardless of how much time I have to prepare, I'm still left with the same pile of contraptions, and I always end up resorting to the club."

Teya marched up the steps with her gear and dropped it down. It consisted of her lopsided bow, her fishing pole, and a small pack to strap them to.

"Man who give horse. Has arrows?" Teya said.

"I didn't ask," he said.

"Maybe need arrows. Have not many." She pointed at the food on the table. "I eat?"

"Fill up. We need to cover as much ground as possible. How's the tug of destiny?" Fel asked.

She shut her eyes, then pointed in much the same direction as before.

"So he's moving slow, or straight in that direction," Fel said.

She climbed onto the table and ladled a bowlful of stew.

Fel gulped down the last of what was in his bowl and wiped his mouth. Two trips across down, some tense negotiation, and a full belly had pushed him a few steps closer to sobriety, and with that sobriety came a clarity that wasn't altogether welcome. He looked at Tome jotting down a spell that in all likelihood would be the difference between life and death. He looked to Teya, who was gleefully willing to throw herself into the flames of battle in service of some ill-defined destiny, yet in his heart he knew she'd have done the same even if he'd simply asked her to.

He shut his eyes.

"In a few minutes, we are going to head out and chase down someone who has been terrorizing the region in general and us specifically. A threat no one else has even been able to put a name to. He must have cut a bloody line across the countryside between here and the Greater Lands, searching for Wick, following the same sort of magical lure we still don't understand. With any luck, our own magical lure will bring us straight to him. I don't know if there's anyone I'd expect to face a threat like that by my side. But I can't imagine anyone better than the pair of you."

"You need a better imagination, Fel," Tome said.

"No. Is good. Family, friend, destiny. We go. We win. Who else could do? No one. Who else do we need? No one." She tipped her head. "No! One more. Also Parch. For ride. And play head bump."

"I don't know if you should be riding Parch. We're going to need to move fast," Tome said.

"Parch fast!" Teya said.

"Not when he pulls a wagon," Tome said.

"No wagon. Just Teya. So fast!" Teya said.

"We won't be able to keep him away," Fel said.

A jangling sound drew his attention to the stairs. Oiler was dragging itself up. It plopped down beside Fel.

"Speaking of things that'll follow no matter what," he said.

"You're not honestly thinking of taking Oiler, are you?" Tome asked.

"It's practically a lucky charm. Oiler's saved my life at least as often as you have. And only about as many times as it's nearly killed us."

"There are quite enough things on this trip likely to kill us, we don't need one that might do it accidentally."

"We're not going to a mysterious world of magic and ancient traps. We're heading northwest. We're more likely to run into someone selling apples by the roadside than a trap for it to accidentally fix."

"And if it decides to disarm us at the precise moment we are about to defeat our enemy?"

"There's three of us. And if we're lucky, it'll pick the elf to disarm," Fel said.

"Luck is for grum. And ideally not even for that. I don't like the idea of relying upon it to control the behavior of a supposed ally," Tome said.

Fel stood and rolled his neck, producing a worrying sequence of crackles. "Well you'd better get used to the idea, because by my reckoning, Verfessa's had time enough to get our gear ready. So it's time to go, and we're taking the entire team."

Tome sighed and finished the last few lines of his spell. Fel pulled Oiler to his back.

"Stay hidden until we're on the road," Fel instructed.

"When has it listened to instruction like that?" Tome asked.

"Today could be the first time. You never know," Fel said.

Fel lit a pipe from Wick's lantern, and the group climbed the steps to the shop. He had anticipated having a brief and potentially contentious exchange with his mother and father about where he was going and what he was planning. Instead, he encountered something far worse. Leonard, in a rare appearance outside the watchhouse or post at the gate, stood in the center of the shop, addressing both parents. He stopped in the middle of a sentence that seemed dedicated to demanding Fel reveal himself to address Fel directly.

"The captain wants a word with you, Fel," he said.

"I'm a little busy, Leonard." he said, attempting to march past.

Leonard stopped him with a hand to the chest. "It's about that thing," he said, pointing to Teya, who was eagerly bouncing in place in the stairwell. "It's been showing its face outside this shop entirely too often. The city has enough to worry about without you losing track of your pets."

"What're we most worried about right now?" Fel said. "Is it the pigs running around? Is it the murderer who stole a wagon and took off to the north? Or is it Teya and her terrible crime of 'leaving the city quickly.'"

"She's what most people would call a monster," he said.

Fel gritted his teeth. "Let me tell you something. What I should do is give a long, eloquent speech about how Teya's kinder and nicer and more dedicated than half the people in this city. But I don't have the patience. I'm not a man of words. I've got a couple of shots of whiskey in me, so I'm a little surprised I was able to even say the word 'eloquent.' So instead I'll take the easy way out. I'm leaving the city, and I'm taking her with me. If we come back, it'll be after dealing with the murderer. So you can stand in my way and make sure Teya stays here, or you can step aside and get this whole group of troublemakers out of your hair."

Leonard blinked. The conversational gambits available to the City Watch were fairly limited, and Fel's response didn't properly align with any of them. Faced with the task of improvising something appropriate or simply letting the problem solve itself, the watchman took the predictable option and stepped aside.

Fel turned to Vivian and Martin. "I'll be back when the job is done. Let me know if anything comes up."

"Be safe," Vivian said. "All of you."

"Make the family proud, and make sure none of our contraptions do any harm," Martin said.

"If there's time between finding this elf and making him pay for what he's done, I'll give it a try."

"I keep him safe!" Teya said with ironclad confidence.

"And in the off-chance Teya comes up short, I'll lend a hand as well," Tome said.

Fel gave his mother a kiss. "See you when it's over."

They filed out, Teya bringing up the rear. She turned on the way out and pointed at Leonard.

"This one? Comes back. And then? You treat me right." She turned and tromped off, thumping her chest. "This one? Nice. Good. Not thing."

Thaddeus puffed on his pipe and paced toward the so-called Skinflint Camp. He was confident in the assertions he'd made to Epiphany in the face of her accusation, but he was far less confident that she would take his word. The Maskers were thorough, but the Graves clan was more thorough. If he was going to be under suspicion of wrongdoing, he would make it a point to either know the truth or find enough evidence to clear himself and his family of suspicion. Now that the killer who had been lurking about was gone, he could safely do his own investigation.

There were now just two tents in the campsite. One was occupied. The other was in the process of being packed up to depart. It would be something of a mixed blessing if the person Tome had identified had already moved on. It would mean Epiphany's investigation would reach a dead end, but it would rob Thaddeus of any ability to put her suspicions to rest with further evidence.

"I say there, sir!" Thaddeus called. "May I have a word?"

The man paused, then looked over his shoulder. Thaddeus froze. This man was familiar. His name was Trenton, and he was one of a small handful of trusted messengers in the clan. Technically a member of the family, but dangling off the end of a forgotten branch of the family tree. He was more of an employee than an in-law.

"Oy! Is that Thad, is it?" the man called back with a smile. "What sends you out this way? Shouldn't you be down south by now? Farther than this, I mean?"

"There was a minor adjustment to the schedule. Jonathan's in-laws needed a hand. Must always keep diplomacy in mind."

"Not so for me. I'd invite you in for a drink, but I already packed up the booze," Trenton said.

"I haven't got the time for it regardless. But I must admit to sharing your curiosity, albeit reversed."

"Huh?" Trenton said.

"What are you doing here?"

"What am I doing anywhere? What I'm told. Frustrating job this time. Beffshire's a damn fine city to visit, but they had me camping out here while a lunatic was on the loose. 'Stay outside the city,' they said. 'Only go in to drop off the messages,' they said. I had to bend the rules to grab a meal now and then."

"Did you have a great deal of messages to send?"

"Stacks. They had me doing that 'which-way' thing, too. Send this one if this one comes to you. Send that one if that one comes to you. It's a terrible mess to keep track of it all."

"To whom?" Thaddeus asked.

"You know better than to ask me that. It's not that you're not allowed to know, it's that I'm not allowed to tell you unless they told me to, or I got permission to, and the pipe's out, so there's nothing to do but head back north."

"My pipe is still lit. Ought I ask for permission?" Thad asked.

"If you're going to do that, may as well ask them who it was I was sending messages to, because I sure don't know. Just dropping them to a local messenger for pickup."

"And I imagine it was the standard. The message was in code?"

"Received in code, yes. But to be delivered in plain language. And there were hundreds of them, with all sorts of instructions for when to deliver them. I'll be damned if I could remember what half of them said, much less which ones ended up getting delivered. And I wouldn't be able to tell you that either. Without permission. Rules is rules."

"And, rules being rules, that pile of ashes I spy would be the unsent messages?"

"That's right. Damn near broke my heart, spending all that time writing them out only to burn nine out of every ten."

"Here, let me help you," Thaddeus said as Trenton fought to bundle up a bit of tent.

"Thanks. You always were one of the more 'regular folk' members of the clan. Guess they wouldn't have you out on the road otherwise. All the high-and-mighty ones delivering the orders stay put up north. Sort of my rule of thumb, you know. The further north you go, the further they stick up their nose when they see you."

"Every family has its hierarchy." Thaddeus held a knot so he could tie it off. "Oh, while we're on the subject, do you have your codebook handy? I smudged up one of my pages terribly, and I haven't quite been able to fill it back in. You know how they feel about sending codes via the flame these days."

"Sure, sure. I always keep mine handy."

Trenton removed a small leather book held shut with a strap. Thaddeus took it and tugged at the strap.

"Terrible waste of resources, wouldn't you say?" he asked.

"Probably. Depends on what you're talking about."

"We've placed so many limits on flames for the sake of security. As far as I know, there are three traveling merchants, of which I am one, and five traveling messengers, of which you are one. Putting two of us in the same city—I could easily have delivered your messages and freed you up to go elsewhere," Thaddeus said.

He let the book fall open in his hand. He knew these books quite well. Sturdy and rugged, and a wonderfully handy side effect of being built so sturdily was the tendency of the thick binding to "remember" the page that was last open. It took days of being shut tight to retrain the binding. Thus, he knew that the page it fell open to was the one Trenton had been referencing to decode the messages that he then delivered in plain language. It was a very old block of codes. Ones that simply weren't in regular use anymore. He flipped to a random page and noted the codes he was supposedly refreshing himself on.

"Of course. So simple, I don't know how I'd forgotten. Thank you," Thaddeus said. "Forgive the speculation, but something tells me the reason you weren't to spend any time in town was specifically to avoid meeting me. More to the point, I suspect you weren't even intended to know I was here, and vice versa."

"Could be. They don't line my pockets enough for me to be wasting my time working out what games they play."

"All the same, best if you not mention we met. I'll do the same. If they want us in the dark, I'll oblige and keep my eyes closed."

"Same. Good not seeing you, Thad. Hopefully next time we cross paths, it'll be in a place with some good meat and better drink," Trenton said.

"One can only hope," Thaddeus said.

He turned and marched back toward the city. So many aspects of the day-to-day business of the Graves family depended upon even the highest-level members of the family being ignorant of the tasks assigned to others. Sometimes business could be done more comfortably with plausible deniability, and keeping key information from a negotiator could easily turn something from a lie to something one had every reason to believe was true. He didn't know if it was the best way to run a business, or the best way to run a family, but it had served the Graves for generations. Thaddeus was under no delusion that he was high enough in the family's hierarchy to be permitted to know the whole truth. But for the first time in memory, he found himself hoping their manipulations and machinations hadn't made a liar out of him.

CHAPTER 11

Fel sat on the ground, eyes fixed on a campfire. They'd traveled as far and as fast as they could, but night had fallen and the horses needed to rest. Fel needed rest as well, but even with exhaustion and the waning end of inebriation tugging at his brain, he couldn't bring himself to lie down. His mind was a tangled mess. Oiler sat pleasantly beside him. No puzzle box had been brought to occupy the contraption. Such distraction seemed less necessary when Fel was around. It simply tucked into its pack, serpentine head poking out from beneath the flap, and softly ticked and chimed with its internal workings.

"I believe that will do for tonight," Tome said, snapping a book shut.

The mage, a good deal better rested and less soused at the start of things, had put their camping to good use. Half the time had been dedicated to filling out their complement of written spells. The rest had been dedicated to some sort of research or another. He'd spoken about it at length as he was doing it, but Fel had become quite skilled at ignoring the endless drone coming out of Tome's mouth.

"Any luck?" Fel asked, more out of reflex than interest.

"Nothing more useful than we'd already discussed," Tome said. "Unless you've come up with any riddles while I was working."

"Riddles?" Fel said dully.

Tome glared at him. "I asked you to try to think up riddles centered on no fewer than six potential answers."

"Did you?"

"For the sphinxes, remember? Egad, Fel. Sometimes I wonder why I speak to you at all."

"I always wonder that," Fel said.

"It's the means of commanding them. They respond to commands associated with the answers to ancient riddles. Something like rhyming slang, where the command is a step removed. The example given in the reference 'What is broken the moment you say its name?' A classic riddle."

"A window?" Fel said.

"Windows don't break when you say 'window.'"

"They do if you say it loud enough."

Tome shut his eyes in frustration. "The answer is 'silence.' In the example, you might use the phrase 'broken by its name' to command a lesser sphinx to be silent."

"How does an animal end up with that sort of quirk?"

"Why does a dragon collect gold? Why do kobolds instinctively work together and seek powerful figures to serve? The world works in mysterious ways, and the mystic world doubly so. The point is, it gives us a means to make the sphinxes a non-factor. We just have to find an appropriate riddle to shout, in their language."

"Can't we just listen to what the elf yells and yell it too?"

"If the old text is to be believed, they associate a riddle with the one who taught them said riddle."

"So don't we just have to come up with a riddle that means what we want them to do?"

"That's what you were supposed to be thinking about!" Tome said.

"Oh. Well, I didn't."

"It's just as well. I doubt anything that would come tumbling out of your head in this state will do anyone any good. Do try to sleep. You're even more like a slab of quarry stone when you're tired."

"I will. Eventually. I hope."

Tome pulled a blanket over him and settled down on his bedroll. Verfessa had supplied a tent, but after the long ride, none of them had the motivation to erect it, and the weather was obliging enough for a night beneath the stars. Tome had already drifted off to sleep by the time the surrounding brush rustled and Teya emerged with two rabbits. More accurately, one and a half rabbits, as she was crunching pleasantly away at one in a manner that found the perfect midpoint between gruesome and adorable.

"I hunt! Good hunt!" Teya said. "We cook?"

"Sure. Let's roast them up," Fel said, producing a knife to start preparing the meat.

Teya waved it off and started the job with her claws instead. Fel broke two green sticks, one to prop over the fire and the other to drive into the ground to support it. Oiler took interest and briefly attempted to reassemble the broken stick, but once both sticks had been called into service as tools, Oiler seemed satisfied they were in fact fully functional.

"Hunting here? So much good! Many things to eat. Bad at hiding. Good eating!"

"Yeah. I learned to hunt in these fields."

"Hunting here? Easy lesson."

She handed him the skinned rabbit. He set it to roast.

"Teya, I gotta say, I envy you," Fel said.

"You should. This one? Very good," she said with a grin.

"You're far from home, helping me on a dangerous mission, and you're all smiles."

"Doing good things. Busy. Helpful. Is good."

"Don't you miss your home?"

"Yes! Miss small fish. Crunchy, good. Miss other kobolds. Work together easier. Here? Us? Work together good. Almost like kobold. But not kobold. With kobold? Not even think. Just work. Know what to do. Do it. But here? Important work. Good work."

"Important. Forgive me, but how do you know that all this is important? What if it's just nonsense? Family squabbles and bad luck?"

"Because I say. Feel important? Important! Clear to me. And so, important."

"It's important because you decide it is," he said.

"This!" she said, pointing.

"Allie said the same thing."

"Allie? Smart."

"She sure is." He rubbed his face. "I don't know... Let's say that I do have something in mind, something important that I want to be doing. Do you realize how many other things I'm already a part of? How many other directions I'm being pulled in?"

"More than none?"

"By a bunch."

"Then good!"

"I don't know. It feels like I'm just a link in a chain sometimes."

"Very very good! A chain? Every link, important. Bad link? Not a chain. Two chains, instead. Broken chain. Link in chain? Important person. Very very."

"I wish I could think the way you do."

"Don't wish. Just do," she said.

His eyes settled on the flames again, the scent of roasting rabbit beginning to remind him that he'd not taken the time to eat when Tome had. Even the sound of Teya crunching through the rest of her rabbit didn't spoil his appetite.

"Just do..." she said, as if considering the wisdom of her own words. "I am thinking. Funny thing. Allie, the smart one. What is the other? The woman with pie?"

"Mariss," he said. "Are we really going to talk about my love life right now?"

"No," Teya said with a shake of her head. "Is none. Remember?"

"Yes. I remember," he said sternly.

"But why?" she said. "You? Big. Strong. Good family. Good friends. Important things to do. Good heart. If kobold? Good mate."

"Human females are a little more discerning than kobolds, I guess."

"Maybe. Don't know humans. Not well. Only you. You tell me. Human? How find mate? By smell? By song? You do dance, maybe?"

"No, we…" Fel paused. "I guess it's sort of a dance, yeah."

Teya nodded. "Bad dancer?"

"I guess I am," he said.

She nodded. "Clumsy. Maybe try something new? No dance. You say, Allie, love me. Love me please. Always please. Very important. Polite. Woman like."

He laughed. "Thanks for the advice." He paused. "Allie, huh? Not Mariss?"

Teya shrugged. "I like Allie. Better for you. You? Want, not do. Allie? Want, do. Two mates? One must do. Mariss? Don't know. Maybe do? Allie? Do."

"You are a very clear thinker, Teya."

She tapped her chest. "Teya? Smart?"

He flipped the rabbit over. "Smart. Good hunter. Good worker. Friendly. And with important destiny. You're a real winner, Teya."

Teya waggled a claw. "Teya and Fel? No no. This one? Wants good dancer."

He laughed. "Something tells me you'll find one."

Thaddeus puffed at his pipe and flipped through his notes. One of the most important skills he'd picked up in service of the family was an almost maniacal penchant for note-taking. It was a bit of a curse and a blessing. His deeper motives and true identity had been sussed out by Epiphany thanks to his notes. But he'd been saved more often than he'd been thwarted by having information of past transactions at his disposal. Sometimes it was a single key piece of information. Today, the truth was buried deeper. Not in any single message but in the nature of many messages.

In the time since they'd instituted the coded messages, he'd received only one message using the codes that Trenton had been referencing. It was also the only message he'd received from Piotor Graves, the family's reclusive archivist and researcher. He puffed again. Without an open flame to observe, it was difficult to know if the voice of the flame was present to take a message. It was more of a notion, a sense at the edge of understanding. But he'd been doing business this way for years. He knew what to wait for. What to feel for. When it came, he spoke.

"I want to exchange some words with Piotor," he said simply.

"I have been asked to remind you that all sensitive messages or business matters should be sent in code."

"This is a personal matter," Thaddeus said.

"There are few who have personal matters with Piotor Graves."

"And I am among them," Thaddeus said.

"I shall inquire after his availability." The consciousness left his pipe for just over a minute. "He wishes to know what matters need to be discussed. He is deep in research."

"First, I wonder, does he recall the name of the dish he had at Marina's wedding dinner? It was ages ago, but I recall he genuinely adored that dish."

Another brief delay.

"He says the chef called it buckled lamb. He's never had the like again."

Thaddeus nodded. It was a small thing, but something only Piotor would know. At least he knew he was speaking to the actual man.

"Piotor, forgive the bluntness of my words, but I believe you are engaged in schemes well beyond your role. Trenton was delivering messages I know to be on your behalf, and those messages were directing the actions of an inspector who was doing his level best to infiltrate the Masker home and potentially sabotage their business irreparably. This is at direct odds to the current aims of the family, which depend upon a strong relationship with the Maskers and their continued success. I want to know what is happening and why."

"I shall deliver the message."

There was another telling absence of the voice. This one lasted much longer.

"His reply is as follows," the voice replied. "Thaddeus. You will recall, when you were first called upon to begin working with Epiphany, there were items of interest. These items included the Warrior mask, the chain pack, and the dagger. We have acquired the dagger through those means. And the Warrior mask has just recently revealed itself through a fortuitous but unrelated circumstance. The chain pack, which we now know to be called Oiler, has been located, but the Masker family has evinced no interest in selling it. We also are aware that Martin Masker has been working on an improved bust for interacting and communicating with the masks. Such a bust, and the new components created for it, would be of enormous value to the Graves family."

"Are you admitting to your role in this scheme with Inspector Cartwright?"

The voice seemed to understand its intended behavior, communicating the comments back and forth without requests for clarification or acknowledgements. It was as near to a face-to-face conversation as he'd had with Piotor in decades.

"There are items we need to acquire which could not have been purchased or traded for."

"You don't know that. The Maskers are businesspeople as well as inventors. You could have given me the chance to negotiate for them."

"Business relies upon a handful of things. Supply, demand. Mutually agreed upon measures of value. When those things do not exist, business as usual cannot occur. You have worked with the Maskers. They have revealed that they are willing to forego business, regardless of price, if they feel that items have a price that cannot be met with currency alone. They have the exclusive known supply of 'Oiler'-type contraptions and fully functional busts for masks. Oiler is a member of the family, as far as transactions are concerned. It will not be sold or otherwise transferred. That is acceptable. The contraption is a valuable resource, but it's not irreplaceable. A contraptioneer with the necessary knowledge can perform the same tasks. Were we to arrange for the purchase of an improved bust, questions regarding its intended use would be raised. Information regarding our operation would be requested. These matters are too sensitive to be honestly provided, and dishonest replies would be too transparent to slip past Vivian or Epiphany Masker. The bust had to be acquired through alternate means."

"Alternate means? A soft phrase for the corruption of an inspector. Was Euphoria made aware of this decision?"

"There are some decisions that must be made outside the usual channels."

"You made a choice that could have ruined her family, and she was not even consulted? You made a choice that could have undone months of careful cooperation that has been mutually beneficial to an enormous degree because you believed the Maskers would not build-to-order a bust due to fear of your motivations for it? What are your motivations for it? And what of this killer who has acquired the items you were attempting to acquire?"

"The killer is not part of the plan. It has simultaneously complicated and simplified matters by separating the key items from the Maskers and providing the long-sought Warrior mask. But in fleeing, he has placed them beyond our grasp. As for the motivations, they are a sensitive matter. Too sensitive to be discussed through this means. Please remain where you are. A representative will be dispatched to discuss matters further."

Thaddeus knew the schemes of his family often danced across the lines set by law and policy. But this was the first time he'd felt as though they'd crossed the line of decency. And worse, there was the issue of Piotor. He was the family's expert in the usage of the sentry lantern. The first persistent lantern acquired by the Graves family was in his possession, and he was the only member of the family who had any success at adapting other such lanterns to work with the Graves flame. Even so, very few new ones had been prepared, and none in decades. He wielded an incredible amount of influence over their communication as a result. He'd just revealed his capacity to dispatch messages to any member of the family through the lanterns and pipes without revealing the true origin of those messages. It would be a relatively simple matter for him to manipulate communications to appear to have been delivered by any other member of the family. Had he done so already? How long had he been doing so? And then there was the matter of the Bolivans and their acquisition of lanterns, some of which were persistent. A sour feeling curdled his stomach at the thought that Piotor might have been responsible in some way.

But worst of all was the notion jabbing at the back of his mind that the content of this conversation may have marked Thaddeus in undesirable ways. And now there was a representative headed in his direction.

He silently removed the pipe from his mouth and snuffed it. He did the same for the lantern he carried, lit from the family lantern in Shalia. It felt wrong to purposely extinguish a flame that he'd spent years carefully keeping lit. But right now, he felt the darkness was more valuable than the light.

Allie thumped inside her home and shut the door. It had been a long day, made a good deal longer by the worrying circumstances of Fel's departure. She slumped down at the table and threw down the pot pie she'd brought home for supper. From the first day she began working at the tavern until just a few days ago, she'd experienced the same blessed feeling at this time of day. The weight of a full shift in a bustling, busy bar slowly lifting from her shoulders as she enjoyed the solitude of her home. Being with others was synonymous with hard work, and being alone was synonymous with a respite from her obligations. She loved to be alone. She looked forward to it.

So why did her home suddenly feel so empty?

Allie turned to the bedroll in front of the fireplace. A pack with some of Fel's tools sat beside it. A spare blanket was wadded up in the corner, still with the depression left by Teya's curled-up form. A small mess left by her houseguests. It should have annoyed her. There was so little in this world that was truly hers. This tiny home was the center of it all. To have someone pile something up in the place she called her own was a terribly invasive thing. But she didn't even bother tidying it up. Not tonight, anyway.

She reached up to the cupboard and grabbed one of her gorgeous new spoons. It neatly broke the pot pie's crust to let some steam out. A few minutes and it would be cool enough to eat. The meal wasn't so different from the stew Fel had made. Not quite so brown, not quite so greasy. Not quite the same.

Allie clenched her teeth and thumped the table. This was a foolish state of mind. She'd gotten comfortable having someone to talk to when she came home. That was all. It could have been anyone. She started to sift through the faces of the people in her life, casting each of them in the role of dinner guest. She dismissed each of them. This one? Too full of himself. That one? Too chatty. This one? Too stodgy. That one? Too wild.

She wanted Fel. By the High, right now she'd even take Teya. She didn't need any of them. She was able to survive just fine on her own. But in less than a week, just a few hours all told, she'd gotten a taste for something that was more than survival. Like there was some seasoning she'd gotten by without through her entire life, and now she'd had some in a few dishes and had developed a taste for it. Being by herself was fine. But being with someone, the right person, that was something else. Even if it never went beyond having their voice in her ear, their face and their stupid laugh right in front of her....

Allie took a spoonful of the pot pie and blew on it. It was good. Precisely as good as it had always been. No little burnt bits scraped from the bottom. No completely harebrained substitutions because the cook couldn't get the veggie he wanted and just plunked in whatever he had. It was a good, hearty meal. It filled her stomach. That's all it did. It was all it had to do. That's what a meal was before Fel had come to stay with her. Now it felt so lacking.

She rubbed her forehead. "Just a few days..." she muttered. "The man ruined me in just a few days. Two more days and I'd be sick of him."

She took another few bites and shook her head. No. Lying to oneself was a pastime for the other folks in the tavern. That sort of nonsense wasn't for her. This wasn't the work of a few days. This was years. Month after month of watching him blunder about, asking for her advice, and taking it. Watching him learn the things the other dopes in the tavern never did. Seeing him do the right thing on purpose or the wrong thing by mistake, then coming in the next day subtly different for the lesson.

It had taken quite some time for him to work himself into the proper shape to slip past the stony exterior that protected her from the truly heinous things the world might have in store for a woman like her. And now he'd run off to do some of the same foolishness he'd been doing all along. But he'd taken a bit of her with him.

"He'd better give me the chance to get sick of him," she grumbled, continuing her meal.

"Epiphany."

The young woman tossed in bed. Sleep had only just claimed her after hours of fitfully staring at her ceiling.

"Epiphany, please wake up."

The voice was Wick's. Epiphany made it a point not to light her own lantern from Wick's lantern. She had no interest in anyone watching her while she slept, even the trusted family lantern. But given the danger Fel was in, she and her parents decided keeping a flame in earshot day and night was a wise precaution in the event Fel needed help.

She opened her eyes and sat up. "What! What is it? Does Fel need something?" she said.

"No. He has gone to sleep."

"Then you should be back there keeping an eye on him."

"Teya is on lookout right now. This is a matter closer to home."

"What?"

"Your mother left a flame smoldering in the shop, as usual, and presently Thaddeus Graves is tapping on the front door."

"What does that man want that can't wait until tomorrow?" she muttered.

She pulled on a robe and thumped up the stairs. When she emerged into the shop, the earful she was planning on giving him slipped from her mind. This was not the expression of a man mindlessly bothering someone late in the evening. This was a man with a weight on his shoulders.

Epiphany reached up to hold the bell out of the way and unlocked the door. "A bit late, Thad," she said, not quite able to entirely suppress the irritability of being pulled from bed.

"A thousand pardons, but I won't be here in the morning," he said, stepping inside and shutting the door behind him.

"I thought you were here for the rest of the week," she said.

"My plans are shifting like a stormy sea these days," he said. "And the wind is really beginning to pick up, figuratively. Here is the key. I've put Reynard's shop to bed. It'll have to be closed until he returns, unless you or your mother feel obliged to run it, but he's out of stock. I've taken my share. Even without it, the man has had quite a week."

"Why are you heading out so early? What sort of winds are blowing?"

"I took your words to heart, regarding the source of the messages sent to Cartwright. I did some investigation of my own. To my great shame, you were correct. Those messages came via the Graves flame. A messenger who was sent here separately."

"I'm... I'm frankly surprised you're telling me this."

"Deception has never been absent from the way my family does business, but we've made it a point of pride to use it strategically, sparingly, and never against those we trust. I say the message came from the Graves flame. It may even have come from a member of my clan. But I speak for myself, and I hope for the rest of my family, when I say those messages were not part of the Graves family's plans."

"Are you saying someone in your family has gone rogue?"

"What do you know about Piotor Graves?"

"Not much. I believe I've heard him spoken of as something of a researcher?"

"A hermit, more like. He's as near as we have in our family to your father. With important differences, however. His knowledge comes not from practice and insight but through endless investigation of old texts. He works best in solitude, and his work has been of immeasurable value to the family, so he was given all the solitude, and all the latitude, he desired. Some years ago there was a terrible fire. We thought we'd lost him, but he sent a message some days later. He'd escaped to a safehouse farther north. From that day, his paranoia consumed him. He's cut himself off from even the rest of the family. The messages and discoveries came at an even higher rate, but at the cost of all face-to-face contact being severed. Some terrible things can grow in the darkness of a mind like that..."

"What has he done?"

"I don't know. Not for certain. But he knows the flame, its functionality, and its behavior better than any in the family. He wrote the codes we use for security. Granted, I'm not as near to the center of power within the family as I might be, but I know of no connections the family has made within the Thayne nobility. Somehow he forged a partnership even we wouldn't dream of attempting. What other resources does he have? And what other plans has he been hatching? What other plans has he already hatched?"

He waggled his extinguished pipe. "I'm off this stuff for now. Heading back home, through a rather circuitous route. I don't feel comfortable retracing my steps or visiting my usual haunts. Not until I know more."

"This is serious..." she said.

"Perhaps. Or perhaps I've let my mind wander as far and wide as I've accused his of drifting. Better safe than sorry. And that's my advice to you, as well. Be mindful of your flame. And be wary of anything that comes from ours, directly or through messengers. I don't know what this means. But I feel I've been used and deceived, and that damage has been done to the reputation of the family. I can't let that stand. Listen. This whole mess was about some form of an improved bust your father was working on. I know that much. Do with that information what you will. Good evening, and be safe."

She held the bell aside again and he slipped out. She locked the door behind him.

With him gone, his words lingered in her mind. She was hesitant to believe that the Graves family had truly turned on them again so quickly. But she'd been ready to take the proper actions if they had been. Years of resenting her sister had made a return to that sort of distrust an unpleasant but not unfamiliar notion. This? This she was not ready for. The possibility that the Graves family was fraying at the seams. That it was rotting from the inside? It was the sort of thing they would have discussed around the dinner table. Half-jokingly wishing it upon them before her sister had run off to join them. But now her sister was a part of it. Very near to the center of it. What did this mean for her? And if this rogue element within the family had tendrils that reached as far and deep as the nobility, what might it mean for the Maskers?

She double-checked the lock on the door. Something told her she wouldn't be sleeping at all tonight. But she could at least keep this revelation from her parents until the morning. Let them get one last good night of sleep.

CHAPTER 12

Fel tugged at the reins with one hand and slapped at a bug on his neck with the other. When they'd left, it was with the expectation that the connection between Teya's earring and Wick's lantern would be utterly indispensable to track the elf. Shortly after they'd gotten back on the road that morning, tracking the elf became a good deal easier.

"Not only has that monster attacked my city and robbed my family," Tome muttered to himself. "He's going to ruin a good wagon."

The group had been following a painfully evident trail through a marshy field. The horses had to slow to a crawl on the soft ground. So much so that Teya was easily keeping pace on Parch's back, thanks to the smaller, lighter steed's ability to prance from stone to stone and avoid the sticky mud. Despite their struggling pace, the deep furrows left by the stolen wagon suggested the elf would have been moving at half their speed. A cargo wagon as heavily loaded as the one he'd stolen was a terrible thing to take into a marsh.

"How about 'What is a fragment and an end to war?' Will that do?" Tome asked.

"Answer is peace, yes?" Teya said.

"Yes. Peace, as a command, ought to stop the sphinxes from attacking."

"No," Teya said.

"Why not?" Tome asked.

"For them? Answer not peace. No answer for them."

"Why wouldn't there be an answer for them if there's an answer for us?" Fel called back irritably.

"In their words? Fragment is… ko-rye-uh-way. End of war… koss-uh-too-may-ruh." She rubbed her jaw. The ancient language was clearly a terrible strain on her anatomy when it came to pronouncing things.

"Right, right. Different language. They wouldn't rhyme. Blast it, why are so many riddles a play on words?" Tome said.

"This is stupid. This is all stupid. A monster that requires you to come up with riddles to defeat it is stupid," Fel said.

A decent meal and half a night of sleep had cleared Fel's head just enough for Tome's anxious attempts at preparation to irritate him. Not because they were unnecessary, but because he was now able to embrace how very necessary, and how far beyond his expertise, they were. The realization was not a welcome one. It was making every aspect of the journey rub his mind raw, from the unpleasant terrain to the weight of Oiler's pack hanging from his shoulders.

"Better than greater sphinx," Teya said. "You solve riddles, then. Solve them or die."

"Stupid," he grumbled again.

"You'll be pleased to know that the elf is much more traditional when it comes to combat. We'll be attempting to dodge arrows and snares at a distance, and up close we'll be dealing with a short sword. The arrows if they are fired, are fired with accuracy that would require mystic influence to dodge."

"If they're fired? If I could shoot an arrow with that sort of accuracy, I'd shoot one at every opportunity."

"If elf might miss? Elf not shoot," Teya said.

"Yes. Apparently it is a point of pride for a ranger to be flawless in his attacks. Mevrelle has something of a vendetta against me thanks to my success at dodging him."

"How'd you do it?"

"A high-speed spell, which I'm sorry to say I haven't had time to prepare yet for this journey. Another missed its mark when the wall's influence fouled his mind, if I recall correctly. I imagine that may have had a role in the first one missing, now that I think about it. He didn't fire any at me when we clashed outside Beffshire. I think the mask doesn't do a particularly good job of preserving his vision. So we have that on our side. But, again, none of that will matter if he utters two words and the sphinxes keep us busy enough for him to get the drop on us and slit our throats. Or if the sphinxes just kill us outright. So we really ought to focus our minds on the puzzle of how to neutralize them. Now, commands that might be of use. Retreat, heel, halt, stop, stand down, relent..."

"Can we order them to do something deeper than that?" Fel asked. "Sleep maybe?"

Teya tipped her head. "Maybe yes? Greater sphinx? No."

"I'll check the book," Tome said, digging in one of the saddlebags as best he could while keeping the steed in motion.

The horses trudged forward. Parch hopped and sprang along, putting some distance between himself and the rest of the group.

"Good news!" Teya called back. "This up here? There is a road!"

"A road," Fel growled.

The horses continued, the ground beneath them slowly becoming more solid until two deep wagon-wheel furrows climbed up to a packed-gravel path.

"This road... this is the road we left! It wraps all the way around this marsh here. The idiot dragged a wagon through the marsh when he could have just gone around. And if we'd known where he was going, we could have taken the road and cut half a day off the trip!"

"This is good," Tome said.

"In what world is this good! I've been getting eaten alive by bugs, and we've been exhausting our horses to cross a piece of ground we didn't even need to cross!"

"It means he must be tracking something the same way we are. He doesn't know the roads of this place. How could he? We had to follow him through the marsh because we only know where he is, not where he's going or how he intends to get there. He must be doing the same, traveling in a straight line. That's good. That's information."

"Information," Fel spat. "The only thing this teaches me is that I wish we could kill this elf three times. Once for attacking you, once for attacking and robbing my hometown, and once for wasting my time! Which way did he go, Teya?"

The kobold shut her eyes and tilted her head. "That way," she said, pointing along the road where it curved northwest.

"Of course he did," Fel said. "He's even heading the same way we'd be heading if we followed the road around. At least the going will be easier now. And if he dragged a whole wagon through that, those horses are going to be on the brink of collapse. Maybe we can catch up."

Teya paused and held up a hand. She raised her snout and sniffed, then turned and pointed to a tuft of swamp grass.

"Small man," she said.

"What?" Tome said.

Teya hopped from Parch's back and stalked toward the grass. Before she could reach it, it stirred and a small form crept out from the grass, blade held at the ready.

"Davie. I should have known it was you he'd send after me," Fel said.

"Yeah. You're always wandering off and needing a shadow. But, see, the idea is I stay close enough that if you get in trouble, I can do some gutting, but far enough back that I don't get caught up in the trouble. That's how we work things. When you muck through a whole marsh and I end up getting ahead of you, it makes us both look bad."

"Believe me, it wasn't my idea."

Teya crouched to look at the gnome, a grin on her face. He raised the tip of the blade and waggled it in her face.

"Back off, sharp tooth," he said.

"Smaller than dwarf. Bigger than pixie. One shape, so many size. Why so many?" Teya mused.

"I don't suppose you saw the other guy come through," Fel said.

"If I did, you'd've found a puddle of blood here instead of some tracks."

"So he's farther ahead than we thought," Fel said. "Let's keep moving. We need to gain ground."

"And let's not meet like this again," Davie muttered, hopping off the road. "Some of us take our jobs seriously."

Martin sat in the near-ransacked workshop. Given the excitement and the danger, the family hadn't even considered taking the time to reclaim their goods from Verfessa's storage. They didn't have a place to put the contraptions yet. They'd have to sell off some of the antiquities they'd acquired as replacements. He could have been working to reassemble the assorted contraptions that had served as decoys during the inspection, or even simply thrown himself into the task of cleaning up the mess they'd made of his place during the search.

Instead he sat, sheets of paper arrayed before him, sketching down the workings of the coupler, all three iterations of which were among the stolen goods. The dancing shadows cast by the lantern went still.

"Martin," Wick said.

"What news do you have, Wick?" Martin asked without looking.

"Little has changed. They are still on the elf's trail. They've yet to encounter him. Some minor determinations have been made about the nature of his navigation, but nothing more. Fel is growing frustrated."

"That boy's patience can be awfully selective," Martin said. "Put him on the road to a vault, and he'll sit in happy silence the whole way there. Put something that he wants just an inch beyond his reach, and he'll tear the world apart to get it. I suppose the family focus finds its way to manifest in different ways across the generations."

"You have made admirable progress in recording your design for the bust coupler, Martin."

"My notes are among the things in that wagon the elf took." He shook his head. "The notes and the working model piled into the same vehicle. The most basic of security precautions, and we completely ignored it."

"Circumstances were not ideal. There was little time."

"A fine excuse. But a fat lot of good excuses will be if those contraptions are put to bad use."

"You worry that the Warrior mask and the bust could combine poorly."

"Some tremendous good has come from teasing information out of the Student. I shudder to think of the evils that could be teased out of a similar contraption with a warlike bent. And the only thing I know for certain about the creature who took it is that it is violent and holds a terrible grudge against us all."

He shook his head. "All my life I've bucked against the notion that contraptions are inherently dangerous. It has been the work of my family, stretching all the way back into the Bygone Era, to build and preserve them. This shop is built upon the idea that contraptions can be safe and simple ways to solve problems and make lives better. And with my idle tinkering I may have opened the door for a terrible price to be paid, in precisely the way the people of this world feared."

He looked down. "And yet how do I occupy my hands while I wait to see if my only son can stop that disaster from happening? Recording the details of the very instrument of that disaster."

"Do not blame yourself, Martin. Sometimes history will simply not be denied. It has a clear and urgent need to repeat itself," Wick said.

"There are some parts of history that I'd prefer not be repeated, Wick," he said.

There was a knock on the door.

"Come in," he called.

Epiphany opened the door and stuck her head through. "Sorry to distract you."

"No. Please. I need the distraction."

"We have a buyer for the two pocket watches, but they need to be cleaned and adjusted," she said, stepping inside.

She set the pair of Bygone Era timepieces on the workbench. He opened a drawer and fetched the proper-size tools to begin their disassembly. Epiphany lingered.

"Dad? I've been doing some thinking," she said.

"A worrisome pastime for this family, if present circumstances are any indication," he said.

"Oh, trust me, I know."

"What's occupied your mind? Anything pleasant, perhaps?"

"Hardly. I've been thinking about what Thaddeus said last night before he left."

Martin shook his head. "Terrible doings. Between the treachery of the Bolivans and the turmoil in both the Graves and Masker families, I am beginning to think mere contact with contraptions brings calamity."

"He said that Inspector Cartwright had been after the new bust you were working on. He referenced it specifically. But... how did anyone know about it? We certainly haven't told anyone we were working on it. We are constantly checking to see if any unknown flames are burning within these walls. Unless Wick has been subverted, I can think of only one other way they might have learned."

Martin popped the back from one of the watches, doing so with care to prevent any components from springing free. "You're thinking of the masks."

"We saw that the Student could tell the location of the Diplomat, and Euphoria confirmed it. Not that it seemed to matter at the time, this presumably meant that once the Student was awoken, the Diplomat must have known it was here as well."

"As did Euphoria. It was no secret among the two families."

"But if they could communicate position, what else might they be able to communicate? They had that connection."

"The Student was quite clear that it could not pass information between the masks."

"It was our understanding that the Student was the first of the masks, correct? Surely the subsequent masks might have had other abilities. The means to draw some insight into their brethren."

"You suppose that through the Diplomat, the Graves family discerned that the Student had gained some new capacity through the coupler I designed?"

"It's a possibility, isn't it?"

Martin dabbed oil onto assorted pivots within the timepiece and tested the tension within the spring.

"Reunion..." he muttered.

"What?"

"The Student spoke of a reunion of the four masks. The Warrior and Student are together, one in the stolen wagon, the other on the face of the elf. We know the Diplomat is with the Graves family in Shalia. But for there to be a reunion, the Scholar must be awake. And by Euphoria's account, the bust they have for the Diplomat is barely functional. The pieces must fit together. They seem so close to meshing. But it doesn't make sense they should. Cartwright was after the bust at the behest of someone within the Graves family. Now an elf has acquired the bust, completely unconnected to that scheme."

"Is it unconnected, though?" Epiphany said. "What is more unlikely? That two radically different forces would seek precisely the same thing at precisely the same time? Or that there is some link between these events?"

Martin snapped the watch shut and held it to his ear. "I tell you, Fanny, I'm starting to miss the days when we struggled to get by with simple repairs and harmless contraptions..."

"One wonders if perhaps the nobles were onto something when they placed such strict limitations," Epiphany agreed.

The sun was sliding from the sky as Fel and the others once again left the road. This time, at least, they found themselves on a rough, unplowed field. The fence around it was decrepit, so much so that the stolen wagon had managed to find a gap large enough to slip through. It suggested either the field was abandoned or the owner was being very generous with how long it was being left fallow. Everything from shrubs to young saplings had sprouted up to clutter the field. The uneven ground and brush was little trouble for the horses and Parch but would have been torturous to drag the wagon across. They could only be gaining ground. But the rocky ground was too firm to leave much in the way of a trail beyond those times when the elf had chosen to ram through a few bushes rather than find a way around them.

"You're sure we're still heading in the right direction," Fel said.

Teya shut her eyes. "That way," she said with a nod. "Close now. Tug strong. Destiny strong."

They approached the fence on the far side of the land. Here, it seemed, the elf lacked the patience to find a bit of fence that had already collapsed. Some freshly exposed breaks in very rotten planks showed where he'd bashed his way through. Beyond the fence was a very steep grade. At the base, the shattered wreck of a wagon awaited them.

"Everyone watch yourselves. If he's still in there, we don't want him to get the drop on us," Fel said.

"Mevrelle is a master of stealth," said Tome. "It will be difficult to spot him. I have a hearing spell here, and one for enhanced vision."

Teya bounded down the hill atop Parch. Fel hopped down to take the trip more slowly on foot. When he did, something caught his attention on the ground beside the broken fence. He crouched and pawed at the ground with one finger. Oiler dropped from his back and inspected the broken fence for any possibility of repair.

"Teya!" he called. "You sure destiny is still pointing to the wagon?"

"Yes!" she cried.

Tome hopped from his own horse. "What did you find?" he asked.

"Looks like a hoofprint. And another down here."

"Not terribly surprising since we already know the wagon came through here, given how it's still here."

Fel pointed. "The wagon went down there. The fence is broken there. The slope leads that way. If he'd gone straight over the edge, the hoofprints would be closer to the fence, and in line with the slope. Even if he tried to straighten the thing out and ride it along the slope before he lost control, the hoofprints would be farther back that way."

"No elf!" Teya called up from the bottom. "Only one horse! Dead."

Fel scanned the surrounding ground, searching for more signs of out-of-place prints. None presented themselves. He and Tome slowly worked their way down the hill to where the wagon had overturned. Oiler followed, satisfied that the rotten fence was unworthy of its attention.

"Oh... By the High, that is gruesome..." Tome said.

There was indeed just one horse, but from the looks of it, it had still been attached to the wagon when it went out of control. The creature was badly battered after being dragged down the hill. One could only hope its death had been swift.

"We eat horse?" Teya asked. "Hungry. Shame to waste."

Tome winced. "I don't think you—"

"Sure. Eat up," Fel said, crouching beside the fallen steed.

He tossed Teya a knife. She went to work. Fel investigated the cargo in the broken wagon.

The whole vehicle must have gone end over end a few times as it tumbled down the hill. The cargo was in a terrible state. But most of it was Bygone in origin and had lasted through the ages. It would take more than a tumble to do much more than cosmetic damage. Similarly, the books had been well packed despite their haste. One of them had been torn to scattered pages, but the rest could be salvaged. He snatched up what pages he could find and tucked them into one of the still-intact boxes, then brushed a few shattered fragments side.

"No..." Fel said.

Oiler surveyed the surroundings. The contraption eagerly plucked up the nearest lightly damaged contraption and started repairing it, internal chimes and a merry bob of its head showcasing just how pleased it was to have something engaging to do. Fel picked up the source of his dismay. It was Wick's lantern. The glass was fractured, but it was otherwise intact. He held it low and poked his head up through the torn canvas.

"Teya, point toward destiny again," he said.

She raised her head, a strip of something juicy dangling from her jaws. She shut her eyes, then pointed squarely at where Fel was holding the lantern. Fel squeezed the ring atop the lantern so hard he could feel his knuckles creak.

"Blast it..." he muttered. "Tome! You told me he wanted Wick! You told me that, didn't you!?"

"I told you that because he told me that. He wanted to make more earrings. But he was at his wit's end when he said it. That mask was tearing his mind apart."

"This doesn't look like the work of a madman," Fel said. "If I figured out someone was tracking me via the lantern, I'd ditch it along with everything else."

"This yoke is clearly cut. He definitely took the other horse." Tome turned to poke through the compartment beneath the driver's seat. "But look. There's food in here. Hunting gear. Why would he leave that behind? If the tortured mind I dealt with had been continuing to deteriorate, it's possible he finally lost control."

"Lost control to what? To the mask?"

"There was magic at work. He'd been linked to it to help defeat the influence of the wall. It certainly seemed to be tearing at his thoughts. And there's no telling what the mask's plan was."

Fel ran his fingers through his hair. "All right... All right... This is good news because Wick is safe, but this is how we were tracking the elf. What do we do now?" Fel puffed the pipe and held it down to light the proper lantern. "The soil only gets firmer and rockier from here. We won't be finding any more hoofprints deep enough to survive a stiff breeze."

"You're a wild beast," Tome said to Teya. "If this little meal is any indication anyway. Can you track the elf?"

She shook her head. "Home? Maybe. Not here."

"We'll have to think it through," Tome said.

"I carry a club specifically so that I don't have to think things through." Fel grumbled. "Where to start... Wick, you there?"

"I am," the flame said.

"Get the inventory of this wagonload. If it's all here, then all we have is an insane elf with an ancient artifact strapped to his face stalking the kingdom. If something else is missing, we might have real problems."

It took the better part of an hour, but Fel, Tome, and Teya managed to account for nearly everything that was supposed to be in the wagon. One of the items that was quite clearly missing was, to their dismay, the Student. It wasn't until Oiler had finished reassembling his father's new bust that the other missing items presented themselves.

"The couplers," Fel said. "Dad made three couplers, and they're not here. Not the one that was on the bust, and not the others he'd been working on. The elf must have taken them. But why?"

"It does seem to be far too complex and premeditated an action for someone who'd succumbed to madness. But I see no way that this could serve any plan the elf might have had. And any insight I had into the Warrior's intentions were filtered through the raving of a mind desperately trying to resist them."

"Wick, ask Dad what those couplers could do," Fel said. "Tome, you're smarter than me, so get to work figuring this out."

"Lovely to have a rare compliment compounded with an order," Tome said. "Let us see. What do we know about the masks?"

"Old!" Teya said.

"Yeah. And if the elf was able to get this one, that must mean it never left the Greater Lands, right?"

"Or it left and was returned," Tome said.

"I think Dad said the masks aren't aware of things when they're not active. So that mask probably doesn't know anything about the outside world," Fel said.

"Unless it learned from the elf," Tome said.

"And the elf doesn't know anything about the outside world either," Fel said.

"True, true. I've had a few glimpses at maps within the Greater Lands, and quite a few glimpses outside. Their view of our world isn't entirely incorrect. Very old maps are closer, but the farther from the wall, the less distorted the maps are. And we're quite far from the wall. So it is possible the mask is aware of the precise location of things outside the wall, if they are old enough to have been present in the Bygone Era and durable enough to still exist. Either that or it is possible that it is being drawn to something it can sense. Another mask, perhaps?"

Fel fetched a map and spread it as best he could inside the broken wagon. "We started here in Beffshire, and we've chased them up through this way... Past that intersection. Through this marsh. And we're here now," he said.

"A straight line," Tome said. "Or very nearly. We did follow this road here for a bit."

"Yeah. And that's a very old road. Dad used to rave about how there are markers dating back to the Bygone Era."

"So the elf, or the mask, or the combination of them, was following a road they knew existed and ignoring new roads. That's a vote in favor of heading for a known landmark rather than following some unseen guide."

Teya hopped down into the shelter of the wagon and wiped her mouth clean. "Straight now. Since road," she said.

"Right," Fel said. "I wish we had an old map. Maybe there used to be a road here?"

"Don't think a road would be traveling up and down steep hills, and very much doubt the hills are new. So whatever he's after is probably along this straight line. Or not far off it. And either it is very old and still there, or it's gone and he doesn't know he's headed for ruins."

"Either way, I ought to know about it," Fel said. "My entire stock and trade is exploring remnants of the Bygone Era. And if he was after something like that, he'd be heading south. There are so many more of them down there. There are some old military bases and a few crypts farther east of here and a big church or something due west, but he could have just followed the road farther for that."

The flame became still. "Martin says that the couplers are a connection-agnostic interface between mechanisms and motivators," Wick said.

Fel glanced wearily at Tome.

"Don't look at me for a translation. Contraptioneering is as foreign to me as magic is to you."

Fel rubbed his face. "All right. A motivator is the thing that makes a contraption do what it does. I know that. And I know he was trying to eventually get it so he could get Wick to move some arms so he could write things down. And it worked with the mask too. So I guess 'connection-agnostic' means it doesn't matter which motivator it is."

"I don't understand how that could be achieved," Tome said. "Surely things still have to attach."

"That's the thing about contraptions. They work the way you expect them to, right up until you get to the point when the Bygone nonsense starts. Then it's all madness. Sometimes things need to link. Sometimes they just need to be near each other. Sometimes they only work if they aren't near each other. It's why there are only three or four people in the world who have the slightest notion of how to repair them and maybe two who can even hope to understand how to make new ones."

"So a contraption that can think has acquired a contraption that is able to connect thinking contraptions to moving contraptions," Tome said.

"And is heading as directly as possible in this direction toward something old," Fel said.

He stared at the map. One by one, vault-diving trips he'd taken in the past popped to mind and settled into their place between the roads and towns. Nothing seemed to be anywhere near the direction they were headed.

"Wait..." he muttered. "I'm thinking of the places I've been to, places that seemed to have good stuff. But this could be a place that was cleaned out of anything worthwhile ages ago. I should be including places I've avoided. Or places that felt cleaned out."

He tapped the map. "Here... the headless quarry."

"A mask is headed roughly in the direction of something called 'the headless quarry' and it didn't occur to you that it might be related?"

"There aren't any contraptions there. They're just statues," Fel said, gathering up the map.

"Are you certain?"

"Yes, I'm certain."

"You didn't know the Student mask was a contraption while it hung on your sign for ages," Tome pointed out.

Fel grumbled something under his breath.

"What was that?" Tome said.

"I said shut up and get on your horse."

"What about the rest of this? Are we just going to leave it here?" Tome said.

"I hate, hate, the idea of leaving this here. With Wick's lantern taken out of the mix, it's mostly books, tools, and a bust with the most important parts missing. We're at the bottom of a gully at the northwest corner of a field. Let's just hope that no one notices. If they do? I'd rather hunt down some goods and the one who stole them than find out whatever it is the Warrior mask is hoping to accomplish has already begun. Let's ride."

CHAPTER 13

Epiphany finished up business with a customer. Now that the bulk of the madness in the city had simmered down and there was no longer a rotation of officials dedicated to harassing customers, the fresh assortment of antiques was once again attracting the sort of customer who had an eye for shiny objects. Getting money out of their pockets was a bit of a challenge, but it was at least the challenge she'd been trained since childhood to overcome. That made it far less stressful than the absurd gambit the family had been executing up until now. Even so, Epiphany lacked her mother's ability to fully compartmentalize those things that took place outside the shop. Concerns for her brother and knots of intrigue that had yet to be untied remained a constant sore spot in her mind, like a rock in her shoe.

"Right, sir. The green color is a patina, a sign of age. Many people prefer to leave it intact. There is a certain beauty to it, of course. But if you prefer, we can polish the piece before delivering it to you," she said automatically.

Her customer launched into some variation of the same speech she'd heard a dozen times before, an attempt to talk down the price of the piece and the fee for polishing it. It was wasted breath on his part. This would all simmer down to a final price that seldom budged more than a few duots. But it made them feel as though they were getting a deal, and that made for repeat customers. In the meantime, she could let her mind wander a bit further.

She glanced out the window and saw the lesser harpies lined up along the roof across the street. They'd had their bribe for the day, so they were happy to sit and watch or squabble over their various prizes. She replied to her customer's counteroffer and glanced up again. Toody and Rudy were playing tug-of-war with a piece of half-crumpled paper. It looked to be far higher quality than a piece of trash they might find. Something snapped together in her mind.

"Sir, for you and you alone, for your clear savvy, I am willing to combine the delivery and polishing into a single fee. Five duots total," she said quickly.

"Oh! Er, yes. Yes that will do nicely," he said.

"Splendid. I have your address here, we will take payment upon delivery. A pleasure doing business with someone who has so keen an eye," she said.

He grinned, pleased at his ability to talk himself down to the very same price she would have offered if he hadn't started haggling, and paced out the door. Vivian had just concluded her own sale. The instant both customers had exited, Epiphany turned to Vivian.

"You were making note of what was being stolen from Cartwright when he was here, yes?" she said.

"I was."

"Was it only duots?"

Vivian flipped to the appropriate page in the appropriate ledger. "There were duots, one or two cenots, on one particularly satisfying occasion, an entire pork pie..."

Epiphany opened the ledger in front of her and ran her finger down the page. "Two sheets of paper on two different days," she said. "Mom, do we have any buns left from breakfast?"

"We may. Why?"

"Because the harpies may have earned it."

She hurried down to the pantry and found three buns that were destined to be ground into crumbs to thicken tomorrow's stew. She grabbed them and rushed to the street. Her mere appearance on the street earned their attention. The fact that she was holding goodies earned their interest.

"Hey!" she hissed, absurdly trying to whisper to a wild animal on the streets of her city. "That! Bring that!"

She pointed at the page. The harpies glanced at one another.

"Rotten thief?" Toody croaked.

"Got my scarf," Judy weighed in.

"Bring me the page and you get all of this!" she said, holding up the buns.

Moody narrowed its eyes and nipped at the page.

"Yes!" she said. "I swear Fel wouldn't have this much difficulty."

The four harpies muttered and cackled. Finally, they flitted down and aligned at Epiphany's feet. Moody delivered the page. She dropped the buns and snatched the page up. As the complex task of negotiating the division of three buns among four harpies consumed the black-feathered creatures, Epiphany looked over the page. It had seen a bit of weather, but the words were still fully legible.

The resources have been made available and will be waiting. The matter regarding Leslie has been resolved.

The other side had a single fragment of wax seal still intact. Epiphany slipped back inside and passed the page to Vivian. Her mother read the page and flipped it about.

"This is one of the messages Cartwright received?" Vivian said.

"It has to be, hasn't it? It fits the descriptions that Tome gave. The bit of seal, the quality of the page."

"Not terribly much to go on, is it?"

"It's more than nothing. Mom, Inspector Cartwright was working for someone. He was an actual official of the nobles that was working for someone else against us. I think it's worth doing what we can to determine just who that person is and what their aims were," Epiphany said. "We know it was someone in the Graves clan, but we don't know how they got influence over someone in such a privileged position."

The door opened. Another customer walked in. Epiphany folded the page and pocketed it.

"I have to run some errands," she said. "We'll discuss this later."

"Now you two knuckleheads sit down and settle it like gentlemen, or someone's going to earn a free drink for dumping the both of you out on the street!" Allie barked, filling two cups from a keg.

Some combination of her better-than-average mood for a day or two during Fel's presence in her home and her distraction during the more troubling parts of that turn of events had changed the overall attitude of The Fox and Log in ways that required adjustment. People were expecting to get away with things, and they should know better. There'd been far too many carrots and not nearly enough sticks in the last few days.

Voices continued to rise.

"One more chance, boys!" she shouted over them.

The two men stood, knocking their chairs down as they jabbed fingers in each other's faces and lobbed accusations. She sighed.

"Lou? What'll it be?" she shouted over them.

One of the burlier patrons stood and grabbed both men by the collars.

"Double rye!" he requested, dragging the two would-be brawlers effortlessly to the door.

As he evicted the troublemakers, Allie fetched a tumbler and a bottle of midrange rye to administer Lou's payment. When he marched back through to pick it up, a scent wafted behind him that several other patrons of the bar had already noticed. A burnt-sugar sort of smell that could only mean one thing.

Sure enough, Mariss looked uncertainly through the door as the two dizzied men tried and failed to climb to their feet in the street.

"Come on in, Mariss. Don't mind the trash we had to take out," Allie called.

The baker gave the two men a wide berth and trotted inside. Her look of uncertainty gradually slid to a giddy, conspiratorial grin as she approached Allie. She plopped down on a stool.

"Cider?" Allie asked, reaching for the appropriate bottle.

"No, no. Too early in the day." Mariss set a cloth-wrapped bundle on the bar. "Cookies and candied nuts."

"What's the occasion?" Allie asked.

"Miss Mary up on the North End ordered too many."

Allie took the bundle and stowed it before the vultures lingering around the bar could try to mooch some.

Mariss glanced to and fro, leaned forward, crinkled her nose, and said, "So?"

The precise tone of voice and gleeful expression put Allie in mind of the kind of childish gossip she was happy to put behind her. For anyone else, it would have felt tawdry and petty. Mariss brought a refreshingly genuine aspect to the attitude that made it more tolerable, if not more welcome.

"Curious about what's been going on with that little thing you observed?" Allie said.

"Ye-e-e-s," she said, prompting for more.

"Fel's off on another trip."

"Oh? More of the same?" Mariss said.

"More of the same," she said with a nod.

"Dangerous same?" Mariss said a bit more seriously.

"It seems like that's the only thing he gets up to these days."

"Are we going to need my horse and cart?" she said with resolve.

Allie shook her head. "We don't swoop in and rescue him every time."

"All right. But you just say the word." She leaned forward and touched Allie's hand, adding with a whisper. "I know what he means to you."

Allie shut her eyes tight and gently slipped her hand from Mariss's grip. "Mariss, I appreciate that, but you are assuming things between him and me are about ten great big steps further than they are."

Mariss furrowed her brow and made sure she wasn't being eavesdropped upon. "He was shirtless in your home," she whispered.

Allie assembled a full explanation in her mind, then started pruning it to remove things that would endanger the secrecy Fel required. The remaining story was terribly sparse, composed almost entirely of the simple, devastating truth that Mariss, in her open and relieved acceptance of a relationship that didn't really exist, had delivered a critical blow to Fel's heart and mind. The delay as she attempted to sculpt it into something that wouldn't further embarrass Fel or mortify Mariss didn't go unnoticed.

"It is all right," Mariss said. "It's none of my business anyway. You two take your time. But when you're ready, I absolutely want to hear about it." She stood. "Enjoy the cookies!"

She paced happily out of the tavern, leaving Allie with the half-considered Fel situation still lodged in her head. She did not like the amount of mental real estate that boy was taking up these days. She shoved the riddle to the back of her mind and returned to the task of reestablishing order in the one place she was completely in control.

"Hey! You back there! You saw what happened to those two. You going to make me get Lou drunk today?" she shouted, gratefully snapping back into a more comfortable state of mind.

Epiphany arrived at the Verfessa household. The frequency with which she found herself at the gate of this man's home was becoming worrisome. But when it came to vague, underhanded business dealings, he was the only one she could think of who might have some insight. That the guards didn't even bother asking her business and simply let her in made her feel doubly uncomfortable.

She stepped through the front door and found Eveline Verfessa in the sitting room.

"Ah, Miss Masker. A pleasure to have you. If you are after Donovan, I am afraid he is doing business elsewhere."

"To be frank, ma'am, I don't even know that he would be able to help, but I don't know who else I can turn to for information."

"If it is a matter of information, I may be able to be of some aid," she said. "Please, have a seat."

Epiphany took a seat opposite the serious and reserved older woman.

"Tea for two," Eveline instructed.

A servant lurking in the doorway scurried off.

"How may I be of help?" Eveline asked.

Epiphany produced the note. Eveline took it and donned a pair of thin spectacles.

"Are you familiar with what's been happening with our shop?" Epiphany asked.

"Quite so. An inspector purposefully disrupting business. Distasteful. Unbecoming of a lord's representative."

"That note was one of many that had been passed to the inspector from the person he was working with, or for."

"And do we know anything about this individual? The ally?"

"Very little for certain. The messages may have come from someone who works with the Graves family."

"'The resources have been made available and will be waiting. The matter regarding Leslie has been resolved,'" Eveline read aloud. "Do we know at what point this message was delivered?"

"My mother saw only two pages stolen, one on the final day he was here and one the preceding day."

"You don't have the other stolen note?"

"The individuals responsible for the theft aren't the best archivists."

"Still. Late in the process. That would imply these resources are things he needed either before the completion of his task here or following it."

"As far as I know, he didn't receive any resources before he left."

"So after, then. What do you suppose Cartwright would have needed following the successful completion of his task?"

"I don't know precisely what his task was," Epiphany said. "Only that he expected to find something within our shop and failed to do so."

"It is a rather troubling riddle." She turned the page over, then back again. "Leslie... Have we considered the possibility of a mistress? Extortion, perhaps? It is certainly an effective way to compel someone into action they wouldn't otherwise engage in."

"Having dealt with him extensively, I do not believe he was being compelled. This was a man quite enthusiastic in his meddling."

The servant returned with the tea. Eveline sipped her tea and stared at the page.

"The Graves family. They work out of Shalia, yes?"

"Mostly."

Eveline glanced to her servant. "The book with the green spine and gold lettering, second shelf from the top next to the end table in my study."

Again, the servant scurried away. The two women sat quietly for a moment, sipping their tea.

"This," Epiphany said. "All of this. Was this always your life?"

"The trappings of wealth, or the means of its acquisition?" Eveline said.

"Either. Both."

"Neither I nor Donovan began our lives with resources of any sort, though I suppose it is fair to say I did grow up with the trappings of wealth. They simply were not my own. I was the daughter of a maid in a manor not three streets away. I was educated expressly to serve the purpose of aiding in the running of the household."

"And now that you run this house, and owe your wealth to—"

"My husband's business?"

"Yes. Does it... do you feel..."

"You are attempting to be diplomatic in your depiction of Donovan's business. You need not. I do not delude myself. But again, I have lived among the gentry all my life. Anyone who acquires considerable personal wealth knows there is no truly legitimate way to do so. Past a certain point, excess demands a price beyond simple duots. Decisions must be made, and if one cannot make oneself comfortable with such things, then one can, and should, settle for less. One can make a living and remain virtuous. But to make a fortune?"

She shook her head. The servant returned with the book. Eveline began leafing through.

"May I ask what that book contains?"

"Names. Locations. Occupations. It is something of a catalogue of influence. Again, past a certain level of excess, it becomes necessary to know your peers, if only to know what to expect from them if you cross paths." She stopped on a page. "Are you familiar with Count Dodderick Leslie?"

"I can't say that I am."

"Nor am I. And nor should we be, unless we were in the market for mercenaries."

"Mercenaries?"

"Indeed. He does work out of Quarr but operates quite near to the Shalia border." She flipped Epiphany's paper over again. "The resources have been made available and will be waiting. The matter regarding Leslie has been resolved."

Eveline snapped the book shut. "Were I to hazard a guess, your Inspector Cartwright is in business with Leslie regarding supplying or acquiring weapons, equipment, or individuals with the skill to use them. Given that he received this message, and it listed the resources as having been made available, it seems likely he was acquiring them." She handed Epiphany the page. "Not a complete answer to your question, I'm afraid."

"No. But far, far more than we had before. Thank you for your help."

"Think nothing of it. After all. We are in this business together."

CHAPTER 14

Years of getting into trouble had provided Fel with a handful of instincts he couldn't explain but had come to rely upon. In the insanity that had consumed his life since his trip to the Greater Lands Wall had earned him the contraption strapped to his back, those instincts had saved his life more than once. Right now, they were screaming at him. A few hours ago they'd crossed a road and begun their journey through a barren field. Now the horse's hooves crunched against the coarse, sandy gravel. Fel scanned the horizon and strained his ears. Something was near. Something very, very bad. And he wasn't the only one who felt the change in the air.

"Destiny," Teya muttered. "Close…"

"How far off is this quarry?" Tome asked.

"We're in it," Fel said.

"This place does not strike me as particularly headless," Tome said.

"The statues are in an alcove or cave or some such," Fel said. "I don't remember, it's been a long time."

"Then where is that?"

"I don't know."

"What do you mean you don't know? You were here before, weren't you?"

"Funny thing about quarries, Tome. They change from year to year because people keep taking pieces of them," he snapped.

Teya raised her snout and sniffed. "Smell something… That way, something bad," she said, pointing.

Parch trotted in the direction she pointed. Even the unicorn's usually energetic prance was subdued.

"Now when you say you smell something bad," Tome said. "Is it an unpleasant smell, or the smell of something unpleasant?"

"Those are same, Tome," Teya said.

"No. One implies a stench, and the other implies the scent of something that is—"

"No talk," Teya hissed. "Leave horse. Stay low."

"You stay here," Fel said to Tome.

Fel hopped from his horse's back. He dropped Oiler's pack to the ground and handed the horse's reins to Tome. Teya was already on all fours, slowly approaching a fault in the ground. It was narrow. Fel doubted he could fit two fingers into it, but it was quite straight and very deep. The sun was almost perfectly overhead, but positioning himself aligned with the fault granted him only brief glimpses of the bright line of sun painted on a surface far below. In what he realized was a pointless maneuver, he fetched Wick's lantern and held it down. All it revealed was that the fault was relatively new, judging by the lack of significant erosion. Teya put her snout over the fault and sniffed with the focus and care of a wine connoisseur.

"What is it?" Fel whispered.

"Fresh meat. Fresh poop," she said. "Smells like... horse."

"The meat or the poop?" Fel asked.

She looked at him like he'd asked the most foolish question she'd ever heard.

"Both," she said. "And also more poop. Horse, and not horse."

Fel glanced along the length of the fault. It didn't seem to lead anywhere. One end vanished into the gravel of the ground not far from where they stood. The other did the same a few hundred yards along. But to the north, the gravel thinned out to stone again, and beyond that, a sharp, unnatural drop-off. Not so long ago, this was the place the quarry workers had been sheering fresh stone away.

He and Teya crawled toward this sharp edge. They both peered over. Some old and not-entirely-trustworthy scaffolding erected by the workers led down to a curious site. The reddish-tan stone that composed the ground and gravel alike gave way to a perfect gloriously white expanse of stone. The white stone was flat, flatter than nature would ever produce and flatter even than the rough chiseling and blocking of the workers. This was the sort of honed flatness that took the skilled hand of a mason and ages of lapping and polishing. It looked as though some ancient temple had been sunk into the stone, swallowed up by it, and they'd only now begun to chip away the covering.

"What is it?" Tome called as softly as he could.

"It's the headless quarry. Looks like they've done a good deal more digging since I was here last. It didn't look this fancy when I came here. You couldn't even see much of the white stone besides around the edge of the doorway."

One of the horses produced an irritated nicker. Fel turned to see Tome leaning a bit too heavily against the animal. His hand was pressed to his temple, and he seemed unsteady.

"Are there any angry elves lurking about?" Tome asked. "I've been getting this... feeling whenever the elf is about, and it is hitting me like a hammer."

Fel swept his gaze along the place where the white wall met the rougher stone ground. He froze as he realized there was something else there, something that had been obscured by the scaffolding. It was a doorway, simple but just as precise as the wall it was built into. And sitting perfectly still within the doorway was one of the lesser sphinxes. It was gazing up at him, calm and focused, eyes precisely on Fel as though it had been waiting for him.

"I don't suppose you've worked out any worthwhile riddles," Fel said.

"I have some theories, but I'm not terribly confident. I'd suggest you keep clear if you spot one."

"And if one of them spots me?"

"... Has one of them spotted you?" Tome said warily.

The second sphinx crept through the doorway and gazed up.

"Two did!" Teya said, a dash more excitement in her voice than seemed appropriate.

Tome riffled through his stack of spells. "I was able to write a taming spell. If you can press one to the creature until it activates..."

"Have you seen how fast these things are?" Fel said.

"I can do!" Teya shouted.

She dashed to Tome and snatched the spell, then scurried for the scaffolding.

"Fel, Teya! I think we need a better plan than 'I can do'!" Tome said, struggling to stuff the rest of his spells into his pockets while wrangling both horses.

"Fine. We can do," Fel said, dashing after Teya.

The scaffold rattled and rocked as they descended. Any attempt at stealth was gone. The scaffold had dry rotted such that Fel wasn't so much climbing down ladders as slowly collapsing them. That he'd neglected to leave Wick's lantern behind didn't help matters, leaving him with one hand to descend. The sphinxes sat, expressions steady and eyes locked on them. Fel didn't know how intelligent they were, but as he crumbled another few rungs and stumbled on a wobbly scaffold trying to get to them, they simply observed. He had the terrible feeling that they were smarter than he was. If he'd been watching someone else do what Fel was doing, his first thought would be "look at that idiot."

Teya hit the ground first and sprinted toward them. She brandished the spell in one hand and dug out her sparker in the other. The sphinxes watched, stone still. Then, as if Teya had finally crossed some line drawn on the ground, they snapped into action.

Fel reached the ground just in time to see them spread their wings. He'd clashed with them before, but it had been in an enclosed space and with barely enough light to see them. In broad daylight and in the open, their speed was even more terrifying. Eagles and birds of prey were limited to slow, ponderous soaring punctuated by sudden swoops and dives. These creatures moved through the air with a freedom in defiance of their size. Powerful legs launched them from the ground. Angled wings arched them higher or forced them lower. Teya, to her credit, dodged the first attack levied at her by rolling to the side. Before she could scramble back to her feet, the second one collided with her, sharp claws raking across thick scales. Fel threw himself at the creature, swinging his cudgel and roaring in anger. The swing missed its target but forced the sphinx to retreat.

The kobold climbed to her feet, a shallow slash on her side trickling dark red. Fel stumbled forward, a hard blow to his back snaring his shirt. Wick's lantern slipped from his grip and rattled to the ground. The second sphinx planted both feline hind feet and raked them down, shredding his shirt and gashing his back. Rather than waste his time trying to pull the thing from his back, he flexed his legs and threw himself backward, bringing his full weight down on the thrashing thing. Teya hopped on his chest, sparked the end of the spell to flame, and slapped the sizzling spell against the trapped creature. It struggled for a moment more, then became still. Fel rolled aside. The sphinx climbed to its feet.

"Go!" Teya crowed. "Kill that one!"

She pointed desperately at the second sphinx, which was wheeling around for another attack. The tamed sphinx darted toward its partner. The wild sphinx barreled into Teya, knocking her against Fel. All four combatants struck the ground in a flurry of wings, scales, fur, and fists. Fel shielded his face with one arm and madly swung his cudgel with the other. In the distance, the approach of clippy-clopping hooves heralded Parch joining the fray. The powerful little creature rammed through the tangle of fighters, skewering one of the sphinxes in the leg. It tumbled aside.

Alas, the one he struck was the tamed one, leaving the other free to continue its assault. The handful of successful attacks seemed to add a measure of caution to its assault, however. It abandoned the failed tactic of grappling with Fel and resorted to quick swoops and darts to try to land slashes. The injured creature, still under the effects of Tome's spell, took to the air, but some combination of being under the influence of magic and suffering a wound to the leg made it no match for the agility and speed of its counterpart. Its clumsy attacks did little more than distract the other creature. But that was enough to give Fel a chance to get his feet under him. He and Teya wordlessly adopted a back-to-back stance so that attack from any angle would be met with claw or club.

Fel huffed and puffed, trying to time his attack so that it would meet flesh. He could feel the tide of the battle turning in his favor. Just one heavy blow and it would be over. Then came the command. Awkward, unnatural syllables echoed from inside the doorway in the white wall. The wild sphinx looped up and pivoted in air, retreating to the doorway and taking up a defensive stance.

A scrawny, filthy, ragged figure emerged. Mevrelle. The fierce, stationary expression of the mask glared at them, but the flash of maddened eyes gleamed from behind its empty slits. The ranger held his bow, an arrow nocked. His clothes hung from him, like he'd lost a dangerous amount of weight. His head twitched now and then, like a frightened puppy in a raging storm. It was a wonder he was still on his feet, so haggard and used up was the elf. He turned and fixed his gaze on Fel.

"Him! Kill that one!" Teya cried.

The tamed sphinx spread its wings and rushed Mevrelle. The weary ranger didn't even turn to face the attacker. While still steadfastly staring down Fel, he let the arrow fly. It struck the sphinx square in the chest and sent it crumbling to the ground.

"Contraptioneer..." Mevrelle wheezed, drawing another arrow. "Masker..."

"Yeah. That's me. I believe you have some things that belong to me," he said, trying to ignore the burning pain of the blows that had struck him.

"The weak may lay claim to nothing," Mevrelle said. "Drop your weapons."

A soft jingle filtered through the quarry. Fel smiled and set his weapon down.

"Good. A wise man knows when he is beaten," Mevrelle said.

"I wouldn't say I'm beaten," Fel said. "Sometimes it's best to not be the one with the weapon in your hand."

A canvas pack dropped heavily from the scaffold, thumping to the ground before Mevrelle. Oiler extended a claw toward the elf, seeking as always to disarm any aggressors. The elf stepped back, but not quickly enough to keep Oiler from snatching the arrow from the bow. The contraption tossed it aside and reached again. Mevrelle spat a command. The remaining sphinx tackled Oiler. The contraption barely seemed to notice, simply allowing its pack to slide along the ground while it reeled its head and claws out, seeking the bow. Fel and Teya dashed forward. With a speed and dexterity that so worn and withered a creature shouldn't have been capable of, Mevrelle nocked a new arrow and fired. His target was Teya. Oiler's claw intercepted the arrow, but the impact shattered the claw to bits. He nocked and fired again. This arrow managed to skewer Oiler's bag, pinning it to the ground. It tried and failed to extend its head and remaining claw farther, but its chain-link body was too tangled around the arrow.

He nocked yet another arrow and leveled it at Fel. The raging human dropped his shoulder, ready to tackle Mevrelle to the ground no matter the cost. The elf took two retreating steps through the doorway, suddenly vanishing into the relative darkness. Fel followed. Before his eyes could even begin to adjust, something hooked Fel's ankle, and he was sent sprawling to the ground. He felt the tip of an arrow press to the back of his neck, and heard the straining bowstring. He dared not raise his head, or even turn it, for fear of the damage the arrowhead would do even if the ranger didn't fire.

"I have Masker. If you make any move to attack, he will be destroyed," Mevrelle warned.

Fel winced as he heard the clippy-clop of approaching hoofs again. Parch was not the sort of creature likely to understand the concept of an ultimatum. He heard the flutter of feathered wings, followed by the clattering skid of hooves. No slash. No yelp of pain.

"I have use for you, Masker. That is why you live. I have no such use for your friends."

"Yeah, well, I've got bad news for you. If you do anything to them, you might as well do the same to me, because the next thing that happens after you draw blood on part of my crew is a lot more blood getting spilled."

"If that is what it takes to motivate you," Mevrelle said. "Do as I say and you all live. Fail or even hesitate and they die."

"Can I trust you?" Fel said.

"If you couldn't, you would already be dead. On your feet." The sharpness pulled away from the back of his neck. "Slowly," the elf instructed.

He did as he was told. The short time in the darkness had allowed his eyes to adjust slightly, but right now the sense providing the most information was smell. Teya's assessment from the cliffside above was quite accurate. Somewhere in this darkness were the remains of a butchered and now-rotting horse. Fel dearly hoped the droppings he smelled were from the sphinx rather than the elf.

"What would you have me do, elf?" he said. "Or am I speaking to the mask right now?"

"Who you speak to is irrelevant. Walk forward until I say otherwise."

Fel took a single step.

"No, wait..." Mevrelle said, his voice now labored. "The lantern."

"Still after that, are you?" Fel said. "Or have you always been after it, and the mask is just letting you have a word?"

The elf didn't reply. Not in any language Fel could understand. He spat a sphinx command. The thing charged out and snatched up Wick's lantern. It approached, lantern held awkwardly in one simian grip while it walked on its other limbs.

"Take it!" Mevrelle ordered. "When we are through here, that leaves with me."

"We'll just see about that," Fel said, taking Wick's lantern.

A fresh command sent the sphinx back to keep an eye on Teya and Oiler. Mevrelle gestured with the drawn arrow. Fel marched into the chamber, the steady flame of Wick to light the way.

Tome lowered himself as best he could down the scaffolding. The entirety of the clash below had unfolded while he was trying to traverse the portion of the ladders that had survived Fel's descent. Easily half of the rungs on each ladder were smashed by his and Teya's rapid climb, so each level put Tome at serious risk of falling. Once Fel had been taken hostage, Teya, Parch, and Oiler were left under the watchful gaze of the remaining lesser sphinx. He hadn't heard what riddle had been given, not that he would have understood it, but the thing seemed to be waiting and watching with a disinterested stare.

He finally reached the ground. Teya was pacing the ground, one hand holding the worst of the slashes in her side while her large eyes darted between the rocky ground and the sphinx.

"Teya," Tome called.

She turned. "You! Where were you! Whole fight, no you!"

He pointed. "You broke the ladders! My options were to take it slow, fall to my death, or find some other way down here. Are you hurt?"

She waved her free hand irritably. "No."

"I have healing spells here. I can close your wounds," he said.

"Use magic for killing," she said, pointing viciously at the sphinx.

"Considering the success the rest of you had, I don't like my chances without a proper plan."

"Plan is, kill thing!" she said.

He slipped a healing spell from his pocket, tore the end, and pressed it to her back. The thin trickle of blood tapered off to a thin white scar on her hide.

"Thank you." She pointed. "Fel inside."

"I know. Do we know what's happening in there?"

"Don't know. We kill, we get in, we know."

"Trust me, I'd like to rescue him as much as you would, but we need a plan."

She crossed her arms. "Fel and this one? No plan."

"And Fel got captured, Oiler got damaged, and you're both bleeding. Only Parch had the good sense to back off before he got hurt."

Teya glared at him. She glanced to the ground and plucked a piece of twisted metal, one of Oiler's damaged digits. She trotted toward the contraption, waving for Tome to follow.

"What magic? What magic is left?" she whispered.

While he sifted through the spells, she handed the digit to Oiler. The contraption had been doing its best to reassemble its damaged claw, but doing so utilizing only the remaining claw and the head of its tail was a slow and cumbersome process. It had a small pile of metal fragments Teya had retrieved already that it had yet to incorporate. It was still where it had been pinned to the ground by the arrow, though the attack and damage to its pack didn't seem to have placed it in any distress. If anything, it seemed perfectly content to have something to tinker with, even if it was its own anatomy.

"I have three flame spells. One ice spell. Two healing spells. A very simple illusion spell. One for hearing. One for vision."

"No more tame spell?" she said. "Two things, you make one?"

"I need time to prepare for adventures like these," he said through gritted teeth. "But there is another way to tame it."

"Riddle? You have some?"

He flipped open a small pad. "If you can translate, we can try..."

Fel marched in the pool of light cast by Wick's flame. The journey went on for quite some time. He didn't remember the entryway of the headless quarry being this long. In his dim recollections of the place, it was just a few small chambers and short corridors. Strange how having a demented elf threatening him could make time seem to crawl. Finally he reached the section of the chamber illuminated by the fault overhead.

"This. This is what I remember," he said.

It had been years since he'd last visited this place, but it still made him terribly uneasy. The headless quarry was something of a training ground for amateur treasure hunters. The traps had long ago been sprung or disabled, and anything of genuine value had been harvested before he was born. But it still had all the earmarks of a Bygone site. The walls were carved with the seals of various members of Bygone families, many of which he now recognized from the streets and the crypt in Clickspring. Huge pennants or banners hung down, oddly folded partway to the ground on complicated struts emerging from the wall until their tassled bottoms brushed the floor. It was a masterclass in iconography, structure, layout, all without the risk the better-hidden vaults carried with them. And this? This was the room that gave the place its name.

Hundreds of statues stood in neutral poses, filling the center of the chamber in a grid. Here and there, one of the statues was missing. Divots in the floor suggested it had been bolted in place and had to be wrenched free. That explained why so many of them still remained. Removing one was a chore. If they'd ever had heads, they hadn't survived much longer than the first few treasure seekers. Now they stood, bronze-cast statues. Some had the remnants of gold or silver inlay. Most had been stripped of it. In place of a neck was a single mounting peg or the hole where one had been. Loops and fixture points on the joints and shoulders suggested they may once have been wearing equipment or costumes, but like anything else of value, the gear was long gone.

Mevrelle reached into his satchel as he walked. He produced one of the stolen couplers. "You will repair it."

"Repair what?" he asked. "These aren't contraptions. Trust me, if they were, I would have hauled them home years ago." He thumped the chest of the nearest statue as they walked past. "Solid metal," he said.

The elf shook his head. "What have the years made of the Maskers?"

They reached the rear wall of the chamber. Like the rest of the place, it had been stripped bare, with only the tiniest indications of where banners, wall sconces, and other items had once been. A brass hook, no doubt formerly the mounting point of something ornate and valuable that was now gathering dust in a noble's collection, stuck out of the wall beside a small inset shelf. A circular plinth, also stripped of its prize, was all that remained on the shelf.

Mevrelle revealed a short length of rope and looped it over the hook. He slipped the other end around his wrist and pulled it tight. Then, after the hesitation of a man about to tear free the bandage covering a half-healed wound, he removed the mask.

Fel winced at the sight of the man's face. His features were sunken and hollow. He looked on the brink of starvation. Before Fel's very eyes, the sharpness and intensity of his gaze left him, his eyes visibly clouding over. Mevrelle wavered.

If ever there was a moment to act, this was it. Fel reached out to snatch the mask. A brief, desperate moment of clarity came to the elf's face, and he flicked his wrist toward the plinth. The mask snapped into position as if drawn by an unseen string. The moment it made contact with the plinth, the whole chamber shook. Fel grabbed the elf by the neck and bashed him against the wall, then sprinted for the doorway. The slab of stone he was running across dropped a heart-stopping few inches. Then another. Then another. Shift by shift, what had been a long, flat chamber descended into a series of wide stairs. Each with a row of headless statues standing on it. Those between him and the entrance of the chamber fell farther, faster. Suddenly a door that was level with the floor turned into a window dozens of feet above it, nothing but sheer wall leading to it. Gleaming bars dropped to seal it, as if to hammer home that escape was impossible even if he scaled the wall. Below the exit, revealed by the final few shifts of stone, was a cell door. Bars matching those that had sealed the exit slowly retracted into the floor. The greater distance from the thin shaft of light from above meant he could see only the dimmest of forms within.

He peered up. There was no way he could reach the sealed exit. He was trapped here. Fel climbed back to where the mask was mounted and set down Wick to grasp it with both hands. In the back of his mind, he'd expected to feel some sort of horrible, arcane influence when the mask made contact with his flesh. But it was cold, inert metal. Whatever had given the mask access to the elf's mind, it was an enchantment on the elf, not the mask. Having his mind spared of the mask's will was a hollow victory, as it was hopelessly attached to the plinth. No amount of hauling at the thing would dislodge it.

"You must repair it," Mevrelle wheezed.

The ranger was slumped against the wall, bruised by Fel's assault. His eyes gazed into the distance, as if somehow he could see the Greater Lands Wall half a continent away.

"You are in no position to make demands," Fel said. "And I ought to kill you right here and now."

"I know what the mask required me to know. I know that it cannot be removed from the plinth unless it wills it so. And neither can the chamber be restored to its prior state until the mask is removed. You are now as much a prisoner of the mask as I am."

Fel poked him in the chest. "This is what you get for trying to come out here and do... whatever it was you were trying to do. What were you trying to do, anyway? What was worth linking yourself to this thing, declaring war on my family, and trying to get Wick?"

"You've never felt the pressure of that wall on your mind. Never felt your own will denied you. The mask... is just more of the same. I'll do anything to be free of it. Free of it all. And if you want to be free of it, you must repair the contraption at the bottom of the stairs. The mask believed the coupler was all that would be required. But it will not work. I have tried. There is some... fundamental difference. You must repair it."

"I've got bad news for you, then. I'm not the man you want repairing contraptions. If you wanted something fixed, you should have gotten my father. Or grabbed Oiler."

"You are a Masker. A contraptioneer. Heir to the terrible legacy of your twisted kind."

"The apple fell kind of far from the tree this generation."

"You will repair it, or we will both die."

"Don't make me weigh the benefits of trading my life for yours," Fel rumbled. "Right now I am just about ready to take that deal." He crouched and snatched up the fallen coupler and Wick's lantern. "But for now I can at least find out if me dying in here is by choice or not."

He made his way down the steps. The glow of the lantern slowly revealed the form within the cell at the bottom. At first, he had difficulty identifying precisely what he was looking at. There were limbs, but too many of them. The posture seemed wrong to be a human form as well. If he hadn't been to Clickspring, he probably wouldn't have been able to make heads or tails of it. But slowly shapes started to look familiar. There were brass struts and linkages, wood panels, and exposed Bygone Era workings. It had features in common with the bust they'd recovered from his family's old home. This contraption was more complete than the bust. There were additions that were eerily similar to what his father had been working on, and others that were far more alien. This bust may have been intended to serve the same purpose as the one Martin had been building. Specifically, it may have been an attempt to make a bust more similar to a living creature. But it was mimicking something decidedly inhuman. Too many arms and legs. And far too large.

The walls of the chamber were hung with tools. They had signs of significant use, but for Bygone artifacts they were practically immaculate. Easily as intact as anything in his father's collection. This cell must have been some sort of a maintenance room. He crouched in front of it and shoved the contraption inside with his boot, pivoting the section of it that looked most like a torso. A symbol had been carefully inlaid on what he assumed was the thing's chest. It was the Masker family insignia, the same one he'd seen in Clickspring.

"Wick, are you seeing this?" Fel whispered.

"I am," he said.

"Does this look familiar to you?"

"This, specifically, is new. But I believe I see the same similarities you are seeing."

"I don't suppose you have any insight into how I can get out of here."

"This experience is entirely new to me, Fel. You have a tremendous knack to find experiences that are unprecedented."

"If there's one thing I'm good at, it's finding new problems." He turned. "Elf!"

"Fix the contraption!" the ranger snapped.

"You said the mask told you what you need to know?"

"It did."

"Well tell me, because starting now, I need to know everything."

"Your purpose is to repair."

"Listen," Fel said, stomping back up the steps. "Here's what's happening. You and I are locked in here. My friends are out there with one of your little monsters. They already managed to kill one, remember? If they're smart, they've already gone to get help. See, this is the problem with letting an ancient mask do your planning for you. It's not necessarily as bright as you think it is. However, credit where it's due, I know Bygone vaults well enough to know that without activating the switch that opens this place back up, there's no way they're getting inside this place or getting us out until long after we've died of hunger or thirst. The only people your little plan has captured are you, me, and the mask. And like you say, no one's getting out of here until the mask decides to activate the switch. Now you? You look like you'll be dead in twenty minutes no matter what we do. But lucky for you and the mask, I have a will to live. So against my best judgment, I'm going to try to fix this thing. Don't get me wrong, as soon as that door opens, all bets are off. But for now, you win. I'll do the job. But to do the job, I need the help of my dad. I can get that through Wick here. But I'll also need to know exactly what I'm dealing with."

He grabbed the elf by the chin to force him to look him in the eye. "Now tell me."

"That is not relevant," Mevrelle said.

"Everything is relevant," Fel said. "Dad taught me that. If you want to get something working again? You need to know where it was, what was near it, who lived there, everything. Because that tells you what it was probably used for, who probably made it, everything you need to know about what it is supposed to do, and how to make it do that again. So what is this place?"

The elf was silent for a few moments. "This place," he uttered. "It was... a place of testing and a record of conquest."

It was as if he was describing a dream, attempting to relive a memory that he never actually experienced. His eyes darted, looking about at things that weren't there, and each word came through pained labor.

"Each statue bore equipment. True, proper equipment. Equipment from foes the humans had faced in battle. Stolen equipment. Elven equipment. Each statue represented another fallen warrior. It would be dressed. The Warrior would be fixed in place atop the statue. And the Warrior would learn. The strengths of weapons and armor. The weaknesses. And when warriors were captured… they were tested as well… By that… thing…"

"You make it sound like we fought a war with the elves," Fel said.

Mevrelle shook with a dry laugh. "It would seem your own minds have not escaped the rot of your contrivances."

"So says the one who is trying to get me to repair something that was used to test his own kind in combat."

"I desire only freedom. For myself. For my people. At any price."

"Trust me," Fel said, turning back to the cell at the bottom of the stairs. "It's going to be quite a price. Wick, get that information to Dad. Describe the contraption to him. And tell me what I need to do. And you, elf. I don't know if you realize, but you attacked, and pinned to the ground, a contraption specifically designed to repair things. I need that in here."

"No. The Oiler remains outside."

"Why?"

"The Warrior has decreed it so. And so it shall be."

Fel glared at the mask. "I'm getting pretty sick of that thing calling the shots…"

Thirty minutes later, back in Beffshire, Wick was completing Martin's debriefing on the situation. Martin had been jotting down notes as swiftly as he could.

"… And there was a large section of the contraption at the forward end that had been removed. Unconnected ends to linkages were visible."

"Yes, yes," Martin said excitedly. He traced out two shapes on the page and held it up. "They all ended in mounting points that looked like either this or this, correct?"

"That is correct," Wick said.

"Sixteen of type one, twenty-eight of type two?"

"Thirty-six of type two."

"Of course. Of course. Additional limbs. It complicates matters but in a predictable way. You say there were parts and equipment on the walls?"

"Only tools."

He tapped his chin. "No replacement parts… Any raw stock?"

"There is nothing beyond what I have described."

Martin shook his head. "If it was a place of testing, then they must have had the means to repair and improve it. It might stand to reason that there were no parts. Something changing rapidly wouldn't have much use for standard replacements. But if there was no raw stock either, then how would they repair it? There must be another chamber. A proper workshop."

He shut his eyes. "A proper... Bygone Era workshop. Just a few days away. Imagine it."

"There are greater matters at hand presently, Martin," Wick said.

"Right. Yes. Fortunately, my entire life has been spent repairing equipment without the proper parts or tools. And Fel at least has the proper tools, so that's a tremendous asset. And he has Oiler, which should be a help, but I've already seen that it struggles with items that are incomplete rather than simply broken. In its present state, there is no means to connect the mask to the rest of the contraption in the cell. Fel has the coupler, and the coupler will work with the mask. But those linkages will need to be connected to a plate, and the plate will need to be engraved with the following symbols, in the following order. He'll need a graver or a burin. If there isn't one, he can use the sharp end of... any tool with a sharp end. He'll need to sacrifice the operation of one of the limbs and use that plate to replace the mounting point for the head. Oh, and furthermore." He shook his head again. "Never mind. I'll write this all down and burn it."

He set about filling the page. "A war with elves," he muttered to himself. "If ever the elves and humans occupied the same place, and the existence of Clickspring affirms their proximity in the Bygone Era, there must have been clashes. But why am I not aware of anything specific? If there was a war of such a scale that it was worth creating a laboratory quite near to my own home to fight the foe, there should be evidence. Evidence beyond the laboratory itself, that is. And this contraption... this animated framework... whatever it ought to be called, why haven't we found anything like it elsewhere? Only early, immobile prototypes in Clickspring and now in this hidden chamber locked by one of the masks. We have found endless weapons from the Bygone Era. They're invariably taken by the nobles, sequestered with good reason. But we've never found anything like this. If it was a weapon of war, what sense would there be in having just one?"

He finished jotting down a page and looked it over. Satisfied, he opened the door of Wick's lantern and burned the page.

"Unless it wasn't finished. The reference material Fel and Tome have found has some of the basic concepts. It's how I was able to add arms to my own bust."

He paused. "Incomplete, in development, at the moment of some great change and destruction. A moment that literally split the world. And I've been working on something so similar."

He put pen to page on the next bit of instruction. "The masks reawakening. The Bolivans, the Graves family, elves, everyone seeking the same things. Things are happening all at once. I'm not a man who believes in things like fate. But there are forces at work here, Wick. And I worry that those of us at the center can't help but play our part."

"As Teya would say, destiny," Wick said.

"Let us hope that destiny has our best interests at heart."

"Forgive the observation, Martin, but it seldom does."

"You have insight into destiny?"

"I was created to observe. And I have observed at length. I have observed that great things take effort. They take time. They are achieved when many come together to a common cause. But nature seeks to level. To balance. Mountains erode into sand. Buildings crumble. If destiny is a force in this world, it is an equalizing force. And I do not believe it comes to push us to new heights. I believe it comes to knock down those things that have grown too tall."

"In my opinion, society has yet to reach the heights of the Bygone Era once more. We've never fully recovered. If destiny seeks such a thing, it is early."

"Or it is anticipating that the next step will be a tremendous leap forward."

Martin finished another page and pushed it into the lantern. "I am a contraptioneer. These are matters for historians and philosophers. You may be right. But right now, the important thing is my son's life. And it depends upon this task. That page should complete the procedure. Relay every word with care. Fel has the knack for this, even if he doesn't think he does. He can do this."

"And what happens after?" Wick asked.

"I have no clue," Martin said. "But whatever it is, I trust him to handle it. Improvisation is in his blood."

— ◆ —

CHAPTER 15

Hours had passed. For Tome and Teya, lingering in the quarry with nothing to do but worry about Fel and work on riddles had been taking its toll.

"Try this one," Tome said. "What can lay low even the mightiest of warriors, yet restores strength to the weak and weary?"

Teya glared at Tome.

"Do you not listen?" Teya said. "You hear me now? How I talk? This is with practice. This language? I know good. Say good. These riddles? Too long!"

"The short ones don't work!" Tome said. "Unless you're saying them wrong."

"Hard to say!" she said.

"Then focus on teaching me to say them."

She crossed her arms. "Teach to say? Without say? How?"

"I don't know," Tome said. "Can you write them?"

"Can you read them?" she asked.

"... This is an intractable problem," he said.

"I say we kill! You use magic."

"My spells are really rather slow to activate, you'll note. That thing is too fast."

"So? I try to kill, you try to kill. Maybe Parch try to kill. One will survive."

"I don't like plans that make survival a hopeful outcome rather than a certain one. No. The way through this is to solve the riddle of the riddle. Do you remember what the elf shouted for any of the commands?"

"No."

"Nor do I. But they didn't seem so long. Not as long as the translations you're giving me. And there must be some deeper nuance, because he had the thing fetch a lantern and deliver it. I cannot imagine there is some riddle with the answer 'fetch a lantern and deliver it.'"

"I gave you words. His riddle? Word. Not words."

"What?"

"Word! Word. Whole riddle, one word," she said.

207

"How can that… wait… It's a language innate to a mystical being that is obsessed with riddles. Of course the language would be built around riddles. And the shortest, easiest words in any language tend to be the most important. All through this trip I've been grappling with vocabulary. One doesn't start with the vocabulary when working with a new language! I should have been starting with the alphabet."

He fetched some pages and a pen. "I've been tackling this like spoken magic, but there is a better way. Here, here. Write down the letters and tell me the sounds they make."

"I do, but why?" Teya said, taking the materials. "How you make word?"

"I am a paper mage, that's how. Spoken magic is tremendously powerful to the spellcaster, if the spell is complete and the caster has the knack to cast it. But my spells change potency by location, by time, by caster… The art of being a paper mage is understanding language at its very root, understanding nuance, and, yes, divining through raw intuition how to achieve the proper meaning with speed, efficiency, and intensity. Trust me, I have trained my whole life for this."

Teya regarded him with a dash of respect.

"Temerity," she said.

"Quite so," he said.

She scribbled out the letters and tapped them, one after the other. Through tortured struggles she was able to croak the proper pronunciation of each one, both its name and the sounds it represented. Tome marked down the phonetic sounds and started linking them to the shape and structures of the words they'd conjured up in previous attempts at riddles. Finally, he scratched out a word, cleared his throat, and spoke it aloud.

Once the word was spoken, he watched the sphinx. The change was subtle. Rather that almost looking through him, like Tome was a piece of scenery, it looked at him. Its posture straightened, and it waited.

"What you say?" Teya whispered.

"In effect, 'listen.' And it appears to be doing so." He started to scratch out a new word. "It isn't much, but it's a start."

Fel hammered at the contraption, making steady progress at dislodging the only mechanism so far that didn't use removeable fasteners.

"Your father emphasizes this should be done with care," Wick said.

"It's a Bygone contraption," he grunted between blows. "Held together with rivets. And I don't have a drill. I'm working with a cold chisel and a hammer. There's no such thing as doing this with care. This is going to be done… with… force!"

A final blow dislodged what he'd found himself referring to as "the other arm" on the right side. Once it was free, a few pulled pins and twisted fasteners removed the plate that had affixed it to the arm. He flipped it up to find the bottom of the plate had the proper connectors for the spider-leg-like linkages sticking out the top. Just not enough.

"Dad's sure I can just double up on these?" Fel said.

"I would use the word 'confident,'" Wick said. "I do not believe statements about such things can be made with certainty until they have been attempted."

"Eh. 'Confident' for Dad is as good as 'sure' for most other people." He worked the fasteners into place.

"Have you developed a plan for what to do once this works, if it does?" Wick asked.

"I'll wait for the door to open and run like an ancient mechanical warrior is chasing me," he whispered.

"And if the door doesn't open?"

"Then I'll hope I did a really terrible job repairing this thing," he said.

He fitted the final linkage into place, using the removed limb for spare parts. Now that the assorted components were repositioned or reattached, Fel had a clearer picture of what this thing was. In a way, it looked like if someone had finished what his father had started but continued working on it anyway. It had a relatively human trunk, albeit one formed of wood and brass. Two fully articulated arms stuck out of the left side, and, thanks to his efforts, there was only one arm on the right. These limbs were spindly, like a wire armature that something else was intended to be sculpted atop, and had a more silvery, ironlike appearance complete with small motes of rust. Both of the left arms had plates attached, formed with the level of workmanship he'd come to expect from the era. The plates were rough approximations of the muscles of the forearm and upper arm. They didn't fully encapsulate the spindly armature, large gaps showing through almost artistically to the metal underneath. The single right arm lacked the plates and had no fixture points to attach them. As if to compensate, the hand was larger, more of a gauntlet than the thin, dexterous ones on the left.

The lower half of the thing was more of a mystery. It had twice the usual complement of legs, and there had been no attempt at humanity. They were heavily armored, such that he doubted they would have been able to straighten into a normal human stance without the armor plates interfering. He couldn't tell much about them, as they were tangled beneath the rest of the contraption, but they were spaced at the four corners of a heavy mounting plate where the pelvis should be.

"That concludes your father's instructions," Wick said. "If all is well, positioning the coupler on top of the plate you've reinstalled should cause it to affix. The mask can be affixed to the opposite end."

He turned. "Elf your—ah!"

Fel had no sooner turned than he found himself face to face with the elf. Or more accurately, the Warrior mask the elf had once again donned. Mevrelle leaned heavily on the wall beside the contraption.

"Well done, Masker," he breathed, though it was not clear if the statement was his own, the mask's, or if such a distinction even existed while he was wearing it.

"What about your end of the bargain?" he asked.

"You will be set free when I am satisfied you have completed your task."

The elf shoved Fel with a strength such a ragged form shouldn't have been able to muster. Fel stumbled back and nearly tripped over the lower step. He turned to the alcove at the top of the steps and squinted at it. Perhaps naively, he'd believed the simple removal of the mask would unlock the room. The rudiments of a plan he'd been able to piece together while working on the contraption had centered on taking full advantage of the moments after the elf removed the mask. However, the news was not all bad. Something in the alcove had changed. At this distance and in this light, he couldn't be certain what had been altered, but if the mask had been removed and the room was still in this configuration, surely some sort of switch had been actuated. After all, this was a room meant to be used. If the mask would be occupied elsewhere for part of that time, some alternate means of activating the mechanisms of the room would need to be available. Now there were tools accessible. Even if there was nothing but the plinth, he had a fighting chance of unlocking the door and restoring the room one way or another. But turning his back on the elf and the contraption for more than a few moments seemed like a bad idea. For now, with a Bygone Era mallet in one hand and Wick's lantern in the other, he could only try to prepare himself for whatever might come next.

Mevrelle pulled the mask from his face once more and dropped to his knees. With shaking hands, he pressed the back of the mask to the coupler. For a long moment, there was nothing but his ragged breathing. Then, motion. The coupler pivoted at its center, precisely as it did when the Student was attached. And just as with the Student, no silver discs appeared in the eyes of the mask.

"What of my vision, Masker?" said the mask.

The Student's voice had been varying degrees of bright and inquisitive when attached to either the original bust or the one his father had created. The Warrior's voice was something wholly other. This was a mask that was not meant for conversation. It spoke with a sound like blades being drawn across shields, a grinding, inhuman sound.

"If you wanted vision, you should have gotten my father and given him a few more months. This is as far as he got."

"Pity. But for now, it will suffice. There are senses beyond sight."

One of the left arms reached out and planted itself against the wall. With the support, its legs shifted and repositioned, moving smoothly and precisely into a wide, four-point stance. Now standing, the thing towered over Fel, no less than ten feet tall. He took a step back as the four sets of legs worked in opposition, clanking the thing toward the steps.

"All right, you're up. You're moving. Now open the door," Fel said.

"I am a warrior, Masker. The Warrior. I exist to serve those who seek conquest. If you wish me to serve you, you must prove yourself a worthwhile master."

"I don't want you to serve me. I just want you to open the door!" Fel snapped. "We had a deal!"

"If you wanted negotiation, you should have sought the Diplomat," the Warrior said, matching Fel's own tone, if not his voice. "Now, prove to me you deserve freedom. Prove to me that you deserve life."

The terrible mechanism thundered toward him. Fel dashed up the steps and slid to a stop behind one of the statues.

"This is an unexpected and undesirable occurrence," Wick said.

"Unexpected? I thought you were supposed to be observant!" he said.

A long grinding sound rang out, then one of the feet rose past the bottom step and came down atop it.

"Yes," the Warrior said. "The chamber. I know it well."

The second foot rose and set down much more surely. Step after step, it began to climb the stairs. Fel held still and kept quiet. Having put the thing together, he was better equipped than he had ever been to take it back apart, and he'd broken his fair share of contraptions even without that benefit. Bygone Era equipment was nearly indestructible. Fel Masker had made a living exploring the limits of the word "nearly."

The Warrior thundered past him. He hefted his hammer, trying to decide if he could risk trying to scramble onto the thing's back, or if he should try throwing the weapon instead. Fel took what he thought was a silent step forward. The mask turned toward him, facing him perfectly. The entire torso pivoted in place. The lone right hand reached out, sweeping its surroundings until it groped onto the arm of one of the statues. In a continuous motion, it wrenched the thing from its mountings and hurled it toward Fel. He dove aside a fraction of a second before the heavy metal statue clashed with the one he'd been hiding behind, wrenching it free as well. Fel scrambled to his feet and dashed up the steps. The Warrior followed. For a being that could not see, it moved with impressive precision. Mercifully for Fel, this precision had its limits. Every few strides, one of its feet clipped the edge of a step, and the thing stumbled and corrected. Each stumble gave Fel a few precious steps of lead. And with distance, the thing's hearing became less reliable for locating him.

He reached the alcove where the mask had been. The removal of the mask had caused the plinth to slide aside, revealing a small panel of small brass switches. There were eight in total. They could have controlled anything. This could have been the input panel for some manner of locking code. The controls could have been used to activate or deactivate an assortment of traps. If the High were with him, they were straightforward controls for the room's configuration. He rubbed a layer of grime from the top of the panel. Ancient writing revealed itself.

"What's it say?" he whispered, holding the lantern high.

Behind him, he heard the click of the Warrior shifting toward him.

"Awfully good hearing for something with no ears," he muttered, tensing for a quick retreat as it stumbled toward him.

"From left to right," Wick began. "Door lock 1. Door lock 2. Floor Level Adjustment 1. Floor Level—"

The creak of metal signaled yet another statue being torn from the ground.

"Time's up!" Fel said.

He reached up and raked his fingers across the entire panel, toggling every switch. Unseen mechanisms ground and rattled all around him. The bars blocking the exit retracted. The bars to the repair cell snapped shut. The floor began to rumble. Fel sidled along the wall, eyes fixed on the far side of the room. Once the ground rose up to be level with the doorway, he'd make his escape. The steps started to equalize… and he felt a slow slide of stone against his back.

The stairs weren't collapsing up. They were collapsing down. The top of the steps was lowering. He scrambled back toward the alcove with the controls and leaped for it, but the step he was on had already dropped far enough to place the controls out of reach. He turned. For now, the grinding of the room had completely robbed the Warrior of any means to locate Fel, which would have been incredibly valuable if there had been some way to reach an exit or a hiding place. Instead, it simply meant that Fel was safe to observe the change and perhaps spot something that might help him.

As with the far side of the room, the descending floor revealed more of the wall. The top of a doorway slid into view, just to his left. Dreams of some secret escape tunnel were shattered a second later when the continued descent revealed more of the same stout bars. He tried to ignore the stinging realization that this door had likely been open until he raked his fingers across the buttons. Instead, he crouched down and held Wick up to cast light within.

"Of course…" he growled.

The room was filled to the brim with weapons of every sort. There were what he assumed to be elven weapons: axes, swords, and shields. He also saw Bygone contraptions that looked like they could allow a man to single-handedly lay siege to a city. They were precisely the sorts of things that might turn the tide of the battle for him, and they were all locked behind bars he couldn't hope to get past. The rattling came to a stop. The floor was flat again. Not only was the rumbling that had hidden his movements gone, but now the stairs that had fouled the blind contraption's own movements were gone as well. It was quite literally a level playing field. That put Fel at a terrible disadvantage.

The Warrior clanked its single right arm along the ground until it found one of the broken-free statues and raised it. Then it became still. As a nonliving thing, the stillness was unnatural, unnerving, complete. Far more stationary than any proper creature could be. Instincts born of the need to avoid predators did strange things when something ceased to move the way a flesh-and-blood threat would. The mind slowly came to believe the threat was gone. Fel tried to hold on to the fear. He held his breath, tried to match the thing's stillness, and racked his brain for some sort of tactic that would get him clear, or at least buy him time.

The answer came to him, as it so often did, once the lack of any sane choices made an insane one seem suddenly palatable. He raised his mallet, tensed his legs, and gave the bars a solid blow.

They didn't budge, but a piercing, reverberating ring filled the chamber. The Warrior's torso rotated one full revolution, spinning the statue up to a terrifying speed. It released the projectile. Fel threw himself against the wall. The lobbed statue perfectly struck where he'd been standing, smashing into the bars. Even with all that force, the blow wasn't enough to bash through them. But the shot was potent enough to bend two of them apart. Fel heaved himself into the widened gap as the Warrior stalked toward him. The burly adventurer wasn't made for squeezing through tight spaces, but desperation had a way of coaxing a man to test his limits. After persuading his ribs and pelvis to shift and contort in ways that he'd probably feel for weeks, he tumbled through the bars.

It wasn't quite fast enough. A gauntlet closed around his boot, clenching it like a vise. The Warrior tried to drag him back through the bars. He planted his other foot against the bars and heaved. Laces snapped an instant before tendons would have, and the boot slipped free. He dropped to the floor on the safe side of the bars and hauled himself up. His wrenched ankle was not happy with having to support his weight, but Fel ignored its protests. He grabbed the nearest weapon he could reach, a spear, and brandished it. A contraption probably would have been better, but at the moment the time he'd spend figuring out how to operate it was potentially time he didn't have. A spear didn't need instructions.

"Cowardice is unbecoming of a true warrior," the contraption rumbled.

"It's not cowardice," Fel said. "It's strategy."

"My memory of this place is precise and complete," the Warrior said. "You are in the armory. Those weapons were made to slice flesh and pierce armor. They were to be used by me. Not against me. Nothing there can damage me."

All three hands of the mechanism clamped onto the bars. Fel propped the base of the spear between to bricks in the floor. He leveled the tip at the mask and waited. Bars groaned and creaked, bending apart. When they were wide enough for the Warrior's upper body to pass through, it became still again. It was waiting. The next sound, it would strike.

"You are unworthy to command me. Face the fate that awaits the weak," it taunted.

Fel narrowed his eyes. "Come and get me," he said.

The thing moved like a sprung trap, bursting forward with all its force. Fel stood his ground and supported the spear. The full force and weight of the Warrior drove it against the tip, which slid right through its hollow eye and raked against the side of the coupler.

The warrior shuddered and twitched, head turned grotesquely aside. It scrambled back out the doorway, dragging the spear with it. Formerly fluid motions were now stuttering and stiff. It groped at the air until it found the spear handle and pulled it free.

"Bygone Era stuff is pretty tough, big fella!" Fel mocked. "But that coupler is brand new! They just don't make things like they used to, do they?"

The grinding, ringing excuse for a voice the Warrior spoke in was swallowed in a roar of fury. It backed away.

"What's the matter?" Fel called after it, pulling an ax from the wall. "Feel the need to retreat?"

The Warrior grasped the same fallen statue and hurled it at the bars again. They became even more mangled but held firm. The Warrior rattled and rocked in place, briefly appearing as though it would fall to pieces. The tremor slowed and steadied, and it grasped another statue. Fel stood clear of the barred door and waited for yet another attack. Clattering motion began again, then the terrifying whistle of something moving at tremendous speed. He heard the metal fingers release with a snap. An instant later there was an impact, not on the wall but against the ceiling directly above. Stone rained down. He peeked around to see the Warrior groping for another statue and whirring to speed again.

Another blow caused a huge section of the stone roof to rain down, littering the battlefield with stone fragments ranging from the size of boulders to scatterings of gravel. Fel couldn't work out what the thing was attempting. Had it lost its mind? Was it fully malfunctioning?

The answer came when it grasped a rock the size of Fel's head and pitched it at the bars. Unlike the huge statue, the stone passed through quite readily. And when it struck the far wall of the armory, it shattered and sent fragments scouring every corner of the chamber. Fel took the pelting with a few bruises and one fresh slash, but a few more of those and he wouldn't be walking away from this encounter. He scrambled to a section of the wall with shields and pulled one down. Properly defended, he dove back to the corner beside the wall and huddled behind it in time to deflect another scattering of stone with the lantern right beside him.

"I have to admit," Fel said to Wick as a shattered stone chip made it past the shield and cut his cheek. "That mask can fight."

Three more stones struck before the Warrior decided it needed more pieces to throw. Fel took advantage of the brief pause to lean aside. A heavy statue launched upward and crackled through the roof. New pieces of stone, and a bright splash of sun, fell from above. The statue didn't return. The thing had broken clean through the roof.

"I don't suppose you have any ideas, Wick?" Fel said.

"Military strategy is not one of my strengths, Fel. Should I seek the advice of your father?"

"No. If I die, tell them I died. Otherwise, no sense worrying them worse than they're already worried. There's nothing they can do for me from there."

The thing grasped a stone. He took cover again.

"It is damaged," Wick said as the bombardment began again. "It is possible you can simply wait for it to fail entirely."

"That might take a while. But I suppose if it doesn't have guts to come in here and get me, it's the safest option until we think of a better one."

He racked his brain and improved his shield grip as the ground was steadily covered with a layer of jagged stone. Then without warning, the bombardment stopped. Fel held still, fearful that the Warrior was trying to draw him out.

"Finally," uttered the Warrior. "Remove him."

Fel gripped the ax beside him. After all the chaos and mayhem, he'd forgotten there were other threats. He didn't have to wait long to learn which was coming for him. The flutter of wings, followed by the padding of feline feet. He stood and raised the ax. The sphinx stepped into view. He tensed, waiting for it to make its move. The ax was far too heavy a weapon for so speedy a beast. He knew the moment he committed to an attack, it would sweep aside and strike. His only hope was to daze it with a defensive blow and finish it before it recovered. Seconds slipped by as the thing quietly observed him. Then, it simply turned, stalked to the doorway, and took a seat.

"About time you figured it out!" Fel shouted.

"I believe I deserve more credit for gaining a functioning knowledge of a new language in mere days, even with a tutor," Tome replied from the entryway, high above the ground.

"What is this?" the Warrior rumbled.

"Aim for its neck! The coupler is the weak point!" Fel shouted. "And send a rope down here so I can—"

"Yaa-haa!" Teya crowed, her voice rapidly growing louder.

He peeked around the wall to see her sliding down one of the floor-to-ceiling banners.

"What are you doing!? Don't come down here!" he shouted.

"Too late!" she cried, dropping down and charging the Warrior.

The kobold's less-than-stealthy approach did an excellent job of drawing the Warrior's attention, and the fact that she was a moving target made it clear that its precision had suffered greatly after the damage to the coupler. Neither stone nor statue met its mark as she bounded and sprang toward the Warrior. For a brief and shining moment it seemed as though the mad creature would single-handedly eliminate the raging contraption. But the moment she was near enough to leap onto it, the thing swatted her out of the air. She rolled twice and slid into the wall, dazed but not badly injured. She was able to scramble aside an instant before a stone struck where she landed.

Teya's continuing distraction gave Fel the opportunity to crawl through the bars, followed swiftly by the sphinx. Once the Warrior turned its attention to him, the sphinx switched from defense to attack. It began to harry the Warrior. Fel hurried to Teya's side.

"All right, here's the plan. I'll keep its attention fully on me. Me and the sphinx anyway. You take this ax, climb up there, and—"

A jangling of chain from behind her revealed, just a moment too late, that she hadn't come alone. Oiler's head popped up from the pack on her back, and its one fully intact claw gripped the handle of the ax, tugging it away and tossing it aside.

The clang of the weapon hitting the ground drew the Warrior's attention away from the sphinx. It grabbed a stone and hurled it in their direction. Teya and Fel had wisely abandoned the weapon rather than attempt to retrieve it, so the stone harmlessly struck were it had landed.

"Why did you bring Oiler down here!" Fel said.

"It take weapon. You fight Warrior. Warrior has no weapon? Not my fault!"

"The Warrior is also a half-broken contraption. We don't need Oiler fixing him up!"

The Warrior swatted ineffectually at the sphinx and charged toward the pair as they argued. They scattered and circled around, meeting behind.

"We need a way to keep it distracted by more than just that sphinx. Something it can't just bash to pieces," Fel said.

Teya's eyes brightened. "Idea!" she crowed. She shrugged the pack off her back and handed it to Fel, then snatched Wick's lantern. "We go!" she shouted.

She scrambled across the floor. Fel dashed in the other direction, sliding to a stop at the barred doorway of the cell that had previously held the inner contraption now in control of the Warrior. He dropped the pack.

"Stay here, stay safe, disarm that thing, not us, and don't fix that thing if we break it!" he said.

Oiler looked curiously at him, then looked to its damaged claw and seemed to notice the scattering of spare parts from Fel's own repair efforts. With its own repair to occupy itself, it seemed perfectly content to ignore Fel as he made his way to the fallen ax and plucked it up. He raised his head and scanned the chaotic battleground for Teya. Her cackling glee made her easy to find, for both him and the Warrior. With wide eyes and a wider smile, she grabbed one of the tufts from the bottom of a banner and stuffed it into Wick's open lantern. The cloth took eagerly to flame.

At first, Fel couldn't imagine why lighting the banner did any good besides feeding Teya's worrisome preoccupation with fire. But it wasn't just a fire, it was Wick's fire. And as the banner began to burn, Wick took it upon himself to shout.

"We must go this way! Quickly! Let us escape!"

The Warrior dashed toward the source of the voice and assaulted the burning banner. Teya scampered along the wall and set fire to each of the banners on that side. The Warrior backed away. It was not a mindless beast, even if the ongoing attacks, multiplying targets, and damage seemed to be pushing it to the brink of frenzy. It realized quite swiftly that the voice was from the flame, but now that Wick was shouting from three burning banners at once, the targeted cacophony seemed to be enough to keep it from locating Fel and Teya.

"I make more! Like dragon!" the kobold shouted, dashing for the banners on the other side.

Fel caught her and hissed in her ear. "No! No, just on one side. Come on. We need to get out of here."

"But fight!" she said.

"We get out of here so we're not trapped with that thing, then we fight it out in the open," he said.

She nodded. "This! Good!"

Fel peered up at the caved-in ceiling. Teya had set flame to the only banner that was anywhere near the place where the broken roof was near enough to climb out, but he very much doubted he would have been able to make it out that way besides. The battle hadn't been treating him well.

"Can you climb this wall? Up to the entryway up there?" Fel asked, pointing to the open door high above.

"I can!" she said.

She dashed over and grabbed Oiler's tail. The contraption obligingly let it reel out of the pack and continued picking at the scattered parts, searching for pieces that would help repair its broken claw. With the ease of climbing a ladder, the kobold scaled the wall. There wasn't quite enough tail to make it all the way to the door, resulting in Oiler being dragged up and away from its precious spare parts. It reeled its head and arms out as the pack followed Teya up the wall so that it could keep working. She vanished through the door and braced herself. Fel grabbed the chain and started to climb. A painfully wrenched ankle and more minor bruises and cuts than he could count made his trip up the wall a good deal slower than Teya's, even with the chain to help. But the crackling fire and shrieking sphinx kept the Warrior busy. He grabbed the edge of the exit tunnel and hauled himself up with the help of Teya and Tome a half-second before he heard a shriek and a sickening crunch. Fel winced. Even though the blasted sphinx had nearly killed him plenty of times before, something inside him still recoiled at the thought of it being smashed while attempting to defend him. He got to his feet. The tree of them started to haul Oiler up. Below, the Warrior thundered toward them, noisily smashing aside two statues along the way. A sudden, sharp yank tore Oiler's tail from their grip and sent it tumbling back into the chamber.

"Oiler!" Fel shouted.

He hurried to the edge and peered down. Oiler was reeling itself back together, seemingly none the worse for wear. The Warrior could have smashed the smaller contraption to bits, but its fury remained focused on Fel and Teya. It pointed its unseeing mask in their direction and crouched. Four metallic legs snapped straight, and the whole contraption launched toward them. Fel sprinted down the tunnel, Teya close behind. Tome, as evidence of his lesser bravery and greater sense, was already well on his way down the dim passageway. The Warrior crashed against the doorframe, dragged its way through, and gave chase. In the battle chamber, it would have easily overtaken them. But the tunnel wasn't made for something of its size to move quickly. Maneuvering four legs and a towering frame through human-sized passages slowed it down. Not much, but enough for Teya and Fel to reach the outside.

They scrambled out the doorway and dashed for the scaffold as Tome shakily scaled it. Getting to the horses and to their allies was all that mattered right now. Fel's ankle screamed for relief, but he refused to make a habit of acknowledging the frailties of his body at times like this. Teya scrambled up the side of the scaffold, climbing one of the uprights just as surely as a ladder. Fel cleared three levels of the wobbly structure, mostly grabbing the next level and hauling himself up now that the ladders were all but kindling. The others reached the top and scrambled onto the stone. He was two levels from the top when the Warrior hurled itself like a meteor. It struck the scaffold halfway up, shattering the platform it struck and each one below it as it descended. The already-damaged construction slumped together, the two sides folding in like a collapsing tent. Fel grabbed hold of one of the uprights and managed to hold firm as it struck its counterpart. A desperate scramble and the extended hands of Teya and Tome brought him to the edge of the sheer rockface. The scaffold tumbled away beneath him.

"Fast, fast!" Teya urged as Fel dragged himself up.

He got to his feet and ran toward the horses. It was at this point that he discovered some very important points that a sounder mind might have caught before this crucial moment. First, there hadn't been anything for Tome to tie the horses to before he came to Teya's aid. Second, like Tome, the horses had too little fortitude and too much common sense to remain nearby while sections of the ground were collapsing and bloodthirsty contraptions were raging. They'd retreated to the edge of the quarry. The only one waiting for him was Parch beside of a wide, jagged hole bashed through the roof of the chamber.

"Stand aside!" Tome shouted, fingers already tearing the end of a spell.

Fel didn't so much dodge as fall aside as Tome flicked the flaring paper toward the edge of the cliff face. A curl of flame rushed forward and engulfed the mask of the contraption as it pulled itself up. The mask took on a cherry-red glow in the daylight but continued forward as though the attack had been of no more consequence than a breath of wind.

"Ice!" Fel said, leaping to his feet. "Hit it with ice!"

"If fire didn't do anything, what good will ice—"

"Take it from someone who has broken six contraptions by cooling them down too fast. Hit it with ice!"

Tome drew the proper spell and activated it. A rush of frigid magic curled around the mask. Loud popping and crackling rang out, and its steps faltered. Though the legs were barely dusted with frost, they suddenly locked up, the whole massive contraption grinding to a stop.

Fel pulled the small cudgel from his belt, the last weapon available to him, and charged toward the badly malfunctioning contraption. It snapped into a new position as he drew nearer, shifting so quickly and sharply that its whole body rattled and shifted in place. If he'd been a step closer, the motion would have sent the gauntlet crunching through his jaw. He retreated a few steps. Again the Warrior snapped to a new position. And again. The motions came faster and smoother. It was already recovering from the briefly seized components. Fel couldn't get close enough to attack.

"You cannot defeat me," the Warrior said. "I am the final iteration of warfare."

"Please. You're one contraption attached to another. You spent hundreds of years buried in a forgotten part of the world. You're only here because my friends and family stuck our noses where they didn't belong and stirred up a hornet's nest."

"I am conquest! I am the route to victory! I am the Warrior!"

"You're a tool!" Fel said, pacing wide around the hole in the ground leading back into the combat chamber. "And you're a tool that's only good for combat."

Tome followed his lead and joined him on the far side of the hole.

"You are limited, you are incomplete, and you are doomed to fail," the paper mage taunted.

The blind contraption stomped closer to the hole.

"You're a weapon!" Fel said.

The motion fully smoothed again. It stomped closer to them.

"I am a weapon. I am the mightiest weapon ever forged. I am the weapon that fells armies, that conquers worlds. And were you a fraction of the contraptioneer of your ancestors, you could have wielded me to serve your own purposes. But you are too weak to handle a weapon of my magnitude."

The first of the contraption's feet savagely stomped down on the edge of the hole. A hunk of stone dropped away, and the foot slipped through. If the Warrior had only two feet, it would have tumbled into the chamber below. But with three feet still firmly planted, it was able to recover.

"Pointless, desperate gambits. Even without vision I cannot be beaten. Submit to your defeat so that I can find a worthy hand to hold a weapon such as I."

Jangling chain rang out from within the hole. A brass claw extended through and grasped the sharp edge of the stone around the hole. The Warrior turned to face the source of the sound. Oiler reeled itself up.

"The Oiler," the Warrior said. "Precisely what I need. Now that I am a complete contraption with a faulty component, it cannot help but repair me."

"Oiler, don't you dare!" Fel said.

Oiler turned its expressionless head toward Fel, then toward the Warrior. It shifted, and something large and metallic launched up from below, latching on to the Warrior's mask. Not until it clamped tight and Oiler started attempting to reel it back in did Fel realize what it was. Oiler had successfully repaired itself with the spare parts available. Specifically, it had replaced its entire faulty claw with the gauntlet of the arm Fel had removed. And of the two actions Oiler was capable of taking, it had decided "remove the weapon" was far preferable to "repair the contraption."

The Warrior grasped the gauntlet and tried to pull it free, but the coupler groaned at the additional strain. Fel snatched up Oiler and dragged it across to the other side of the hole. Tome grabbed hold, as did Teya. The three of them hauled against the might of the Warrior. Finally Parch galloped up. Teya hooked a chain link over his horn. The whole group hauled at Oiler. Metal plinked and popped. The Warrior's limbs twitched and trembled. The chain grew so taut that Teya was hauled into the air, dangling from it. She abandoned the chain and grabbed Fel's cudgel.

"Destiny!" she cried, scampering up the struggling contraption's back and hammering at the coupler.

Three solid hits finally shattered the component. The body slumped forward, nearly taking Teya with it as it went lifeless and tumbled through the jagged hole. Fel and the others went sprawling backward. The mask popped free and rattled to the ground behind them.

After constant chaos from the moment the mask had been affixed, the silence that followed felt unnatural. Fel's heart was thumping in his chest. He was bleeding from a dozen places. One boot was missing, and his ankle was starting to swell. But he was alive, and the danger was gone. Fel finally let the strength leave him. He sat heavily on the ground and promptly found himself beneath a pile composed of Parch and Oiler, each jockeying for position on or near him.

"We did it... It's over," Fel said.

"What? No! What do you mean it's over!" Tome said, creeping up to the edge of the hole.

"I mean we won!" Fel fetched the fallen mask. "We got the mask, we broke the coupler, and we defeated the warrior contraption. It's over."

"What about the elf, Fel? Did you kill him?" Tome asked.

Fel glared at Tome. "Wick," Fel said. "Are those banners still burning?"

"They are."

"Do you see the elf anywhere?"

"He is not present anywhere within the chamber below. I was distracted by the attacks on your life and thus had my attention focused primarily on the Warrior during combat. So I can only state with certainty that the elf was present and unmasked at the time the Warrior mask was installed on the coupler and is now absent."

Fel sighed. Teya scampered over to help him up.

"If he doesn't have the mask, then he should be easy to find, right?" Fel said.

"Yes! No help, he go. There, to the wall," Teya said.

"But we start here. The last thing we need is for all of us to gather ourselves up and march off to the south and have him hiding somewhere, ready to pick us off. Not to mention there are still some stolen goods unaccounted for." He huffed a breath and limped forward. "If anyone sees my boot, give a holler."

Two hours of searching had turned up very little. On the plus side, that meant no arrows had been fired at them, no spells cast, no mystics sicced on them. On the other, their target was gone without a trace. The only things their search turned up were one of his father's couplers, badly damaged by falling stones, and Fel's ruined boot. That meant the elf, the Student mask, and a coupler were unaccounted for. After receiving the last minor healing spell Tome had, Teya took it upon herself to ride Parch south to see if there was some sign that the elf had indeed heeded the call of the wall once more. Fel had wanted to come, but he quickly found out that having a war machine attempt to wrench off his ankle was the sort of thing that slowed a man down. Without the horses, he would be little good in a pursuit. Instead, he, Oiler, and Tome stayed behind until he could be patched up.

"A few more lines and I'll have a spell finished for that ankle," Tome said.

"Is it going to do any good? The last one didn't even completely stop me from bleeding," Fel said.

"The last one was written to generally heal injuries. This one is written to heal your ankle," Tome said. "By now you should know that specificity impacts potency."

"Yeah, well, by now you should know that almost getting killed makes me cranky, and you shouldn't pay any attention to what I'm saying." He held up the shredded leather boot. "This was also my best pair of boots."

Tome wrote the final word, tore the edge, and pressed it to Fel's ankle. Faint blue light whisked its way around the wound. He shuddered at the sensation, but gradually the swelling eased away and with it the pain. Fel sighed in relief.

"You do good work, Tome," he said. "I think maybe it's worth saying that a bit more often."

"I wouldn't turn down a bit of praise, but gratitude isn't necessary. Not so long ago, I was becoming concerned my time in Beffshire was making me too comfortable. Limiting my mobility. Limiting my growth. But in light of the recent necessity to learn a new language and use it to gain control of a mystic creature, albeit briefly, I suspect I continue to gain more from our bizarre association than I lose from it."

"By the High, if you thought life with the Maskers was going to make you soft, I could have set you straight on that with one glance at the scars on my back."

The clopping of hooves caused both Fel and Tome to snap their heads to the south. It was Teya, and she was leading both of their horses with her.

"I don't like that we've reached the point that I'm reacting to any given sound like a cat in a dog kennel..." Fel muttered.

"Hypervigilance seems to be one of the many gifts my time with your family has given me," Tome said.

As Teya drew nearer, it became clear that the horses weren't the only things she was bringing along. A small figure was riding on Fel's horse.

"Davie!" Fel shouted, jumping up to his recently restored feet. "Where were you! I thought you were supposed to save my neck if things got hot!"

Davie stood with remarkable stability on the saddle of a moving horse. "You know what your problem is, Masker?" he said. "You got too many enemies."

He hopped down and grabbed the edge of one of the saddlebags. After a quick rummage while the horses finished their approach, he tossed something to Fel. It was a noble's badge of service.

"Where'd you get this?" Fel said.

"Off that fellow who was torturing your family last week," Davie said.

"Did you kill him?" Fel asked with the complex tone of someone who was both worried and hopeful the answer was yes.

"I doubt it. Unless he's a pushover. Point is, he was on your tail with some reinforcements, and I don't think he had official business in mind. I was busy taking care of him. I take it you had a tough time?"

"All things considered, it was a fairly typical caper for me. So yes, borderline lethal."

"At least you're on the happy side of the border, huh? Teya here says you didn't get the elf?"

"No. We got most of what he stole, though."

"And no idea where he went?"

"Not unless Teya spotted something," he said.

She shook her head. Fel rubbed his face.

"So that's it. We lost him. If we're lucky, he'll starve to death somewhere between here and the wall, and we'll never have to worry about him again. If we're not lucky, and we never are, he's figured out how to survive out here regardless, and we'll cross paths again."

"He still has the Student mask, right? Can't we track that?"

"The masks can track each other, but are you in a hurry to stick this thing back on a bust?" Fel asked, nudging the Warrior mask. "I say we cut our losses and head home. Chances are, if there's anyone out there who wants me dead, he'll come along and try to kill me on the way back, and we can take care of him then."

"So that's it? We just return to Beffshire?" Tome said.

"Not directly. There's still a wagon full of my family's stuff to repair and reclaim." Fel glanced over his shoulder. "And there are some things from down below that I'd like to get my hands on before the other vault hunters figure out there are new chambers open."

EPILOGUE

Allie took a deep breath and crossed her arms. It was the start of another day of business, and she had the unenviable task of covering the place from open to close thanks to Oovay's decision that today was the day he'd cash in the favor of covering for her last time. Such was life. They had a fresh delivery of ale and assorted spirits, the cricket roaster had brought a few sacks that were filling the place with their salty, toasty smell. All in all, she was looking forward to it.

People started to file in, a mixture of heavy drinkers who planned to make a day of it and hard workers who needed a place to cool down and slake their thirst in the middle of their day. She greeted regulars by name, learned the names of new faces, and generally plied her trade in the way that few in Beffshire could. The day had fallen into a comfortable little rhythm when the door slammed open.

Allie's head snapped toward the doorway, and her brain quickly ticked off the locations of the three heaviest objects for her to use as a club if clubbing was indeed required.

"Everybody listen up. Next drink is on me. I feel like celebrating!" crowed Fel as he marched inside.

"Well, well, well. Look who's back safe and sound, and with enough good sense to buy a round when the place is practically empty."

"It's not my fault the usual crowd didn't line up outside when they heard I was back in town," Fel said, marching over to the bar and plopping down.

Each of the patrons shuffled over to get their drink and offer some combination of a slap on the back, a handshake, and a hearty welcome to Fel, then just as quickly returned to their seats. Fel raised an eyebrow.

"Really? None of you wants to hear what I've been up to?" he said.

The only answer was a noncommittal murmur.

"They know full well whatever is worth telling will be tumbling out of you every time you get drunk for the next few weeks," Allie said. "And it'll get more interesting each time you tell it. No sense catching the first draft, right?"

"Yeah, yeah," Fel said. "That's fine, because I can't tell half of it anyway. Everybody got their drink? Happy?"

Another murmur.

"Good, because I need to borrow Allie for a minute."

"I'm the only one here for now, Fel. Not even Davie is here, so—"

"Yeah I am!" called Davie as he trotted through the door. "I'll keep an eye on folks."

"I'll make it quick," Fel said.

"You better," Allie said.

He held the door open, and Fel started to walk her around the side of the tavern.

"Just what was that all about?" Allie hissed.

"The trip? Or buying the round?"

"The trip. I'd like to say I've never seen you looking that serious on the way out, but it's getting to be a habit with you."

"Eh. The usual. A murderous elf stole some potentially disastrous stuff from us, and we had to get it back. Some of the stuff is still missing, but we got the worst of it back. It took some repair to get the cart back in one piece and get it all home, but fortunately Oiler came along, and it treats that sort of thing like a reward."

"The usual," Allie said with a shake of her head.

"We managed to grab some new items, and I even brought something back for you."

"It isn't another spoon, is it? Because I'm all stocked up on them," she said.

"No good spoons in this place. But I grabbed you this…"

He rounded the back of the tavern. Allie jumped a bit when she encountered what she first thought was a burly man waiting for them. In actuality it was a life-size bronze statue with a dusty old helmet propped on top. Fel slapped it on the back.

"Authentic Bygone Era military armor stand, it turns out," Fel said. "Sorry for the scratches and the bent arm. A huge murderous contraption tried to beat me to death with it."

"You sure do have to use the word 'murderous' a lot," Allie said.

"The price of an interesting life," he said.

"How did you get this back here without me noticing?"

"I've gotten a lot of practice moving huge things secretly over the last week or so."

"What'll it cost us? I'll talk to Sid to get you paid."

"Whatever he pays, keep it. Call it payment for letting me stay at your place," he said.

"In that case, I'll be making sure Sid coughs up plenty," she said.

"And speaking of me staying at your place…"

"Are we going to be speaking about you staying at my place? I figured that was in the half of the story you couldn't tell."

"I'll leave that up to you. But I had a lot of time on the road to think about what happened."

"Yeah, plenty of time around here to think it over, too, what with one of the bigger, rowdier patrons not showing up for the last few days."

"You first, then."

"You left a bag and your bedroll at my home," she said. "I expect you to come by and pick it up."

Fel glanced aside, his expression distant and twisted up as though he'd just been handed a puzzle. "You're giving me a signal right now," he said. "I don't know if it's a bad one because you want me to take my stuff home or a good one because you want me to come back to your house."

"I'm not a riddle, Fel."

"You say that, but I can't figure you out."

"Sometimes a woman just doesn't want a pile of junk on her floor."

"Oh."

"But that I didn't forbid you from ever coming to my home again isn't a bad sign, just so you know."

"How about I say my piece, then," Fel said.

"How about that," she agreed.

"You know I'm an idiot, right?"

"I do."

"You know I get drunk all the time, and I gamble too much."

"I've noticed."

"About once a month, I almost die."

"I'm starting to understand why your sister is the one giving the sales pitches."

"Point is, you know me. Good and bad, top to bottom."

"I don't know much about your bottom, but go on."

"I can't wear a mask and pretend to be someone else. Can't make myself into someone you want. And I can't pretend it wasn't Mariss I'd been after all this time. But I also can't pretend you don't know that some of the best times of my life, you were there. And I can't pretend you being there wasn't a big part of what made those times great. There's nothing I can say here that I didn't say before. The timing seems wrong. I'm not who I want to be, and I don't want you to feel like this was because I couldn't get Mariss. For the life of me, I can't imagine you'd ever want to waste your time on the man you know I am. But I truly believe if you do, we'd add an awful lot more good times before it was over."

Allie smirked and patted him on the shoulder. "Try not to think so hard, Fel. You can walk me home after work tonight and get your stuff. Until then, I have to get back in there before someone gets the bright idea to test Davie's willingness to guard the bar."

They turned and paced back toward the street.

"So what sort of heads do you think we should make for that thing?" she asked.

"Not a warrior. Trust me," Fel said. "And just so you're prepared, at some point Captain Boltt is probably going to show up and give me an earful. I've done a couple things to earn it."

"Eh. I'll give him a free brandy. Should take the edge off him. And just so you're prepared, Mariss is pretty clearly in love with the idea of being the only one who 'knows' we're secretly together. Be ready for that."

"Grand…"

Tome dropped heavily into his chair. Of the group, he'd absorbed the least abuse during their journey, but there was still a mental and physical fatigue that came after such madness as he'd endured during the week. A dull exhaustion swallowed his thoughts into a haze. Even so, he pulled open a blank book and started jotting things down.

"Tome!" Teya called from behind him.

The sudden call gave him a start. She trotted into the room and jumped on his bed.

"We go?" she said.

"Go where? We just got home."

"Fel went to tavern. We go?"

"I don't think that's a good idea."

"Helped stop elf. Earned good deed. Let's go!"

"We didn't stop the elf. We don't even know where he is."

"Not here. Because of us. Let's try!" she said.

"Fel is really the one who's willing to anger the City Watch over something as petty as getting a drink."

"I know! Let's go get him!" she said.

He rubbed his face. "Would you at least give me a moment to take some proper notes?"

She nodded magnanimously. "You do." Teya dropped down to sit on the edge of his bed, dangling her feet. "What you do?" she asked.

"The language you started to teach me? It's given me some ideas. I'd been in a bit of a rut, or so I thought. You'll remember when I went to the Greater Lands, it was in pursuit of means to expand my mystic capabilities."

"We steal books," she said with a sage nod.

"And, to my great dismay, I hadn't the knack to cast their style of magic. Not with any degree of potency."

"Bad magic," she said.

"There is no such thing as bad magic. Intent lies in the mind of the caster," he said.

She shook her head. "That? Maybe for sword. Maybe for bow. Maybe for most things. But magic? Some magic, bad. Elf magic, bad."

"We shall agree to disagree. But the point is moot, as I've realized I had selected my focus poorly. There are many paths to greatness. Shoring up one's weakness is one of them. Playing to one's strengths is another. Mastering old arts? Still another. And forging a new path. I think, perhaps, rather than eliminating my weakness, for me the path forward is to fuse what I know with what they know."

He pulled out the stolen book of elven magic and opened it. "Spoken magic, written magic, the power is in the words. They have that in common. I shouldn't be focusing on replicating how they cast their magic. I should be adding their vocabulary to my own. If a few words of arcane origin can command a lesser sphinx, imagine what can be achieved if those words are written into spells. I didn't walk away with a new tool, but I may have added whole new colors to my artistic palette. It is thrilling."

She nodded. "So add colors, then tavern?"

"We shall see... What about you? Surely this adventure has seen you clear to your destiny."

She nodded harder. "Very very."

"That was your aim, wasn't it? That was your direction. What now?"

"Don't know. Before? I would say, go home. But what is home? Home is friends. Home is family. Home is safe. Home is fun. Home is happy. This? This is home, also. Now I have two."

"Thinking of staying, are you?"

"Don't know," she repeated. "Maybe yes? Maybe explore? Maybe much. But today? Drink at tavern."

"In a moment," he said firmly.

She nodded again. For a few blissful seconds, there was silence.

"Small eyes, little light," she said.

"What?" he grumbled.

She pointed to his face, then gestured at the room. "Small eyes, little light. You need light?"

"I usually light an additional lantern, now that you mention it."

She pulled out her sparker. "I do!"

He stood and snapped his book shut. "What do you say we go try for that drink? I suddenly have a powerful need to finish dulling my senses."

Martin tightened the panel on a music box and took a long, satisfied sigh. It was nice to be back to doing proper contraption repair again, and moreover it was nice to have most of his tools returned. But the moment looming ahead of him was what he'd been waiting for from the moment Fel had come back safely. The loss of the couplers was a bit of a setback, but they could be remade. Likely, he could make them with a higher degree of skill and functionality than he did the first time. The loss of the Student was a considerably greater setback. However, he hoped it could be a temporary one. And Fel's journey had not been without its spoils. However, the chief item among them would need to be treated with care.

"Are you watching, Wick?" Martin asked.

"Always," Wick replied.

"I don't imagine any unexpected damage will come from this, given the precautions, but the very nature of unexpected damage precludes anticipation. Alert me to anything out of the ordinary that might be beyond my perception," he said.

"This is a service I shall happily fulfill."

He took another breath, then fetched the burlap sack that was still warm from its ride in the wagon. Tugging the ties revealed the fearsome visage of the Warrior mask. The years had been considerably less kind to it than even those masks left to the weather as part of their shop's sign. It was blackened with char, thick with patina here, and scraped clean of it there. But even simply holding it in his hand, he could feel that it was different from the Student. It had a weight to it. Physical, yes, but more than that. It felt impactful. Potent. It felt more real, more important than the Student did. Like it carried with it the weight of the motivations for its creation. He shifted the original bust, the one gathered from his family's ancestral home, and fitted the mask in place. When it was properly affixed, he removed the Bygone dagger from the back of the bust. Silver disks slid into position behind the eyes. They fixed on Martin's face.

It spoke, its voice somewhat smoother on the Bygone Era bust as compared to Martin's bespoke coupler.

"You are a Masker," the Warrior said.

"And you are a mask," Martin said.

"Your breeding has endured the ages. You still have the look of your ancestors."

"We'll discuss my ancestors later. You tried to kill my son."

"I tested your son. And it would appear he passed. The Maskers of this era retain their worth. I am yours to command."

"At present, I have no interest in commanding you. What I seek is information."

"Then you seek the sage, the Scholar."

"Among other things, yes. And I understand it has awoken."

"It has."

"Tell me where it is."

"I am a warrior. I can perform tasks only as they pertain to tactics and conquest."

"Similarly limited in scope, like the Student."

"Focused. Specialized. Not limited," the Warrior corrected.

"If you operate only in tactics, then consider this espionage. Military intelligence."

"That is acceptable."

"Are you able to determine the locations of the other masks?"

"I am able to make that determination, with a great deal of precision if they are functioning as intended. If they are active but functioning improperly, the precision is greatly reduced. At present, the Scholar is the only properly functional mask. The Diplomat is operating at limited functionality, and the Student is engaged only be elven magic. A useful but flawed activation."

"This is, perhaps, the most important thing you can do for me right now. And I suspect the thing you are most willing and eager to do. I need to know the location of the elf and any indication of intent you may have. He is a threat to my family."

"He is a threat to more than your family," the Warrior said. "I cannot speak to his current aim, but his aim while in contact with me focused on assembling a force to breach the Greater Lands Wall."

"To what end?"

"Conquest."

"In what form?"

"Immaterial. He sought military might. That was sufficient to justify my usage."

"And you were aiding him?"

"Had he demonstrated the capacity to utilize me adequately, I would have done so. I have no capacity or inclination to make determinations about the moral, ethical, or political value of a military campaign. The Scholar and the Ambassador make such determinations. I merely assess military strength and military weakness and exploit such things to complete the task at hand. When I acquired the means to perform such a test, Fel Masker was available. As a member of the clan that was responsible for my creation, I deemed him a more pressing and potentially valuable ally, and so he was tested first."

"And the elf is now similarly allied with the Student?"

"It is a reasonable assumption."

"When linked to the elf, you pursued your own goals, specifically the acquisition of the means to test your would-be collaborator. Would the Student behave similarly?"

"The Student's purpose is to learn and demonstrate knowledge. That is a goal that does not require any specific action beyond observation and dialogue."

Martin took a note. "And where is it now?"

"A short distance northeast of the testing ground. Moving in a decidedly meandering path, broadly north."

"Can you provide any additional insight into its location and actions?"

"I cannot."

"Is your limited insight a function of the nonstandard way it has been awakened? That is to say, the mystical rather than contraption-based activation?"

"Likely. All masks beyond the level of complexity of the Student are able to make broad determinations about the nature of the operation of the other masks."

"Were you thus able to determine that I had created a new coupler and a new bust due to my installation of the Student onto the bust?"

"I was."

"And the Scholar would thus make a similar determination?"

"It would."

Martin made a few more notes. "We will need to decide how to deal with the elf, but before that, tell me everything you can about the Scholar and where it can be found."

"The Scholar has been stationary on a lightly damaged but fully operational bust in the mountains north of the Dunmar settlement."

"The Dunmar settlement..."

"An ancient name for what is now known as Marshoss, a midsize city on the Shalia side of the north end of the Quarr-Shalia border," Wick said.

Martin pictured the point on the map. "That would place it squarely within the overlap of the Graves and Bolivan territories."

"I am not capable of making that determination," the Warrior said.

He nodded. "Very well. Let us return to the subject of the elf..."

Mevrelle stalked northeast. His strength was gradually returning. The Student was a more frustrating but far less insistent voice at the edge of his mind. He did not know if it was the nature of its role or simply that the mask was weaker than the Warrior. The inquisitive voice remained a passive presence in his mind rather than an active one. It asked questions, offered advice. It had been in the possession of the Maskers, learned from them. And now, with the gentlest of prodding, those lessons could be teased from the mask. As he restored his strength through hunting and foraging in a way the Warrior was rarely willing to indulge, he learned important things about this world and what had become of it. And history as well. History as the contraptioneers told it to one another. Most important, he learned that there was another active sentry flame. The Maskers were astoundingly capable of protecting their own. But perhaps this other flame could be acquired more easily.

His slowly clearing mind was still formulating the plan. Locate one of the flames. A proper Bygone lantern that the flame was linked to. Nothing that could be extinguished to sever its connection to the flame. Assess its defenses. Acquire it, and return home to use it to complete the purpose that had sent him to this horrid place.

He turned. Points of light danced on the road to the west. He moved a bit farther into the brush. There were very few sizable forests in this part of the world. None of them were what he would call proper. But here in particular, there was very little in the way of cover. The motion of the lights and the fact that they had been showing up at this same time of day ever since he'd left the quarry suggested it was a search party. That they'd followed him this far suggested it was a quite skilled search party. He doubted, in his present diminished state, he could move quickly enough to lose them. Better to hunker down and wait for them to pass or ambush them if they found him.

Hidden among the bushes, bow at the ready, he watched through the slits of his curious mask as the lights drew nearer. He almost felt a degree of admiration as they slipped off the road at the precise point he had. He was still ailing from the Warrior's will taxing his own, so he was not at his best in terms of stealth, but even so, rare was the human who could follow him with such precision.

The search party approached. There were six. No, a seventh lagged behind. Their leader, no doubt. They were headed directly toward him. Seven men. He had eight arrows remaining. When they were near enough, he would eliminate the hunters. Tomorrow he would need to craft new arrows if this wretched place had any worthwhile wood to perform such a task.

The search party seemed to know they'd found him. They formed a circle around him, laboring under the false assumption that he couldn't possibly end them all before they could apprehend him, no doubt. He selected his first target.

"You there!" came the voice of the leader. "My mercenaries tell me you are a rare talent when it comes to surreptitious travel. I must assume you are similarly rare in your combat. One wonders if perhaps you are a sharp negotiator as well. It would serve us both well if you were. My name is Inspector Cartwright. It has cost me a great deal of accumulated prestige and privilege to undertake this little mission. Indeed, I may soon no longer have the right to call myself an inspector. But I wouldn't have taken this mission if I didn't feel the rewards outweighed the risks. You have, in your possession, a mask and a contraption capable of attaching to it. I require both. Or, more specifically, my employer does. Mr. Lens is quite insistent he acquire them, you see. So if my mercenaries must destroy you, they will. But given your bloody clash with the Maskers, I believe you, Mr. Lens, and I have compatible aims. I propose an alliance."

Mevrelle raised his arrow and stood. "If I release this string, my arrow will pass through your eye and whatever worthless flesh waits behind it," he said. "You speak of negotiation. I require only one thing. If you can offer it, I will offer my services. If you cannot, all your lives are forfeit, beginning with you."

"What is your demand?" Cartwright said, his bravado eroding visibly in the face of the raised weapon.

"I require access to a sentry flame," Mevrelle said.

"If that is a contraption, I am confident Mr. Lens has access to one. He is one of the foremost experts in such things the world has ever seen."

Mevrelle measured Cartwright. The shaken human believed he was telling the truth. One could tell at a glance that he was too much of a coward to hold back something that could save his life, and too accustomed to being unquestioned to lie convincingly. Cartwright at least believed he could offer what was requested. Mevrelle shifted his plan. Each day, the weaker will of the Student would feed him more information and allow him more freedom to recover. By the time this alliance revealed itself to be either worthwhile or worthless, he would have the strength and fortitude to take whatever actions were necessary to extract what he required from it.

He grinned, unseen behind the mask.

"So be it," he said.

FROM JOSEPH R. LALLO

Thank you for reading! If you liked this story, or perhaps if you found it lacking, I'd love to hear from you. For free stories and important updates, join my newsletter at: www.bookofdeacon.com
Discover other titles by Joseph R. Lallo:

The Book of Deacon Series
An epic fantasy series spanning six main novels and assorted spin-offs and prequels. Follow the journey of Myranda Celeste and the rest of the Chosen as they fight to save their world from a terrible war and its aftermath.

The Big Sigma Series
A sci-fi action adventure series with six novels. Trevor "Lex" Alexander is a former hover-racer who finds his world turned upside down when he becomes embroiled in the schemes of mega-corporations, criminal syndicates, and a mad engineer with a quirky AI.

The Free-Wrench Series
Take to the skies in this six novel steampunk series about airships in an era of steam, brass, and excitement. Nita Graus joins the Wind Breaker crew, a group of smugglers in a constant clash with the twisted and nefarious fug folk who run the world from their place in the toxic mists that blanket the land.

The Shards of Shadow Series
An ongoing Urban Fantasy series following the trials and tribulations of a photographer named Alan who unwittingly becomes entangled in the dark machinations of the shadowy shades thanks to Blot, one of

their weakest agents. These exciting stories take place in modern day Philadelphia and shed light on the supernatural invasion that could tip the balance of power for the entire world.

The Greater Lands Saga

An epic fantasy adventure in a world where magic and supernatural contraptions coexist. Fel Masker is an explorer and adventurer, tasked with securing mysterious, arcane devices for his family to repair and sell. Rivalries with other contraptioneering families are heating up, and soon the lost history of the world may return with a vengeance.